M I
LYING
HUSBAND

An unputdownable psychological thriller
with a breathtaking twist

E.V. SEYMOUR

Joffe Books, London
www.joffebooks.com

First published in Great Britain in 2024

Cover art by Nick Castle

ISBN: 978-1-83526-283-2

For Ian

CHAPTER ONE

The second I heard Frankie roar, I knew it spelled trouble.

Half-dressed, I shot to the window. Outside, on the driveway, my grown-up son madly remonstrated with two smartly dressed men wearing banker's overcoats.

'Look, dude, you can piss right off!' Frankie yelled. '*Nobody* is taking my car.'

Zipping up my jeans, I threw open the sash window.

'What's going on?' I called down.

Three pairs of eyes glanced up at our Victorian villa. The two strangers were not exactly twins but with their red hair, pale, clean-shaven skin, ice-blue, almost colourless eyes, and curiously unlined features, they could definitely be brothers. One, I noticed, had a prominent mole above his top lip.

'These bastards are trying to steal my car, Mum.' Frankie stood with his hands on his head, as if he'd walked away from a train crash.

'That's not true, sir,' said the man with the mole. His voice had the smooth, cultured authority of the public-school educated. It threw me. I'd expected a thug with a wide-boy accent. 'As we explained,' he continued in modulated tones, 'your father owes us a lot of money and, in lieu of payment, we have the right to take the vehicles.' Plural meant my car too, my beloved Porsche Macan. What the hell was going on? There must be a terrible mistake.

'You don't have the right to do any damn thing,' I shouted. 'I'm coming down.'

They'd obviously gone to the wrong address, I thought, thundering down the stairs. My main priority was to reach Frankie and calm him. All dressed up in a suit and tie, he had a job interview in Tewkesbury and the last thing he needed was an upset over a stupid misunderstanding. Poor boy, he'd only had his MINI a week. It had been a birthday gift from Lance and me. Lance hoped it would inspire our son to become more independent, that both living and working from home at twenty-six was not desirable. As far as I was concerned, Frankie could stay for as long as he liked. We had a special bond because, for the first six years of Frankie's life, before I met Lance, it had been the two of us.

A cold March wind gusted into my face as I opened the front door and crunched across the Cotswold-gravelled drive. Annoyingly, Mrs Fletcher, my gossipy next-door neighbour, lurked on the other side of the low boundary wall. I silently made a shooing noise, and prayed she'd hurry off to work sooner rather than later.

Forcing a smile that was not reciprocated, I addressed the two men. 'What's this all about then?'

The taller of the two answered, 'We need the keys to your son's car and to yours.'

'Don't be ridiculous.'

'As explained . . .'

'On whose authority?'

'Veldo Loan Management.'

I frowned. 'Never heard of them. A loan company, you say?'

'The clue is in the title, madam.'

'God's sake.' Frankie glowered.

'I want your names,' I said.

'Our names aren't important.'

'Yes, they bloody are,' Frankie said.

The two men looked at each other, exchanged a glance and shrugged. 'Jack Mount,' the one with the mole said. He tilted his head in the direction of his co-partner in crime — as far as I was concerned — 'and my brother, Marcus.'

'There's obviously been a mistake,' I said doggedly. 'We don't owe a penny to anyone.'

'But your husband does,' Jack Mount insisted.

'I don't believe you.'

'This is Lance Stratton's house, isn't it, and you are Susannah Stratton?' It was Marcus Mount who'd asked. I hated the fact he knew my name. Now that I had a closer look at him I could see he wasn't like his brother. His features were sharper, his eyes smaller, his face filled with more edges and lines. His top lip wasn't so thin. Curving up as it did, it made his mouth look like it was in a permanent sneer.

'Show me your paperwork,' I said, 'and I expect to see your names on it.' I glanced across and noticed that Mrs Fletcher had thankfully disappeared.

The sneer widened. 'That's not how we operate.'

'Then you'd best leave before I call the police.'

Marcus Mount let out an enormous sigh as if I were wasting not only my valuable time, but also his. 'Look,' he said, small eyes glinting, 'the last thing we want is a scene on your driveway.' To make the point he glanced up and down the leafy road. Bordering Montpellier and the Park, it was a portrait of well-heeled residential Cheltenham. *Ugly scenes shouldn't happen here*, his expression suggested, *so do us a favour and do as you're bloody well told.*

Frankie stepped forward and alarmingly drew his fist back. I shot out a hand to prevent him taking a swing. It didn't stop his yelling, 'I've had enough of you. You heard what my mum said, piss off!' The raw energy of misjudged youth sparked off him and zipped through my fingers. His temperament suddenly seemed in step with his Latin-looking features: jet-black hair, the colour of a wet blackbird feather, an olive complexion that required shaving twice a day, and dark brown deep-set eyes that drew you in when he talked.

Physically, he resembled his biological father, the only anomaly Frankie's height, which was a shade less than six feet four. His inherited trait from me was his easy-going nature, or so I thought. He'd never displayed a violent streak in his life. Disturbingly, I didn't recognise the fired-up young man beside me.

'Let's all take a moment,' I said, patting the air with my hands in a placatory gesture.

'I will when they clear off,' Frankie retorted.

'Shut up, son.'

Frankie paled. Practically knocking me out of the way, he lunged. Powering into the man called Marcus, Frankie caught him in a rugby style tackle, dead centre. I let out a scream as a number of deft blows rained down on Frankie's head from Marcus Mount.

'Stop it. Get off him, you bastards!'

A flurry of grunts and punches and Frankie was lying on his back in the dirt with blood from his nose staining the collar of his new white shirt. His eyes were briefly glazed.

I rushed to his side, knelt down and reached out. Shaking me off, hurt and humiliated, Frankie staggered to his feet and, cursing, fled inside. Meanwhile Marcus Mount straightened his tie and adjusted his collar. His brother, Jack, who'd stood by coldly watching, punched a number on his phone.

'Look what you've done,' I railed, fighting back tears. 'Grown men, you should be ashamed of yourselves.'

They couldn't have looked less bothered.

'Here,' Jack Mount said, passing me a phone.

Puzzled, I stood up, knees cracking. 'Yes?'

'Susannah, it's me.'

'Thank God! Lance, what the hell is going on? I've got . . .'

'I know, sweetheart,'

'You *know*?'

'I'm truly sorry, but I want you to listen very carefully.'

'Two men from some bogus company have just hit your son and knocked him to the ground.'

'Oh God.'

'They are threatening to take our cars.' I glared at the Mount brothers venomously.

'Yes, I . . .'

'And how am I supposed to get to work and Frankie to his interview?'

'Call a cab.'

'What? To take him all the way to Tewkesbury?' I didn't say *are you crazy* because that wasn't my style. I was very much in favour of looking at a problem logically and reacting with composure. Sod that. 'This is outrageous!'

'Susannah,' Lance cut in roughly and in a voice I didn't recognise. 'Hand them the keys to both cars. Do not call the police.'

'What . . .'

'I repeat do *not* call the police.'

'I don't understand.'

'For fuck's sake, do as I say!'

Lance never, ever swore at me. Fear shot across my shoulder blades. 'Are you in trouble?' My voice was small. I glanced anxiously at the Mounts. They stood feet apart, waiting patiently *because they knew how this was going to roll*.

'I'll explain everything later, I promise but, please, Susannah,' Lance pleaded, 'do exactly as they say.'

CHAPTER TWO

Humiliated, I meekly fetched the keys and wordlessly handed them over.

Crossing my arms and clutching at my elbows to steady myself, I spoke to the man with the phone, Jack Mount. 'This is it, right? Full and final payment.'

He snatched a smile. 'Look on it as a first instalment.'

I felt a thud of disbelief as they climbed into the vehicles for which I'd paid out my hard earned. Unable to bear to see the cars driven away by faceless snakes in suits, I sped inside, closed the door and collapsed onto a chair in the hall where I shut my eyes.

Did what just happened actually happen?

God alone knew how Frankie was feeling.

Confused and angry, I found my son in his bedroom sitting on his bed. The fury previously scribbled all over his face had gone. He stared vacantly at the wall. Thankfully, his nose had stopped bleeding and he'd changed his shirt. His trousers were dusty where he'd hit the gravel, but a brush down and he'd be good to go.

I sat next to him. Inches apart, I might as well have been on the other side of the globe.

'I knew they were sketchy the second they showed up,' Frankie grumbled.

'What exactly happened? Did you see anyone drop them off?'

'Nope. They looked like they'd walked here.' He turned to me beseechingly. 'I really tried to keep it cool, Mum, and talk them out of it. Thought it was some joke, you know,' he continued tonelessly. 'One of Miles's pranks.'

Miles Rayner was one of Frankie's closest friends. Right from school days Miles had been a clown.

'I understand.' I rested my hand on his knee.

'Why do you always have to be so reasonable?' he said, suddenly accusing.

'I didn't think I was.' I always did my best to muzzle my feelings. It was important to stay in control. The fact I'd screamed and shouted felt quite alien to me, a measure of how cross I was when faced with a bizarre situation. Not just with the men, but with Lance, too. Lance's business, MultiMax, a commercial waste company based in Worcester, was well-established and going from strength to strength, or so I'd been led to believe. Over the years it had undergone carefully planned expansion. As far as I knew loans from the bank had been paid back without a problem.

'I wanted to rip that smug fucker's face off,' Frankie spat.

'I know,' I said quietly.

'I bloody loved that car and you've given it away.'

'It's not as simple as that.'

'Yes, it is.'

'We will get you a new car.'

'With what?' His brown eyes were dull with disappointment.

'We'll find a way.' I spoke with conviction. A dental hygienist, I earned a fair wage. I had a good handle on domestic finances but I'd always left big picture finance to my husband. Until I got to speak to Lance I'd no idea what possessed him to get involved with men who, however educated they sounded, were nothing short of loan sharks.

'Have you spoken to Dad?' Frankie asked.

Adopted at a young age by Lance, Frankie had never enquired about his real father. As far as he was concerned, Lance was his dad.

'He's going to explain everything later. Don't worry about that. Our main focus now is getting you to your interview on time.'

Frankie scowled. 'Looking like this?'

'It's not so bad. Any prospective employer would be impressed that you'd made the effort.'

'Oh sure,' Frankie said, voice drenched in sarcasm. 'I lost my temper and got into a fight this morning but, hey, I'm a really solid guy to have on board. I mean what the fuck?'

'I wish you wouldn't swear.'

'I wish you would.'

Two short bursts from a car horn signalled Coco's arrival.

Frankie stood up. 'I already phoned her,' he said, in answer to my surprised expression.

Coco was my stepdaughter. And Frankie would have told Coco what happened, and Coco would tell her mother, and Chantal would gloat. In the big scheme of things it was a minor irritant, I guessed.

'Isn't Coco at work?'

'Day off,' Frankie replied. 'She nobly offered to drive me to Tewkesbury.'

'That's good of her. Problem solved.'

Frankie gave me a look that suggested we were a very long way from a solution. Privately, I agreed and followed Frankie downstairs.

The passenger door to a scarlet-coloured Toyota GR Yaris was already open. With a big smile on her immaculately made-up face, Coco leant across, clutching a takeaway carton of coffee. She handed it to her stepbrother.

'Thought you might need a boost.' A good-looking girl, with neat pixie-like features, sharp hazel-green eyes and cropped dark hair, she and Frankie were often mistaken for genuine brother and sister. Two years younger than Frankie, they'd always rubbed along incredibly well. I shouldn't be smug but I was proud of my blended family, something I boasted about more than I should. Coco had teased me for it: 'You make us sound like a beverage.'

'Thanks so much for coming to the rescue,' I told her.

'No worries. Hadn't got anything else on today.'

'You'll be all right?' I asked Frankie anxiously. Huffing into his seat, he'd dragged the seat belt across and hunkered down as if he were a celebrity trying to avoid paparazzi.

''Course he will,' Coco said. 'Go on, smile for Mummy.'

Frankie snorted a laugh, turned to me and flashed a grin. All white teeth and bonhomie. Now that his stepsister was here, his mood had improved and, I had to admit, so had mine. A whirlwind of a young woman, relentlessly upbeat, Coco was the same age as me when I'd had Frankie. Her carefree spirit reminded me of who I once was before single motherhood kicked in. Feeling as I did now, it was rather depressing to remember more carefree days.

'Bloody glad I wasn't here,' Coco declared, 'otherwise my lovely motor would have been carted off too. So what's the craic? Sounds as if Dad has been a right knob.'

Unfortunately, after the morning's episode, I thought Coco had a point.

'I'm sure it will get sorted,' I said loyally.

'But what about you, Suze?' Coco asked, 'You okay?'

'Good of you to ask.' More concerned for Frankie, I hadn't had time to process what had happened. Part of me was still in shock.

'You're not going to work, are you, Mum?' Frankie said.

'Suze would go to work if her leg was dropping off,' Coco chipped in.

I gave a tight laugh. My children's natural exuberance made me feel boring and dull.

'Need a lift?' Coco asked me.

'Do we have time?' Frankie was edgy again.

'We do, big bro. This thing,' Coco said, smacking the steering wheel, 'is as fast as fuck.'

I assured them I'd walk. The fresh air would do me good. 'You will drive carefully, won't you, Coco?'

'Always.'

Her accompanying grin was not exactly reassuring. 'Right then, I'd better crack on. Best of luck today, Frankie,' I called.

And then they were gone.

CHAPTER THREE

'Now what have I told you, mate? There's no point crying your eyes out. You are not taking sweeties to school. Don't want Mummy getting into trouble again, do you?'

Amy Meadows crouched down and gazed into her four-year-old son's big blue eyes. Little Wilf was the spit of his dad, not when he was snivelling, of course, and she really didn't have a favourite, but out of her three children he was the child that squeezed her heart the hardest.

'That's right,' six-year-old Tana declared. 'Miss Ward is *very* strict and she would be *very* cross.' Amy's oldest daughter, Tana, was a proper little princess, loved her girlie clothes and nail varnish, but without the diva attitude. Kindness and sunshine shone out of her. She had a mop of copper-coloured hair like her mother, although Amy's was styled shorter, and a similar dusting of freckles over her nose and cheeks. Lowering her voice and rolling her green eyes, Tana said, 'I don't like Miss Ward at all.'

'That's not nice,' Amy said, except she didn't like Miss Ward either — a right old biddy. The expression on that woman's face could turn flesh to stone. Miss Ward had once practically asked her if wedding bells were on the horizon any time soon. Amy supposed that's what happened when you were born in the Dark Ages. Around where she lived, near Kidderminster, she knew more women her age single, or shacked up, than those that were married. Why bother had been her mantra, especially when weddings were so dear. Anyway, she liked the idea of "partner", not "husband". The former suggested a joint and equal enterprise and Amy was a naturally independent young woman. Had to be, these days.

'Christ,' Amy let out. 'Look at the time.' It was always the same when Rollo was away: the nights were long and exhausting, the days short and chaotic. If she got to eat her dinner before nine o'clock she considered it a major achievement.

Hurling lunch boxes into the kids' rucksacks, making sure Tana had her book bag and Wilf had a spare pair of underpants and his Igglepiggle, which travelled with her son everywhere, Amy scooped up her baby, conked out and snoring softly, and bundled her into a buggy. At least when Rollo was around he could take his turn. Calm and patient as they came, he had a magic knack of soothing his baby girl. Amy put it down to him being an older dad. She'd never been keen on men her age. They tended to be insolvent: *can I borrow a tenner, bab?* Overweight or — as off-putting — so ripped that you could virtually see their internal organs. They also spent too much time at the pub, had mental health issues (often spawned from drinking alcohol and/or smoking weed) and a tendency to over share. Amy didn't have time for all that malarkey. Give her a straightforward middle-aged Midlands man with no extra fat around his belly any day, one happy in his own skin, a practical man who knew how to feed and look after his family. In the bedroom department they were better too. More experienced and knew what they were doing.

If only Rollo were here.

But, Amy sighed happily, Rollo would be back this evening. A long=distance lorry driver and her favourite Knight of the Road, he was currently on his way back from France. He could drive a rig anywhere and mostly did continental runs. Things had got complicated post Brexit with a shortage of lorry drivers, meaning Rollo's skills were in high demand and pay was good. He'd promised to take her out for steak and chips as long as her mum could have the kids. Her mum loved having them and had said yes straightaway.

Touching the necklace he'd given her, Amy's heart lifted at the thought of seeing her man. They were great together. Maybe because they were forced to spend so much time apart. Nothing got stale or samey.

With a warm glow, she bowled out of the door of their rented bungalow, locked it and, with a child on each side and buggy in front, trotted down the short drive.

'Don't run ahead,' she called as Wilf left her side. 'Tana, take his hand for God's sake,' Amy bawled, alarmed by the volume of morning traffic whizzing up and down the road.

Dead handy for school and with a childminder that lived around the corner, their little rental was well situated, but what Amy really wanted was a home to call their own. Her heart skipped at the thought of the little black and white cottage she'd clocked on one of those property websites. Semi-rural, close to a nice primary and with a secondary school a few miles away in the market town of Tenbury Wells, where she worked in a sweet shop, it had three bedrooms and one large enough for the girls to share. Maybe in time they could extend with a double-storey extension to provide extra space downstairs and another bedroom upstairs to accommodate Tana as she got bigger. The garden was generous enough. She'd had her eye on the property for a while and, with her savings and Rollo coining it in, she'd budgeted that they could afford it if the price came down a bit.

As soon as she'd got the kids where they needed to be, and had double backed to pick up the car to get herself to the shop, she planned to call the estate agent and arrange a viewing. Later, and once she'd got Rollo nice and mellow, care of a well-deserved pint in front of him, she'd bring up the subject. He'd always said they should move and now was exactly the right time.

Dropping off Adele first, at the childminder's, Amy's mobile phone went. Seeing Rollo's number, she instantly beamed.

'Hey, babe,' she said. 'All right?'

'Afraid not, hun. It's a right pain but I have to do a run up to Scotland.'

'What? Now? But you promised.'

'I know. I'm sorry. It's a favour for a mate.'

'I see.' Amy hoped the ice in her voice would reach all the way to Rollo's cloth ears.

'I wouldn't normally step in but it really is an emergency and you know how short-staffed we are.'

'Right.'

'The extra lolly will come in handy and I should be home tomorrow night.'

'Should?'

'Promise.'

'Not much I can do about it then, is there?' She looked down at Wilf and Tana. Their sweet little faces looking up at her; they'd sensed they wouldn't be seeing their daddy today.

'It's not fair on the kids, Rollo.'

'I'll make it up to them, I swear. And to you, babe.'

Amy softened — not that she let Rollo know. As far as he was concerned she was pissed off and mortally disappointed. 'You'll be home for a bit then when you finally arrive?'

'At least for a few days.'

Good, Amy thought. She had a nice little house she wanted to show him.

CHAPTER FOUR

I arrived at work out of breath, feeling all of my fifty years. I'd hoped that the walk would bring clarity. The logical part of my brain strived to second-guess how Lance had got himself into such a mess.

I'd always tempered his natural enthusiasm and energy. Was there something he hadn't shared with me? Had he overextended on his borrowings for the business and, unable to pay back through the accepted route, fallen foul by accepting a loan from unscrupulous people? Had Lance known from the outset what he was getting into, or had he entirely miscalculated? I made a mental note to check out Veldo Loan Management during my lunchtime break.

That should have been the end of it. My fretful mind refused to shut up. What if Lance had needed the money for something entirely unconnected to the business, like a secret gambling habit? This didn't sound like the man I loved. And, by God, from the first moment I'd clapped eyes on him I'd loved him. Prematurely grey, his silver hair, the colour of mercury, was all the more striking because of his dark eyebrows and sideburns. His soft brown, expressive eyes floored me. We'd met on a train journey from Malvern to Harrogate. He was reading *The Curious Incident of the Dog in the Night-Time* and I was reading *The Kite Runner.* When he asked if it was any good we fell into easy conversation. Before I knew it I was telling him about my life and how anxious I was leaving my young son with my parents while I attended a conference, even though they were good people and looked after him often.

At the prospect of emotional baggage, Lance didn't make a fast exit from the conversation, or glaze over at "child talk". Quickly, I discovered he had a young daughter and that his marriage had foundered, although he'd maintained good relations with his ex-wife, Chantal. Lance was loyal to his core, foolishly so, I'd thought later on when he defended Chantal for coming down too hard on their only child, Coco, but that was Lance all over. He always saw the good in people. I admired him for it. But he was no fool and getting into trouble with loan sharks simply didn't compute. Sternly, I told myself I'd have to be patient and wait to see what Lance had to say.

The emotional part of me, the bit I did my best to subdue, was a lot messier. It reminded me of the wild panic I'd experienced on discovering I was pregnant after an intense holiday romance. That same alarming sensation of *what do I do*? Halfway through a four-year course in dental hygiene I'd been forced to confess all to my parents. Mum, who had, according to her, given up a career in banking in order to devote herself to her only child, was deeply unimpressed and let it be known. Dad had been more sanguine and took the view that "these things happen". I'd always tried to model myself on him and yet feared Mum's critical influence held sway. To be fair, my mother, and to a lesser extent, my father had generously stepped in to look after Frankie so I could pick up and continue my studies.

But the day Lance suggested we moved in with him and I could safely dispense with my mother's services and give Frankie a proper loving home, I'd never been happier. And neither had Frankie. I was so proud of him with his degree in Computer Science and Business Studies, his ambitions and his lively mind and warm smile.

Which was why I couldn't forget the awful expression on his face when he'd been knocked to the ground that morning. Sparking a raft of raw and complicated emotions, it was ridiculous, but I felt as if I'd personally failed him.

After a plethora of good mornings from dental nurses and dentists, I hurried off to a back room where I changed into my work uniform and stowed my home clothes in a locker. Since hitting the big five-oh, I barely looked in the mirror. My blonde hair, once the colour of summer sand, had faded and the curls grazing the collar of my shirt had turned to frizz. I kept it short and in good condition and wore minimal make-up: a dab of foundation to even out my skin tone, a little eyebrow pencil, mascara and a slick of lipstick and that was it. My forehead was high and my nose, though a little large, was straight. My eyes were blue in some lights, blue-grey in others. I believed I had an honest, open-featured face. When I bothered to do yoga, the lines seemed to disappear; lately, I'd been either too busy, or too tired. Most of the time I felt invisible. My mother had told me that once your childbearing years were over, that's what happened, a natural part of the life cycle. To be honest, I felt a million miles away from the earth mother I'd been two decades before, with her mad hair, slim, taut body and natural lust and enthusiasm for life. What had happened to the woman who didn't take things seriously, least of all herself? Had the real me gone walkabout? Could the original one stand up and be noticed? I let out a sigh. Why the hell was I thinking like this? Was it possible that one disturbing event could bring on such negative thinking and rake up the past?

My first patient was a middle-aged man with gingivitis and breath that could fell a camel. I carried out a thorough examination, poked and prodded and probed. At the margins, where the tooth met the gum line, the skin was red and puffy and blood freely flowed. It reminded me of Frankie's nose that morning. Blinking away the memory, I went through the usual routine about the importance of dental hygiene, the need for rigorous and regular brushing.

'Which interdental brushes are you using?'

'Um . . . purple and green, I think.'

I nodded and smiled then set to work: scraping and cleaning and fishing out pockets of debris.

'Turn to me,' I said softly. 'And put your hand up if you want me to stop. There's a fair amount of plaque and your teeth are going to be a little bit sensitive.'

Normally, I'd give a running commentary, or make an inane comment about the weather: it's so cold *and* wet. My mind was elsewhere: how was Lance going to explain? How could I fund another car for Frankie? How was I to replace the Macan? Good God, I'd worked so hard for it. And why hadn't those men turned up when Lance was at home and taken *his* BMW? Lance said he *knew*. Did he have prior knowledge? Had he been warned? Why hadn't they embarrassed *him* at work instead of humiliating Frankie and me outside our home, our sanctuary? And what would the neighbours think? Exhausted by a relentless interior monologue, I flushed at words that my mother had used when I'd blurted out about my pregnancy. My skin suddenly suffused with fire. Bathed in heat, perspiration mottled my brow, my cheeks flaming red. As if I didn't have enough with which to contend, menopause was playing havoc with my body. Fortunately not, as yet, my mind; brain fog, that had assailed some of my friends, was alien. Long may it last: I reckoned I was going to need all the mental capacity I had for the days ahead.

Turning away, I discreetly mopped my face, although I could do little about the sweat gathering underneath my arms and forming a small tributary down my spine. Returning to my patient, I soldiered on through five more patients. Normally, I'd feel a sense of achievement, particularly with those who had specific problems. They weren't all elderly. It amazed me how many youngsters had truly awful dental hygiene, despite the emphasis on bright, white and straight teeth.

Lunch — a flask of soup and a piece of fruit — was usually spent at the surgery. Unable to face people and needing to escape, I took a short stroll to the High Street and into the John Lewis department store, where Coco normally worked in the cosmetic department. A beautician by training, Coco also offered private make-up sessions, which her mother, Chantal, took full advantage of. I cringed again at the thought of Lance's ex receiving the news of the morning's events. She of the generic, perfectly arched eyebrow and super whitened teeth; Chantal had the emotional depth of a puddle. In twenty years I'd never witnessed her lose her cool — never really seen her express joy, come to think of it. Chantal rarely laughed and, if she found something amusing, it was usually at someone else's expense. A cyclone could blow through Cheltenham and she would still be standing. Nothing got to her. It was as if she had chilled water flowing through her veins. I instantly regretted my mean thoughts. It wasn't fair to take out my angst on Chantal even if we'd never really got on.

Cutting through the cosmetics department, I headed for the café and ordered a double espresso and a winter Chicken Caesar salad. That was the other thing about hitting fifty, try as I might, I didn't seem able to keep my weight down. My clothes felt too tight and I was at that stage where I either bought a new wardrobe or took radical steps to kick-start my metabolism and drop the pounds. In the meantime, I continued to squeeze dispiritingly into my old wardrobe of dresses, skirts and jeans.

Taking a tray of food to the table, I took out my phone and, first of all, checked the joint bank account, used for paying the mortgage and household bills; all looked in order — a massive relief. From the outset of our marriage we'd had separate accounts by mutual agreement, something my father had instilled in me from an early age. 'Important to have your own money,' he'd said. 'In case of rainy days.' This was more like a monsoon. I briefly wondered what kind of shape Lance's personal finances were in and decided I ought not to go there, mainly because I couldn't. In common with not reading each other's emails, we didn't spy on each other's finances.

Googling Veldo Loan Management, nothing of significance came up. I tried various combinations; still nothing of note. I punched in loan companies. A raft of services popped onto my screen under "Debt Consolidation", which sounded a lot more friendly and businesslike than the services provided by Veldo that morning. I narrowed down the search to loan companies in Worcester, where Lance's business was based, then did the same for Cheltenham and discovered an outfit called VLM. The registered office address was in Battledown on the east side of Cheltenham. According to Companies House, it had two officers, Jack and Marcus Mount, and two active directors, Bobby Stella and Dale Jovi, both Americans, in their early sixties and with addresses in Florida. Under nature of the business, it stated that it dealt in financial and technical services.

About to pick at my salad, my phone rang: Frankie.

'Hiya, how did it go?' I asked.

'I blew it.'

'Oh.'

'Win some, lose some.'

'I'm so sorry.'

'Not sure junior software designer for a travel agency was my thing anyway.'

'He thought it would lead to paid-for holidays on the Continent,' Coco said, giggling in the background.

'Yeah, and then they told me the role would be one hundred per cent remote,' Frankie said with a groan. 'How's things with you, Mum?'

'So-so.'

'But you're okay?' Frankie persisted.

I smiled. My son always knew when okay was not okay. 'Honest,' I said.

'You should go home. Scraping people's teeth is gross in any circumstances, but after this morning, well, what can I say?'

It was good to hear Frankie sounding like his old self. 'Thanks for the solid advice but, really, I'm good.'

The line went quiet. I heard a muffled exchange.

'I was wondering,' Frankie began speculatively, 'seeing as those guys didn't have business cards, thought I'd run online checks on Veldo Loan Management.'

'I've already done it.' I gave Frankie a précis of my findings.

'An American outfit? Isn't that slightly odd?'

I pushed my plate away, appetite abruptly deserting me.

Through friends, I'd heard of a couple who'd released the equity on their home, using an American company, and had run into all sorts of trouble when they'd wanted to sell. Similarly, I knew of a couple that had re-mortgaged their home through an American lender and, eventually, wound up losing it. What had occurred was legitimate and entirely legal, though it had resulted in financial disaster for both British parties. This was not what Frankie was getting at.

'You mean why would a legitimate company approve of the methods used by the British arm of VLM?'

'Exactly.'

Maybe they're not legitimate, I thought with a shiver. 'So what are you doing for the rest of the day?' I asked, swiftly moving on.

'Hanging out with Coco.'

'Good idea.'

'We're gonna get lit.'

Bad idea. 'Well, don't overdo it,' I said mildly. Frankie and Coco's drinking sessions were legendary, their capacity for alcohol knowing no bounds. Odd really, as far as I could tell, a lot of youngsters these days didn't drink at all. As for me, I was hard pressed to manage a few glasses without feeling light-headed and out of sorts. Tonight might prove an exception. As a friend once told me: strong women required strong drink to raise strong children — or to deal with foolish husbands.

CHAPTER FIVE

I poured a glass of white wine, plumped the cushions in the sitting room again, and went to the loo for the third time since I'd got home. Cottage pie, taken from the freezer the night before and properly defrosted in the fridge, was already in the oven on a low heat. It was six o'clock and Lance was normally home by now.

The crunch of tyre on gravel alerted me to his arrival. Normally, I'd feel a ripple of fond familiarity — in the old days, lust. I enjoyed the fact that other women found him attractive because he was mine and I felt secure in that knowledge, yet all I felt was dread: of what he might say, of what we would be forced to do. *Look on it as a first instalment.* Just how bad *were* things?

I listened as Lance's key hit the lock, the door opening and closing. The chink of keys chucked into a drawer then a soft thud, indicating he'd deposited his briefcase, another couple of thuds that he'd kicked off his shoes.

Tension leaked from the walls and ceiling. It dripped through the light fittings and pooled around my feet. When he entered the sitting room and awkwardly said, 'Hi,' I forced a smile and stood up. Those solid arms, once so dependable, reached out and pulled me towards him and wrapped me in a fond embrace. We stayed like that for a little bit. For a few moments it felt as if nothing had changed. The way he held me tight, the smoky fragrance of his aftershave, his soft lips glancing across my neck and tracing a line of kisses to my mouth.

I pulled away, studied the face I knew so well. New lines had appeared at the corners of his eyes, shadows underneath; he looked exhausted. And yet he still had "it". Sexy as hell, heavy-lidded, with a winsome smile, he was a man in his prime. Naturally lean, he hadn't run to fat like a lot of middle-aged men. It made me more acutely aware of the pounds I'd piled on recently. Lance could easily pass for five years younger. How come he'd retained his sexual appeal when I was losing mine? 'We need to talk, Lance.'

He pulled a pained face. 'Drink?'

I gestured that I already had one.

'Be right back.' He loped out of the room, across the hall to the kitchen. I'd always admired the way he moved: like a big cat.

It will be all right, I told myself. *It will be okay.*

Moments later, he appeared, tie loosened, top button of his shirt undone, a glass of Scotch in one hand, the other gripping the neck of a decanter. He placed it on the coffee table, within easy reach, and took a deep swallow of whisky. A man full of restless energy, he would often pace up and down when trying to solve a business problem. It alarmed me to see him slump straight onto the sofa opposite.

'I fucked up.' He stared into his drink then looked up with doleful eyes. 'Did they hurt you?'

'Only Frankie.'

'And he's okay?'

'His nose isn't broken. His ego is bruised. He'll live.'

'Christ, I'll make it up to him — and you, of course.'

I couldn't think how and said so.

'I'll work something out. I can replace the cars through the business.'

I felt a punch of surprise. How could he? The business was the source of the problem. I said as much.

'I still have levers to pull,' he assured me.

'Then how is it that those men were able to show up this morning? They intimated that they wanted a lot more than the cars off the drive.'

'Yeah,' he said evasively. 'It's complicated.'

I bit my lip to stop me from saying something I might regret. Most women would lose their tempers. I wasn't like this. Painting on a smile, I said, 'Why don't you start from the beginning?'

Lance took another drink.

'Business is basically fine,' he declared, 'but we've encountered a few issues lately that have thrown things off course.'

'What things?' How off course?

'You remember we diversified into recycling paper?'

'I do.'

'Someone left a piece of metal in documents to be shredded. It broke the teeth of the machine, costing us around £20k to repair.'

'Not a great start but surely not a catastrophe?'

'True.'

'So, essentially, it's a cash-flow problem?'

'Not quite.' He grimaced. 'We lost a key Middle East customer.'

Using the Saudis as brokers, we did a fair amount of business with Iraq. Never shipping direct, it was always a complicated and fraught operation that required high levels of diplomacy. It also paid extremely well.

'Okay, but if the business is *basically fine*,' I said, inverting my fingers into speech marks to make the point, 'how come the loss couldn't be absorbed?'

'Dirty tricks,' he answered bluntly. 'Someone's been posting fake reviews about how poor our service is.'

'A smear campaign?'

'That's the size of it.'

'How long has this been going on?'

Lance averted his eyes. 'A year.'

It was a lie. He knew it and knew I knew it.

'Then another company bought a similar domain to ours,' he continued, 'and redirected all traffic from our website to its website.'

'Isn't that illegal?'

'Yes, but the damage is already done.'

'They stole your Iraqi contract?'

'Can't prove it but most likely.'

'Why not sue?'

'Takes time and money.'

'Why didn't you say something before?' I strained to keep my voice neutral and not accusatory.

'I didn't want to worry you. You had enough going on with . . .' He paused. 'Women's issues.'

I felt a stab of anger. 'Please don't make this about me.'

'Honestly, I'm not.' Lance spread his hands. 'You asked a question and I'm trying to be as straight with you as I can.'

'Had you been straight with me sooner, we might have two cars sitting in our driveway and our son would not have had his nose almost broken.' I wasn't shrill. I spoke in the same balanced tone as if talking to a patient who'd skipped a year's worth of appointments.

'Rather an exaggeration.'

It was. I didn't care.

'And there's another issue,' Lance said quietly.

I raised a questioning eyebrow.

'Due to recent volatility in the stock market, I've lost money.'

'Surely, you only lose money if you sell.'

He gave a slow nod. His gaze locked on to mine.

'You mean you sold?'

'Bad timing,' he said, shamefaced.

'Please don't tell me this was to pay Veldo.'

'No, no,' he said. 'I needed funds to prop up the business after the Middle East deal went sour.'

The business that was basically fine, I thought cynically. The more Lance talked, the greater the contradictions and worse the situation became, mostly because I was struggling to accept his version of events. How could so much go wrong in such a short space of time? It went beyond bad luck.

'How did you come across Veldo Loan Management? Incidentally, I discovered they have a registered office in Battledown and headquarters in Florida.'

'I know.'

'And you're cool with that?'

'It is what it is.' He reached for his drink. 'I don't want you getting involved.'

I didn't like the sound of that. 'I *am* involved. Those men — Jack and Marcus Mount, assaulted our son. You have to do something.'

'We're not going to the police,' Lance said definitively. He took another snatch of his drink. I have to admit he looked afraid.

'We have to.'

'We can't. I took the loan willingly.'

'For God's sake,' I burst out. 'How the hell did you get involved? How were you duped?'

His face relaxed marginally. A basic question requiring a basic description seemed easier terrain for him. 'I was approached in a pub.'

I hoped the cold expression on my face conveyed how foolish and naive I thought he'd been. Clearly, it didn't because Lance continued, oblivious.

'It was after a trade gig at the NEC. As you know, the waste industry is quite small and obviously word had got out that we were in trouble. I was in a pub afterwards and there was this one guy and he approached me, bought me a drink, seemed friendly and reasonable.'

'What was his name?'

'Milton.'

'You didn't think an approach like that unusual?'

'I did but . . .'

'But what?'

'At the time I felt I had few options.'

'What about the bank, the traditional route?'

'We'd used up our credit.'

I didn't believe him and it rocked me. Honesty was Lance's watchword. It was the bedrock of our marriage. However difficult things were we swore to be truthful to each other.

Full of innovative ideas, sometimes in need of my restraining influence, Lance had always been a dependable guy. It was one of the qualities I'd seen in him when I was a trapped single mum, alone, with an overbearing mother and no seemingly good way out. Looking at him in the half-light, with the woodburner yet to be lit, the lamps dimmed low, I viewed him in a way that made me feel as if the ground beneath my feet was no longer rock solid. We had come so far to build a life together: the business, the home, my professional work, which was going well, bringing up two children who hadn't succumbed to drugs and were gainfully employed. It could so easily have gone wrong. I had friends on second marriages and always the arguments were about the children — often the way a child, even in adulthood, played one parent off against the other. Despite Chantal hovering like a ghost at a wedding feast, Lance and I had pulled it off.

And now we hadn't.

I looked at him straight. 'How much do you owe?'

Lance glanced at his drink with regret, the glass almost empty. 'Hard to say.'

'You must have some idea.' I didn't like the shifty look behind the soft brown-eyed gaze.

'Rates of interest are extortionate and unpredictable.'

'How unpredictable?'

'The goalposts keep changing. First, it was ten per cent per week and now it's twenty per cent.'

'And you didn't know this from the outset? Wasn't it explained?' I couldn't help the cynical note in my voice.

'Not clearly, no.'

'Okay, so how much was the original loan for?'

'£250k.'

'And how much now?'

'Around a mill.'

'Good God,' I gasped.

'Fucking hell.'

Lance averted his gaze to the door to where Coco and Frankie stood, open-mouthed.

CHAPTER SIX

Coco danced in and flung herself down next to her father. 'Hi, Pops, sounds like you've been an utter dipshit.'

Normally, I'd ask my stepdaughter not to talk to her dad like that. I felt too ill to speak.

Parking himself next to me, Frankie took and squeezed my hand. He smelt like a brewery and, in my experience, alcohol and family problems were never a good combination.

I looked pointedly at Coco. 'I hope you didn't drive here.'

''Course not. We walked from Mum's.'

'How is she?' Lance asked, topping up his glass.

Coco shrugged. 'Like Mum, and don't change the subject.'

'I'm not,' Lance said, clipped. I had the impression that being interrogated by his daughter was worse than being questioned by his wife. 'How's the nose, Frankie?' Lance asked with evident concern.

'Tender, but I won't need plastic surgery.'

'Thank fuck,' Coco said dryly. 'The household budget couldn't stand it.'

Studiously ignoring Coco, Lance said to Frankie, 'I was telling your mother that I'll sort you out a set of wheels through the business.'

'Only it won't be a brand new MINI.'

'Coco, for goodness' sake, can you stop mixing it?' Lance snapped.

Feeling raw, I was glad Lance had stepped in. Saved me from doing so. At times, Coco behaved more like a teenager than a young woman of twenty-four.

Unperturbed, Coco eyed up her father's glass. 'Any more where that came from?'

'You don't like whisky,' Frankie said.

'I'm prepared to give it a go. So, Pops,' she said, fixing Lance with a cat-like stare. 'WTF happened?'

Unable to bear Lance trawling through it all again, no doubt with highly edited highlights, I stood up and announced I had dinner to check on.

I took my time, refreshed my glass and gazed blindly out of the window to our lovely garden. *A mill*? An incredible amount of money that only a lottery win would fix. On a practical level I could increase my hours from four days to five. We could take in a lodger. I could let Mrs Drummond, our cleaner, go. I could shop for food more cheaply, stop buying wine and eating out, cancel holidays, hawk my jewellery; frenzied and ultimately paltry economies that would barely make a difference. My gut instinct was still to go to the police.

Raised voices cut through to the kitchen. Despite my reluctance and the sheer exhaustion of the day, I found myself automatically propelled, as if on rails, into the living room where Lance appeared to have it in for Frankie.

'You flit from one job to another . . .'

'Pops, it's called progression,' Coco cut in, taking her stepbrother's side. 'Gone are the days when you stay with one company for your entire working life and pick up a carriage clock or a watch at the end of it.'

'More's the pity,' Lance muttered.

Frankie snorted a laugh. 'Dad the dinosaur.'

My son was trying to defuse the situation with humour that was entirely, if understandably, lost on Lance who had refilled his glass with what seemed like a triple measure.

'This dinosaur was already running his own business at your age,' Lance snapped in a loud voice. 'What I don't understand is why you must always apply for jobs that are above your abilities.'

'It's called ambition,' Frankie retorted.

But Lance wasn't having any of it. 'A pity you don't use some of that ambition to flee the nest and lead an independent life without hand-outs from your mother and me.'

'Lance,' I burst out.

'Dad, that was bang out of order,' Coco said.

Lance glowered. 'Was it?'

Frankie stood up. 'If that's the way you feel I'll go and pack my gear.'

'Sit down,' Lance growled. 'Don't be such a fool.'

'It's cool, Dad. Got the memo loud and clear.'

'Frankie, please don't go,' I said. 'Not like this.'

'No worries, Mum. I'll be fine. Besides,' Frankie said, jutting out his chin in Lance's direction, 'you've got more than enough on your plate with him.'

Coco sprang to her feet. 'You can come and stay at ours.'

'Absurd,' Lance said.

'Won't your mum mind?' I asked anxiously.

'Nope, Mummy already offered Frankie her car for any other out-of-town interviews.'

'That's very thoughtful of her.' I felt crushed inside.

'See ya.' Coco gave her father a peck on his cheek. 'Bye, Suze,' she called cheerily, hurrying out after Frankie.

Silence descended like an avalanche of rocks.

Spent, I slid down onto the nearest chair; the grip on the stem of my glass so tight I thought it might shatter. Neither Lance nor I spoke as Frankie packed a bag, pounded downstairs and followed Coco outside. Only when they'd sped off down the road, footsteps disappearing into the evening light, did I trust myself to utter a word.

'That was both unnecessary and cruel.'

'You're right it was cruel, but entirely necessary.'

'The boy is simply trying to find himself.'

'I wasn't aware *the boy* was lost.'

'Young men are so vulnerable in our changing world.' I felt it quite deeply. Women were born survivors.

'God, Susannah, this is all rather beside the point.'

Unhappily, I supposed it was. 'I still don't understand why we can't go to the police.'

'No,' Lance said.

'Why not?'

'Because I don't want my legs broken down a dark alley, all right?'

I gave a start. 'You really think they'd do that? I mean I know they roughed up our son, but what you're suggesting is taking it to a different level.'

'I wouldn't want to put it to the test.' He swallowed another mouthful of whisky. 'No,' he said pensively, 'going to the police would only generate hysteria. There has to be another way.'

For the life of me I couldn't think what that might be. 'I was wondering,' I began and told him about the possibility of increasing my hours and taking in a lodger.

'That's hardly going to make a dent. All the time you're nobly working to make a little more cash, the interest rate will shoot up.'

'Then talk to them and negotiate a better deal.'

'You think I haven't tried that already? Besides, it's not the henchmen I need to speak to.'

'What about this Milton character, the guy who approached you?'

Lance shook his head. 'A shadowy figure based in the States, unfortunately.'

Unbidden, tears welled up in my eyes. 'How could you, Lance? How could you get us into such a fix?'

He put down his glass and, crossing to where I sat, knelt in front of me. Reaching up, he took my face in his hands and rested his forehead affectionately against mine. 'I am very, very sorry.'

And I knew he was.

He kissed me once and sat on the arm of my chair.

'Would it help if I took a look at the accounts?' I said.

'You'd only get half the picture. End of year returns,' he explained. 'Dave's pulled a lot of stuff together. I don't want to interrupt his flow.'

Dave Spencer was the company's Ops Manager. The way Lance was talking, you'd think he was compiling dossiers of hard copy when, in reality, financial information was submitted digitally.

'That business trip I told you about,' Lance reminded me.

'The one in Scotland?'

'I've managed to bring it forward.'

I looked up at him. 'And you think that will help?'

'It could secure several new big orders for the firm.' I didn't like the sound of *could* — way too nebulous. 'I leave first thing tomorrow,' Lance said.

'Will it be enough?' My voice sounded hoarse.

His face lit up. 'If I pull it off, more than, and then we'll be free.'

CHAPTER SEVEN

Lance had spoken with such conviction I almost believed him.
By the time we got to eat, the cottage pie was burnt and I'd lost
my appetite. Turning in for an early night used to be code for
sex. These days it was symptomatic of the exhaustion that regularly grabbed hold and didn't let go. Lance wasn't much better.
Some days he'd come back from work absolutely done in.

Lights off, I admit I froze when he reached across and
took me in his arms and nuzzled my neck.

'Are we okay, darling?' he whispered.

'Yes,' I said mechanically.

'Do you trust me, Susannah?'

The hesitation was fractional. 'I do,' I said.

'We'll find a way through, like always.'

But we'd never had a problem like this before.

'I think it best we keep it to ourselves.'

'You mean secret?' I'd never been good with those.
Secrets entailed lies.

'Obviously Frankie and Coco are in the know.'

'And Chantal,' I reminded him.

'Oh, she'll keep her own counsel.'

He was right about that. Chantal was a woman of few
words and big gestures.

'Speak to the children and remind them of the need for discretion,' he said.

Gagging order, I thought uneasily.

'And definitely don't mention it to your parents.'

I wouldn't dream of it. 'What about yours?' I could do worse than have Jeremy and Theresa Stratton as my in-laws. Native Midlanders, they now lived in suburban splendour in Surrey.

'Dad would be okay but Mum would worry herself into oblivion.'

'Can't I talk to Suki?' Suki Quant, a dependable friend, ran a yoga class in town. 'I'm not sure I want to carry it alone.'

'You're not carrying it alone, sweetheart. You have me.'

'Yes, but another point of view might be useful. What about Meera and Dan, Holly and Jonathan?'

'We barely see them these days.'

Which was true. We all led such busy lives. I sometimes bumped into Holly at the supermarket. I'd last seen Dan when I'd taken my car in for its service.

'I think it best we keep the circle tight.' He kissed my temple, rolled over and fell asleep. Amazingly, before long, he was softly snoring. How could he dream so peacefully with so much on his mind? I'd be hard pressed to get any shut-eye tonight.

I lay on my side, on my back, the other side. I tried covers on, covers off. Wide-awake, lying in the dark, mind churning, I considered getting up but that would disturb Lance and I needed him sharp tomorrow morning with such an important day ahead. Go to a happy place in your mind, I'd read somewhere.

Taking long deep breaths in and out, letting my limbs go tight and then slack, I pictured warm weather, sunshine, waves gently rippling along a sandy coastline under bright blue skies. And there Lorenzo was: dark eyes shining, mouth perpetually smiling, his hand in mine, tugging me into the water. I squealed at how cold it was and squealed some more when he pulled me down into the waves, wet hair slick against his scalp, his bare taut chest against my skin. That had been the start of it — an instant attraction — and, for three glorious weeks, we had been inseparable. I'd even helped out at his father's bar in Salerno so that I could stay close to him. To be out of his reach had physically hurt. When I was with him I felt as if I could barely breathe. It had been the most intense relationship I'd ever experienced. What I'd shared with Lorenzo Bonetti defied the cliché of the holiday romance. The proof, if any were needed, was in our son.

And Lorenzo never knew of Frankie's existence.

How we had clung together when we said goodbye at the airport. Lorenzo had promised to keep in touch, but I'd never heard another word from him.

'By now, he's probably on to his next British conquest,' my mother had opined sourly.

At the time, I thought my perfect life had been upset. And here I was again: sleepless, agitated and confused. Only this time it felt considerably worse.

CHAPTER EIGHT

Chantal Kelly, formerly Chantal Stratton, climbed out of the private members' pool, towelled her body dry and pulled on a pair of soft flannel sweats and trainers. She never showered in the changing rooms in the spa because she didn't wish to become embroiled in conversation with strangers or, worse, locals at such an early hour of the morning. She had no need of a quick glance in the mirror. Confidence wasn't an issue. If you hadn't attained a degree of comfort beneath your skin at the age of fifty-six, you could forget it. Her iron-grey hair was cut short, almost to the bone and, obviously, she wore no make-up. That could wait, though it was an essential part of her grooming and wellbeing.

Heading out of the club, her wet swimwear stowed in a designer sports bag, she took out the key fob and opened the door to her Night Blue Audi TT and climbed inside. Already traffic was building up as she turned out of the hotel grounds and onto the Shurdington Road. It would take her roughly ten minutes to reach her Grade II listed home in Lansdown Parade. Hopefully, Coco and Frankie would still be asleep and she could enjoy her first cup of carefully brewed, organically sourced coffee in peace.

She sincerely hoped that Frankie was not going to be a permanent fixture. She'd known him since he was small and he'd grown up into a nice enough young man, quite amusing on occasion, a marvel in the kitchen and made a mean jackfruit curry, but his devotion to his mother and his mother's adoration of her son bordered tastelessly on the Oedipal. Chantal couldn't abide it; it wasn't healthy. Fortunately, she'd spent enough time with her daughter, Coco, to instil a measure of independence in her from an early age. Admittedly, Coco's relationship with her father was a little too close for Chantal's liking, which was why she was rather pleased to hear what an idiot Lance had been. Nothing like torpedoing the hull of the family ship to create a stark financial reality check. Ever since Chantal's own father had been declared bankrupt, she'd had a visceral dislike of being poor and had taken steps to ensure that her life was ring-fenced with money. She didn't enjoy it for its own sake. That would be too dull. She loved it for what it could give her: a beautiful home, a proper education for her only child and a lifestyle independent of any man, including Lance Stratton.

Parking outside in her designated space and behind Coco's car, she crossed to the portico entrance and let herself into the open hall that housed a Lara Bohinc console table inspired by a geometric design and on which sat two lamps uniquely designed by Sam Rush. A large sitting room also contained statement pieces. Each chair, sofa, table, mirror and bed had been carefully curated; nothing was there by accident. Double doors led into a family room, where Frankie was asleep on the sofa bed. Chantal liked properties with flow and her home was positively fluid. Off the family room, there was a dogleg into her office. From here she ran an online vintage clothing company selling frocks (among other items) modelled on the late designer Vivienne Westwood, with a touch of Helen Bonham-Carter chic.

All was pleasingly quiet and she stole downstairs to the large kitchen and dining room that constituted the lower ground floor and into a utility area and walk-in shower.

Stripping off, she ran it cold and stood underneath for a regulatory minute before turning it hot and soaping herself with an expensive brand of organic shower gel for the mature woman. Afterwards, she applied a similar brand of body lotion and, reaching for a fluffy white robe, again made from organically sourced and sustainable fibres, prepared coffee, which she took to a favourite piece: a Wiggle Chair by architect and designer, Frank Gehry, and perfectly placed for a wonderful view of her walled garden. This was her safe space where she could freely think and be as one. Normally, Lance would not feature, either in her mind or physically, despite the fact he and his wife lived a mere three-minute walk away. Over the years they had met briefly for birthdays and school events and to make practical arrangements around holidays. Now that Coco was a fully-fledged adult such communications were mostly unnecessary.

It had to be said Chantal had no clear memories of fights, rows or disagreements with the father of her child because she had surgically obliterated them from her mind. She told anyone who asked, that at the time of the split, she'd simply outgrown him, as she did any man who hung around in her life for longer than was strictly necessary. Too late, she'd realised that she wasn't marriage material; wasn't even good girlfriend material, she'd subsequently discovered. She guessed she suffered from one of those fashionable conditions that ensured she got bored very quickly though she would never put a label on it. In her experience most people were so endlessly disappointing. Admittedly, it would be too harsh to place Lance into that category, the initial attraction between them sparking from his chancer style, the fact he was prepared to take risks personally and professionally, which she rather admired as a character trait in others, but regarded as a flaw in Lance. Susannah was nice enough but Chantal never really understood what he saw in her, other than she was a safe bet. Still, how could Chantal possibly criticise? Susannah and Lance had been together for twenty years, a good deal longer than she'd ever managed with anyone. Her main concern now was to protect Coco from any "blowback". She shrank at the thought of her only daughter exposed to undesirables and if that meant her staying away from the Stratton family home for the foreseeable future, so be it.

A shadow fell across the room, disturbing her peace.

'Frankie.' Chantal was startled to see him barely dressed. He wore a pair of jeans, which she suspected he was wearing commando style, and nothing else. She could not help but stare at the dark line of hair from his chest to his navel. 'Darling, you look a complete mess and smell worse. Go and get in the shower before Coco wakes up, there's a good fellow.'

'All right to help myself to coffee first?'

No, it was not. 'There's juice in the fridge — wonderful for a hangover.'

'I'm not hungover.' He scratched underneath his arms in a way that Chantal found disconcerting.

'How can I put it?' She smiled delicately. 'This is my little oasis in the day. I will happily make you a lovely cup of coffee once you've availed yourself of the bathroom facilities.'

He gave a wolfish grin. 'Is this a polite way of you telling me I stink?'

'If you must be so direct, yes.'

'That's what we all love about you, Chantal, you always tell it like it is.' He stood on one foot and ran his toe down the back of his leg. *What was wrong with him*, Chantal thought, *did he have fleas?*

'Come on, Frankie, you know very well how we roll here. Quiet time for Mama ensures calm time for children.'

'Fuck's sake, Chantal, I'm almost twenty-seven.'

'And still a baby to me, my darling. Seeing as you love my directness, when will you be going home?'

He pulled up a chair. Chantal waggled a finger. 'No need to get comfy.'

'God, you're harsh.'

'So I've been told.'

'In answer to your question: when the fuss dies down.'

'It does sound rather a mess.'

40

'Understatement of the year.'

'At least they didn't knock your teeth out. That would have been a pity.'

'Thanks for the sympathy. I must say you don't seem to be taking this very seriously.'

'Rather outside my box — thank goodness. All I can offer is practical help.'

'The offer of the car *is* appreciated.'

'If you're looking for emotional support, I'm not the right person, as well you know,' Chantal said with a dry smile.

He nodded absently. Oh God, how she hated uncomfortable silences. She could tell he wanted to ask something but didn't know how to go about it. That was modern youth for you.

'Chantal?' he asked at last.

'Yes, Frankie.'

'Do you think there's more to it?'

'I'm not absolutely certain what you're driving at.'

'Well, Dad is pretty successful from what I can see. The business has gone from strength to strength. It seems such a bum move to get into trouble in the first place and then go to a couple of loan sharks.'

Frankie wasn't as slow as he sometimes seemed. Similarly unnerving thoughts had crossed Chantal's mind. 'Sometimes people do strange things.'

'But this is Dad.'

'Even dads make mistakes.' And, Christ, she should know.

'It's a monumental fuck-up,' Frankie said. 'I mean nobody seems to know what to do about it. Dad seems genuinely scared. Mum, well, she looks beaten. I've read about extortionists. They bleed people dry and rip the shirt off your back. What if we lose the house — double-fuck, the business?'

Chantal squirmed in her seat. Firstly, it was the most horrible reminder of what had transpired when she was a child and, secondly, she didn't want Lance's mess rebounding on her. 'I think you're running ahead of yourself.'

'Am I?'

He looked genuinely stricken. 'My best advice, and God knows I hesitate to agree with your father, but now is the time to leave the old folks to get on with it, break free and make a life for yourself. Carve your own route forward, Frankie. Be bold. You're young enough to make a few mistakes and, if you do, you'll bounce back stronger, you'll see.'

'Yes,' he agreed, though his frightened eyes told her *no*.

CHAPTER NINE

Lance had already left by the time I stirred. A secret part of me was grateful. Every time I looked out of the window and saw the space where my car should have been, I was reminded of what had befallen us. I tried not to be angry. Lance had been stupid. He'd kept things from me. One hundred per cent responsible, he'd owned it and was contrite. I truly believed him when he said he was genuinely sorry. It felt important to hang on to his good qualities. He'd done a good job of bringing up another man's child. His patience had been legendary during Frankie and Coco's more challenging teenage years and, latterly, with having a stay-at-home adult son and visits from a daughter who treated the home like an Airbnb. Lance was also thoughtful and could spring the odd surprise, like when he whisked me away for a long weekend in Fowey recently.

'Oh, Lance, what a lovely idea but I can't,' I'd said. 'I have work.'

'No, you don't. It's all sorted. Cleared it with the practice months ago.'

And we'd had a fantastic time. The drudgery of routine that assails every marriage fell away. We had laughed like we used to. We realised that we still had dreams together. I'd felt desirable and loved.

Seemed like a lifetime ago.

Letting myself out into the early morning, I was surprised to see Mrs Fletcher pop up from behind the buddleia.

'Everything all right, dear?'

'Good morning, yes, fine, thanks.'

'Only I couldn't help witness your bit of bother yesterday.'

My face flushed and my skin felt clammy. *Please God, not now*, I thought. 'It was all a stupid misunderstanding.'

'So pleased to hear. Unsavoury individuals, I thought.'

'Well, lovely to chat but I really must get to work.'

'Oh yes, without your car, I see.'

I forced a smile and fled. Put it out of your mind, I told myself. Mrs Fletcher was simply being Mrs Fletcher. No doubt it would be the topic of conversation at the golf club. Fortunately, the residents on the street were too engrossed in their own lives to be interested in the idle chatter of a renowned gossip.

The walk to work took around twenty-five minutes. After days of rain, the burst of sunshine was welcome; it would take a lot more than that to lighten my step. Despite Lance's intention to sort out the vehicle problem, I considered calling Dad. He wouldn't hesitate to loan me money to buy a cheap run-around. Then Lance could focus on getting a better car for Frankie. It would help heal the rift between them after the row. I hated dissent in any form. A people-pleaser to my core, "a pushover" as Frankie once reminded me in jest, I'd contort myself into any shape to ensure that life ran smoothly — unlike my mother, who was as resistant in her views and behaviour as a piece of granite. I still shuddered at the memory of Frankie as a small boy, red-faced, crying and clinging to my legs as my no-nonsense mother prised him off me. With a difficult start, Frankie had been slow to walk, to potty train, to read and to add up.

Instantly, I felt my resolve weaken. If I called Dad, Mum would want to know why and then she would dig and I didn't trust myself to keep my mouth shut and Lance very much wanted me to keep it secret. I got it. If word got out that we were in debt to the tune of a million pounds, the business would fold overnight and Lance's company was the only thing that was going to get us out of the mess. I also guessed that he felt terribly humiliated by what had happened.

Work was work and I was thorough, professional and pleasant. Underneath, and despite my best efforts, I couldn't help but seethe. I found myself with resentments I never knew I had. My job involved the crappy, tedious and time-consuming tasks so that patients could be presented with a nice and shiny set of teeth to the more highly-paid dentist for a check-up that mostly took minutes. Mean-spirited and borne of envy, I gave myself a stern talking to: *if you hadn't mucked about at school, you could have attained better qualifications. If you hadn't fallen pregnant, you could have trained to be a dentist.*

'Of course, you could always have an . . .'

'No,' I'd told my mother smartly. *'Out of the question.'*

'And rinse,' I said too cheerily to a girl whose teeth were so white they blinded.

At lunchtime, I toyed with phoning Lance to see how he was getting on. Such interruptions were discouraged and had been from the very early days of our marriage when he was building the business, but I was desperate to see how things were going. To my surprise, he answered after a couple of rings.

'Hiya,' he said breezily.

'You got there safely then.'

'No prob. Reached Berwick-on-Tweed and had a cup of coffee in my hand by the time you were seeing your first patient. Had a really productive meeting and about to head to my next.'

'That's great. I won't keep you then.'

'Everything okay your end?'

'Same old.'

'Good,' he said, with emphasis. 'Heard from Frankie?'

'Not as yet.'

'He'll come sloping back, you'll see.'

I smiled stiffly, hoping Lance was right, fearing he was wrong.

45

The house smelt of lamb and spices when I got home. Warm relief trickled over me as I kicked off my shoes. My son was back, peace restored. I was glad that Lance's judgement was not totally impaired.

'Hi,' Frankie called from the kitchen.

I padded inside. It was so good to see him. 'This is a nice surprise.' Sweetly, Frankie had laid the table for three.

'Thought you deserved a treat.'

'That's very thoughtful of you.'

'No Dad?'

'He's in Scotland.'

'What's he doing there?"

'Restoring the family fortunes.'

'Good luck with that.' He went to the table and cleared Lance's place away. 'There's white wine in the fridge.'

'On a school night?'

Frankie elevated a dark eyebrow. 'Desperate measures.'

'Go on, then.' I hopped up onto a bar stool and sat at the central island while Frankie poured two glasses.

Chinking mine with his, I took a long deep swallow. I wasn't sure if it was the calming effect of alcohol or the fact that Frankie always made me feel better but I felt a little more hopeful that we could survive this.

'I take it you've discussed going to the police.'

I squirmed on my seat. 'Discussed, yes.'

'And?' Frankie frowned, his expression intense.

'Your father is scared.'

'Then even more reason to go to the cops.'

'It's not as simple as that.'

'Isn't it?' The harsh note in his voice was unmistakeable. 'What's going on is totally illegal.'

'Look, I really don't want to fall out with you. I see where you're coming from but Dad got us into this so I think we owe it to him to give him a chance to get us out of it.'

'You really reckon he can pull something off? A mill is a fuck of a lot of money.'

I agreed and took another sip.

'Miles suggested a deep dive into Veldo.'

I felt my stomach flip. 'You've spoken to Miles?'

'He's ridiculously good with a computer.'

'Frankie, please don't discuss this with your friends.'

He drew in his chin, eyes narrowed.

'Your father is embarrassed. *I'm* embarrassed.'

'What do *you* have to feel embarrassed about?'

'I simply think we don't need to broadcast it, that's all,' I said briskly. 'It's best kept within the family.'

'Is this you talking, or Dad?'

'Both of us,' I said pointedly.

'Cool.' Frankie took a gulp of wine. 'I hadn't realised it was to be one big fucking secret.'

'Don't say it like that.'

'Is there any other way to say it? Is that why Dad never wanted me in the business?'

'That's a big leap in logic.'

'Not really. It's based on the same principle. '

'Dad wants you to get some experience before he takes you into the firm.'

'If you say so.' It wasn't said in a snarky fashion, more resigned acceptance.

'Now can we change the subject, *please*?' I implored.

I topped up our glasses and we ate in companionable silence.

'That was delicious. Ever thought of a job in catering?' I asked when we'd finished. My shoulders felt less tight, my mind more composed.

'Long hours, fussy customers and non-existent social life, no thanks.'

While Frankie did the washing-up I dutifully emptied the recycling bag and took it to the bin outside, ready for the morning's collection.

Night had fallen and there was a sharp chill in the air. Illuminated by streetlights, the road was quiet apart from a cat jaywalking. Stepping off the drive and parking the bin on the pavement, I noticed the silhouette of a retreating figure, urgent and in a hurry, coattail flapping. Fearing one of the duo had returned and the effect of alcohol making me bold, I called out, 'Hey, you.' The figure sped up. I couldn't tell the gender for sure, although the height and build suggested it was a man.

Disturbed, I hurried back inside.

'You okay, Mum?' Frankie asked. 'You've gone quite pale.'

I shot him a nervous glance. 'Drank too much booze too quickly. You know what a lightweight I am. Think I'll get a glass of water and go to bed.'

Lance was in Scotland, wasn't he? I thought, running the cold tap and splashing my face with water.

CHAPTER TEN

Amy had got the kids to bed early with promises that Daddy would come up and see them before they went to sleep.

Wilf lifted his chubby hand to hers. 'Pinkie promise?'

'Pinkie promise.' Amy touched his little finger with hers. 'Now tuck up with your dinosaur.'

'He's not a dinosaur.'

'Yes, he is.'

'He's a stegosaurus.'

'Clever dick. Well whatever he is, night-night.'

Amy went downstairs to the kitchen to where Adele was gurgling in a baby recliner. Amy stroked her baby under the chin then arranged two sirloin steaks on the grill ready to pop on once Rollo was home. They were going to eat them with oven chips and peas. She'd laid the table in the lounge with candles and a couple of paper serviettes she'd found in the back of a cupboard, glasses, too, for the bottle of Spanish plonk she'd bought from the corner shop. Afters would be a bar of that nice dark chocolate Rollo loved. Working at the sweet shop had its advantages. The whole dinner had cost her less than twenty quid, which was a saving on a meal out, especially if you added the cost of petrol. What they didn't spend could be put towards the day out she planned

49

for them tomorrow. It had been ages since they'd had some fun because they were always looking after the children and working. She'd got it all mapped out.

She checked on Adele again and noticed her eyelids were heavy.

'Come on, little miss,' Amy said, picking her up and giving her a cuddle. 'Time for bed.' *Not that you'll stay asleep for long*, Amy thought. The second her daddy walked through the door, those eyes would pop open, swiftly followed by her mouth. Amy continued to be astounded by the lung power of a five-month-old.

With Adele settled, Amy gazed out of the window. The evenings were getting longer and soon the clocks would go back. After the rain, the sky, a mixture of pink and turquoise, didn't look real.

Sixth sense told Amy that Rollo's Dacia Sandero was not far away. She touched the necklace at her throat and thrilled with anticipation. *Not long now*, she thought, looking forward to another pair of hands to help with the kids, especially in the middle of the night when she was knackered. What she really wanted was her man, her Rollo. She loved the way he talked. He was refined, that's what he was. A clever man, who knew stuff she'd never heard of; he was a cut above. If he were a dog he'd be one of those Afghan hounds. Definitely got the right sideburns. With a father she never knew and two stepdads, neither hanging around for long, she considered herself more of a mongrel. Rollo always had something interesting to say. Even when he was old (she had long faced the fact that his time would be up before hers) he would be exciting to have around.

Sure enough, his car drew onto the drive. Hurrying to the door, she threw it wide open. Beaming at her as he got out she felt a pure burst of joy. Next, just like in the romantic comedies she loved, she was in his arms, smelling his earthy skin, his body taut against hers.

'Wotcha,' she said, giving him a squeeze. Then she went in for a long snog and didn't give two hoots what the neighbours thought.

'Oh, I've missed you,' he said.

Hard against her, she could tell he had.

'I've bought steaks and wine and *everything*,' she said.

'Baby asleep?'

'Yeah.'

'*Everything* then.'

She dragged him inside and they did it in the kitchen. Urgent, desperate and filthy, with her rear on the kitchen table, Amy loved every moment of it.

'You'll have to go away more often,' she said, putting her knickers back on and readjusting her clothing. 'Go up and see the kids and I'll fix dinner while you have a shower.'

The steaks were on the plates by the time he came down.

'Wilf stirred but the others are fast asleep.'

'Even the baby?'

'Managed to get her back down — she looks as if she's grown.'

'Don't be soft. You've only been gone a week.'

'Too long.' He slipped his arms around her waist while she ladled out peas and chips.

'Get off,' she laughed. 'I'm bloody starving and Adele will be wanting a feed soon.'

They sat down at the table. One of the first things Amy noticed about Rollo was his lovely table manners. He didn't bolt his food, always took his time, like the way he made love — that evening's frisky interlude the exception. He never crammed too much on his fork, didn't stick the blade of his knife in his mouth or belch afterwards. She'd never told him before, but watching him eat was a turn-on.

Halfway through the meal Amy judged the time to be right to tell him about the house. 'I was thinking,' she began.

Rollo raised an eyebrow. She loved that about him too. He had really dark eyebrows. Mobile, they suggested so much.

'Why don't we have a day out tomorrow?'

'Sounds good.'

'I thought once we'd dropped the kids we could go and view a house I've seen in Bayton.'

Rollo put down his knife and fork. 'But we've already got a house.'

'A bungalow,' she corrected him, 'and it's not really big enough and I want the kids to grow up in the countryside *and*,' she said, waving a knife in the air, 'it's rented.'

He picked up his fork and stuck it into his steak like he was stabbing a burglar in the back.

'Don't be like that,' she said.

'I'm not being like anything.'

'You are, babe.'

'It's, well, money's a bit tight at the moment.'

'That's not what you said on the phone yesterday. Thought you were coining it in.'

'Yes and no.'

'Either it's one or the other.' It wasn't like him to dither.

Rollo stopped eating and reached across the table to her. She put down her knife and fork and laid her hands in his.

'I know it's important for us to have a place of our own but, in life, it's all about timing.'

'Exactly. I'm not prepared to wait until you're drawing your old age pension. Our kids need a proper start in life.'

'They already have. You're a fabulous mum.' He smiled and all the little lines around his eyes crinkled adorably.

'You can't flannel me, Rollo. Besides, I've already made the appointment with an estate agent.'

'Bloody hell, Amy.' He drew away sharply and went back to his steak and chips.

Downcast, she finished her meal. 'Are you all right? I don't know, you seem a bit . . .'

'Tired, love.' He pushed a smile. 'Sorry, didn't mean to crush your dreams.'

'Take more than that.' She stood and swept up their plates. 'I'll go on my own.'

Storming into the kitchen, she noisily deposited any remaining food in the bin while silently beginning the count-down to ten. Normally, Rollo would cave in around five.

Six, seven, eight . . .

'Tell you what,' Rollo said, sneaking up behind her. 'How about I take you out for some retail therapy instead? Buy you a new dress, or those jeans you've been on about. Then we could have a nice pub lunch and a siesta before the kids come home.'

'What about Adele?'

'She can come, too. She normally has a sleep in the afternoon,' he said in a low voice.

'Hmm.' She wasn't feeling in the least bit mollified. What was it her mum said? There are a dozen ways to skin a cat. Not a very nice saying, but Amy got the meaning. Perhaps if she looked as if she was giving in now, she could talk Rollo round to seeing her point of view later.

'Done,' she said.

'That's my girl.'

'Cheltenham, that's where I want to go. They've got proper shops there. What?' she said in response to Rollo's strangled expression. 'You look as if you've choked on your chips.'

'I was thinking Birmingham,' he said.

'Brum is boring.'

'No, it isn't.'

'Well, okay it isn't, but I want to go somewhere different. Please, Rollo.'

'But Birmingham is so much nearer.'

'You drive from Land's End to bloody Scotland and don't complain.'

'That's my point. That's work. This is fun.'

'It's about twenty minutes extra,' she argued. 'If you like, I'll drive.' And then she could take a little detour on the way back — well, a big detour on the way back.

'I'm not in the mood for Cheltenham. It's too frantic, too busy, too cut and thrust.'

What was wrong with him? He'd gone all pale and not in an interesting way. *Crap*, she thought, *Rollo is scared*.

He ran his fingers through his hair. 'What time did you say you'd booked the viewing with the estate agent tomorrow?'

'10.30 a.m.'

He swallowed hard. 'Okay, you win.'

CHAPTER ELEVEN

I called in sick early the next morning. Nobody wanted to be seen by someone contagious in my line of work so it was easy enough to persuade the receptionist to cancel all my appointments. It wasn't a complete lie. I really didn't feel very well. *Stress*, I thought, *that's what's making me feel out of sorts.*

In the cool light of day I told myself I was making too big a deal of the night before. The random person hurrying away from my home was a coincidence: I'd been putting out the rubbish and whoever it was had been rushing past because it was a cold night. People scooted about in Cheltenham all the time; it was one of those places. The man, (I was pretty certain it was) had probably dismissed my cry as intended for someone else. Random shouts, usually from drunks and particularly late at night, was another feature of the town, now designated with city status, and best ignored. The ludicrous thought that Lance was watching from the shadows was symptomatic of the pressure I felt. I'd phoned him first thing and my call had understandably gone to voicemail so I left a message.

Hi, darling, touching base and hope your trip is continuing to be productive. All well here.

Frankie stumbled into the kitchen, hair askew, jaw shadowed with stubble. How he looked like his father at the same age, I thought warmly, wondering what Lorenzo was up to these days. He'd always wanted a bar of his own, not his dad's, he'd once told me. Without any obvious skills, that's probably what he'd wound up doing. Most likely married to a beautiful Italian woman and had a clutch of kids. His would be a simpler life than mine, for sure.

'Coffee's in the pot,' I told Frankie.

'Life-saver.' He helped himself. 'Pulled a sickie?' he asked, amused.

I was embarrassed to admit that I had.

'Don't feel bad. Me and Coco thought you were mad to go into work yesterday.'

'It's not easy to ditch patients.'

'Well, I wouldn't want to be seen by a jittery woman with a scalpel in her hand.'

'I'm not jittery and I don't use scalpels.'

'Sharp pointy things then,' he said with a grin. 'Got plans?'

'Might go for a walk.'

'On the other side of town from the surgery, I hope.'

I flicked a conspiratorial smile.

'You won't be seeing much of me,' Frankie said. 'I've got a software gig with a parking management company. Pay's rubbish but hey.' He gave a shrug and ambled back upstairs to his room-cum-office. Once the door was closed I sat on the window seat, with my back to the garden, and surveyed my home with fresh eyes. We could do with a new cooker hood and extractor — the old one barely functioned. The walls could use a repaint. Much of the skirting was chipped and tired. We'd been talking about getting the basement properly tanked for years. A glory hole full of old appliances, odd bits of furniture and general rubbish; that would definitely have to wait. What had once looked homely seemed hopelessly dated, not that we could possibly afford to do anything anytime soon.

In a subdued mood I scrolled through my phone. Suki Quant had dropped me a WhatsApp message about a possible drink after work. We'd been friends since our children went to secondary school. A yoga teacher, Suki approached all problems from a horizontal "circle of life" angle. She made me seem like a raging ball of energy by comparison. I so wanted to talk to her, yet the ensuing guilt I'd feel for breaking Lance's trust wasn't worth it. Instead, I messaged her and, extending the lie, said I'd come down with something nasty, but would be in touch soon. Then, before I changed my mind, I put a call through to Dave Spencer, Lance's Ops Manager.

The phone rang out for ages. About to cut the call and try again, a breathless Sharon, one of Lance's admin staff, answered.

'Yes.'

'It's Susannah, Sharon. Sorry to disturb you.'

'We're up to our ears at the moment what with being short-staffed and the boss away.'

'Could I speak to Dave Spencer, please?'

'He's not here.'

'Is he down on site?'

Fractional hesitation followed by a response suggesting the negative. Sharon seemed peculiarly cautious.

Perplexed, I said, 'Can you get him to give me a ring when he's available?'

'Thing is,' Sharon said awkwardly, 'Dave left the firm a couple of weeks ago. I thought you knew.'

Concern gave my hand a tug, got up close and whispered: *come on, leave it alone, walk this way, silly.* 'Of course,' I stammered. 'How stupid of me. I'd clean forgotten. Do you have his personal number?'

Clearly overwhelmed with work, Sharon let out a groan.

'I'd be so grateful if you could text it to me, please. It's quite urgent.'

'Right you are,' Sharon complied, eager to escape.

I thanked her profusely and ended the call.

Dave had been the mainstay of the business for several years. A no-nonsense Brummie, he was reassuringly capable, "a good man to have at the helm", so Lance maintained, especially when Lance was out and about, drumming up business, yet Lance had deflected me from taking a look at the finances by using Dave as an excuse. *A man who had not stepped over the threshold for two weeks,* according to Sharon, a woman who would know and had no reason to lie.

Ten minutes later, while I was debating whether to brave the rain or wait until the most recent cloudburst had dissipated, a message came through from Sharon. No greeting, no bells and whistles, only the number.

Dave answered as though he'd been expecting my call. Given prior warning, I surmised.

'Susannah.'

'Dave, I've literally just heard you no longer work for us.'

'That's right,' he said gruffly.

'I'm very sorry to hear.'

'Thank you,' he replied.

I was getting the strong impression that Dave had left on bad terms. 'Would it be too rude of me to ask why?'

Dave gave a snort of laughter. 'Where to start?'

'I understand from Lance a deal in the Middle East went south.'

'We had a couple of big guaranteed orders for incinerators — God alone knows what they use them for — but before they got shipped, the plug was pulled. I put it down to a competitor's dirty tricks.'

'Lance said . . .' I proceeded to run through what he'd told me.

'Right enough,' Dave said morosely.

Finding points of contact in the two stories offered welcome relief. I let myself relax.

'Not sufficient to sink us, mind,' Dave continued. 'The company was running like clockwork, at least on paper, so much so that I believed the workforce were in line for a well-deserved pay increase.'

My chest suddenly tightened and I felt a little dizzy. 'Which I assume didn't materialise?'

'It did not. I was that angry. We lost a number of good people, I can tell you.'

I tried and failed to muzzle my surprise. Lance had never uttered a word about a mass exit of staff. Did he hope to save on salaries? 'Going back to the Middle East order, Dave, were you able to offload any of it?'

'Some; not nearly as much as we'd have liked.'

At least that explained Lance's Scottish trip: he was trying to find a buyer for the remaining units. I put this to Dave.

'I shouldn't think so. We barely do any trade north of the border, maybe the odd incinerator. No big market for it.'

Confounded, I almost missed what Dave said next.

'Thing is, Susannah,' Dave continued, 'once I took a closer look at the finances, money has been steadily leaking from the business for a number of years. Not massive amounts, but . . .'

'What?' How many years, Dave?'

'Reckon over the last five.'

A tremor of fear crawled up my spine. I hadn't believed Lance when he said that problems had been going on for a year, but never expected it to be five.

'Is this what you fell out about?'

'Too right we did. It didn't sit with me, I can tell you, what with the squeeze on personal budgets and such. We've all got our bills to pay, haven't we?'

My throat closed over in distress. The more I delved, the worse the picture became.

'If you don't mind my asking,' Dave said, 'Are you okay?'

'Me?' I said in a tight voice.

'I hope I'm not speaking out of turn, but I gather things are strained between you. Fair play to you for chucking him out.'

I could hardly formulate a response. How the hell had Dave got that idea?

'Nothing like an uncomfortable night to bring a man to his senses,' he said.

'All marriages go through their ups and downs,' I said with a giddy laugh. 'We're fine now.' It almost killed me to cover for Lance.

'So he can pack up his camp bed?'

Closing my eyes tight to prevent a surge of hot tears, I mumbled something to the effect that Lance could.

'At least something's going right,' Dave said philosophically. I agreed, my voice strained by the lie.

.

CHAPTER TWELVE

'What do you think then, babe?'

Having been given the tour, the estate agent said they were free to wander around on their own. They were in the main bedroom, a cosy space with slanting ceilings.

'It's very tidy,' Rollo said.

'It's bloody perfect.'

'As long as I don't bash my head.' Rollo reached up and touched a beam.

'Don't be so negative.'

'I'm six foot two.'

She gave him a sharp look.

'I know you've set your heart on it, babe, but it needs a fair amount of updating.'

'So what? You're great at DIY.'

'I'm good at putting up shelves and unplugging drains.'

'You're selling yourself short and you know it. Look what you did with Mum's bathroom? Gave it a complete refurb.'

Amy saw Rollo's jaw clench. She didn't like it when that happened. 'Think what we could do with the place, Rollo. It's got so much potential. We could build out.'

'Steady on, we've got to be practical about this.'

'I *am* being practical.'

'Building supplies are through the roof at the moment.'

'I mean when the kids get bigger. I'm not talking about bunging on an extension straightaway.'

'Which will take a hell of a lot of money.'

'We'll earn it. You're on a good wage.'

'You won't have your mum around the corner.'

'She's not in Australia.'

'But she doesn't drive.'

'She can move closer.'

Amy bit her lip and wished she'd kept her mouth shut. Judging by the less than enthusiastic expression on Rollo's face, he wasn't keen on that idea.

'And there's the convenience factor,' he pointed out. 'You've got childcare all nicely sorted and the school's good.'

'The school's good here. I checked. Outstanding, it said online.'

'What about friends?'

'What about them? We're not moving to the other end of the country and we'll make new friends. It's a proper little community here. Dead friendly. Everyone knows everybody.'

The clench in Rollo's jaw developed into a full-grown tic. Why had he gone all funny on her?

'And there's the work factor.'

'Duh! I'm closer to the shop living here than we are now.'

'Not *your* work, *mine*,' he countered. 'I'm getting too old for this lorry driving lark.' He gave a miserable shrug.

'Says who?' Now was not the time for Rollo to plot a career change.

'I think we need a different plan.'

She stared at him. God's sake, she hoped he wasn't having a midlife crisis. 'We need a change of scene,' Amy insisted.

'Granted, but it's too soon.'

Desperate to break his resistance, Amy held the baby aloft and gazed out of the window. 'Look, donkeys, Adele.'

'They make a racket,' Rollo pointed out.

Amy turned on him. 'What's got into you?' Most of the time, she kept her temper in check, even when Miss Ward was giving her some, not like the old days when she was a teenager and the slightest thing would set her off. She'd never told Rollo about the time she'd wound up in court for affray. Some things were best kept hidden. But, my goodness, he was testing her this morning. 'You've had a face like a squashed wasp since you got up. And don't tell me you're bloody tired. If anyone should be knackered, it's me looking after three kids, single-handed.'

His face flushed with rare anger. 'I cooked breakfast this morning and took the kids to school, didn't I?'

'Hoo-bloody-ray. What do you expect — a medal?'

'Everything all right up there,' an anxious voice called from downstairs.

'Now look what you've done.' Amy stamped out, Rollo trailing unhappily behind.

'So what's the verdict?' the estate agent asked.

Amy thumbed a hand in Rollo's direction. 'Ask him.'

'I need to run some figures,' Rollo answered smoothly. 'You'll receive an offer by close of play.' Rollo's checkmate smile stunned her into silence. She didn't care that she was standing with her mouth open.

'Great,' the estate agent said, shaking both their hands, 'I look forward to hearing from you.'

Walking down the path Amy thought she'd burst a blood vessel in her cheeks she was that happy. Slipping her arm through Rollo's, she gave it a squeeze.

'You really had me going up there. Quite the dark horse, aren't you?'

'Don't get too excited. They have to accept our offer first.'

'Oh, they will. It's been empty for months.' She sighed happily. 'Our very first proper home together.'

CHAPTER THIRTEEN

With Dave's words clamouring in my head, I reached for my wet-weather jacket and, hood up, headed out of the house in the direction of the Bath Road.

In the past twenty-four hours, revelations about my husband were coming quicker than I could process them. How many times had Lance told me he was away on a business trip when he'd been secretly sleeping the night at work? And why? We didn't argue. There had been no great division. Contrary to what Dave thought, I had not chucked Lance out, although I was pretty close to feeling I might now.

Past the Lido at Sandford Park, I crossed onto the busy London Road. Driving rain sprayed into my face. Dirt from passing cars and lorries splashed up the bottom of my jeans. Then it was into Hales Road, cars parked half on pavements, and up towards Battledown Approach. A quick left turn and I was in the street where VLM claimed to hang out. Sure enough, a few doors down, next to a property with a skip outside filled with building rubble and an old bath perched precariously on top, a late Victorian house with vile new picture windows.

Looking left and right, I crossed a short steep drive with broken paving and, narrowing my eyes against the glass, peered into the interior. Apart from boxes stacked up in one corner of a room, the place was empty and looked as if it had been that way for some time. Damp mottled a rear wall and the cornicing was in a rough state. The only sign that someone had once lived there was a glorious chandelier hanging from a central ceiling rose, under which sat an abandoned desk.

Deciding to walk away, a punch to the middle of my back knocked my forehead hard against the window and made me briefly see stars. Next, strong arms propelled me from the front of the house into the covered porch so fast I didn't have time to scream. Leather-gloved hands gripped the collar of my jacket, hauling me up until I was practically standing on tiptoe. Pressed hard against the front door, I stared up into the cold eyes of Marcus Mount, his mouth so close I could smell his sour coffee breath. Terrified, I could barely speak, let alone protest.

'Mrs Stratton, we meet again.' His voice was soft yet edged with hate. 'If you really know what's good for you and your family, you'll go back to your tame little worker-bee life, make sure hubbie keeps up with his payments and stay out of our way.'

Panic bubbling up inside, I nodded blindly.

'And if you don't,' he said, oozing menace, 'we'll rear-range your tired old face and knock your teeth out so that even the best private dentistry won't be able to fix it.'

He released me. My knees almost buckled as my heels hit the ground square. Then he turned and strode off in the direction of town.

I stood mute. My head hurt. From my toes to my neck, my whole body shook. The sheer speed and audacity of the attack, the way he'd violated my personal space, the threat of violence rocked me to my core. I was an ordinary woman in an ordinary life and yet I was a victim of the extraordinary and awful. I'd no doubt in my mind at all that if we didn't comply Marcus Mount would make good on his threat. Lance had every right to be afraid. His fears were not ill-founded. Oh my God, what about Frankie and Coco?

Shocked and nauseous, I stumbled back home. Should I speak to Chantal? I wondered. Should I warn her about the seriousness of the situation?

Frankie was downstairs making lunch and called to me from the kitchen.

'Want a sandwich?'

'No thanks, I'm not hungry,' I called back.

Slipping off my soaking jacket, I hung it in the hall and went upstairs to inspect the damage to my forehead. I'd taken quite a clout. At the point of impact, the skin was red, raised and swollen and going blue at the edges. I reached for a tube of foundation and painfully dabbed it on. Annoyingly, it served to highlight the bruise rather than disguise it. I now had the beginnings of a world-class headache and it wasn't down to the injury, but the boulder of fear I was suddenly pinned underneath.

In the bathroom I took painkillers from the medicine chest and, turning on the cold tap, cupped my shaking hands underneath, scooped water into my mouth while downing a couple of tablets. Drying my face gently on a towel, I viewed myself in the mirror. 'Tired old face,' he'd said. Hot tears of humiliation streaked down my cheeks. Whatever were we to do?

CHAPTER FOURTEEN

Amy named the time between four and six o'clock in the afternoon the witching hour. It didn't matter how much she prepared and planned it was always mayhem.

After collecting Tana and Wilf from school and, on two days a week, Adele from the childminder's, there would be school bags to unpack, dirty clothing to sort, a nappy to change, hungry tummies to feed, but not with too much crap because she didn't want to ruin their teas. If Wilf couldn't get his own way playing *Paw Patrol* while Tana wanted to watch *Frozen* (again), he would go into a meltdown, Amy would lose her temper and Tana would flee to her room in tears. Catching the bad vibe, Adele would begin bawling and Amy, by this time losing her mind, would shut herself in the downstairs loo, and count to twenty — thirty if she thought she could get away with it — before emerging to sort out her brood. Too often, she used bribery. The promise of a sweet treat after tea worked wonders.

But when Rollo was home, everything was better. No tantrums. No arguments. No fuss. While Amy did all the practical stuff, he played with the kids, inventing new games for Wilf that steered him away from his beloved tablet or TV screen. Rollo spent time with Tana talking about her day and really showing a genuine interest in a way that Amy found heartwarming. Happy to bath the baby, Rollo gave her a bottle and sang her to sleep. He really was a marvel.

'Have you phoned the estate agent yet? They close at six,' Amy reminded him.'

'What's the rush?'

Amy felt a twinge of irritation. 'Someone else might make an offer. It might get sold.'

'You heard what the agent said. Practically tearing our hands off. Bet they haven't had a bite in months.'

'That's no reason to drag your feet. Have you run through the figures like you said you would?' Amy failed to curb her frustration.

'Love, give me half a chance.' Rollo gave Adele an adoring look.

'Here,' Amy said, whisking the baby out of his arms. 'Take your mobile outside and give them a ring. Quick, before they close.'

Rollo pulled a face. 'Slave driver,' he teased, getting to his feet.

'Can I come?' Wilf asked. Wherever his dad went, Wilf doggedly followed — with Igglepiggle in tow.

'Daddy's off to buy us a nice new house.' Amy practically pushed Rollo out through the front door. 'Stay with me for five minutes, Wilf, while Daddy phones the nice lady at the house shop.'

'Can I choose my own bedroom?' Tana piped up.

'You can,' Amy said with a smile.

Humming happily, she went into the kitchen, put Adele down on a play mat and took sausages out of the fridge and opened a tin of baked beans. Beside herself with joy, she couldn't wait to phone her mum and tell her the good news. Better still, to phone her sister, Bev, who lived in Rowley Regis with a bloke called Brett who Amy wasn't sure about. Bev was like their mum in that regard. She went through men like Wilf went through fruit pastilles. Not that Amy was making a judgement; each to her own.

Once more, Amy congratulated herself on finding a good solid bloke. She only wished she'd met Rollo's parents, but they'd both died before she and Rollo had met. He had an older sister who'd never married. They'd lost contact, he'd told Amy sadly over a drink in the Dog and Piper.

After laying the table for tea, Amy put the oven on, the sausages in when it came up to heat and wondered why Rollo was taking so long. A quick glance out of the front window revealed Rollo pacing up and down, one hand clamped to the back of his neck, phone aloft, his free hand scything through the air as if he were chopping wood. And he was shouting. Something was up and she didn't like the look of it at all.

Fretting, she returned to the kitchen and scooped up Adele. Rollo finally reappeared, poked his head around the door, sheepish. His face was the same colour as her mum's fag-ash.

'Don't tell me it's been sold?'

'Never had the chance to make the call,' he said distractedly.

'How come?' She didn't get funny with him. He was properly upset; she could see that.

'It's Mickey,' he said.

One of the other lorry drivers, she registered.

'He's been badly beaten up.'

Sorry to hear but what had this to do with Rollo? 'Do they know who did it?'

'Men who wanted him to transfer unusual cargo.' He glanced at the children, obviously not wishing to spell it out in front of them. Amy had no such scruples.

'Drugs or people?'

'Hell, Amy.'

'Well, whatever, I'm very sorry but I don't see where you fit in.'

'We're a man short.'

'Give me strength, not that again. Why in hell's name do *you* have to fill in? Why can't it be someone else?'

'Mickey's a mate, Amy.'

'More like an invisible friend.' Resentment surged inside her. 'So while you were whiffling on to someone who got himself mixed up in something he shouldn't, you missed the most important call of our lives.'

Rollo didn't argue the point. Fair play, he never did when he was wrong. 'I'll phone first thing tomorrow — honest.' He reached for his jacket.

'Hang about. Where do you think you're going?'

'Work.'

'What — now? What about tea?'

Wilf glanced up from the TV. 'You said you'd read me a story.'

Rollo walked over to his son and squatted down. 'Another night, Wilf. You be a good lad for Mummy.'

Rollo straightened up and went to kiss Amy who turned away. 'You can cut that out,' she said.

'Amy, love.'

'And don't bother coming back until you've put in an offer on the house and it's been accepted.'

CHAPTER FIFTEEN

I went through the motions. I sorted laundry, updated the freezer list, wrote a shopping list, made a cup of tea I didn't drink, a sandwich I didn't eat and stared out of the window. 'Trust me,' Lance had said before he left. I was no longer sure I could.

In minute detail, frame-by-frame, I went over and over the distorted action replay in my mind. There was nothing oafish in the threat and that, somehow, made it more chilling. The man in the slick suit with the dark smile, who thumped me in the back, could not have cared less about the blatant injury he'd caused. It told me something: he wouldn't hesitate to do it again, or worse.

The familiar click-clack of stilettos across the porcelain-tiled hall floor heralded Coco's arrival. We'd got into a routine where she spent weeknights with us, and weekends, either with Chantal or, more often, friends. I braced for the inevitable comment about the lump on my head, the bruising above my eye, the devastation to my self-esteem.

'Absolute bitch of a day,' Coco complained, collapsing into the nearest chair. She slipped off her shoes and massaged her toes. 'Had an absolute mare of a woman . . . Holy crap, Suze, what happened to you?'

'Slipped and banged my head on the bathroom cabinet.'

'Ouch! Bet that hurt. I've got some concealer upstairs.' Coco had every cosmetic known to woman.

'It's okay.'

Her gaze locked onto my forehead. 'It is so not okay.'

Without further discussion she darted out and headed to her room. I heard a muttered exchange between Coco and her stepbrother. Next, Frankie flew down, bare feet pummelling the stairs.

'When did you do that?'

'This afternoon,' I replied.

'When this afternoon?'

'After I got back from my walk.'

Frankie viewed me with suspicion. 'I didn't hear anything.'

'With your headphones on and lost in a digital daze, you wouldn't hear the world came to an end,' Coco remarked. She was brandishing a small make-up brush and a pot of something called *Faultless*.

'Hold still,' Coco told me. 'It looks really nasty.'

'It will fade,' I said.

Crouching down, tip of her tongue resting against the side of her perfectly painted mouth, Coco dabbed at the bruise. I didn't like to complain, but it hurt like hell.

Standing up, Coco took a step back and, like an artist surveying the final brushstroke on a portrait, declared my head vastly improved.

'Thank you,' I said.

Frankie exchanged a glance with Coco. I wasn't sure whether they failed to buy my story, or something else was rippling between them. When they were teenagers I'd oddly found them easier to read. Now they were all grown-up I couldn't quite work them out.

'Have you spoken to Daddy?' Coco asked.

'About?'

Frankie sighed with frustration. 'The situation.'

'Men with menaces.' Coco's eyes rolled theatrically.

'It's in hand.'

Another shifty exchange between them set my nerves on fire. 'If you're planning on doing something silly, don't,' I said sternly.

'We simply want to help,' Frankie said.

'You can by quietly getting on with your lives.' Desperate to deflect I suggested we ordered a takeaway. After a lot of discussion about what and from where, I ordered sushi from a local Japanese restaurant for Coco and a Balti from the Indian in Suffolk Road for Frankie and me.

Dinner and conversation about nothing important briefly lifted my spirits. By the time I was ready to turn in I was totally wiped. Calling goodnight to Coco, who'd already disappeared to apply a deep cleansing facemask, I grabbed a glass of water and found myself alone with Frankie.

'Did you really hurt yourself?' His face searched mine.

'Of course.'

He flicked a smile. 'Good because if I thought those guys . . .'

'Goodness, Frankie,' I said, pressing a hand to my chest. 'It was a silly little accident. I'll have to learn to be more careful.'

Which was totally true.

* * *

The bruising was impressive and extensive the next morning and I received a sympathetic response from work colleagues and patients. Running through the same lame explanation again, it occurred to me that this was what women did when beaten up by violent husbands. I only received one sideways look from one of the newer receptionists who was obviously suspicious and probably thought I was married to a wife-beater. On the plus side: asking for an extra day at the surgery was a doddle and met with warm approval.

'Excellent,' Colin McLagan said, a senior partner in the practice with a string of dental qualifications that ran off the page. He was also a specialist in maxillofacial surgery. I hitched inside. Would Dr McLagan be a match for the men in suits? *Even the best private dentistry won't be able to fix it.*

'With a backlog of patients wanting to sign up, we'd considered employing another hygienist,' McLagan continued, 'but if you're sure you can handle the workload.'

I assured him I could.

Feeling a little more positive I worked methodically through the morning's patients and, glad to lose myself in work and take a hike from my personal problems, lunchtime came around quicker than expected. Saying goodbye to my last patient, I was told by reception that my two o'clock appointment had cancelled. Staying inside with my feet up was the safe option. Nobody could reach me in the confines of the dental practice. A blaze of spring sunshine changed my mind. Fresh air and a brisk walk would do me good.

Quickly changing out of my uniform into home clothes, I slipped out onto the street. Looking surreptitiously left and right to check nobody from Veldo was watching, I cut to the end of the road and crossed where Imperial Square met Oriel Road.

Daffodils were out in force in Imperial Gardens, a carpet of yellow interspersed with fat purple crocuses. On to Montpellier Gardens, I strolled past the bandstand. Lots of people had the same idea: dog-walkers, kids on skateboards and hardy types eating lunchtime sandwiches on benches in the cold breeze. No sign of pale-skinned men in suits. Automatically, I glanced over my shoulder to make sure.

The Gardens Gallery was hosting a spring exhibition of work by a Cheltenham group of artists. A quick glance inside told me it wasn't my thing and, ambling past, I watched a couple of keen enthusiasts playing tennis on the courts behind. Lost in the rhythm of ball on racket I barely noticed a man who stood next to me until he spoke my name.

Startled, half expecting a punch to my jaw, I whirled around and gazed into the warm eyes of a man with receding dark hair that formed an arrow-shaped point in the middle of his hairline, and the biggest smile imaginable — one I'd clocked over twenty-six years ago.

'Lorenzo,' I gasped. 'Is it really you?'

'It is really me.' His accompanying laugh was deep and joyous.

'Oh. My. God.' In seconds we were hugging the life out of each other. Warm breath against my neck, fragrant and expensive aftershave against my skin, I was astonished that he could step into my life at the very moment I needed a friend. I drew away first and studied his face: eyes the colour of burnt charcoal, the gorgeousness of his smile — and he was always smiling — those gleaming naturally white teeth. (I obsessed about stuff like this). When I'd known him he was a young man with a young man's build. Since then, he'd put on weight in a good way and grown strong. Tanned, wearing a beautifully cut navy suit and red tie with a soft light-blue linen shirt, supple black leather shoes on his feet, he looked the epitome of Italian chic. By contrast, I resembled a bag lady.

Suddenly embarrassed and shy, I burbled, 'I must look such a mess.'

'You haven't changed a bit.' The mischievous light in his eyes said that we had both altered over the years, but in essence were still the same. Except I really, *really* wasn't. In the midst of recent events I no longer knew who I was anymore.

I felt an urgent need to lie about the bruising to my face. He listened intently.

'I confess I worried you'd got a jealous husband. You are married, I see,' he remarked, viewing the wedding ring on my hand.

'Yes, I mean, yes, I'm married. No, I don't have a jealous husband.' My accompanying laugh was high pitched and silly. I felt an idiot and totally lacking in sophistication next to him, yet Lorenzo viewed me with such affection he didn't seem to notice.

'What on earth are you doing here, in Cheltenham?' I asked.

'Business,' he answered. 'I'm in pharmaceuticals,' he added. 'Look, do you have time for coffee?'

I did — just — but, after all these years, it would be a horribly hurried affair and instinctively I thought maybe it wasn't such a good idea.

'Oh, I'd love to, but I have to get back to work.'

His face fell. 'Such a pity.'

It was.

'Is it nearby?' He glanced over my shoulder.

'A few streets away.'

'We could walk and talk.'

'That would be lovely.'

He slipped into step beside me, almost like old times, though he did not slip his arm around my waist. He did not draw me close. *Stop it.*

I discovered that his mother had died and his father was not in the best of health and lived with one of Lorenzo's five sisters. Lorenzo had been married and divorced twice.

'Goodness,' I exclaimed.

'I never found the right woman.'

The distance between us narrowed. My mouth dried. *Don't look at him*, I thought, *keep walking*, except I couldn't. Traffic was building up on the approach to the Town Hall and we were forced to stop at a pedestrian crossing.

'You have children?' he asked.

'A son,' I replied, feeling distinctly giddy. 'And you?'

'Two girls, one by each wife. They are wonderful mothers,' he added loyally.

'Daughters are lovely. I have a stepdaughter,' I said, relieved the pedestrian light was on green and it was clear for us to cross.

I sped down the road so fast Lorenzo was forced to increase his step.

'And you still live in Salerno?'

'I have a home there, or rather one of my ex's has a home there, but I mostly live in Matera.'

I nodded. I was not familiar with it and there was no time to ask him now.

'This is me.' I glanced up at the dental surgery.

'You followed your dream.' His expression was one of pure admiration.

No, I thought, *I definitely didn't do that. Had I followed my dream, I would have stayed. I would have told you I was pregnant. I would have shared my life with you.*

'It's very good to see you, Lorenzo,' I said, holding out my hand.

He took it and drew me close, depositing a soft kiss on my cheek that made me feel ridiculously weak. 'And you, Susannah.'

Confounded by the effect he was having on me, I drew away.

'I'm staying at the Queens and flying back home tomorrow,' he said. 'Why don't you and your husband join me for dinner tonight?'

'Oh, that's lovely but I'm not sure . . .'

'Please, we are grown-ups. You have your life and I have mine.'

I went through the calculations in my mind. Lance would not be back until tomorrow. I would not be doing anything underhand, not really. We were old friends, as far as anyone else was concerned. Would a night out with an old lover be so bad? Except this lover was the father of my son. He was the man that got away.

Lorenzo beamed at me, viewing me with such delight and interest I shrank beneath his gaze. 'All you have to say is yes.'

I took a breath. I badly wanted to accept, yet things were complicated enough without adding another dimension. Mentally and emotionally at a low ebb, I also recognised my vulnerability. Somehow, my mouth operated separately to the need in my heart. 'I'd love to but I genuinely can't.'

'Oh,' he said, disappointed.

I touched his arm. 'I'm so sorry.'

'Not at all,' Lorenzo assured me warmly. 'If you change your mind, you know where to find me.'

I flashed a weak, embarrassed smile. If only Lorenzo knew how close I'd been to accepting. Perhaps he'd read the truth in my eyes.

'Goodbye, Susannah.' He embraced me briefly once more, turned and walked away. I watched until he reached the end of the road and disappeared into the main drag of shops and shoppers. *I'd made the right decision*, I told myself stoutly.

But it still stung.

CHAPTER SIXTEEN

Chantal ran through the parks twice a week during lunch-time. In the summer she joined an outside yoga workshop run by Suki Quant, a friend of Susannah's. The warmer weather couldn't come quickly enough because Suki, despite her chakras and spirituality, was a gossip and, as such, a mine of irrelevant information. Sometimes it paid to know the dirt on who was doing what and why, and Chantal, a closed book in her private life, wondered whether Susannah had confided in Suki about the family's financial woes. Was there some-thing Chantal didn't know that would be to her advantage?

She took it steady as she ran along Montpellier Terrace, partly to pace herself and to avoid people lacking in spatial awareness. Middle-aged men in shorts on electric scooters were worst. And it was such an awful look too. She couldn't stand the trend for short pants on anyone older than nine years of age, particularly when a sizable majority of older wearers had legs that resembled Queen Anne chairs. She'd imbued this same appreciation of the importance of style in her daughter.

Calves pumping, she entered the park at the top end near the tennis courts. Following a designated gravelled path she almost tripped in surprise. Chantal didn't do theatrics

— unlike her drama queen of a daughter — she didn't exclaim in shock, joy or anger, but was certainly taken aback by the sight of Susannah Stratton in a clinch with a broad-shouldered man in a chic and, though she couldn't be sure from that distance, hand-stitched suit. The back of his head displayed expensively cut dark hair that had once been black and was now flecked with grey. Chantal bet he smelt exotic, too. Who'd have thought *Susannah the Sensible* had such a passionate side? The locked embrace suggested two people who'd crossed a desert in search of water and found it. Did it throw a different light on the difficult domestic situation at the Stratton household? She believed it might and wondered whether Frankie and Coco had any idea about Susannah's "friend". *Doubtful*, Chantal thought, jinking to the right. If they'd had an inkling she would be the first to know. Coco messaged her faithfully every day and would have said so.

Increasing pace, Chantal had lost count of the many secrets contained inside her head. She wasn't one of those individuals who kept them locked and loaded, primed to be shot at an opportune moment. Unlike money, she enjoyed secrets for their intrinsic value, for knowledge and understanding. What she had inadvertently witnessed that afternoon she salted away. Nobody need ever know, and definitely not Lance.

Unless it benefitted Chantal to betray his wife.

* * *

In a mixed-up mood, I entered a house tinkling with light and laughter. Lance's voice, with its mild Midlands intonation, came from the kitchen. I felt surprise and more than a measure of relief that I'd turned down Lorenzo's invitation. It would have led to all kinds of conversations I wasn't equipped to have. Sweetly loyal, Lance regarded the man who'd made me pregnant as entirely irresponsible. It wasn't fair and it wasn't accurate, but it suited Lance to believe, and me to agree.

Glancing in the hall mirror, I viewed the bash to my head. The concealer was doing a goodish job although the mark was impossible to completely disguise.

Stepping into the kitchen, I was assailed by glasses chinking and bottles opening. A guffaw of laughter from Frankie indicated that the row had been patched up, for now at least. Hostilities had ceased because we had a bigger enemy with which to deal, I thought grimly.

'Hey,' Lance said, 'God,' he added. Soon I was enveloped in a big hug and tried not to flinch. Another man had recently embraced my body. Would Lance be able to tell? Would he smell Lorenzo's aftershave? God, I was thinking like an adulterous spouse. Even so I found myself comparing Lance's hug with Lorenzo's; Lance's embrace came up short. A million pounds in debt, lies about our marriage, what was it people said? Cold in the kitchen meant ice in the bedroom.

'Good God, you've been in the wars, sweetie.' Lance studied my face intently.

'Its nothing.' With a quick smile, I turned to Coco. 'Can you spare a glass for me?'

'Coming right up.' Coco slid off the bar stool that sat under the central island. 'White or red?'

Both, I was tempted to say. 'White would be lovely.'

Obviously eager to deliver the good news, Frankie said, 'Dad says his trip went really well.'

No big market for it. We barely do any trade north of the border.

'And why I'm home early,' Lance said.

I sipped my drink. 'That's great.'

'Great? It's amazing,' Coco gushed.

'I'm pleased,' I conceded, meeting Lance's eye. He was difficult to read and Coco clearly regarded me as a party pooper. Anything I said felt inadequate. If Dave Spencer was wrong or mistaken, I still feared that whatever Lance had achieved wouldn't be enough. 'I'm a little tired,' I said, rolling out a standard excuse to explain my evident lack of enthusiasm.

Conversation drifted to the hen party Coco had been designated to organise and a band Frankie was going to watch in the summer with Miles. I watched, nodded and listened, feeling very much the bystander. When Lance sidled towards me and touched my hand, it felt as if I'd been hit with a Taser.

'We can talk later,' Lance murmured.

I smiled and nodded agreement. We certainly would; I had much to ask and say.

'You look shattered,' he murmured. 'Why don't I run you a bath? You could have a soak while we sort out dinner.'

'Well . . .'

'You're bushed, Mum.' I read the concern in Frankie's eyes, in all their expressions, in fact. Perversely, I felt as if I were the problem, the obstacle to better times, the one who made things difficult.

'I've got some lovely new bath oil to trial,' Coco said. 'Help yourself.'

'Go on,' Lance said with a grin. 'You'll never get a better offer.'

I relented. Topping up my glass, I made my escape.

Later, after a strained dinner, in which I contributed minimally, we were alone in our bedroom. I sat on the window seat, Lance on the edge of the bed.

'How much business have you really secured?' I asked.

He met my eye. 'Enough.'

'To pay them off, or hold them off until next time?'

'Susannah, must you . . .'

'I *must*!' I cried. 'You think that by doing as they say, acceding to their every wish, it will stop them?' I struggled to keep my voice down.

'Yes . . .'

'You're wrong.' I pointed at my face. 'How do you think I got this?'

Life and colour drained from Lance's expression. 'Frankie said it was an accident.'

'Because I lied.'

Lance looked as if someone had punched him in the gut and winded him, exactly as I'd felt when Marcus Mount had assaulted me.

'When?' he demanded to know, his voice cracking. 'Where?'
I told him.

He ran his fingers madly through his hair, genuinely stricken. 'That's why you lied to the kids,' he said in realisation, 'to protect them.'

'Unlike when you lied to me about Dave Spencer.'

His brown-eyed gaze suddenly hardened. 'You've been checking up on me at work?'

'Damn right I have. Dave left weeks ago and consequently is *not* drowning in financial stuff in preparation for end of year returns.'

'There's a perfectly simple explanation.'

'Isn't there always? No wonder you want me to keep my mouth shut about everything.'

Lance studiously ignored the jibe. 'Dave and I fell out.'

'He said. He also said that you'd been taking money out of the firm for an extended period.'

Lance gave a dark chuckle.

'It isn't funny.'

'Christ, Susannah, keep your voice down,' Lance said, deadly serious again. 'Dave is mistaken. Any money taken out was for investment purposes.'

'The same investments you lost money on?'

'Precisely.'

'And what about nights spent sleeping at the office? What about the marital problems you told him about?'

'That was simply to make him feel better,' Lance said, clearing his throat nervously. 'I was merely empathising with him about his own marriage problems.'

I folded my arms tight. 'It doesn't explain why you have a camp bed at work.'

'It's not how you're portraying it. Hear me out,' he said in answer to my furious expression. 'To save money, I don't always book into hotels when I take a business trip.'

'Why didn't you tell me?'

'Because sometimes I leave really early and drive back the same day, or night. You'd worry if you knew how much time I spent on the road.'

'For God's sake, Lance, you've not heard the phrase *tiredness kills?*'

Lance spread his hands. 'You're right, of course.' He reached across and pulled me towards him. In the early days I'd often sit on his lap. It always felt cosy and comfortable. This time, I perched and there was nothing snug about it. 'No more sleeping at work,' he assured me.

'No more half-truths, Lance.' No more lies.

'I promise.' He kissed me on the mouth as if to seal it.

I wanted to feel relief. I wanted the situation to feel more knowable. I didn't. 'So what happens next?'

'Driving back from Scotland I had a phone call with demands for more money.'

'Oh God.' This was exactly what I feared.

'I cut up pretty rough,' Lance continued. Reliving the memory, an ugly expression entered his face. 'With an advance on one of the orders secured, I can make the payment. But that's it, I told them. No more where that came from.'

'And they accepted it?'

'They did.'

I searched his face for deceit. I thought something was there yet couldn't properly identify it.

'And if they change their mind, or renege?'

'*Then* we go to the police.'

CHAPTER SEVENTEEN

Coco had been asleep when she heard the sound of raised voices. At first she thought she was dreaming until she heard Suze shout. *'You think that by doing as they say, acceding to their every wish, it will stop them?'* That's when Coco realised it was for real. Suddenly her bedroom didn't feel her safe space anymore.

For the life of her Coco could not understand why her dad had not simply gone to the cops. That's what normal people did. She'd always thought her dad and Suze were conventional — not something you could say about her mum — but now they weren't. That was no big deal in itself — unless it impacted negatively on her. The way she saw it, huge amounts of money going out meant no money coming in and she needed financial assistance to fulfil her dream of starting up her own business. Further down the line, she'd need cash for a home, a wedding, whatever, for Christ's sake. It's what every decent parent was supposed to do. Poor Frankie. Coco sighed. He'd really loved that car.

Sliding out of bed, and creeping across a no man's land of discarded clothing — she really didn't have enough dresses — she'd pressed her ear to the wall and wondered if Frankie could hear the argument too. Probably not. When Frankie slept it was like someone had taken out his batteries.

How do you think I got this?

Fuck me, Coco rattled inside. She'd suspected the smack to Suze's face wasn't an accident. It was no less shocking to discover the truth. And why was Dad being so wet about it? Straining to hear, Coco heard Suze's spirited response. Good for her. Coco was overwhelmed by an instant swell of girl power. Suze wasn't buying his lame excuses any more than she was.

According to Dad, the situation was getting sorted; one final payment and that would be it. Yeah, right, Coco thought, recalling how upset her brother had been when he'd describing in humiliating detail getting punched and knocked to the ground, dirt all over his new suit. But those bastards had taken it up a level by attacking defenceless, go-along to get-along, people-pleasing Suze. That her dad was still convinced going to the cops was a last option proved, beyond reasonable doubt — she'd got a mate who was training to be a lawyer — that darling Popsicle was scared as shit.

All this travelled through her mind over strong black coffee the next morning. Remembering the argument she could barely meet her father's eyes. Fortunately, he dashed off to work — or to set up a shady meeting with gangsters. Monosyllabic Suze quickly followed suit with the briefest of farewells.

'What's up with you?' Frankie asked, spooning milk and cereal into his mouth. Some of it didn't make the connection and spilled down his I LOVE FLORIDA T-shirt.

'Nothing.'

'Yeah, right.' He leant towards her. 'Come on, give.'

Coco parked her coffee cup. 'Didn't you hear the row last night?'

'Between the parents?'

'Who else? Obvs.'

Frankie huffed. 'Not my circus, not my monkey.'

'It's very much your monkey. This is as bananas as it gets.'

'If you say so.' Frankie pushed in a last mouthful. His apparent lack of interest was ridiculously annoying.

'Do you want to know, or don't you?'

He picked up the bowl and slurped down the remaining milk. Disgusting. 'Go on, then,' he said, 'slay me with it.'

Coco galloped through what she'd overheard, pleased to see Frankie's eyes widening with each revelation.

'Bloody fucking shitting hell,' Frankie burst out.

'Quite,' Coco agreed, studying her nails, painted in dark blue with silver tips.

'I *knew* Mum was lying.'

'Harsh.'

'It's true.'

'She's only trying to protect us,' Coco countered. 'Or him,' she said darkly.

'We're not six-year-olds and he's big enough and ugly enough to face the bloody music. This is ALL. HIS. FAULT. And poor Mum. Honestly, Coco, he's never around when it matters. It's as if the second you became a fully-fledged adult a part of him fucked right off.'

Frankie made an interesting and deeply disturbing point.

'What do you reckon to money disappearing from the business?'

'You really heard that?'

'Swear to God.'

'How much?'

'Investment-sized.'

'Big stuff then.'

'Precisely.'

Frankie ran his fingers through his hair. His face looked shadowy and deadly serious. 'And this started before the men in suits showed up?'

'Not good optics, huh?' Glancing from left to right, as if the kitchen was bugged, Coco lowered her voice. 'Have you wondered why Dad refuses to go to the cops?'

'Hmm.'

'Hmm what? Think he's hiding something?'

'Like what?'

'Search me but it's got to be big.'

'Big as in something illegal?' Frankie's eyes glistened. They looked like pools of molten chocolate. No wonder the girlies fancied her stepbrother. 'Like, I dunno, siphoning off funds to a private overseas account and defrauding the tax-payer?' He gave his armpits a vigorous scratch. Normally, Coco would complain. She didn't want to break his flow. 'Does that sound his style?' he asked, drumming his fingers on his chin. Coco could tell he was thinking it all through, or "processing", as she termed it.

'We have to do something,' she said urgently. 'It's not right he's imposed the equivalent of a gagging order on Suze. She's not supposed to talk to another soul about what's going on.'

'Neither are we.'

'There rests my case.' Another line stolen from her legal mate.

'I admit it looks awfully fishy, but . . .'

'But nothing. Come on, Frankie, *your* mother is in the firing line. *Your* car got nicked.'

Frankie gave a grunt. 'I guess we wouldn't be having this conversation if it were your mother.'

'Too right.'

'Crap, do you think we should tell her?'

'God, no.'

'So what do we do?'

'You're clever with technology.'

'I create software packages, not spy for GCHQ.'

'But you could take a peek at Dad's devices.'

'You have to be shitting me. Absolutely not.'

'For goodness' sake, grow a backbone.'

That really got him riled, judging by the mutinous expression in his eyes.

'One,' Frankie said, 'all Dad's stuff will be password protected. Two, if he's into anything dodgy he won't be daft enough to leave incriminating digital debris. He might be using encrypted technology like Telegram. Think about it, Coco,' Frankie said, in answer to her disbelieving expression, 'he works in the *getting rid of shit* business. Dad's bound to be careful. Three: you're still assuming he has something to hide. Four — enough of the drama.'

'Fuck you,' Coco snapped.

'Fuck you, too.'

Coco gave Frankie her version of a death stare. Grown men had been known to wither under her gaze. Frankie was a harder nut to crack, but eventually he broke.

'I'm too tired to fight,' he said wearily. 'Sorry.'

'Accepted.' This was standard operating sibling behaviour. It started with Frankie being wrong, Coco snapping a rebuke, Frankie, who could never stay angry for long — like his mother — apologising, and Coco, gracious in victory, accepting, without recrimination.

Frankie flicked a grin, one that she reciprocated.

'I've got a daring plan.' She admitted she felt pretty cool about it. Frankie looked less cool. He could be such a coward.

'Ri-ight,' he said.

'Could you be a little more in awe of my initiative?'

He sighed, scrubbed at the back of his head. 'Go on then, shoot.'

'You are going to talk to Miles.'

Frankie grimaced. 'You don't like Miles.'

Which was true, ever since she'd found Miles trawling through her underwear drawer when she was fifteen. It was years and years ago and Coco was not of a forgiving disposition, but Miles was a nerdy gamer who could prove useful.

'He owes me,' she said imperiously.

Frankie dry-swallowed. 'What did you have in mind?'

'We're going to find out how to keep tabs on Dad.'

'Isn't that illegal?'

'Desperate measures.' To prove the point, Coco told Frankie to make the call and ordered him to put it on speaker. The number rang out for what felt like days.

'Miles rarely surfaces before noon,' Frankie explained, eager to wrap up the call. 'He's not going to answer.'

Impatiently tapping a fingernail on the table, eyes locked on his, Coco said, 'Give it a few more rings.'

At last a voice spluttered. 'Un-gh . . .'

'Miles, my man, how you doing?'

Coco cringed at Frankie's false bonhomie.

'Fuck, dude, I was asleep,' Miles replied.

'No shit.'

'Unless someone's died, or it's snowing, I'm hanging up.'

'Miles,' Coco piped up, 'could we interest you in a little dirty work?'

'Hey, Coco,' Miles let out, suddenly and considerably more awake. 'What kind of dirty?'

Not the type you're thinking, you gross little bastard, she thought with a shudder. Businesslike, she described what they needed.

'Sound,' Miles said. 'Got just the gadget. Want to pop round for a coffee?'

CHAPTER EIGHTEEN

'Shouldn't you two be at work?'

It was lunchtime and not one of Chantal's running days. She'd emerged from her office after arranging a flight to Milan, the home of fashion and with at least five fantastic shops where she could purchase upmarket vintage clothing for the discerning and wealthy client. After carefully selecting items, she bought them, marked them up, and sold them on. A productive morning of talking to interested parties for whom she acted as a personal shopper, she was looking forward to eating a bowl of spinach soup in peace. She did not want to engage with either her daughter or stepson.

'Period pains,' Coco explained. Which was a lie. Unknown to Coco, Chantal kept strict watch on her daughter's menstrual cycle. No Susannah-like surprises for her.

She turned her stony gaze on Frankie whose smile was one part bullish, the other superior.

'I choose my own hours,' he said.

Hmm, Chantal thought. *Might, or might not be true.* She viewed the pair of them in the only way she could: with deep suspicion. Although she strongly disapproved, she was accustomed to Coco's laissez-faire attitude to the workplace. Frankie's breezy explanation for not toiling away on his computer was out of character. Had they found out about Susannah's dalliance in the park? It hardly rated as worthy of a day off. If they *did* know, no doubt mental health issues would be cited. It's one of the reasons that Chantal had chosen to be a one-woman band. She couldn't be doing with employees who could have so many things go wrong with either them, their families, or their lives. Look no further than Susannah Stratton if one needed evidence. Poking around inside people's mouths with sharp instruments required calm composure and a steady hand. With a husband seemingly intent on bankrupting her and the attentions of a good-looking stranger, Susannah could be forgiven for not being quite her professional self.

'You can stay if you must,' Chantal said haughtily, 'but do not make a noise, do not make a mess and keep out of my way.'

'You got it,' Frankie said.

* * *

'Unless you're going to pay for it, get your grubby mitts out of the pick 'n' mix.'

It was all very well running a sweet shop on old-fashioned values of trust and honesty, but some kids took the piss. The innocent looking lad with the smooth cheeks and the "talk to the nice lady" routine wasn't fooling anyone. Amy knew his game. While he was buying a block of chocolate and giving her the chat, his mates at the back of the shop were robbing her blind. And these weren't hard-up kids. Not like some of the children on the nearby estate. Oftentimes, Amy would put her hand in her purse and make up the difference between a couple of gobstoppers and a Lion bar for a child who didn't have quite enough. 'But don't tell your friends,' she'd say.

Crossing her arms, she scowled as the would-be thieves barrelled out. One of them had his cheeks full of sweets and, opening his mouth let her know it. She flicked him a V sign, and to hell with it being inappropriate behaviour for a mother of three children under the age of six. What were they going to do? Report her?

The real reason for her bad mood was Rollo. Since he'd driven away on his mercy mission, he'd called that often she'd turned off her phone. Switching it back on alerted her to an inbox slammed with pleading messages and base attempts to smarm his way around her. She wasn't interested in excuses. The kids wanted him home, especially Wilf who'd been a right little sod since his dad had vamoosed. She'd been up half the night with Adele who was teething. Tana, usually her reliable ray of sunshine, was also playing up. Amy needed Rollo home and in her bed with good news about the house. If he couldn't do that, then he could sling his bloody hook.

Except she knew she didn't really mean it.

* * *

'So,' Coco said wide-eyed.

They were on her bed in her room at Lansdown Parade. Coco was lying on one side, top to toe with Frankie on the other. They used to do it as little kids and the habit had stuck. A power ballad from one of Coco's favourite artists was on low volume, enabling them to talk unimpeded, and loud enough to run interference and block her mother from eavesdropping. Took one to know one.

'I'm not happy about this,' Frankie said. 'I think we should leave things be.'

'Sometimes you sound like Popsicle.'

'He's not a bloody cereal, Coco.'

Coco took a big breath in, so as not to explode out. 'What on earth was the point of sharing oxygen with moronic Miles if we're not going ahead with the plan?'

'I'm not cool with it. If we put a tracker on . . .'

'*You* are putting the tracker on Dad's car.'

'Why me?' Frankie said, indignant.

'Because it's more of a guy thing.'

'Isn't that sexist?'

Maybe, but Coco didn't care. 'You're more adept,' she said, which was a moot point. 'Make sure you link it to your phone so we can watch Pop's Beamer when it moves in real time.'

'Fuck's sake, why my phone?'

'Because I'll be driving.'

'Your car is bright red. You can see it from the surface of the Moon.'

Coco huffed. 'Well, we can't use your car because, pretty boy, you don't have one.'

'I can borrow your mum's.'

'Duh — that's only for interviews.'

'So I say I have an interview.'

'That's ridiculous when we can use my car.'

Frankie let out a scream of frustration that could be heard in the next county. 'Did you not hear a single word I said? If Dad spots your car he'll know we're following him.'

Coco could look fierce when she wanted to. Crooking herself up on one elbow, she gave Frankie the full force of her fierce face.

'I don't understand why we need a tracker at all,' Frankie argued, 'which, incidentally, is illegal without the owner's consent.'

'So is extorting money with menaces.'

'I still say we follow Dad in your mum's car.'

'If she finds out we've been using her motor for nefarious purposes she will go apeshit, trust me.'

'She really bothers you, doesn't she?' Frankie said, amused.

'She bothers most people. You know very well she is not a woman to piss off. Remember when . . .'

'Okay, so we rent a van.'

'I can't drive a bloody van.'

'But I can.' Frankie gave a wolfish grin. 'It's perfect. They're way more anonymous.'

Unfortunately, Coco thought Frankie made a solid point. 'How are we going to pay for it?'

'We don't. We borrow Art's.'

Art Mather was Frankie's mate. After missing the boat on the beard oil boom, he ran a carpet-laying business when he could be arsed. Fact was, Art didn't need to lift a finger. His mum and dad were minted. They had a proper pile in Pittville that left Coco drooling. Art had a similar effect on her.

'Why would Art do *you* a favour?'

'Set up a couple of websites for him for next to nothing.' *So frigging typical of Frankie*, Coco thought. Most people would have charged Art top dollar. 'One good turn and all that,' he said.

Coco rested her hands underneath her head, comfortable in the ensuing silence.

'Except there's a big hitch with this,' Frankie said, disturbing her calm. 'What if Dad acts normal? It could be a massive waste of energy.'

'Aside from that romantic long weekend away he cooked up for Suze, how many times in the last few years has he been home for an entire weekend?'

'But what if he's on the level?'

Frankie was right, Coco conceded. All their efforts would be squandered, and she so hated pointless enterprises. 'How about you get him on his own, man to man, see if you can persuade him to talk?'

'Are you cracked? He's never going to dish any dirt to me, supposing there's any to dish.'

'You don't believe that any more than I do . . . I know,' she said, adopting her most wheedling voice, 'find out if he's available to take you out somewhere.'

'Dad hasn't *taken me out somewhere* since I passed my test.'

'Say you want to spend quality time with him.'

'Coco, that sounds positively yuk.'

'Take him down the pub on Saturday when Suze goes shopping. You could treat him to lunch.'

'Why don't *you* treat him?'

'I'm working, thicko. Saturday is my most lucrative day.'

'What the fuck happens if he says yes?'

'That's rather the point.'

'It's a crazy idea.'

'Go on, you might even enjoy it.'

'That I very much doubt,' Frankie said grumpily. 'A couple of pints of Cotswold ale and he'll be back on his pet subject: me and my limitations.'

'Coward.'

'All right, all right,' Frankie said, 'but I'm broke at the moment so you're springing for it.'

CHAPTER NINETEEN

Punch-drunk by events, I had gone full circle with my emotions and reached a point of uncomfortable numbness.

The sight of a second-hand Polo on the drive barely raised a flicker of interest, though I recognised and appreciated that Lance was trying his best.

'Should get you from A to B,' he announced when I got home after work. 'They're good little workhorses.'

'And Frankie?'

'Give me a break, Susannah. As soon as I humanly can find a new car for him, I will.'

I forced a smile to prove that I was grateful. If I were honest, my churlishness towards Lance was a result of a letter, more of a note really, that I'd received at work that morning from Lorenzo.

> *So lovely to see you. If you'd like to stay in touch, here is my number. Maybe next time. x*

What a lovely, thoughtful man, I'd thought, quietly thrilled before guilt dug its nasty little claws into me. Didn't Lorenzo deserve to know that Frankie was his son? I'd told myself that silence was a sensible decision. Why add another layer of complication by renewing the ties of an old and brief, if intense, love affair at a difficult time like this? Sharing such news with Lorenzo would inevitably invite him back into my life and into Frankie's. However platonic Lorenzo's intention, it would not help my relationship with my husband. I'd had enough danger courting me lately, without adding more. Still, I felt lousy for not telling Lorenzo the truth.

In an extra effort to cheer me up and make amends, Lance had sweetly bought flowers and sparkling wine. Friday nights used to be special. We'd enjoyed less of them lately. I couldn't pinpoint when they'd ceased to be. Grateful, I accepted a glass.

'How did you get on today?' I asked cautiously. We both understood what I was driving at.

'Monies have been transacted.'

'The debt paid?'

Lance chinked his glass with mine. 'Everything can go back to the way it was.'

I felt the expression freeze on my face. Lance seemed ludicrously upbeat and, I hated to say it, simplistic. Only when months passed without any more demands would I feel anything like secure. In the meantime we had to decide how to make up for all that was lost: thousands and thousands of pounds.

'Susannah, darling,' he said, slipping an arm around me. 'I'm going to work all the hours God sends until I put this right.'

'I don't see how you can do any more without giving yourself a coronary.' Men of a certain age needed to be careful and that included the lean and superficially fit. For a start, Lance drank too much.

'You don't need to worry about me. I'm as healthy now as I was in my twenties. Ask Chantal.'

'Think I'll pass,' I replied with a thin smile.

During a dinner, in which awkward silences outnumbered conversation, Lance seemed peculiarly distracted by his work phone.

'Are you expecting a call?' I asked when we'd finished.

'Confirmation of an order,' he said, glancing up.

'Surely, offices are closed on a Friday night.'

'Now that Dave's left I'm trying to keep closer tabs on the day-to-day running.'

'He's a big loss.'

'*A* loss,' Lance corrected me.

'Will you replace him?'

Lance shook his head. 'Means I can save on a salary.'

A fair point, I thought. Since Monday the sole topic of conversation had been money and I didn't see that changing any time soon. It was depressing.

'I've been thinking,' Lance said over dinner. 'I know I said we wouldn't mention it to the parents, but I was wondering if I might go and see my folks in Surrey on Sunday. Not to talk to them about *it* exactly but Dad understands the financial imperatives associated with running one's own business and I thought I could, perhaps, persuade him to stump up some loot to tide us over.'

I wasn't keen. 'They've already been quite generous with Frankie and Coco's education.'

'It would be a on a temporary basis, obviously. Besides, I haven't seen them for quite a while.'

'Then it will look bad if you visit them now when you want something.'

Lance was looking at his phone again.

'Are you listening?' I said tersely.

'Sorry, yes, you're right. I'll still go but I won't ask for funds.'

'I could come with you,' I said brightly. 'It's only a couple of hours down the motorway. Better still, why don't we go tomorrow and stay overnight? We don't need to stay at your parents.'

'That's a lovely idea, but aren't we supposed to be saving money?'

'I can pay for it.' I didn't want to upstage him and definitely wasn't trying to humiliate him, but a spontaneous weekend away was what we both needed. I needed to reclaim what was lost between us. It wasn't simply about the money. Our relationship had gone walkabout too.

'Darling,' he said, 'that's a lovely idea.'

There was a *but* coming, I knew it. Had he seen the urgent desire in my eyes? Could he see how weak and vulnerable he'd made me feel?

Lance reached across and closed his hand over mine. His skin felt warm. 'But, actually, I'm having lunch with Frankie tomorrow — no idea what the boy wants to talk to me about — and, to be honest, I was thinking of travelling to Esher on Sunday and staying over. I've got a meeting in London on Monday afternoon.'

'Oh, I see.'

'Don't look like that, sweetheart.'

'Like what?'

'All brave and hurt.'

'I'm not,' I said more loudly than intended.

'We can have dinner at home together tomorrow night, the two of us. You do understand, don't you?'

Lost in his soft-eyed gaze, I tamped down my disappointment. 'It makes perfect sense.'

'And now you have a set of wheels, maybe you could visit your folks too.'

'Great idea.' I drew my hand away, stood up and cleared the dishes. With my back to him, I unglued the false smile stuck to my lips.

CHAPTER TWENTY

'You owe me forty-three quid,' Frankie told Coco.

She'd finished work and was in the middle of deciding what to wear for a girls' night out when he'd phoned.

'At that price I hope you had more than a liquid lunch.'

'Pizza.'

'And?' She posed in front of the mirror in a new dress that hugged her slim figure and flattered her high boobs. Small breasts were indicative of massive intelligence, she'd read. 'What did he say?'

'He's got a new phone.'

'About time he replaced his old phone, but it's hardly dynamite news.'

'No, I mean he has another phone.'

Coco sparked with excitement. 'Only criminals and two-timing bastards have two phones. Bloody hell — you don't think . . .'

'No, I don't,' Frankie snapped.

'Calm down,' Coco said bossily.

Ever since Oscar Woods had two-timed her with India Deverell, Coco had felt a visceral hatred towards cheats. But this was her dad they were talking about. He couldn't. He wouldn't. It was her mum's decision to call time on her short-lived marriage and, according to her mum there had been nobody else involved. Coco could believe it. Her father wouldn't be alive with his balls intact if he'd cheated on her mother.

'Anything else?' Coco asked.

'He's spending a nice night in with Mum this evening and then off to the grandparents on Sunday.'

'Lucky him. Is Suze going with him?'

'Nope.'

'Why not?'

'Says he's got a work thingy on Monday.'

Coco felt a distinct tingle of excitement. Scrap that thought about Daddio's devotion to his wife. Heart rate spiking, she stripped off the dress she'd tried on and plunged her legs into a pair of black skinny jeans. 'This is our chance.'

'If you think I'm trailing Dad all the way to Surrey, you can forget it.'

'If there's another woman he won't be going to Surrey, will he?' She didn't say "dickhead". No need. Frankie was astute enough to know from her tone.

'You seriously think?'

She wasn't sure, but was determined to leave no dirty little pebble unturned. 'Can you sneak out and put the tracker on tonight?'

Frankie let out a groan.

'Please, big bro.'

'Why is it that I get to do all the tricky stuff. Honestly, Coco, I don't feel good about this.'

'So you've said — endlessly.'

Frankie's silence was not encouraging.

'Don't go all limp and pathetic on me.'

'I'm not.'

'Good — want me to sweet talk Art?'

'Christ, you're so manipulative,' Frankie said.

She actually preferred devious and cunning, but manipulative would do. 'I'll tell Art to leave the van on his parents' drive.'

'With the keys on the offside wheel arch so we don't have to disturb the parents.'

'Good thinking,' Coco said approvingly. 'Did Pops say what time he's leaving tomorrow?'

'Not before eight. Gives us time to fill up with petrol if we need to.'

'Early start then,' Coco said.

'So don't get wasted and definitely don't get laid.'

CHAPTER TWENTY-ONE

Amy had been awake since 5.00 a.m. and up since six and it had nothing to do with the kiddies.

The only way to impress upon Rollo exactly how she felt, she'd held out for as long as possible and refused to answer his calls or respond to his messages. *Sorry* didn't cut it. Sorry didn't put things right. Around dinnertime the day before, when she was at her mum's, everything changed with the magic words: "OFFER ACCEPTED ON OUR HOUSE". A glance at their joint savings account revealed that the forty thousand pounds they'd put aside had indeed gone out. Busting with excitement, she called him immediately and was well pissed off when her message went to voicemail. An hour or so later, Rollo called to confirm the good news.

'And I'll be home early tomorrow morning. How about we do something with the kids, like a trip to Dudley Zoo?'

Dudley Zoo would not be her first choice. For a start, the penguins had been really poorly and some of the enclosures looked as if they'd been empty for years. Didn't matter. They were going to be a proper family again and best of all they were going to live in their own little bit of paradise. Amy felt the strong sense of new beginnings and had already combed the internet for ideas on interior design. She was quite taken with the notion of creating a strongly-coloured feature wall and had already ordered paint samples.

Responding to the twin demands of Adele's hungry cry and a call from Wilf, Amy bounced up the stairs as if she had springs in her heels.

'Guess what?' she said, scooping up Adele from her cot, 'Daddy's gone and bought us a brand new house.'

'For me?' Wilf barrelled in and launched himself on Tana's bed.

'Ouch,' Tana cried, rubbing sleep from her eyes.

'Careful, Wilf. For all of us,' Amy said proudly. 'And we're going to the zoo today.'

'With Dad?' Wilf's eyes were as wide as family-sized pizzas.

'With Dad.'

'Wowee!'

Eager to push her luck, Tana said, 'Can we have chocolate for breakfast?'

'You can have anything you like, my love.' *Today was special*, Amy thought, brimming with joy. Today Rollo was coming home *and* he had finally delivered. *Bliss.*

* * *

Chantal's Sundays followed the same pattern. Rain or shine, she went for an early morning walk in which she neither communed with God, nor Nature. Strictly a mind-nurturing body exercise, it was designed as a reset for the working week ahead.

Afterwards, she'd return to the sanctuary of her home where she'd eat breakfast, followed by an obligatory coffee. Next, she'd write out her work schedule for the week — always done longhand because it helped her think more concisely — followed by the creation of a list of jobs for the cleaner and the woman who collected and put away her shopping. Chantal had no interest in either activity and had employed others to carry out the domestic necessities of life for the past fifteen years. Once a month, a handyman was handed a separate list for the maintenance of her property. A gardener came twice a week from March to October. Nine times out of ten, Coco would be asleep after a night out with friends and so the list-writing would always take place in peace.

But today was different.

Invariably, Chantal's Sunday saunter would wind up at Pittville Park, the city's largest park and listed as Grade II. The eastern side, overlooked by the Grade I Pump Room, was of historic significance. At that time in the morning, Chantal enjoyed walking around the lakes because they were free of people.

Cutting back towards Evesham Road, skirting the walled and hedged entrance to the Mather's elegant semi-detached, she was astounded to see her daughter climbing into a dirty old white van in the Mather's private parking area. An earthquake would not normally rouse Coco from sleep on a Sunday morning. Instinctively holding back and using the hedge as cover, Chantal was even more astonished to see the van reverse out with Frankie in the driver's seat.

They'd been plotting and hatching for days and were definitely up to something. Chantal instantly intuited that it was not going to end well for anybody.

* * *

'Well, this is a rush — not.'

Frankie had done nothing but moan since they'd picked up the van at 7.00 a.m., topped it up with petrol and parked it down the road from home.

'I'm not a morning person and I'd kill for a coconut and turmeric latte,' Coco griped, 'but you don't hear me complain.'

'Sounds like something you have with a portion of rice,' Frankie grumbled.

'Ha-not-ha.'

She'd gone to great lengths to dress the part: beanie hat pulled down low, black leather bomber jacket, jeans tucked into thick socks and Doc Martens. Without her make-up she was virtually unrecognisable. When Frankie had first seen her he'd opened his mouth to take the piss. Silenced by a glare, he'd wisely thought better of it.

'God, after all this, I hope he hasn't changed his mind,' Frankie whined.

Coco hoped the same, but not for the same reason. Frankie was looking forward to returning to his pit and sleeping the day away. She had a morbid dread of being proved right. Christ, another woman would gravely dent the Bank of Dad. Annoyingly, Mum believed monetary donations encouraged dependency. It was imperative Coco knew the score with her father's personal life if only to allay her fears.

'Hello,' Frankie said, perking up. 'Look's as if Dad's on the move.'

* * *

I tipped up on my toes and kissed Lance goodbye. 'Send my love to your mum and dad.'

'Don't worry, I will.'

'When will you be home?' I attempted to sound as casual as possible. No point putting him under any more pressure.

'Depends how things go in London. I might stay for an extra night.'

'No more sleeping at work?' I teased.

He rested his hands on my shoulders and grinned. 'Promise.'

'You'll call me?'

'I will.'

'Safe journey then.'

We hugged and I padded back upstairs with a second cup of tea. With Frankie and Coco out last night and Frankie not expected back until later, the house felt abnormally quiet.

Tucked back up in bed, Lance's space beside me already cold, I reflected on the lovely evening we'd shared. Lance had come home in good spirits after his impromptu lunch with

Frankie. We'd spent a relaxed afternoon reading and listening to classical music — Vaughan Williams and Mascagni — and Lance had cooked chicken cacciatore while I'd watched and sipped wine. Afterwards, we'd tuned into a Norwegian crime drama and, when we went to bed, made love even though I didn't feel much like it. Sex was a good way to reset the emotional temperature between us, I told myself, and it had. Guilt smothered me as I remembered how hard I'd tried not to think of Lorenzo when all my focus should have been on Lance.

Never one to lie in bed for long, I showered and dressed. Due at my parents' mid-morning and about the time they religiously drank coffee I ate a slice of toast and mentally prepared to maintain "radio silence" regarding the family's financial difficulties. My mother had a laser-like ability to ferret out problems when things were going south. I didn't doubt my new downmarket vehicle would be a source of curiosity. A convincing cover story would be the only way to head my mum off. I'd run through a number and decided I'd tell them that the Macan was in for repairs and I'd picked up a cheap "Get Me From A-B". In response to inevitable questions about Lance, the business, Frankie and myself, I'd stay calm, upbeat and convincing. The bruising had faded a lot. My dad would never notice, but my mother wouldn't miss it. Again, if I stuck to the script, I'd breeze it. The trick was to fill any awkward silences and, in this regard, Mum's inclination to dominate any conversation was to my advantage. By bombarding her with questions about the latest talks at the Women's Institute, her progress with tracing her family tree and the holiday plans she'd arranged for the year ahead, I could do my duty as a caring daughter, swerve from the spotlight and be in and out, with the family secret intact.

As far as Lorenzo's random if brief appearance in my life, this was one secret I was happy to hug tight. It was mine alone. Not that it stopped me from wondering what my parents would make of it. Lorenzo was clearly doing well for himself and had amounted to a lot more than Mum would ever have given him credit for. Petty of me, but Mum's mis-judgement pleased me to a ridiculous degree.

But, I thought sternly, my focus now must be on steering my husband through the current crisis.

So why did I sense that it was very far from over?

Lance had a glib answer for every question I'd asked. When I was with him he seemed entirely credible, his reassurance reassuring. If I contested a point I felt I was being deliberately difficult — not that Lance ever said so or made me feel awkward. It wasn't a case of him gaslighting me, or anything horrible like that. But when I was alone, like now, I found myself less certain. Those men meant business. Would they so easily be persuaded to leave us be and pick on someone else?

A deep chill settled on me at the memory of being trapped against the door of the empty house, the threat made, those hauntingly well-spoken words and the total disregard for me and for authority. What made the Mount brothers so damned brave?

And then it dawned on me. They had dirt on Lance. It was the only reason he refused point-blank to go to the police.

A horribly disturbing thought — I couldn't think of anything during our marriage, no bag of old bones lurking in a cupboard that would instil such fear. Could it be something from way back?

* * *

'Epic fail,' Frankie exclaimed. 'He's going to board a bloody train.'

They were at Cheltenham's central station in Gloucester Road.

'Not necessarily,' Coco said. 'Park up.'

'I'm not getting on a train to Surrey.'

'Look,' Coco pointed wildly. 'He's ditched the car and is heading towards the road.'

'What the fuck is he playing at?'

'Search me. I'll wait in the van while you follow.'

'No way, I'd get made in seconds and then what would I say? *Oh, sorry, Dad, we thought we'd stalk you to see if you have a bit on the side.*'

'Don't be so unpleasant. There could be a number of reasons why he's behaving oddly.' She couldn't actually think of any other than the blindly and depressingly obvious, but she wasn't going to admit that to Frankie.

'Seeing as you're dressed like a ninja, *you* follow. '

'God's sake, okay.'

She climbed out.

'And don't be long or I'll have to pay,' Frankie warned, leaving the engine running.

Slamming the door, Coco followed her dad and crossed the road, trotting along behind at a safe distance.

One of the main routes into Cheltenham, traffic was constant, though less dense and noisy than it would be on a weekday. The area had been gentrified in the last few years yet there was no escaping that it wasn't a prime location unless you counted the close proximity to the train station a bonus. Parking was a nightmare. Leaves and litter decorated the pavement. *It all felt a bit dirty*, Coco thought, sinking her neck further into the collar of her leather jacket and narrowing her eyes against a random shaft of spring sunshine.

Her father looked purposeful and appeared to be heading towards a redbrick three-storey Edwardian villa. Jinking left, he tore up a short path with broken tiles to a front door that could do with a good coat of paint.

Coco dodged down near a lamppost and retied a shoelace. Waiting a few beats, a surreptitious glance in the direction of the entrance to the house revealed a man of indeterminate age with a shock of red hair. She jolted with realisation. With his colourless features, the homeowner fitted the description Frankie had given of the man who had knocked him to the ground. And here was her dad shouting and gesticulating at him. *This was not good*, she thought, *not good at all.*

Straining to hear and thwarted by the loud rumble of a skip lorry driving past, Coco quickly realised the precariousness of her situation. If she stayed put, her dad would trip over her. If she walked away, he would easily catch up with her. Only one thing for it: she stood up, looked both ways and legged it across the road where, with her back to the traffic, she took an avid interest in a sign proclaiming "Jesus Loves".

A fast glance over her shoulder revealed that the door to the house had closed and her dad was hurrying away. From his hunched profile and pounding gait, he'd come off worst in the altercation.

Waiting until he was almost at the entrance to the train station, she moved off at a jog, crossed the station concourse and clambered back into the van to a petulant reception from Frankie. Cosmic Gate were belting "Fire Wire" out of the speakers.

'Holy crap, Frankie, turn it down.'

Peeved, he did as instructed. 'Now what?'

Coco studied the moving dot on her phone. 'Drive, but not too closely.'

Dropping in several vehicles behind, Frankie said, 'Dad's going the wrong way for the M4.'

'That's because he's heading through Swindon Village towards the M5.'

Frankie smacked his forehead. 'He's going to work, isn't he?'

'Maybe.'

'Still want me to follow?'

'He lied, so definitely yes.'

Sure enough, the Beamer moved down the M5 at smooth speed and turned off at junction 7 to the southwest of Worcester. Frankie let out a groan. 'I so told you,' Frankie said.

'Shut up and keep driving.'

'What are we going to do if he goes to work, which, by the way, Sherlock, is exactly where he's heading?'

'We observe,' she said.

'How can we do that?'

'For goodness' sake, it's a business park. White vans are not exactly unusual. Park down the road from his unit and see what happens.'

Frankie fell quiet. Coco hunkered down in her seat. Frankie followed suit. From where they were situated she had a pretty good view of the works' vans and her father's BMW, which was parked next to a Dacia Sandero.

'Shit,' she said, eyes widening at the sight of her father climbing out of the Beamer and into the other car.

'He's switching,' Frankie said, animated, giving her sleeve a tug. 'Oh crap! The tracker is on the wrong car. We'll lose him.'

'No way.'

'But Coco . . .'

'Turn around.'

'What?'

'I said turn around. We're doing this old school. Don't let him and that poxy car he's driving out of our sight.'

* * *

With nothing else to occupy me, I left to travel the forty-five minute journey to Mum and Dad's. They lived in a modern house, built in anaemic-coloured brick, in Great Malvern. It had been the family home for decades. I'd grown up there and Frankie, too, during the early part of his life.

'As a single mother, you'll need to provide for your child,' my mother had told me, with a distinct lack of charm. I'd have preferred to leave Frankie with anyone else while I continued my studies but, financially, it had made sense. For once my mum had been right: any other choice would have been impossible and, as she'd also pointed out, I hadn't a clue how Lorenzo would react to me falling pregnant. Italians loved children. Lorenzo was the eldest of nine but this was different: I barely knew him. Parenting a child, based in another country, would always have been tricky, especially as his family were poor and just about making ends meet. I could never have abandoned my studies halfway through my degree and any prospect of gainful employment to go and live in Italy. And what would Lorenzo have done for work if he'd come to live with me in the UK — even if he'd agreed to it? How would we have managed? As upsetting was the intolerable thought of Lorenzo's rejection – not all young men wanted the responsibility that came with fathering a child. I could hack pregnancy. I couldn't hack that.

Traffic was light and although I missed my big car, the Polo drove well enough. Unlike Lance, I never thought of cars as status symbols.

On the M5 and before the junction for Tewkesbury and Evesham, I became aware of a black dot in the distance growing bigger and bigger and faster and faster until an SUV morphed into view and bore down on me at speed.

I pulled over from the outside into the middle lane. Glancing in the rear-view mirror, I grimaced when I noticed the vehicle had swerved and tucked in behind me, driving virtually bumper-to-bumper with the Polo. Intimidated, I pulled into the slower inner lane. Checking again, I felt a stab of pure fear.

It was *my* car, the Macan.

And there was a man in the driver's seat. I couldn't tell if it were Marcus or Jack or somebody else.

My palms went clammy. Sweat broke out all over my body. A pulse inside my head hammered.

Lance had sorted it, he'd told me.

Lance had it under control.

Everything can go back to the way it was, he'd said.

He'd lied.

Without indicating, I swerved out into the next lane, hoping to wrong-foot my pursuer, then stuck my foot down as I crossed onto the outside. The speedometer climbed from 60, to 70, to 80 and beyond. Munching up the miles, tarmac and white lines blurred and transformed into one. Muscles in my neck tightened. My jaw clenched. Travelling at break-neck pace, the smaller, less powerful car juddered with strain, the Macan keeping up with ease.

Fields and trees sped by. On open road, with little traffic, I felt as if I were flying. In whichever way I used the lanes, the Macan stayed fastened in an extreme form of tailgating. When I overtook, the Macan overtook. If I slowed, it slowed. Speeding up, it sped up. We were joined by a horrible, inextricable connection that seemed unbreakable, and Lance, the man who was supposed to protect me, was at its centre.

A turning for Ross-on-Wye and Ledbury appeared. Without indicating, I took it, hurtling towards the roundabout and on to the two-lane M50.

There was about a mile before the exit for Malvern. My thoughts ran hot and collided. What was the plan? Was it to run me off the road, to make me crash? What would happen when I turned off the motorway finally? Would I be followed all the way to my parents? I racked my brains, wondering how to find the nearest police station.

I took off again, the Macan glued close behind. Snatching for a way out, coated with fear and fury, and considering how best to navigate the rest of the journey, I felt an explosive bang. Jolted forward, the seat belt cut tightly into my chest and made my nerves and bones rattle. I cried out in terror. Another shunt from behind and I heard the grind of metal on metal and momentarily lost control as the rear of the Polo fishtailed.

Palms damp and knuckles white, I righted the car; any thought of reaching safety forgotten and in the distance.

And still the Macan was there, right behind me.

Jaw clenched, I gripped the steering wheel and stared straight ahead and the turning to Malvern. I should slow down. Instead, I sped up and, at the last moment, hung left. A streak of silver surged past, the Macan smoothly flying into the distance, as if nothing had happened.

Dry-mouthed, I crawled along for a few miles, driving like a nervous learner driver. As soon as I was safely able to do so, I pulled over, parked, switched off the engine and shook.

My body felt as if it had been put on a rack and subjected to medieval torture. Every muscle ached. My bones felt dislodged and disjointed. My head was agony and the pain in my heart worse. Sweat that had coated my skin had dried, sticking my clothes to me. They felt dirty. *I* felt dirty.

And angry.

Silver-tongued thugs, I cursed aloud. I blamed them, for certain; I blamed Lance more.

Slipping my phone from my bag, I called him. It went straight to voicemail. I began to speak, my voice shrill. Abandoning the message, I phoned his parents.

Lance's father answered.

'Hello, Susannah. How lovely to hear from you.'

Normally, I'd exchange pleasantries, talk about the weather; enquire about Jeremy's golf handicap; ask after Theresa. I didn't have time for niceties.

'Is Lance with you yet?'

'Lance?'

'Yes.'

'I don't think so.' Jeremy sounded uncertain.

'Could you tell him when he arrives . . .'

'No, sorry, I meant we're not expecting him. Hold on a second . . . Theresa,' I heard him call, after which there was a thud as the receiver was placed on a hard surface. It was followed by silence.

But my mind was not silent. It was filled with raucous thoughts and accusations. It was riven with Lance's lies.

'No, m'dear, we're not expecting him. More's the pity. Haven't heard from Lance in a while actually.'

A wave of nausea bubbled in my gut. I did my best to suppress it. I felt as if I were aboard a yacht. Navigating through choppy seas until, on entering calmer waters, another huge wave rises up and threatens to submerge and overturn the boat on which your life depends. 'Must have got the wrong end of the stick,' I said lamely.

'Mind, I'm glad you phoned. Funnily enough I was about to call you.'

'Oh?'

'It's about the money we loaned Lance.'

'Money?' I could hardly stutter the word; my tongue felt too thick for my mouth.

'Yes, the £25k for house repairs.'

I blinked wildly and glanced at the spectacular backdrop of the Malvern Hills. Lonely as a little girl, eager to escape my mother's overbearing manner as a teenager, I'd come to value solitude and enjoyed walking them many times. Looming down, the quiet peace they'd represented evaporated; now they crushed me with their malevolent presence.

'Are you still there?' Jeremy said.

'Sorry, yes.'

'Only it's been a while and Theresa really could do with a new motor.' He coughed uneasily. 'We wondered whether Lance could see to paying us back.'

'I'll speak to him, of course.'

'That's grand.' I sensed Jeremy's relief that a potentially tricky conversation had gone so smoothly. 'Good to know I can leave it in your capable hands,' he said, then as if remembering that I'd called him, he said, 'Family okay?'

'Oh, yes,' I lied. 'Everything is fine.'

I finished the call with a terrible twist of fear in my stomach.

Where the hell are you, Lance?

* * *

Technically, they were travelling through Worcestershire. As far as Coco was concerned, it could have been the lunar landscape of a distant planet with no name.

When she wasn't staring ahead at the rear of the Dacia, she noticed signs for Droitwich Spa. She suspected it had nothing in common with Cheltenham Spa. Other names flashed past: Stourport-on-Severn and Kidderminster. There was a definite West Midlands vibe that Coco found alien.

'Apparently it used to be a centre for carpets,' Frankie informed her.

Coco didn't respond. She was becoming more depressed by the mile. Suburbia really didn't cut it for her. One estate ran into another — you couldn't call it a development — with rendered houses, some with odd bits of what looked like grey plastic cladding stuck on the front. If it was meant as a design feature, it failed.

So far, Frankie had done a good job of maintaining pace, without breaking speed limits. They'd only had one hairy moment when he'd been forced to jump a set of traffic lights to ensure they didn't lose the Dacia.

Approaching another set, the Dacia indicated to turn right. They were two vehicles behind in the van. When the Dacia moved off they followed through a series of side roads.

'He knows where he is,' Frankie murmured.

'Of course he knows where he is.'

'Don't be such a grouch, Coco. I mean the way he's driving you can tell he's on familiar territory.'

Coco sat up a bit. On occasion Frankie's intelligence could take her by surprise.

'Hold up, he's slowing down,' Frankie observed.

Coco watched as the Dacia stopped, indicating to turn into the drive of an ugly-looking dormer bungalow in which an old, dark blue Peugeot 205 was parked.

Frankie glided past.

'What are you doing?' Coco complained.

'I'm not going to knock at the door, am I?'

'Pull over.' She reached dangerously towards the steering wheel.

'Fuck's sake, who's driving this thing, you or me?'

'Now!' she barked.

Frankie screeched to a halt, sending Coco's thin body painfully against her seat belt.

'Ouch!'

'Now what?' Frankie said, unapologetic.

'We investigate.'

Jumping out of the van, she sped back down the road with Frankie in pursuit.

They were outside a low boundary wall topped by a brown and thin beech hedge, its leaves resembling crunchy cornflakes, when she felt Frankie's sweaty hand clamp on her arm, urging restraint.

'Get off me,' she hissed, peering through the dismal foliage.

'I don't want you making a scene.'

'I'm not going to make . . .'

Coco broke off. Her father was locked in a deep embrace with a young woman whose hair was the colour of beaten copper. Christ alive, the woman, who'd partly been obscured from view, was clutching a baby. To cries of 'Daddy', Coco's father broke away and, bending down, swept a little boy into his arms. He held him aloft as if he were a tennis trophy. At his side, a girl, a bit older and who resembled her mother, clamoured to be picked up too.

Following Coco's gaze, Frankie muttered, 'Fuck me sideways.'

Blood chilling in her veins, feeling deeply nauseous, Coco grabbed hold of her brother for support. 'I think I'm going to throw up,' she groaned.

CHAPTER TWENTY-TWO

'You seem brittle, Susannah.'

My mother had a gaze that could penetrate tungsten. Her small eyes stared out beneath a high forehead. Unlike me, her straight grey hair clung to her head like a tight-fitting helmet. The lines on her seventy-four-year-old face were not so much connected to age as to gardening without sun protection.

Under interrogation and shaken up when I arrived, I struggled to explain the dent in the back of my "new" car and failed to convince Mum that the injury to my face was a result of a simple accident. I couldn't blame her. In my mother's shoes I wouldn't have believed a word of it either. Failing to ascertain the truth, Mum had taken a familiar tack by making a negative personal observation.

I disguised my tight response by sipping coffee in my parents' new garden room, as they called it, in reality a hideous plastic-framed conservatory that would boil them in the summer and freeze them in the winter.

My mother continued to criticize. 'Time of life, I suspect. You really should take better care of yourself.' She exchanged a dark glance with my father, to which he failed to respond. Eager to change the subject, Dad, a quiet, bespectacled man and former civil servant, enquired about Lance.

At the mention of my husband's name, anger surged up from the pit of my stomach and flooded my entire body. The flush spreading across my cheeks had nothing to do with the "time of life" to which my mother had alluded.

'He's in trouble,' I said dully.

Mum started forward, a look of satisfaction bordering on triumph in her expression. I imagined the joy such a revelation stirred in her heart, how she would plan to share the news with her coterie of female friends.

Dad frowned. 'What sort of trouble, darling?'

'To be perfectly honest, I'm not entirely certain.'

'So that explains the injury. He hit you, didn't he?' Mum had no filter when it came to saying what she thought or doing what she liked. It wasn't an age thing. She'd always been like it.

'Lance would never raise a finger to me,' I said quietly. 'Or anyone, for that matter.'

'Then what?'

I looked from one to the other. Now that I'd broken my silence I instantly regretted it. How much *could* I say? How much *should* I tell?

'The business has run into problems.' I repeated some of what Dave Spencer, Lance's former operations manager, had told me.

Dad shook his head. 'That's not good,' he said, when I'd finished.

'It's sharp practice, Rupert,' my mother said. 'Surely, something can be done about it?'

'It might not be that simple,' Dad said.

I'd expected a guarded response from my father. 'Thing is, Lance has borrowed money — too much.' Despite my best intentions, my voice cracked.

'He can't keep up with the payments is what you mean.' Mum's eyes burnt with accusation.

'Something like that.' Fortunately, it would never occur to my parents that Lance had turned to less legitimate means of getting his hands on ready money. The conversation I'd had with Jeremy, Lance's father, flashed through my mind. How were we going to find £25k?

'Is the house in jeopardy?' Dad asked. 'Lance hasn't borrowed against it, or anything like that, has he?'

'No — I don't think so.' Truth was it hadn't occurred to me. If Lance had done such a terrible thing, he would have told me, wouldn't he? I swallowed hard at the thought that maybe he hadn't.

'It would be worth checking out,' Dad said.

'Yes,' I said briskly. 'I'm sure he hasn't but I'll ask him.' When I find him, I thought bleakly.

'Do you need assistance, darling?' My father's kind expression made me want to cry. At their age I should be looking after them, not the other way around.

'No point throwing good money after bad,' Mum bridled.

'I know you're annoyed, Rhona, but you're not listening.' My father rarely reproved my mother, but on this occasion he made an exception. I'd rarely seen Mum look so humiliated. Her scowl promised that he would pay for it later. 'I'm talking about helping our daughter and grandson,' he continued firmly.

'Thanks, Dad, and it's very kind, but I've got my head well above water at the moment.' *No, you haven't. You're drowning.* 'If I need help further up the line, I'll shout.'

He looked over the rim of his lenses at me. 'You promise?'

'Promise.'

I didn't stay long after that. Mum continued to prod and probe and I batted back her enquiries with bland, non-committal answers. Maddeningly, I felt guilty for being disloyal to Lance.

On home turf by lunchtime, I called him again and got nowhere. Frustration and anger gave way to despair. In desperation, I took my courage in my hands and phoned Chantal. After a couple of rings, Frankie and Coco burst in. I could tell straightaway something awful had happened and hung up.

'Mum, you'd better sit down.' The set of Frankie's mouth was grave, his expression tight. Coco, behind him, wrung her slender hands and her eyes were red-rimmed.

'What's happened?' Sickeningly, I knew, or at least thought I did and collapsed into the nearest chair.

'It's Dad,' Frankie said.

'Oh my good God.'

'Jesus Christ,' Coco burst out unkindly. 'Nobody died.'

'Then what?'

'He's got another life, Suze, another family, another woman. And she's a fuck of a lot younger than you.'

CHAPTER TWENTY-THREE

Head spinning, I mouthed the words Coco had spoken as if I were translating them from Urdu into English.

Anguished, Frankie said, 'Mum, Mum, are you okay? Let me get you some water.'

I watched in numbed silence as he pulled a tumbler from a cupboard and filled it from the tap. I took a sip. It tasted warm and stale.

'I don't understand,' I said.

Between them, Coco and Frankie tumbled over each other to spill the morning's events.

Horrified, I wanted to bang my head against the wall repeatedly: physical pain to deaden the emotional pain. My thoughts felt sluggish as if I couldn't put them together in the right order. 'Go back to the beginning,' I said, utterly wretched. 'You hired a van and followed him?'

'Too right,' Frankie said. 'All the way to suburbia central.'

'Yeah, but before that,' Coco cut in, 'Daddy went to some doss house in Gloucester Road and got into an argument with the guy that nicked your car. Daddy left the house as if his arse was on fire.'

So that's why I'd been hunted down that morning: retribution for Lance's interference. 'Did you hear what was said?'

'Too far away,' Coco replied.

I tried to imagine the tenor of the conversation. Clearly, Lance had lied when he told me we were off the hook and, feeling guilty, had attempted to negotiate afterwards and failed. In fact, he'd made things worse. The man in the property at Gloucester Road must have contacted his accomplice and agreed on quick and decisive action. Maybe the driver of my car was already staked out at our home, ready to follow me when given the order. On a reflex, I got up and went to the window, looked out onto the street, searching. Neither the Macan nor its driver was anywhere to be seen.

Turning back to Frankie and Coco, I asked, 'When you waited for Dad to leave home this morning, did you see anyone else hanging around?'

They exchanged glances and shrugged. Frankie answered for both of them. 'Not that we noticed.'

I rolled the conversation again, eager to understand. 'So then you followed Dad to Worcester where he allegedly switched cars.'

'Nothing alleged about it,' Frankie said.

'And you're really sure that it was Dad you saw in Kidderminster with this other woman?' *Please let it not be true*, I prayed. *Please let it be a horrible dream.*

'Definitely,' Frankie said.

'Hard to unsee it.' Coco scraped a chair along the kitchen floor and parked herself in front of me, eyeball to eyeball. She took my hand.

'You said there were children.' I spoke softly.

'Two and a baby,' Coco confirmed.

'A baby *is* a child,' Frankie corrected her.

'Fuck off, Frankie.'

My heart fell in dismay. I'd wanted a child with Lance, another sibling for Frankie so badly, but Lance was not keen and had argued we'd enough with one each. 'Bringing another into the family might disturb the perfect balance,' he'd said. And I'd eventually, if reluctantly, agreed. What an idiot I was.

'One of his spawn was a dead ringer for his daddy,' Coco said, glowering.

I pulled my hand away. It was a terrible situation, an unimaginable situation. I did not need Coco making it worse by being vile about a little kid, a half-brother no less. Whatever Coco felt — and she had a right to feel wronged — the children were innocent.

'How old was the little boy?'

Coco's eyes slid to Frankie's. He gave a shrug. 'Under five,' Frankie answered. 'The girl was older, same age as Art's half-sister, about six, I'd guess.'

A pebble of grief lodged in my throat. If this were true, Lance had been having an affair — no, another life — with someone else for years.

What had I done wrong, I screamed inside, *apart from getting old?*

'Mum?' Frankie viewed me with deep misgiving.

'I need to think,' I said.

'Suze,' Coco railed in frustration, 'what's there to think about? You need to *do* something.'

If he wanted another life how could I prevent him? The mystery was why he'd failed to leave me. 'Like what?' I said.

'Haul him back. Sit him down. Tell him the entire situation is unacceptable. Tell him . . .' Coco flailed her arms. 'I dunno . . . he has to stop behaving like a dick and come home. To us.'

'I agree.' Frankie stood with his arms crossed tightly across his broad chest. For a moment he resembled his biological father so closely, I felt blown away. And how stupid I felt now that I'd declined Lorenzo's invitation to dinner. Why should *I* feel guilt when Lance had been cheating on me for years? No wonder we had money problems when he was running two households. With acute clarity, I realised that this was his big secret; this was what he'd been desperate to protect. The men in suits had used it as leverage: pay up or I'll tell your wife about your sordid, cheating double life.

'Mum?' Frankie said, cutting into my thoughts. Both he and Coco were looking at me expectantly, as if I could magic it all away. An uneasy thought crossed my mind.

'You said you'd seen your father in Gloucester Road.'

''S'right,' Frankie answered.

'In no circumstances must you go there again. I mean it,' I said in response to Coco's mutinous expression.

'Okay,' Frankie said, answering, I hoped, for both of them.

'Does Chantal know about the other woman?' I asked.

Coco shook her head. 'We came straight here.'

'So you haven't been in contact with your dad?'

'Not yet but I will.' Coco's expression was poisonous.

'Don't.'

Coco looked stung. 'You can't tell me not to speak to my own father.'

'Not yet,' I added gently. I reached for my phone and began to type in a message.

'What are you doing?'

'Letting Lance know that his parents spoke to me this morning and asked for their twenty-five grand back.'

'Bloody hell,' Frankie exploded. 'He took money off the oldies?'

He scratched his chin. 'Wasn't he supposed to be seeing them today?'

'And we all know he didn't,' I said, tapping away.

'Clever,' Coco purred appreciatively. 'Daddy will know that you know he didn't go to Surrey, but he won't know that we know about his . . .'

'God's sake, Coco, stop talking in riddles,' Frankie lashed out. 'You sound ridiculous.'

'*Don't*,' I said, issuing Coco a warning look. 'Frankie, that's really not a helpful way to talk to your sister.'

They both stared at me as if I'd had a brutal personality transplant, which, in a way, I had. No more Mrs Go-Along to Get-Along, I thought grimly.

'Stay here,' I said, reaching for my bag.

'Where are you going?' Coco asked.

'To see your mother.'

CHAPTER TWENTY-FOUR

I found Chantal at home.

'Wondered when you'd call.'

Dressed in a svelte black jumpsuit that accentuated her toned physique, she invited me in. We went straight down-stairs to the kitchen and dining room.

A bottle of Côtes du Rhone, already open, sat next to a glass, half drunk, on a black granite work surface.

Chantal inclined her head. 'Can I tempt you?'

I only drank in the day in exceptional circumstances like Christmas and weddings. This rated as a unique occasion, more along the lines of a funeral.

'Please.'

I waited quietly as Chantal found another glass and poured a generous measure.

'If you think I know anything about Lance's financial affairs after all these years, you're mistaken,' Chantal said, handing me a drink.

I took a long, deep swallow. Strong and slightly sweet, it lit up my senses and hit my empty stomach with a satisfying burn. 'That's not why I'm here.'

Chantal flicked an edgy, slightly patronising smile. 'Why don't you sit down?' She indicated a strange-looking chair near the window. I perched reluctantly, fearing that the slender piece of art might not hold my weight. Chantal sat opposite on a toffee-coloured leather sofa, watchful and listening.

Seeing no point in pulling my punches, I came straight out with it. 'Lance has another woman, another family.'

Chantal didn't react.

'You knew?'

'I did not.'

'You suspected?'

'Why should I?'

'Because you were close once and have remained friends.'

'Pushing it,' she said, expressionless. 'We get along because we're civilised people.'

Nothing civilised about Lance from where I was standing. 'Allegedly, he has three young children.'

'Lance always wanted a big family.' Chantal's matter-of-fact response came less as a shock than the fact that Lance's ambitions for a large brood had never been clear to me. Stunned, I almost missed the importance of what she said next. 'I never thought he would stoop to bigamy though.'

Something I hadn't considered and should have done. Trying to hang on to reason, I spluttered, 'I don't actually know if the woman is his wife.'

'Then dismiss it from your mind,' Chantal said airily. 'Lance is many things, but he's no criminal.'

She spoke with such authority I was glad to agree.

'How long has it been going on, if you don't mind my asking?'

'At least six years.' Saying it aloud slayed me.

'And how did you come across this . . .' Chantal hesitated '. . . unusual situation?'

'*Unusual*, is that how you'd describe it?'

Chantal sipped her drink. 'It's appreciated that this must be a shock.' She didn't add *to an unsophisticated person like you* although that's how I read it. 'I understand your sense of humiliation,' she continued. 'However in the realm of human relationships, is it so very peculiar? Surely, *you* must know that?' Chantal held my gaze for a fraction longer than felt comfortable.

'He cheated on me, Chantal.'

'People do.' Her closed expression spooked me. 'Marriage as an institution, I've always thought it rather . . .' again she paused, 'passé and restrictive.'

Chantal had reduced my very personal pain to a philosophical exercise. I might have known that Chantal, with her legendary sang-froid, would take such a view. She took the mantra "all's fair in love and war" to the extreme, although I hadn't realised that Lance's ex would be happy to express it to my face in circumstances like these.

'You're condoning what he did.'

'I'm *explaining* what he did, what a lot of people do.'

'Is that why you left him?'

'I'm not sure how that's even relevant. As it happened we left each other.'

'He never cheated on you?'

'Never.'

No, he saved that for me. I felt something in my chest contract and squeeze tight.

'I realise you're looking for answers,' Chantal continued smoothly. 'Sometimes there is no explanation. Perhaps Lance simply wants to live his truth.'

'I'd have expected that bullshit from Coco, not you.' I swallowed a large gulp of wine to mask my surprise at a) swearing and b) aiming my ire at Chantal — always a risky business. By the tightened grip on the stem of Chantal's glass, it had the desired effect.

'Forgive me,' Chantal said stiffly. 'I'm not dismissing the enormity of what he's done to you.'

'But it's not only me, is it?' I leant towards her. 'It's Coco and Frankie too.'

Chantal flinched. 'She knows?'

'It was Coco and Frankie who told me.' I described exactly the sequence of events, what they'd done and how they'd found out.

Something passed behind Chantal's eyes.

Quick to pick up on it, I asked, 'What?'

'Nothing.'

'Nothing is something.'

'Only that it explains why they've been spending so much time together recently.'

That wasn't what you were going to say, I thought. 'Unsurprising in the circumstances.'

'True,' Chantal said, clipped. 'I take it you've spoken to Lance?'

'I need to locate him first.' I sounded as bitter as I felt.

'So presumed guilty before proven innocent.'

'You sound as if you're on his side.'

'I'm on nobody's side.'

'You think there's an innocent explanation for what Coco and Frankie saw with their own eyes?'

'I think you need to establish the facts before you go wading in.'

'Like the fact he borrowed 25k from his parents who now want the money back?'

'Ouch, poor Jeremy and Theresa.'

What about me? I thought, rocked by a sudden wave of self-pity.

'Don't you see, those awful men have made terrible demands, not just on Lance but on us?'

'It's very unfortunate.'

Every time Chantal opened her mouth I felt the need to ramp up the ante.

'They used the threat of exposure of his other life to force him to comply. That's why Lance gave in to them without putting up a fight.'

'Yes, I see that, of course. It would seem so.'

'It's the *only* explanation,' I said firmly. 'I'm mad with myself for not tumbling to it before.'

'The men who threatened you,' Chantal began tentatively. She ran her fingers lightly through her close-cropped hair.

'What about them?'

'Who are they exactly?'

I told Chantal as much as I knew, which wasn't nearly enough. When I'd finished, Chantal steepled her fingers together and rested them under her chin. I could practically see her brain making connections. Whatever I thought of Lance's ex, she was a clever woman. She hadn't got to where she was today without guile and creativity. When Chantal finally spoke it wasn't what I expected.

'Now that the cat is well and truly out of his bag, with all her little kittens in tow, Veldo should leave you alone.'

'I don't care. I'm going straight to the police.' With Veldo's bargaining chip gone, and the memory of the car chase that morning still raw, I didn't want those bastards returning for an encore.

'Susannah,' Chantal said, 'I'd think very carefully before you do something like that.'

'In God's name, why?'

'Because it might inflame the situation.'

'It's already inflamed.'

'Granted, but intimidation is very hard to prove. You'd need dates, times, proof. Have you received threatening emails, for example?'

'Well, no but . . .'

'Did anyone film the cars taken off your drive?'

'No, we were . . .'

'Did anyone see you being threatened?'

'My neighbour witnessed some of what happened.' But was it enough and would Mrs Fletcher back me if I went to the police? I could already hear her saying that she didn't witness the scuffle and, in any case, didn't want to get involved. 'For God's sake, I was nearly driven off the road this morning.'

'I'm sorry to hear that, but did another driver report it and if one did, won't the police write it off as another nasty case of road rage?'

'Cameras, there would be cameras on the motorway.'

'At exactly the place where it happened?'

Confronted by Chantal's sterile logic, I felt winded. There were no cameras when the Macan had shunted my vehicle. It was as if the place had been picked especially. 'He was in *my* car,' I insisted.

'To which you handed him the keys.'

Chantal was right. I couldn't prove a thing. A maddening tear trickled down my cheek.

'Would you like a tissue?'

'Got one.' Hand trembling, I produced one from the pocket of my skirt.

'Obviously, you have a lot to deal with. If it helps, Frankie could stay here; give you a breather, while you sort things out.'

'He's twenty-six, Chantal, not a child.'

'I was simply thinking he'd be better off in a more settled, less febrile environment.'

Something in Chantal's smooth, ever so slightly patronising manner cut into my bones. I drained my glass. 'I disagree.' He needs to be somewhere his opinions can't be undermined, unappreciated, perverted or distorted. 'You'll have your hands full with Coco. She's very upset,' I said, and stood up. 'Thanks for the drink. It's been good to talk. Don't get up, Chantal, I'll see myself out.'

* * *

Amy helped the kids pile out of Rollo's car, a major exercise. They'd had the best day ever. The zoo was shit, but the kids had loved it anyway. Nobody had moaned about how cold it was, or that the ice-cream kiosk was closed. They had their daddy home and that was all that mattered.

'You go inside, babe, and I'll unload the motor,' Rollo said.

Wherever they went there was always that much kids' stuff to take with them: tablets to keep Wilf and Tana occupied, drinks and eats, spare clothes and wellingtons, and that's before they started on baby gear. Three pieces of equipment: sling, stroller with umbrella and/or sunshade, changing mat were devoted to Adele's needs alone. She'd been a sweetheart and chuckled at the tigers, bless her. *Fast asleep, she'd be a little devil later*, Amy thought, as she popped Adele into her crib. Happily, Rollo would sort her out and would rise to the challenge of giving her a bottle in the small hours, leaving Amy to catch up on some well-earned shuteye.

While Rollo entertained the kids, Amy prepared their Sunday dinner. They were having roast chicken, gravy and all the trimmings. Her mum had made an apple crumble that she'd delivered the night before. Amy wanted to make the occasion nice, a celebration of them buying their first proper home. She'd bought a bargain bottle of sparkling wine to go with it.

Table laid, chicken in the oven, roast potatoes prepared and ready to roll, she poured out two glasses of fizz and took them through to the lounge where the kids were watching *Horrid Henry*.

Rollo was staring avidly at his phone. He slipped it away and took the glass from her.

'Ta, love.'

They chinked and Amy wanted to say something daft but then, as if her brain was catching up with her vision she said, 'What's happened to your phone?'

'Broken so I bought another.'

'So who's messaging? It isn't work again, is it?'

Rollo gave a wry smile and pulled her down on to his lap. 'No, it isn't. It's the financial advisor I'm seeing tomorrow.'

Amy pulled a face. 'He's messaging you on a Sunday?'

'Keen to secure his commission on the mortgage, isn't he?'

Amy let out a squeal of delight. 'Oh my word, that sounds so proper.' She chinked her glass with his and took a deep drink. Bubbles popped against the roof of her mouth, up her nose and exploded in tiny stars inside her mind. She didn't think she could be this excited. It was like being a kid again on Christmas Day morning.

'Want me to bunk off work and come with you? If I phone Merv now, he could cover for me?'

'Nah, babe. It's mostly boring stuff, going through procedure and filling out paperwork.'

'Don't you need me to sign?'

'Not tomorrow.'

'Okay.' Miffed, she'd wanted to be a part of every bit of the process. She didn't want to be the little woman who chose the house and the paint colours but had no skin in the game. A joint enterprise, it felt weird that she wasn't involved. 'Won't this financial person need to establish my identity, go through my bank accounts and suchlike?' Her mum had given her a rundown of what was involved.

'I can take a copy of your passport with me.'

'Yeah, but . . .'

'They do everything digitally and remotely these days, Amy.'

Having never bought a house before, Amy had no reason to doubt that Rollo was right. This is where his senior years came in dead handy. A man of the world, her Rollo.

'I might be gone all day,' he said.

Amy felt a little hitch of misgiving. 'But you'll be back home for tea?'

'Oh yes.'

'You haven't forgotten it's parents' evening for Tana?'

'I hadn't forgotten.'

'Good,' she said, relaxing again.

'Bloody exciting, isn't it?' he murmured in her ear, giving her waist a squeeze.

She looked at him fondly and gave him a smacking big kiss on the lips. 'Hell, yeah.'

* * *

In the dark.

Frankie had decamped to his room. Coco had long gone to vent her pain and fury on her mother. *Good*, I thought weakly.

As expected, my phone was crammed with lame excuses from Lance.

—*Crap, forgot to mention the money from the parents. Will sort it a.s.a.p.*

—*Car had problems on the way so I had to ditch the visit. Got a lift back to Worcester. Will call you later when it's fixed.*

—*No, I definitely arranged a trip. They're both getting on so must have forgotten or misunderstood.*

—*Love you x.*

Fuck you, I thought.

His pathetic attempt to get his cover story straight insulted my intelligence. To convince him I'd bought into it I strung him along with *oh dear* and *what a pity*. In answer to my request about when I could expect him home, he'd replied: *Later tomorrow.*

Stung by Chantal's cool and unsupportive reaction, my calm and confidence was at rock bottom. How I'd longed for Chantal's smug mask of inscrutability to crack. There was only one evident fissure: her advice to me to avoid the police. It had seemed reasonable in Chantal's artsy kitch-en-cum-dining room. Here, in my less than tidy home, it seemed peculiar.

Three-quarters of the way down a bottle of red from a little-known French vineyard, I'd experienced a whole spec-trum of emotions from hurt to blistering betrayal. I wept and mourned the life I'd had despite that life being a lie. Only days ago Lance had asked if I trusted him. I'd taken a leap of faith and told him that I did. He must have sniggered silently at that one. In fact, he must have laughed every time he'd deceived me over the years and got away with it. And there had been so many deceptions and lies.

Scrambling through a mental calendar of events, I reck-oned I was forty-four or forty-five when Lance first embarked on an affair. Around that time I'd started working at my current dental practice. Frankie was about to graduate from his uni course. Coco had passed her A levels with Grade As in three subjects and a B in one. It had maddened Lance, I recalled, that Coco wanted to pursue a career in the beauty business instead of using her intelligence to go to university and get a degree. In the end Coco had won him over. I had believed that the children and me were at a point in each of our lives full of new beginnings. My heart twisted and I snatched at my drink in a doomed effort to dull the searing pain inside. What I'd failed to factor in: Lance was doing exactly the same, embarking on his very own fresh start.

Without me.

Through the cheating years there had been holidays and graduations, dinners out and conversations, the mundane, the exciting and all the grist and grind of family life that was supposed to glue us together. Looking back, I saw how much Lance had used work as a cover for his absences. The "emergencies" when he'd had to suddenly dash to Newcastle or Leeds when something went wrong at a plant. In reality, he'd been summoned back to the West Midlands, perhaps for the birth of a child, or family event, like an anniversary or crisis. It would explain why he'd missed our eighteenth wedding anniversary. "Unavoidable", was the word he'd used and he'd encouraged me, somewhat oddly, to take Frankie out to the ritzy restaurant Lance had booked for the occasion. All those times when I thought he was messaging customers on his phone, he was probably sending love letters.

Deep down, as painful as it was, I wondered if Lance's behaviour was in part my fault? Was my drive to excel at work, my aspirations for Frankie and Coco and my overwhelming desire for them to be happy, to blame? Had I neglected my husband? Had I piled on too many pounds? Was my low libido a factor? I shut my eyes tight at the thought of him making love to another woman, a younger woman, full of vitality and fertility and lust. *Did he fuck her like he fucked me?* I thought wildly. Or was I simply someone to fuck over?

I took another slug of drink and poured another.

However much I disliked what Chantal had said, perhaps she'd made a fair point about the nature of marriage and human relationships. In my inebriated state, it seemed more credible. I smiled bitterly at the thought of what my mother would say: "utter tosh". But Chantal was definitely right about one thing: I needed to talk to Lance. And he needed to talk to me, really talk, no more lies, no more fobbing me off.

Seized with frustration, I picked up my drink and hurled it at a large photograph on the wall of Lance and me together. The glass instantly shattered, cascading in lots of tiny fragments. My gaze locked onto the wine that shot up to the ceiling, like a burst artery, staining it red. Satisfyingly, it dripped down onto the porcelain-tiled floor. I imagined it as blood. *His*.

* * *

'How could he do this to me?'

Coco was inconsolable and Chantal was not good with emotions. Her daughter had been at it for hours now and Chantal needed to be fresh for work the next morning.

Regaling events in gory detail, Coco had switched from hot, manic and bright-eyed animation, which Chantal could have done without, to tears and hysteria, which Chantal could *definitely* have done without. Either Coco would break something or break herself. Chantal hoped that numb frozen shock would kick in as soon as possible. This was not how her Sunday was supposed to roll.

Navigating the visit from Lance's second wife was trickier than she'd expected. She half knew that Susannah would call; sensed it somehow. What she hadn't bet on was that Susannah would act with brazen cool when Chantal had hinted at Susannah's own duplicity. It amazed her how people in glasshouses were fond of chucking dirty great rocks at others. Naturally, confronting Susannah about her mystery man at this stage would serve no useful purpose. Perhaps it never would.

As for Lance, Chantal had been genuinely surprised. Who'd have thought it? She'd never considered him a player. In his own warped way, she guessed that he considered himself to be faithful to two women, or at least had reconciled himself to the situation, though she doubted he felt at peace with it. Uncomfortably, she wondered if it were symptomatic of a deeper underlying conflict.

A nerve in her jaw tensed. She needed Lance calm. She needed him in control. Traumatic events that had never come to light, thank God, could land them both in trouble. Ironically, Chantal had Susannah to thank for saving the pair of them, not that she'd ever known. Blissfully ignorant, Susannah had met Lance when he'd been most vulnerable. She had provided him with purpose and stability and, quite possibly, the ability to forgive himself and live with what he'd done. In light of current events it appeared to have been a temporary fix.

And that was deeply disturbing.

Whatever else occurred, Susannah must not dig, and Chantal very much feared that it was in Susannah's nature to do so. Frankly, she'd been surprised that the shy, reserved woman she thought she knew had a steely streak. That little verbal outburst of hers, entirely out of character, worried Chantal. Betrayal, it seemed, had ignited something immutable within. It was critical for Chantal that there were no repercussions.

She got up, stretched her limbs and yawned. Coco had stopped sobbing. Everywhere was silent. Exhausted, she had obviously cried herself to sleep.

As long as Susannah believed that Lance had got into trouble with money to fund his other life, which Chantal accepted was the stronger possibility, events in the past could stay exactly where they were: undisturbed. But if the men terrorising Lance had an ulterior motive, far removed from the simple extraction of money for its own sake, it indicated that someone from way back knew and wanted payback. If so, was Chantal also at risk?

When Susannah had asked questions about Lance in his previous marriage, specifically about who left whom, Chantal had answered truthfully: that it was by mutual consent. Except Susannah didn't know the reason why. It was critical that it stayed that way, which brought Chantal full circle to her biggest concern: Lance.

When his world crumbled, as Chantal was certain it would when the two women in his life turned on him, would he be able to keep his mouth shut?

CHAPTER TWENTY-FIVE

I called work first thing and said that there had been a family emergency and wouldn't be in. Not in a couple of days, not this week, maybe not the next. After the initial wave of sympathy, there was a lot of tutting and clucking. Within minutes, Colin McLagan, the senior partner, "wanted a word".

I braced myself.

'I hear you have personal problems,' McLagan began.

'Yes.'

'Rotten timing.'

'I'm sorry. It can't be helped.'

'Have you any idea when you'll be back?'

I stared at the wall. Part of my identity would never be back. Not the wife, the loyal and supportive partner, not the "for richer and for poorer".

'I'm not sure.'

'We may need to reappraise,' McLagan said curtly. 'I'll let the girls know to reschedule the extra patients drafted in. If you're unavailable, we will have to consider taking on another hygienist, I'm afraid.'

'I understand.'

'I'll leave you to it then,' McLagan finished awkwardly.

* * *

Washed and dressed, I headed downstairs. I'd barely eaten yesterday and grabbed a piece of toast with a strong cup of tea.

Frankie was bleary-eyed over breakfast. 'Not going in to work?'

'No.'

'Don't blame you. This is all so fucked up. Have you heard from him?'

'Yes.'

Frankie elevated an eyebrow.

'He's apparently coming home later.'

'Shit, he's got some nerve.'

'Have you been in touch?'

'You told us not to.'

'Think Coco will comply?'

'Doubt it.'

'You've heard from her?'

'Hell, yeah. She's totally spun out. Bawling her head off, she was on the phone for hours last night. I actually think I went to sleep at one point.'

I nodded sympathetically. 'She's always been highly strung. It's bound to hit her hard.'

'It's hit me hard too.'

I stretched across and closed my hand over his. 'I wasn't trying to diminish it.'

'I guess I'll never get my car now,' Frankie said sulkily. 'Why did he do it, Mum?'

'I really don't know.'

'All that stuff about ambition and standing on your own two feet was utter BS,' Frankie said. 'It was his sad way of lightening the financial load.'

'We all have a lot of questions.'

'But will he give us the answers?'

I shook my head and shrugged. I honestly didn't know.

'So tonight's the night, is it?' Frankie said. 'Judgement Day.'

'Something like that — unless Coco has frightened your dad off.'

'He's got to face the music sometime.'

'If it's at all possible I'd like to speak to your dad first.'

'You're the headline act, Mum. Coco and me, well, we're the support band.'

'Who normally go on first,' I said with a quick smile, one that Frankie returned.

'Okay, I get it. I'll have a word with Coco and try to get her to hold the line. So what's the plan for today?'

'I'm going out.'

He gave me a wary look. 'You seem . . . I dunno . . . different.'

'I'm good,' I said brightly.

'Is that normal?'

I shrugged. 'Who can tell? I've never encountered something like this before, thank God. Right,' I said, gathering my things. 'There's not much food in the fridge for lunch, I'm afraid.'

'No worries, I'll manage.'

'I can do a shop on my way back.'

'Back from where?'

'The scene of crime,' I answered.

* * *

Amy had a lie-in. Rollo got the kids up, washed, dressed and fed them, then brought her tea and toast in bed.

'Blimey, what have I done to deserve this?' she said.

'Nothing is too much for my princess.' He kissed her softly on the lips. 'After I've dropped the kids I'll drive straight on to my meeting. No point coming back any sooner with you at the shop today.'

'Ooh, yeah. Let me know how it goes.' She took a sip of tea. Strong and malty; Rollo had a knack of getting it just right. She couldn't stand her mum's tea: too much milk and the colour of a puddle.

Once she'd finished her breakfast, she showered and dressed. From the bedroom she could hear her children

140

laughing and playing in the lounge next door. It was so good to have an easier start to her day. She kissed them goodbye, wished Rollo luck, and then set off for the half hour drive to the sweet shop.

Dull to start with, the weather brightened. Amy couldn't have cared less if it was slinging it down with rain. She could hardly catch her breath, she was that happy. Her heart soared as she passed the ribbon settlement of Mamble. Beyond lay the little hamlet of Bayton, marking the start of their new life in the countryside. Living there would cut her journey time to work in half.

Dropping down to Newnham Bridge, paying attention to the speed limit — she'd got done once for doing thirty-five in a thirty zone — she drove slowly through and admired the surrounding scenery glazed in spring sunshine. Finally entering the small market town of Tenbury Wells, she parked her car and hurried off to the sweet shop.

It was a good day, a bloody *brilliant* day, and she was going to enjoy every second of it.

* * *

Frequently checking the rear-view mirror, I didn't relax until I was almost in Kidderminster. From there I followed directions to "the other woman's" home.

As Coco had described, it was a dormer bungalow. There were no cars on the drive. It didn't look like anyone was in, though I couldn't be certain.

Parking in front of a picture window with Venetian blinds, I stepped out and rang the bell. I'd no idea what I was going to say or how I was going to say it. It was a fair bet I'd be met with hostility and tears, accusations and defence. I didn't care. If I were going to find a way through this mess I needed to confront the woman who had such a hold on my husband before I tackled him.

With no response, I walked back to the window and, unnerved by the memory of the last time I'd been nosy, cupped a hand over my brow and stared through the open slats. The room was a picture of homely chaos. Toys strewn over the floor, a half-eaten orange on the window ledge, a plastic beaker upended on a fake marble fireplace, juice spilling out and onto the worn carpet. Beyond, the sight of a baby bouncer made my heart plummet to my toes.

'Can I help you?'

I whirled around, my gaze fastening on the face of an elderly man with a stooped gait, and then to his overweight pug who looked as disgruntled as its owner.

'I was looking for . . . a friend.' I felt my neck flush.

'Amy's at work.' He spoke between his teeth. Gum issues, I automatically registered. '*You* know,' he said, as if I were dim, 'at the sweet shop.'

'Silly, of course.' The flush spread from my neck to my cheeks. I bent down to stroke the dog to hide the fact I was reeling. A *sweet* shop? Was some higher force, a weird god with a savage sense of humour, playing a joke on me?

'Bertie loves a bit of fuss,' the man said indulgently. 'Tana, Amy's eldest, often comes out with me to walk him.'

I stayed down, patting the animal, furiously trying to think how I could ascertain the location of the sweet shop.

'It's rather disappointing,' I said. 'I've come a long way.'

'You didn't think to give her a ring first? Folk these days are always messaging each other and whatnot.' The old man spoke softly. Underneath, I detected a grain of suspicion.

'Sorry, I should have explained.' I stood up. 'I haven't seen Amy in a while and we rather lost contact. I wanted to surprise her.'

'Ah, I see.'

Doubt clouded his eyes. He was questioning why would I, an older woman past her childbearing years, be Amy's friend?

Inspiration striking, I said, 'I'm a healthcare professional.'

The old man grinned. 'Why didn't you say?'

I forced a reciprocal smile to smother the lie. 'We met when she had Tana and now she's got two other little ones.'

'She has indeed. A lovely brood.'

My masseter muscle ached with the effort of sustaining my smile. 'It would be such a pity to drive all the way back home.'

'Well it's another half hour to Tenbury Wells.'

'I've got nothing else to do today.'

'Be nice for you to catch up. Tell her to bring me a bag of coconut mushrooms from the shop,' he said with a wink. Giving the lead a tug, he headed back to the road, the dog in tow.

Back in the car I took a few deep breaths, set the sat nav, started the engine and, reversing out onto the road, traced my way to the A456, passing the Wyre Forest Nature Reserve.

The old man was right about the time it would take. Shortly after 10.00 a.m., I crossed a bridge and the gateway to the market town. Directly on my left, a supermarket offered free parking. I turned into it and left the car beneath a canopy of trees, their leaves dripping rain.

Weaving my way through shoppers and motorists, I stepped out opposite an accountancy firm, and walked down a street of individual shops, some of which looked as if they'd been there and run by the same owners for decades. From the way people met and greeted each other it was a close-knit community and a mile away from my life in Cheltenham. I guessed it offered security, something I craved.

The main shopping area was along a main street intersected by another. I crossed over the road and found *Sweet Treats* down an alley next to a pub. Modelled on the sweet shops of yesteryear, the shop front window was crammed with jars of loose sweets, candy sticks, sherbet and a tooth-rotting and tongue-burning granular concoction called "Kali" that stained and destroyed enamel. I'd only ever come across it once when visiting Birmingham as a child.

A quick glance and my gaze was immediately transfixed by the young woman standing behind the counter. Her short, copper-coloured hair framed a face of pale skin, dusted with freckles, out of which shone the greenest eyes. Her easy, winning smile lit her up from the inside out. Shorter than me, she had a neatly proportioned figure. She wore a soft blue open neck-shirt over dark trousers. I caught a glimpse of the curve of her collarbones, set off by a beautiful necklace that looked expensive. I saw how alluring she would be to Lance. Crushed, I almost fled. I would have done had I not been rooted to the pavement. Apart from the woman I perceived to be Amy, there were three customers: a teenage boy weighing up the various merits of chocolate bars, an impossibly youthful looking mother with a baby in a sling. She was picking out a collection of mini packs of chews. An older woman, my age, was at the till and paying for a box of fruit jellies.

Stepping inside, a bell clanged and everyone turned. Amy's face widened into a welcoming smile and then she continued talking.

I loitered near a cabinet of handmade chocolates and listened to my love rival's voice. Low, with the singsong tone of the Midlands, without upward inflexion, it would be monotone if it weren't for the animation of the speaker.

'I'm that excited,' she was saying to the older woman. 'Our first home together.'

'Next it will be a wedding.'

All the women trilled with laughter, apart from me. I wanted to sink through the floor.

'I'll be with you in a moment,' Amy called, mistaking my reticence to join in for impatience.

'I'm in no hurry,' I replied politely.

It seemed to take forever for the shop to clear and when it did, I was afraid of it filling back up with customers. Within an hour, school would be out for the lunchtime break and the place would be rammed with kids.

'Right,' Amy said, 'how can I help? Those truffles with the walnuts on the top are lovely. My personal favourite is the dark orange cream. It's got a nice boozy kick to it.' Her endearing smile made me want to choke.

'You're Amy, aren't you?'

'That's me.'

'I'm Susannah Stratton.'

Gripped by momentary confusion, Amy pressed a hand to her chest. 'Oh, I thought it was Susan. I'm sure that's what Rollo told me. You're his sister.'

'Rollo?' Lance's middle name was Roland and his nickname at school in the Midlands had been Rollo. Worse, he'd passed me off as a sister, *Susan*. I'd rather be dead in his narrative than part of his lies.

'My partner,' Amy said. 'You all right? You look a bit, I dunno, peaky.'

I produced my phone, scrolled through and found a recent picture of Lance. 'Is this Rollo?'

'That's him. Oh my God,' Amy burst out, eyes shooting wide. 'Nothing's happened to him, has it? You're not going to tell me something awful. I'm always saying to him to watch the maniacs when he's driving.'

'No,' I said quickly. 'But I think you may need to sit down. If I were you, I'd change the open sign to closed.'

CHAPTER TWENTY-SIX

'NO, NO, NO.'

'I'm sorry, but it's true.' I'd barely got the words out before Amy reacted. Her voice rebounded off the walls and filled the shop.

'He's got kids with me. He loves me. We're buying a house together.'

'He has a stepson. He already has a home.' I couldn't make the claim that Lance loved me. Not after this. The fact he had children with this woman when he'd persuaded me of the merits of not having any more cut me more painfully than I could ever have envisaged. 'He also has an older daughter by another marriage.'

'*What?* You're lying.'

'I wish I was.'

'How old is she then?' Amy tossed her chin, defiant.

'Twenty-four, two years younger than my son.'

'It's not true and even if it was,' Amy said shakily, 'you're just sad he's left you, angry he's chosen me over you. It's pathetic you coming here like this,' she hurled. 'He loves my kids.'

'I don't doubt he loves all of them but . . .'

'Who the hell are you to barge into my life and talk to me?'

146

'I'm his wife,' I said through gritted teeth.

'So you keep saying.' Amy crossed her arms, glared at me.

'What do you think he's doing when he's not with you?' No point shouting. Amy was doing enough of that for the pair of us.

'Driving lorries. It's what he does.'

A brilliant choice of occupation designed to deflect. 'Have you seen his HGV licence?'

'No, but . . .'

'He owns a waste company in Worcester. He lives in Cheltenham. With me.'

'Cheltenham?' From the nervy expression on her face, I saw something fall into place for Amy.

'I can give you the address. I'm a dental hygienist and work at the Roborough Dental Practice. You can check all this out online.'

Amy stared, glassy-eyed.

'And that's not all.' I continued to reveal the extent of Lance's financial problems.

'I don't believe you. He's with a financial advisor right now.'

'How do you know?'

Confounded, Amy's green eyes welled with tears. 'He promised me. He . . .'

'Amy, this is really important. Has anyone approached or threatened you?'

'Me? No. I don't understand.' A sudden note of fear had entered her voice.

Would the boys in suits leave Amy and her family alone? I wasn't certain and felt a duty to warn her, which I did.

'You're saying he owes money?'

'A million, last count.'

A ragged breath seeped out between her chalk-pale lips.

'I know this is a lot to take in.' Strangely, I felt the calm associated with an out of body experience. Talking to Amy was like bargaining with Coco. It was imperative that I, the older woman, stayed composed and in control in order to turn down the emotional temperature. From the sharp expression in Amy's eyes, it wasn't exactly working. She appeared to be rallying.

'Only if I believe you.'

'Then call him.'

'What?'

'Call him. See if he answers. He won't.'

Amy took out her phone and put it on speaker. It rang out and went to voicemail: 'Rollo Stratton here, you know what to do.'

At the sound of Lance's duplicitous voice, I was gripped by nausea.

'Doesn't mean a thing — he's busy, that's all.' Amy ended the call without leaving a message.

'Are you expecting him home today?'

'This afternoon.'

'He won't show.'

'He has to. He . . .'

'And when he doesn't you'll know he's lying.'

'He'll come,' Amy said, flashing with defiance. 'You'll see.'

'This is where you can find me.' I handed Amy a piece of paper with my name and number scribbled on it.

Amy barely glanced at it before crushing it between her fingers and dropping it on the floor. I gave a weary nod and made for the exit. Amy rushed ahead of me to unlock the door.

'Go on,' Amy jeered. 'Piss off.'

Flushed, but with my dignity intact, I strode out of the confectioners, crossed to the main street and, bypassing the nearby supermarket, returned to my car. I couldn't bear to stay another second. That's when I snapped. That's when I could no longer contain myself. I sent a two-word text to Lance that I knew would be instantly understood: *I KNOW* . . . Then I switched off my phone.

On the drive back I had plenty of time to think. In another life, without the aggro between us, I would have found Amy an endearingly sweet creature. Envious of her youth, her shapely figure, her clear skin, I was not devoid of sympathy for a woman young enough to be my daughter, despite her rabid reaction. I had not enjoyed smashing up her life and the lives of her poor children. If Amy was right and Lance chose her and her children over his family in Cheltenham, things would never work out between them. I wondered if, beneath the rage, Amy understood this.

Back in town, I shopped in Waitrose, to hell with choosing a cheaper supermarket and counting the pennies.

Frankie was out when I returned home. Probably gone for a late lunch. I stowed the shopping, made myself a pot of coffee and, on impulse, messaged Lorenzo. I kept it light and platonic. I didn't mention a cheating husband or my current dismal financial situation. Reckless, vulnerable, needy, I unashamedly wanted my ego stroked. Any guilt I felt, and certainly I experienced more than a twinge, was overwhelmed by the delicious thrill of doing something deep down I knew I shouldn't. Within minutes, Lorenzo messaged me back.

Good news: I'm back in Cheltenham tomorrow. Perhaps we could meet for dinner?

I shouldn't be seen out and about. It would be a potentially career-killing move. Family and friends could also misinterpret it.

It took me seconds to reply: *That would be fabulous.*

CHAPTER TWENTY-SEVEN

Amy could not stop shaking. Inside, she was screaming.

It was all lies. Had to be. Then why was something ringing true?

All those times Rollo had dashed off unexpectedly and reappeared out of the clear blue, the unpredictability of his work life — it went way beyond shift work — his reluctance to part with money for the house. Oh. My. God. Her dream home was in jeopardy. He'd probably used the deposit money to pay off the people after him. What scared her most was being left alone with her poor kiddies and how would her children react? Adele was too young to understand but Tana and Wilf would be heartbroken, especially her little Wilf who idolised his dad.

Then there was Cheltenham. No wonder the rotten sod didn't want her on his stamping ground, the place his Mrs called "home". Amy fizzed inside at the thought of the woman, with her hoity-toity voice, the way she'd spoken to her, like she was a kid. Fucking snob.

Faces pressed up against the window, the sound of kids knocking on the locked door brought her briefly back to her senses. She hid in the backroom, hoping they'd go away.

She'd once been described as a firecracker. Her temper as a teenager had got her into trouble. She'd been a bad person. But that had all disappeared into the past when she met Rollo. It was like a nasty memory and one she'd sooner forget.

Until now. Was this punishment for a misspent youth?

A horrible sense of helpless rage bashed her over the head. The old Amy would have ripped Rollo's balls off. For the sake of his children she should. Then why oh why did she simply want her Rollo back, never mind what he'd done? She felt as if her heart would literally break without him. The question she needed to ask: would she have him back at any price? Her mum would definitely be against it. 'Kick him out,' she'd say. Mum should know. She'd got rid of enough men in her time.

Swallowing hard, Amy slipped out her phone and messaged him.

How's it going? What time will you be home?

Disappointingly, he wasn't online. Seized with a need for sugar — good for shock, wasn't it? — she dropped to her hands and knees and crawled through to the counter. Reaching up, like a periscope reading the waters from a submarine, she sneaked a Snickers bar, unwrapped it and bit off a large chunk, the winning combination of salty peanuts and sugar instantly calming. Chewing and crawling back, she returned to her phone, watched the screen, licking a flake of chocolate from her bottom lip, willing the man she knew as Rollo to respond. Her heart lifted when she saw he was online, two blue ticks beside her message, and typing a reply, which was taking an age. 'What are you doing?' she hissed aloud. 'Writing a bloody book?'

Sorry, babe. All's good with the money man — happy face emoji — but there's been a family emergency. It's my sister, Susan. She's been rushed into hospital in Leeds. Racing up there today. Will be with you tomorrow. Promise. Love you x

Fear hit her square in the chest. Despair grabbed hold and spun her around. Bursting into helpless tears, Amy cursed and cried and cried some more. Finally spent, and wiping her nose miserably on her sleeve, she retrieved the crumpled up and sodden piece of paper from the floor where she'd dropped it, and called Susannah.

Amy didn't muck about with niceties. 'Will he be at yours later?'

'I believe so.'

'What time would be best?'

Susannah hesitated. *She hadn't seen that one coming,* Amy thought.

'Six o'clock.'

Amy furiously worked out that she'd need her mum to give the little ones their teas and maybe put them to bed at hers. She didn't like the idea of missing the parent teacher evening — education was important — but she could see no way around it. She made a mental note to call the school and explain to the teachers, hopefully not Miss Ward, that she was unable to attend. Maybe they could give her a rundown of Tana's progress on the phone.

'I'll be there,' Amy said. Weirdly, it was good to talk to someone in a similar boat to her. Forewarned and forearmed, there was something she badly needed to know. 'What are you going to do?'

'Throw him out,' Susannah replied.

* * *

Chantal had had a bitch of a day.

Coco had spent the morning mooning around and getting under her feet, then Frankie showed up and regaled her with the same story she'd heard the day before, admittedly with less drama. Asked for her opinion, she'd been moderate, giving Frankie similar shout lines to the ones she'd told his mother. It was like living in a TV soap opera, and Chantal could not abide those. Eventually, Frankie and Coco sloped off, to get drunk, no doubt. Chantal couldn't care less as long as she was left alone. She'd been forced to deal with a tricky customer who was not wholly satisfied with the dresses she'd ordered, or the service received and was threatening to leave a ghastly review on Chantal's website. It wouldn't matter so much but the woman had influence and contacts. Chantal suspected that as *loaded* — to use Coco's description — as the bitch — also Coco's description — was, she was after a serious discount. With a sigh, Chantal sent her client an email to that affect, the percentage carved off the price described as "a gesture of goodwill" when all Chantal felt was ill will.

A late session of Brazilian jiu-jitsu did not improve her mood despite the claims to improve and sustain mental health. Reliant on technique over physical strength, it focused on pinning moves, choke holds and arm locks. There was a lot of what she would describe as ground fighting. When you "tap" your opponent to release, they are supposed to let go, not hang on. Chantal had given her instructor a rare piece of her mind after he'd nearly made her pass out.

Showered and dressed and back at her desk, without any distractions from 'the children' who were still out getting plastered, she was annoyed to hear her doorbell. If it were Susannah again, she would scream. When she opened the door it wasn't Susannah. She wanted to scream just the same.

'Lance,' Chantal said dully, without exclamation.

He looked like hell, as if he hadn't slept in weeks. His clothes were rumpled and she'd seen better-dressed homeless people sleeping rough on the corner of Regent Street, near the shopping arcade.

'Can I come in?'

'Coco isn't here and I'm incredibly busy.'

'Chantal, please.'

He did that whole hangdog thing he was so good at, like a beaten Cocker Spaniel. Odd that he looked like a victim when he was so accomplished at leaving a trail of human debris in his wake.

Chantal issued a gale of a sigh and stepped aside. Lance plunged in.

'Got anything to drink?'

153

'I was having green tea.'

'I think I need something a little stronger.'

'What you need is a good talking to,' Chantal said. 'Sit down, shut up and listen.'

Obediently, Lance did as he was told. He ran his fingers through hair that looked in need of a serious wash. 'You've heard then?'

'From where I'm standing it would be hard not to. I've had your wife here — the one you live with in Cheltenham, in case you've forgotten — and your daughter who is deeply upset and which is where I come in.'

Lance opened his mouth to protest. Raising the flat of her hand, Chantal made it plain she was not finished.

'I don't care about your private life. I do care how it impacts on our daughter and I very much care about how people digging around in your questionable financial dealings might unearth something unpleasant from your past.'

She took care to stress "your" and not "our".

Lance opened and closed his mouth.

'You do realise the risk you run?'

From the devastated expression on Lance's face, he didn't, but he did now.

'You really believe it's connected to . . .'

'Don't even say it,' Chantal snapped.

'Christ,' Lance said, clutching the back of his neck.

'Tell me how you were approached by those unsavoury characters.'

He did. She listened with a growing sense of dread.

'You have bigger things with which to concern yourself than your love life.'

'I feel like I'm a dead man.'

The way you're carrying on, you may well be, Chantal thought.

Lance looked up at her. 'What do I do?'

'You pay them.'

'You're not serious.'

'Deadly.'

'Are you prepared to chip in?'

'Don't be ridiculous.'

'But you're as much . . .'

'With regard to your women, you face up to what you've done and take the flak for it. You grovel. You make peace. You make reparation. You do not, repeat, do *not* give Susannah or this other . . .' She tailed off, temporarily lost for an apt description that wasn't insulting.

'Amy,' he interjected.

'. . . a reason to look into your past. People do when they're vexed,' she said in answer to his questioning expression. 'It will be painful and it will be difficult. You'll simply have to suck it up.'

Lance sat up a little straighter, she noticed. Good, she was getting through. 'As I've already said and of graver concern: the men in suits.'

'They don't know about . . .' He broke off under the weight of Chantal's stare.

'You cannot be sure.'

'Trust me, they would have used it against me by now. The threat was always the exposure of my other life.'

'Threats can evolve. They can change.'

'I've never told a living soul.'

'Neither have I.'

A moment of conspiracy between them, Lance gave a half-smile that made the lines around his eyes crinkle. He looked quite boyish for a man of his age. Immune, Chantal could still appreciate his physical appeal. She got how he'd charmed his way into a young woman's life. Neither his mistress nor his wife had known him when his hair was dark. They didn't know that it had turned silver over the space of a single night, still less the reason why. Due to shock, Chantal reasoned.

Pushing the past back to where it belonged, she was simply glad she'd helped her ex to get his mojo back. A confident Lance was more reassuring than a wet and pathetic Lance.

He gave Chantal a hopeful smile. 'Will you tell Coco I love her?'

155

'Tell her yourself some place else and on your own time.' She stared in the direction of the door. 'I think we're quite finished. I have work to get on with — and so do you.'

* * *

'Wouldn't it be glorious to never have to work?' Coco was glassy-eyed with booze.

Frankie laughed. 'At this rate you'll get the sack. Job done.'

They were at the Lansdown, a Greene King pub on the road of the same name. It had a large beer garden that was usually rammed in the summer with drinkers. Coco was deliberating between a second bottle of Prosecco, shots, or both. Frankie was drinking lager at a more sedate and steady pace. He'd long ago given up trying to keep pace with his sister.

'Don't you think you should eat something?'

'Pussy.'

'Christ, you're off your tits.'

'I'm so not.' Her voice a drunken whine, Coco's face suddenly darkened. 'Why won't Daddy return my calls?'

'Because he's shit-scared. I mean would you return them if you were him?'

'In the first place I wouldn't do the awful things he's done. Secondly—' she waggled a finger —'*if* I had I'd be adult enough to make things right with my firstborn. I'm never having kids,' she said with vigour.

Frankie fell silent. Coco read it as agreement. Darling Frankie concurred with her about a lot of stuff. 'Maybe I'll have a Pinot,' she said. 'And a tequila shot. Get another round in, would you, Frankie?'

Frankie held out his hand.

Coco pulled a credit card out of her pocket.

'PIN,' he said.

Coco revealed the four-digit number and watched him disappear. She was at that stage of inebriation where she'd gone past happy, to the miserable, bleak and futile, stepped up again, briefly, to happy, and was now in danger of plunging into angry. She'd never been a sleepy, or a riotously funny and "loves everyone" drunk.

Frankie returned with a tray of drinks. Coco reached over and took a long swallow of wine. 'What's going to happen, bro?'

'No idea. Don't think there's going to be a kiss and make up.' He stared into his glass as if it would deliver an answer.

'Fuck, that means divorce. *You'll* be all right,' Coco said, sly.

'Oh, sure.'

'No, really. Suze will get half the assets. It's what happens.'

'What assets? Those bastards have robbed us of everything.'

'Haven't got their paws on the house though, have they?'

'True.'

'See, every cloud and all that.'

'Sometimes you talk utter shite.'

'So I've been told.'

Coco glanced at her watch, a gift from her mother. Designed by Chanel, it had a chic black masculine-styled wristband and cost thousands. 'S'pose I could pawn this if things get tight.'

'Yeah, right,' Frankie said sceptically. 'What's the time?'

'Only an hour to go. Think we should gate-crash?'

'What would be the point?'

Coco shot forward, angry eyes on Frankie. 'Don't you care?'

'Sure I do, but it's not going to ruin my life in the way it will ruin Mum's.'

'Or mine,' Coco snarled.

'Or yours,' Frankie repeated mechanically.

'So?' she challenged.

'Let the *grown-ups*,' he said, with a big eye roll, 'sort themselves out. We can show up later if you think we must.'

Coco snatched at her drink and treated him to her iciest smile. 'You're such a coward.'

'I'm a realist,' Frankie said. 'Don't take me for a fool, Coco.' When Frankie was pissed off he could go all deep and dangerous on her. Coco kind of liked it. She was also wise enough to know when to back off.

'Think Suze will chuck him out tonight?'

Frankie shrugged. 'Who can say? You never can tell with women.'

'Do I sense a misogynistic slur?'

'Nope. Women are more emotionally governed, more led by their hearts.'

'Than their dicks is what you mean. Well, thank fuck for that.'

They broke into peals of raucous laughter and chinked glasses.

CHAPTER TWENTY-EIGHT

I heard the door go. Cold air from outside came inside. It felt like an omen.

I was sitting on a high stool near the central island unit in the kitchen. I'd finished one cup of coffee and was halfway through the next. There was no 'Honey, I'm home'. No best foot forward and 'Hey, what a fantastic/bloody day and how about yours?'

Lance slunk in, wordless.

I turned and forced myself to hold him in a vice-like stare for as long as I could stand. I hoped he withered underneath the weight of my condemnation. His silver hair appeared to have darkened to the colour of old pewter. Two lines appeared close to his temples. I couldn't read whether it was due to distress or guilt, or both. He hadn't shaved and dark shadows underneath his eyes gave him a drawn and haggard appearance. I felt like a goddess.

'Susannah,' he began. The tone was apologetic and pleading and, to my ears, thoroughly irritating.

'I'm not doing this now.' Imperiously, I slid off the stool. 'I'm taking a shower and changing into something more comfortable.'

As I walked past he shot out a hand and grabbed my arm. My disgusted gaze travelled from his grip to his face. 'Let go of me,' I said quietly.

He released me as if he'd touched molten bronze. 'I want to explain. Please.'

Once, I would have gazed into those eyes and melted. Once, I would have let him draw me close, smother me in kisses. Once, I would have been persuaded.

'I thought we were in for the long haul,' I said bitterly. 'I thought you would always protect me.'

'Susannah, I'm so sorry. It's complicated. I still love . . .'

'I was hunted down yesterday, nearly run off the road.' My voice shook.

'Darling, are you . . . ?'

'Stop it,' I snarled. 'How the hell did you pull it off? Do our friends know? Are Meera and Dan, Holly and Jonathan aware of your double life?' God help them if they were.

'No, I swear. They knew nothing.'

I stared at him, assessing if he were telling me the truth. I thought he was.

'Please, what can I do to make amends?'

'This isn't a case of slipping me a few quid to buy a nice dress,' I said scathingly. 'Not that you could afford it.'

'Susannah, I'm . . .'

'I only want one thing from you.'

'Name it,' he said earnestly. 'I'll do anything. You know I will.'

'Now that the Mounts have lost their hand of cards, go to the police right here and now and shop them.'

Fear entered his eyes. 'I . . . I . . .'

'Thought so.'

'Honestly, Susannah . . .'

'There is nothing *honest* about this. I thought they were using your double life to blackmail you.'

Lance swallowed hard. 'They were.'

I gave him a dead-eyed smile. 'What the hell *else* have they got on you?'

'Nothing, I swear.'

'Normal people consider extortion a crime.'

'I've already explained, it will only make . . .'

Feeling murderous, I walked out of the kitchen, up the stairs and locked myself in the bathroom. I hadn't told him to clear out his things. I was saving that until later.

* * *

Amy wasn't accustomed to driving long distances on her own. She was used to urban traffic, yet driving in Cheltenham was on a different level. Everyone piloted big expensive motors and seemed to be insanely in a hurry. Rush hour didn't help, although she reckoned it was rush hour all hours of the day and night here. When Rollo was at home he insisted on her sitting in the passenger seat, especially for the longer journeys. That way, she could entertain the children and keep them topped up with snacks and drinks. God — how she missed her babies.

Tana knew something was up the second Amy collected her from school.

'Have you been crying, Mummy?'

'Me? No, sweetie, I've got hay fever and my eyes are all sore and itchy.'

'Daddy will make you better,' Wilf said.

Amy had fought to hold it together. When she'd reached her mum's the floodgates opened. Her mother fretted and fussed.

'I was never sure about him, our Amy, but bloody hell I never expected something like this.'

'Mum, please don't swear in front of the kids.'

'It's a very naughty word, Grandma,' Tana piped up.

'For a very naughty person.'

'Mum, please,' Amy begged her.

Amy told her mother everything while they drank tea. Her mum had put in a spoonful of sugar "for the shock". Amy hadn't cared that it was weak and milky.

'Do you know how long you'll be?' her mum asked when it was time for her to leave. She had Adele in her arms and the children were watching the television with a plate of biscuits each.

Amy didn't know. How long does it take to give the man you love his marching orders? Would she have the strength to see it through?

'Best if you stay here tonight with the kids,' her mum said. Then, quite spontaneously, she'd wrapped one arm around Amy and kissed the side of her face. 'Go. Do what you have to do. We'll get you through this, you'll see, my love.'

The thought of her mum's kindness made Amy tear up again.

Following the sat nav, she drove down Suffolk Road, as instructed and, turning off into another street, found Ashford Road. Amy's jaw went slack at the sight of such lovely houses — and to think that this was where Rollo lived his other life, the cheating shit. He must have found their place poky and cramped by comparison. Something in her soul turned cold.

There was one space left on the short gravelled drive. Amy parked her Peugeot between a Volkswagen Polo with a dirty great dent in the boot and a swanky BMW. No sign of the Dacia Sandero.

Sitting there to compose herself, she allowed her gaze to travel to the upstairs windows. They were dressed with pretty curtains in a chintz pattern. Downstairs, had shutters. A hanging basket of violas and pansies hung next to a solid-looking door in a lovely shade of green; teal, she thought it was called, according to the paint colour charts she'd studied. Anger streaked through her. To think she'd had to fight to get Rollo to shell out for her little house in Bayton. She didn't care what that Susannah said about people after them for money. They were better off than anyone she knew. This was proper upper-crust living. The dark thought that Rollo was attracted to her because Amy came from the other side of the tracks choked her. Was she his "bit on the side", his "bit of rough"? Is that how he thought of her?

Right, be cool, be as civil as you can to the bloody wife, Amy thought, stepping out of her car and locking it. Braced for a fight, she pinned her shoulders back. God help him.

* * *

Since my shower, Lance had made several weak attempts to engage. I'd silenced him with the truth: that he'd lied and lied and lied again. 'What have I ever done to deserve this? What have *we* ever done?'

'We?'

'Frankie and me.'

'There it is,' Lance said. 'We were never a couple. There was always three of us.'

'Don't be pathetic.'

'It's true. You think more of your son than you do of me.'

Slammed by the accusation, I struggled to find a reply. Was this how Lance really felt or was he saying it in the heat of the moment to hurt me and offer a pitiable defence for his appalling behaviour?

The doorbell rang.

'Are you expecting someone?' Lance asked.

'No,' I replied.

Still, he hesitated.

Vexed, I said, 'Go on then, make yourself useful and answer the door.'

Lance remained rooted. I got it: he feared a visit from the Mount brothers. After what he'd said about Frankie I hoped it rattled the hell out of him.

'What if it's Veldo?' he muttered.

'They wouldn't ring the bell. They'd barge in.'

Lance nodded uneasily. I watched and listened intently as he walked slowly out towards the hall.

The sound of his hand on the catch.

The noise of the door swishing open.

Then Amy's monotone voice. 'Surprised to see me? Thought I'd swing by, *Lance*.'

Picturing the consternation on my husband's face, my smile was as cold as a Russian winter.

'Aren't you going to invite me in?' I heard Amy say.

Next, she was in the kitchen, wide-eyed, slightly flushed, but no sign of tears. She wore a nicely styled jacket over jeans and ankle boots. She stood ruler straight, head held high. In spite of everything I thought she looked magnificent.

Lance trailed in behind like an old man told he is to be put into a home, reliant solely on council funding.

'Drink?' I asked Amy.

'I'd love one but can't. I'm driving.'

'How about an elderflower and raspberry spritzer?'

'Sounds nice.'

I patted the bar stool beside me. 'Take a seat.' I took my time fixing a drink. 'Ice?' I asked.

'A cube, thanks.'

Out of the corner of my eye, I noticed Lance wringing his hands. I placed the drink before Amy and sat back down. A film of sweat glazed Lance's forehead, no doubt feeling the heat of two angry women on his case. He sat and stood up. He paced up and down. He thumped a fist repeatedly into the palm of one hand, like he was psyching himself up for a presentation, which, I guessed he was.

'Look, girls,' he babbled. 'Susannah, Amy,' he began again in response to our outraged expressions. 'I recognise what I've done and I can only ask your forgiveness.'

'You abandoned me. You abandoned our children!' Amy's voice was a roar that filled the kitchen with her pain.

'That's not true,' Lance argued. 'Never. I won't ever give up on either of you.'

'What?' I sneered. 'You actually think in your deluded mind you can continue flitting between the two of us? What are you suggesting — a throuple.'

'A what?' Amy said.

'A romantic relationship between three people.'

'Romantic?' Amy said, appalled. 'Screw that.'

164

'I'm suggesting no such thing,' Lance said, desperate to get a word in. 'I'm sure we could work something out.'

'You're fucking nuts,' Amy cursed.

'I know I've hurt you. I know I've caused you immense pain.'

'It's not just us though, is it? It's the kiddies. Have you any idea what it feels like to tell them their daddy is a cheating shit?'

'Amy, love, I adore our children.'

'Funny way of showing it,' Amy sniffed. 'And don't *Amy love* me. What about hers?' She tilted her head at me.

'Adult children still hurt, Lance,' I reminded him. 'Coco and Frankie are wounded and bewildered.'

'I'll explain. I'll make it up to them. You have my word.'

'Your word?' Amy sneered in derision.

'My children are my life.'

'Sentimental bullshit,' I said, mocking.

'Honestly, I mean it. I promise to speak to each and reassure them that my actions don't change my love or my commitment.'

'Says who?' Amy said. 'After what you've done you won't be seeing mine again.'

'Amy, you can't do that.'

'You think?'

'And Frankie doesn't want to speak to you right now,' I cut in. 'Don't believe you can easily win him over, Lance.'

He hung his head. 'I never thought this was going to be easy.' I felt Amy bristling beside me. I'll be honest, I was watching to see how she interacted with my husband and how he responded to her. I couldn't read it. Were Amy and me on the same side, or weren't we?

'What's not easy,' Amy said, 'is looking after three youngsters single-handed when you've had no sleep. What's not easy is dreaming about the home you'd like and having it ripped away. What's not easy is knowing that the man you love has a wife and kids he never told you about.'

'And it's no picnic to live with a man who runs up enormous debts with crooks who threaten to disfigure you,' I joined in.

'I've tried to sort it.'

'Try harder.'

'I never meant this to happen, I swear.'

'So how did it?' I folded my arms. 'Enlighten us.'

Lance's tired face expressed hesitation, confusion and embarrassment. He ran his fingers under his jaw. He pursed his lips, seemed about to speak and then changed his mind. Finally he said, 'I fell in love with two women. It's the god's honest truth,' he added, faced with a brick wall of cynicism. 'I couldn't choose between you if I wanted to. I love you both.'

I looked at Amy who looked at me. Bewildered, Amy's eyes flooded with sudden tears.

Shamed, Lance said, 'Please don't, Amy. You know how much I hate it when you cry.'

'If you only knew how much I'd loved you, how much I'd needed you.' Amy's voice broke. I couldn't help but reach out and lightly touch her arm.

'Don't say that,' Lance begged, desperation in his eyes. 'I will make this right. I will — for the kids as well.'

'You can't.' Amy was really sobbing now.

Lance's betrayal, the enormous damage done, emotionally, physically, mentally and financially was so immense I could no longer stand it.

'Amy's right. You've taken my life, her life and the lives of your children and trashed them because, at heart, you're a weak, greedy and selfish man.'

'Please . . .'

'Get what you need for tonight and clear out.'

'Susannah?' He pleaded. 'I beg your forgiveness.' Finding no quarter, he turned to Amy.

'You heard her,' Amy said stonily.

CHAPTER TWENTY-NINE

Coco woke up at Art Mather's house. Sadly, she was not in Art's bed, but on a sofa in a spare room.

The afternoon and evening had spiralled out of control when, first, Miles showed (yuk) and then Art (yum). They'd moved on from the Lansdown to a student squat near St Paul's where a party was in play. After that things got a bit blurry. She remembered receiving a message from her father in the early hours, to which she hadn't yet replied because she'd lost the ability to either walk in a straight line or formulate words. Better have a squint at it now, she thought, slipping out her phone, attempting to focus.

Would love to talk. Are you free to meet? How about the Norwood Arms at 12.30 pm?

No way could she deduce whether this was good news, indifferent news, or bad news. She considered phoning Suze to get the lowdown then changed her mind. Frankie, currently snoring softly on the floor, having for a period of the night slept in a bath, would winkle out a more honest response.

She replied: *OK* and staggered out of her makeshift bed to the loo.

Having got utterly and totally hammered, the consequences were plain to see in the mirror. Her skin was blotchy.

She didn't have circles under her eyes; she had rectangles. Her lips were cracked and dry and her tongue looked dark and furry. She felt like hell.

In the space of time she'd taken to answer the call of nature and study the wreckage that was her face, Frankie was up and on the phone to his mother. Maddeningly, his glossy hair shone. His eyes were dark and clear and gave the impression he was wearing eyeliner and mascara, which he most definitely wasn't. Even the fashionable stubble on his jaw looked groomed, upstanding, alert and ready for the day.

'Fuck,' he said. 'Yup . . . yup . . . Fuckity fuck . . . Good . . . What? . . . Jesus. Right . . . Laters.'

Coco stared, mystified. 'Did you know that there are other words in the vocabulary apart from the F word?'

'Sometimes only the F word will do. She's thrown him out.'

'Fuck,' Coco said, sliding down onto the sofa. 'So come on, dish the dirt?' She drew up her knees to her chin.

'Apparently, it all got a bit shouty.'

'Suze doesn't do shouty.'

'I know. A tad worrying, actually.'

'Go on.'

'The other woman showed.'

'You're shitting me.'

'I am not. Mum invited her.'

'No way.'

Amid interruptions and questions, Frankie gave Coco a précis of the evening's events.

'So that's why Daddy wants to meet me today.'

Frankie frowned. 'He didn't invite me.'

'That's because I'm his favourite.'

'Ha-ha.' Frankie looked anything but *ha-ha* about it. 'Are you going?'

'Too right, I am. We're going to have some proper daddy and daughter time.' Principally, to secure her future; her father had made promises and, holy crap, she intended him to keep them.

Frankie glowered. 'Give him hell.'

'Oh, I will. Shall I send your love?' she teased.

* * *

I finished my call to Frankie. Strung out and emotionally mangled, I hadn't begun to work out what I was going to do. It wasn't as if I could take a husband back after an affair. It wasn't about forgiveness so that I could move on. There was nothing to mediate, nothing for me to resolve. Lance had summed it up when he professed to be in love with two women. In an immature and deluded part of his brain, he seemed to believe that now everyone knew the truth he could continue with his aberrant behaviour and make relationships work for three when it would only work for one: him. If I'd wanted to share my husband I'd have joined a cult. I had no idea if Amy felt the same way. She was so vulnerable and with three tiny mouths to feed, I could imagine a scenario in which she would take Lance back and that pissed me off immensely.

I had not revealed this to Frankie, preferring to give him edited highlights. He didn't need to know how Amy had broken down, how she'd remained briefly after Lance had left — Coco would dine out on that one for years to come. In an awkward and stilted exchange, I discerned that Amy was a good person. Her children were the centre of her world, as Frankie was mine, and though the situation was infernally complicated and fraught, I felt peculiar concern for Amy and her children's welfare. I knew their names and ages. According to Amy she had emotional support from her mother. I didn't envy much about Amy's life but I envied her that. Perhaps, in a quiet moment with my son, I would try to explain that Amy was not the villain of the piece. She had not known that Lance was married. She was as much an innocent victim as me; the same man had betrayed both of us.

Sitting in front of Lance last night and dispensing judgement, I had felt strangely composed. To me, Lance was like the details of an expensive house for sale: all shiny, elegantly photographed and inviting. In reality: old, poorly maintained and repellent.

I was grateful he hadn't blustered or attempted to appeal to one or other of us in a weak attempt to divide. His mawkish oath to support us both had come as a surprise because I'd believed that Amy, a younger woman with her little family, would have the stronger pull. She and I didn't agree to stay in touch. We didn't hug each other goodbye. Amy went her way, and though I stayed on the doorstep for a considerable time after she drove away, I didn't think I'd see her again.

I could not say the same for the men from Veldo. I hadn't forgotten the look of abject terror on Lance's face when he thought they were at the door the night before. His refusal to involve the police was like an itch I continually needed to scratch. Now that I'd thrown Lance out, I was free to do as I pleased, except would the police take me seriously? Chantal had put serious doubts in my mind. Could I make a clear and convincing case for harassment? I didn't know.

Turning this over, my phone alerted me to a message.

So looking forward to this evening. Meet me at the Ivy. Table booked for 7.

In a funny mood, my initial thrill at the thought of illicitly meeting Lorenzo had faded. As a young man, he'd had swagger and arrogance, qualities I was certain he'd tamed as he'd grown older and which I found appealing, yet it didn't feel right to kiss off my husband and walk straight into a night out with the father of my son, after decades apart. And what would Frankie say if he knew I was going out for a cosy dinner? How would that look? It would give Lance a perfect opportunity to take a pot shot at me and accuse me of hypocrisy. My head was all over the place. On a more pragmatic level, what would happen if someone from work saw me out and about?

No, I had to let Lorenzo down as gently as possible. I wouldn't be good company. Life was complicated, I'd say. Plus I had nothing to wear that would create an impression of glamour and confidence and I very much thought that this was the kind of woman Lorenzo hoped I was rather than who I really was. And what did that amount to?

A woman robbed of her confidence in the most profound way. All that sentimental stuff about falling in love with two women felt like a smokescreen. I needed to know what had triggered Lance to stray in the first place, however potentially self-destructive that might be.

With Lance no longer around to restrict or advise me what to do, I phoned my friend, Suki Quant. A woman who exuded inner stillness, Suki was a deep thinker, a person who would be sympathetic and wouldn't judge me.

'I thought you might be taking a class,' I said.

'I wish. Strained a hamstring. I'll be off until it heals. Going to play havoc with the finances but there you go. So what's new?'

Without mentioning Lorenzo, I revealed the breakdown of my marriage. 'This is a whole lot more than a midlife crisis,' I said, revealing Lance's double life. Suki listened without comment until, drained, I reached the end.

'How are you bearing up?' Suki asked kindly.

'I veer from feeling murderous to bewildered.'

'Understandable.'

'Have you ever heard of someone leading a double life?'

'Not to the extent you've described.'

'Any insights gratefully received.'

'Obviously this is a bit more than an extra-marital affair,' Suki observed. 'Where is Lance now?'

'Since I threw him out, no idea.'

'Might he have gone to his other home?'

A fair question, I bristled at the thought. I didn't *think* Amy would take him back, but it was possible. I said as much to Suki.

'Have you spoken to a solicitor?'

'God, no. It's too soon to talk about separation or divorce, although I can't really see any way out of it. I suppose . . .' I tiptoed up to what was needling me. 'I want to understand what's really going on here. The decent part of me sees my husband as a man who made a terrible mistake and is completely trapped and exhausted. The less decent part sees a greedy and despicable individual. Do you really think it's possible for him to love more than one woman at the same time?'

'I do.'

'Oh.' This sounded horribly similar to Chantal's take on events.

'Not that this makes things easier for you,' Suki said gently, 'or the other poor girl, or the children.'

'What's going on inside his head, Suki? I'm really struggling here.'

Suki didn't answer immediately and was obviously giving it serious consideration. 'To his mind, Lance is faced with two irreconcilable choices. Men, and they're usually men, who lead a double life usually have deep psychological issues.'

'That's not Lance.' As soon as the words were out I realised that I no longer knew who Lance was. 'He's always struck me as being rational, straightforward and uncomplicated.'

'Until now.'

'Yes.'

'Is there anything else?'

I told Suki about Lance's financial problems and Veldo.

'I assume you've gone to the police.'

I trotted out Chantal's argument.

'Extracting money with menaces is extortion,' Suki said firmly. 'Essentially, Lance had defaulted on a debt. If Veldo were on the level, they'd set their solicitors onto him and take him to court. What you're describing is entirely criminal. No question.'

I knew Suki was right. It's what I'd known all along.

'Do you think I should approach the main company in Florida? I suppose it's possible that they don't know what's going on in their name?'

'You *could*.'

'You don't sound certain.'

'I'm not sure what you might be walking into. What's more troubling is Lance's reluctance to do the most obvious. Weirdly, it might explain his alternative lifestyle,' Suki said.

'How do you work that out?'

'He feels shamed by a part of his personality.'

I scratched an ear. Perhaps speaking to Suki was not such a good idea. 'He's a cheat. He's bound to feel ashamed, surely.'

'But still he can't help himself. At the root of it he feels guilty for another reason.'

My body tensed. A light flashed on in my brain. Guilt felt like a whole different issue. It would explain Lance's staunch refusal to go to the police. Chantal had adopted a similar line, I recalled. At the time I thought she was protective of me. There was another more plausible explanation.

Chantal is in on it.

'Thanks, Suki,' I said. 'You've been more helpful than you could ever know.'

* * *

Chantal had got the lowdown from Coco. A man in a bind and unstable was an alarming prospect. Trapped in a never-ending cycle of debt, thrown out by both women, Lance posed a serious risk.

As an act of damage limitation, Chantal had spoken to her mother that morning. She lived in Bath with her second husband, a man whose sole virtue was his wealth, as far as Chantal was concerned. Coco didn't know it yet, but Chantal had arranged for her daughter to stay with them for a few weeks. Coco would have to give up her job, but in the long run it was for the best. Perhaps her grandmother could talk sense into her only granddaughter and persuade her to make better use of the brain she'd been borne with. Chantal prided herself on the fact that Coco had inherited her intelligence, instead of her father's.

As importantly, persuading Coco to make a temporary move to a less contentious atmosphere would benefit

Chantal. She could get on with work unimpeded by heavy emotional fallout. It would enable her to keep an eye on "the situation". Very importantly, she could make discreet enquiries about the men who had ransacked Lance's finances. She did not share Lance's naïve belief that Veldo and the Mount Brothers knew nothing of his past. People like them did their homework. Lance had been approached, she recalled, not the other way around. And if those money-grubbing bastards decided to ramp things up, Susannah, the loose cannon, would react. And Chantal really couldn't have that.

Chantal shut her eyes tight. She was good at compartmentalising but, sometimes, images from the past refused to stay in their box.

Lance, white-faced and beside himself.

'It's one in the morning and Coco's asleep and so was I.'

'Oh God, oh God.'

'What have you done?' Because she knew he'd done something.

Wild-eyed, he said, 'Put Coco in the car. I need you to come with me and see.'

And oh my God, she had seen and it was terrible.

CHAPTER THIRTY

Coco sat in the Norwood Arms miserably nursing a soft drink. First, Mum had interrogated her about what had gone down the night before and then Coco had received the mother of all bollockings from a supervisor at work for taking time off without permission. There were protocols in place for sickness and bereavement, she was told, though nothing for a duplicitous father shagging around and producing another family — Coco made that last bit up. She'd put on her game face and agreed to turn up for work that afternoon.

Apologising profusely, her father limped in late — quite literally — sporting a black eye and a split lower lip. Coco wasn't aware that any physical violence had taken place and wondered who had lumped him one. Emotionally frayed — diddums — his expression burned with nervous energy and fatigue. Grime on the collar; his shirt had to be two days old, at least. The creases in his trousers were non-existent. He looked spineless and contrite and totally pathetic. She used to think her dad was cool, a maverick and someone to admire. Banish that image.

He ordered a double Scotch, paid for it and sat down next to her. Agitated, his knee jackhammered as if he'd taken coke. Normally, they'd fall into easy conversation. She'd tease him, take the piss, he'd laugh good-naturedly and tell her she was his golden girl, which was a fucking lie because his golden girl lived in Kidderminster with three of his snotty-nosed kids. Coco had so many questions, none of which were asked because, in the warped silence, she bloody wanted him to suffer. She slouched and eyed him coldly.

'Coco,' he said nervously, 'how are you, darling?'

'You honestly expect me to answer that with any degree of candour?'

He launched into a litany of sorrys. She tuned out, only the odd phrase and word penetrating her brain '. . . *love you* . . . blah-blah . . . *nothing changed between us* . . . blah-blah . . . *difficult* . . . blah-blah . . . *complex* . . . blah-blah . . . *my best girl* . . . blah-di-blah . . . and so I'm afraid I'll have to cut off your allowance.'

What? She sat up straight.

'I'm sorry but things are tight right now. Obviously, once . . .'

'You said you'd stake me money for my business.' She'd planned to open her own beauty salon in a year's time. She wasn't going to stay a shop assistant on a makeup counter for fucking ever. She'd got it all mapped out: up the ante on Insta, use Substack to reach her core audience, reach out through TikTok, create blogs and podcasts, all of which took energy — mostly Frankie's, though she hadn't told him yet. But the hardcore bricks and mortar, the financials and rental, required her father's input and here he was blowing her out.

'I know. I'm sorry, it's simply not possible, sweetheart.'

In the space of minutes Coco had gone from party girl about town, influencer hellbent on conquering the cosmetic world, to impoverished no-hoper.

Other daughters would have stood up and walked out. Coco was not a quitter. Angry, burning with accusations, she let him have it with a range of expletives borrowed from Frankie's repertoire. Breathless, she finished with, 'You know what you are apart from being a serial shagger? You're a dream-breaker.'

'I appreciate you're upset.' He shot her a nervy look and then, maddeningly, glanced over his shoulder as if he expected instant arrest by armed police.

Bloody hell, focus, she thought. 'If you weren't trying to run two households we wouldn't be in this foul mess.'

'That's not strictly true, sweetheart, as well you know.'

'Oh *them*!' she said with a big eye-roll. 'I don't care what you have to do to get those bastards off your back, but you can and you will. You have to.'

'Coco, it's not . . .'

'Yes, it is. Stand up to them, for Chrissakes. Grow a fucking backbone. It's *our* money.' There was so much fear in his face she wanted to scream aloud in frustration. Suddenly his injuries made sense. 'Did they beat you up?'

'No,' he said with a wet laugh. 'I got drunk, fell over and did my face in on a pavement.'

She raked his face for lies. Maybe true, probably not.

'I saw you with them, you know.'

'What? When?'

'The other day in Gloucester Road.'

'Coco,' he said suddenly stern. 'I forbid you from going anywhere near those people.'

'You forbid?' She raised a haughty eyebrow. It had pissed her off when Suze had issued a similar order. Coming from her father it was risible.

His hand shot out and copped hold of her arm. 'I mean it, Coco.'

Reacting to the uncommonly dangerous light in his eyes, she said, 'Okay, okay. You've made your point.'

'And Frankie mustn't get any ideas either,' her father insisted. 'You keep away, the pair of you. Understand?'

'Message received loud and clear,' Coco said tartly. 'Can't speak for my brother. You realise he is seriously pissed off with you.'

Her father snatched at his whisky.

'So,' she said, sipping her drink. 'Where are you going to stay now you're officially homeless?'

He drained his glass and stared at his feet.

'Daddy?' she prompted.

'At the unit,' he said. 'It will be good to focus on work. Maybe if I wait it out . . .' He looked up and tailed off.

Coco gave a snort. 'Suze won't have you back, you know that, right?'

Denial was scribbled all over his face. Parents were a real pain in the arse, she thought. Glancing at her watch, she got up, went to pat his shoulder before thinking better of it, and stalked out.

* * *

I phoned Chantal twice, the line engaged. Giving up, I marched straight round. With no answer, I stood on the doorstep in spitting rain and phoned Chantal's number again on the off chance that she was really in and pretending not to be. The call went to voicemail. I left an uncompromising message.

We need to talk and it's urgent.

Trudging back, I phoned Lorenzo before I chickened out.

'I'm so sorry but I can't make it tonight.'

'Oh no,' he said, disappointed. 'I was so looking forward to it.'

So was I. 'Things are tricky at home at the moment.'

'Nothing too serious, I hope.'

'Well . . .'

'Susannah, we don't have to eat out, if you don't feel like it. I could cancel the restaurant. How about we order room service in the hotel?'

'No,' I blurted out, fearing it would be too intimate and risky. 'Sorry, I mean that's a lovely idea, but . . .'

'Or we could go for a walk and talk.'

'It's tempting but I won't be good company.'

'Let me be the judge of that.'

'Honestly . . .'

'Susannah, if you think I'm trying to pick up where we left off, I'm not.'

'Oh.'

'We're both grown-ups, aren't we? We live in different countries. You have your life and I have mine.'

'Yes,' I said, stupidly deflated. 'Absolutely.'

'So what do you say?'

'You're very persistent.' And I was weakening.

'That's better,' he said encouragingly. I could feel the warmth of his personality from where I was standing. 'My room is 205. Get here when you can. I'll have a bottle open, ready and waiting.'

Flustered and still unsure, it didn't take much for me to give in. All the way back I told myself *separate lives, no strings, definitely no romantic aspirations*. That was sensible, wasn't it? And sensible was who I was.

Reaching home, I stepped into the hall and immediately froze. Someone was stalking around upstairs.

'Frankie,' I called.

No answer.

Maybe it was Lance back to collect more of his belongings. He'd taken little with him the previous evening other than an overnight bag. I called his name. Still no answer. Holding my breath, I heard drawers yanked opened and closed, possessions rifled through, heavy footsteps, *noise*. *Veldo*, I thought, in terror.

Seized with panic, I slipped out my phone, my finger poised on the emergency number. Then, backing away, one hand reaching for the door, ready to exit, a figure emerged at the top of the stairs.

'Lance,' I burst out. 'You frightened the life out of me. What the hell are you doing? And what's happened to your face?'

Dishevelled, he limped downstairs.

'Can we talk?' His tired-looking eyes were wild and pleading.

I slipped off my coat and followed him into the sitting room. He eased himself gingerly into a chair.

'You're hurt,' I said, alarmed.

'I was jumped last night.'

'Oh my God, not . . .'

He leant forward, took both my hands in his.

I drew away. '*They* beat you up?' My voice wasn't much more than a whisper.

He nodded blindly.

'Lance, this has to stop. You absolutely must . . .'

'Thing is,' he said, eyes strangely alight. 'I've found a way out.'

'You have?' My heart gave a little lift.

He slipped out his passport. So that's what he was rummaging around for. Then, horribly, it dawned on me.

'You're making a run for it?'

'Of course not.'

'Then what?'

'It's for a rescue package.'

Thank God. 'Tell me more.'

'Veldo want the deeds to the house.'

I sat open-mouthed. Dully, I realised that he needed his passport as proof of identity to fulfil his legal obligations to any solicitor handling the transfer. Coming to, I snapped a look that would shatter a steel girder.

'With a little money taken from the business we'd have enough to use as a deposit on another property,' he said.

'For what? To buy a shed? Are you out of your mind?'

'Hear me out. I do this and I can finally pay them off.'

'I? What happened to *we*?'

His shifty eyes travelled to the wall. And then I tumbled to it. The house was his original marital home, the one he'd shared with Chantal. When I moved in and married, Lance remained the sole owner. He'd never put my name on the deeds. If we got divorced, it would be a different story and would fall under statement of assets. Handing it over now, he'd got around it. Or so he thought.

'You can't. I won't let you.'

'Susannah,' he began.

'I have rights,' I said, my voice thin and raised. 'You will not make Frankie and me homeless. You will not do this.'

'If I don't, they'll come for the business and then you'll have nothing.'

'If you believe that, you're more of a fool than I took you for. They've just given you a beating, for God's sake. They won't ever stop.'

'I never wanted it to be this way, I assure you.'

'And this is the best you can come up with?' I had a sudden insight into what it feels like to want to hurt someone. Badly. Blood engorged every vessel in my body. My skin was one seething mass of perspiration and heat. I felt fire deep in my belly. 'For the last time, what's the dirt they have on you?'

Lance's mouth opened into an O. His body seemed to collapse and fold in. Stricken, his hands flew to his face. His shoulders sagged and then heaved. Alarmingly, he let out a dry sob.

I was appalled. 'Lance?'

Eventually he let his hands drop. His face revealed a portrait of a terrible deep inner struggle. I thought he was weighing up whether he could entrust me with whatever it was he was hiding.

Finally, he took a breath. 'I'm not a good person.'

Chill slithered up my spine and nestled at the base of my neck.

'What did you do?'

He shook his head. 'I can't.' He moaned and scrubbed at his hair with one hand, clawing his face with the other.

'You must. You owe it to me.'

'Please, leave it, Susannah.'

'Does Chantal know?'

'No,' he said quickly. 'It happened when we were estranged.'

'And you never told her?' Something I found hard to believe.

'She never knew.'

181

A shadow fell across the room. I glanced up and met Frankie's furious expression.

'What the hell is he doing here?' Bowling in, my son threw himself down next to me.

'I was talking to your mother.' Frankie's arrival had a curiously galvanising effect on Lance. Digging deep, he'd suddenly found a bullish streak and quickly pulled himself together. 'Technically, I might remind you, I still live here.'

'That's a joke,' I said bitterly. I turned to Frankie and explained Lance's plan to give the deeds to the house to Veldo.

Frankie's face was a stone. 'Is that true?'

'I have no choice.'

'Have you no shame?' Frankie railed.

I rested a hand on my son's arm. Not to be mollified, Frankie pulled out his phone and waved it in front of Lance's face. 'Look,' he said. 'You and your dirty goings-on are plastered all over social media.'

Lance's jaw jacked open.

'Show me,' I said, snatching the phone. 'Oh my God, it's on the company page.'

> *Stratton the serial shagger.*
> *Lance Stratton banging a woman young enough to be*
> *his daughter.*
> *How to incinerate your life in one easy step.*

It went on and on, some posts more lurid than others. My eyes filmed with tears. 'Who the hell did this?'

'Shit happens,' Frankie said, brittle.

Lance stood up. 'I think it's best I go.'

'Coward,' Frankie spat.

'Not until you've explained,' I said doggedly.

'Explained what?' Frankie asked.

'It was nothing,' Lance blustered. 'Heat of the moment.'

'Good riddance then,' Frankie called as the man, who'd been more of a father to him than his real dad, headed for the door.

CHAPTER THIRTY-ONE

Feeling a failure, Amy had jettisoned every swatch of fabric she'd collected, together with several paint colour cards, and hurled them into the bin. No point thinking about dream homes she couldn't have if the dream was dead. She'd dragged herself through the rest of the day by staying in bed. Her mum had been good as gold. Looked after the kids and took them to school. She'd phoned the sweet shop to say that Amy was poorly, which in her heart she was. Mum had brought her soup at dinnertime and tried to cheer her up by slagging off the opposition, as she referred to Lance's missus.

'From what you said you're well out of it, my girl. Sounds a very odd set-up to me. That's posh rich folk for you; they get up to all sorts — nothing normal about them. Don't have the same problems as the rest of us.'

Amy couldn't help but agree. Susannah was insulated in a way that she wasn't. Amy's eyes had nearly popped out at the sight of the navy blue AGA, the island unit, all that glass and shutters and expensive cookware. Copper, for goodness sake, it must have cost a small fortune. And Amy bet Susannah was pensioned up to the eyeballs. People like that were, weren't they? They didn't put a bit by when they could and hope for the sodding best.

'And fancy calling a child, Coco,' her mum had banged on. 'Where I come from it's a hot drink you have when you can't sleep, not some kid's name.

'It's not Susannah's daughter,' Amy had said. 'It's Rollo's.'

'I don't care. That Susannah woman sounds a right stuck-up cow.'

It was one thing for Amy to silently slag off Susannah, another when her mother did it. 'She's stinging as much as me.'

'That I doubt and why should you defend her? As for Rollo, or whatever he's bloody called, I never did like him. Something not quite straight.'

'You never said.'

'Didn't want to fall out with you, did I? Someone should take a horsewhip to him.'

From what Amy had gathered, the men blackmailing him might do a lot worse than that. God help them if they came knocking at her door. Amy wondered how Susannah was doing, wondered if, in the end, she'd take her husband back. Wives did, didn't they? Oh she knew what Susannah had said the night before, and she didn't think it was bluff, but you never knew with couples that'd been together a long time. Like her mum said, people like them handled things differently.

I fell in love with two women.

Those words still clouted her around the head again and again. Amy loved her children equally; she could never love two men. It was bloody bullshit.

Blistering with anger, she couldn't believe she'd been such a mug. All those absences *for work* and *doing a mate a favour*, Rollo's new phone, his vague answers to simple questions, the fact he had few friends or friends she was allowed to meet, his insistence on separate accounts for finances; it all fell into place. When Susannah let on that he had two parents alive and very much kicking, she realised what a lying, conniving cheat Rollo really was. There appeared to be no end to his fibs. She'd wanted to rip his bloody head off last night and yet, as reality slowly sunk in, she missed him. She felt so terribly sad and it had barely been twenty-four hours.

'Early days,' her mum had said. 'You're bound to be all over the place. Remember when I had to throw out Reggie Jelf?'

Reggie Jelf was a crook with more dodgy deals going on than a bent copper. 'Use your anger and keep it close,' her mum maintained. 'It will get you through.'

But Amy didn't want to "get through". She wanted to be rescued.

Ashamed to admit it, she was jealous of la-di-da Susannah, of her comfy life, of what she had with Rollo. Without him, Susannah would do just fine. For Amy, it was different. She needed Rollo home. She wanted things to go back to where they'd left off, before her world had collapsed and dragged her down with it. The old Amy, the ball-breaker, would have survived with two fingers up. Motherhood had changed her in ways she'd never appreciated until now. It had made her soppy. She worried about things more. She didn't like reading the news with threats of global warming and wars and weird people whose only aim in life was to destroy the lives of decent folk like her. If she were to protect her young, she needed to find some of that steel. Now her life had imploded she wondered if she ever could.

* * *

'What will you do?'

Not yet five o'clock, Frankie poured us both a drink. He placed a glass of wine in my hand, sat down next to me on the sofa, and put his arm tightly around my shoulders. It felt good.

Devoid of ideas, bereft of insight, plain lost, I shook my head. What was I to do if the house was given away? Where would I go? Lance was behaving like a mad man. And there was that other thing, the dark secret lurking in his background, the thing that gave those bastards from Veldo power over him. Lance had been on the cusp of a confession that I sensed was going to rip a hole in my head. Had I ever really known my husband?

'Can he really transfer the house from underneath us?' Frankie asked.

'Hopefully not.'

'You must get legal advice.'

'Trust me, I intend to.'

'Good,' he said absently and then, as an afterthought, he added, 'We'll be okay.' He gave my shoulders a squeeze.

I wasn't so sure. A grim situation on so many levels, I felt as if I were fighting for my life while holding together a stab wound in my side.

'I could kill him for making you suffer,' Frankie said.

'Get in the queue.' My smile was savage. 'Do you know who posted that awful stuff online?' The thought of everyone in the world knowing about our private life, though trifling by comparison to everything else, made me queasy. How would staff react at work? What would my patients think? I couldn't bear their pity, the whispered conversations and sudden silences when I walked past, or left a room.

'My money is on Miles.'

'Surely, not. You've known him since you were little.'

'My bad,' Frankie admitted, embarrassed. 'We got pissed and I told him about Dad.'

'Some friend he's turned out to be.'

'I could say the same about my father.'

'Oh, Frankie.'

'Not sure I'm going to call him Dad after this, Mum. Funny, I've never thought much about my real dad until now.'

I fell silent. Frankie knew he was a result of a holiday romance with an Italian man. He'd never expressed an interest in tracking him down. The thought of Frankie starting now was unnerving.

'Art calls his parents by their Christian names,' Frankie continued. 'Perhaps I'll call him Lance.'

'I think that might seem a little odd.'

'Better than bellend, or some of the names Coco's come up with.'

'How is she?'

'How do you think? Apparently, she had a meeting with *him* at lunchtime. Obviously on some kind of charm offensive.'

'Not sure charm will be quite enough.'

Frankie snorted and took a large swallow of wine. 'You won't take him back if he dumps his other woman, will you?'

I shook my head. 'I'm not sure Amy would have him back either.' *Not sure* being the operative words.

'Amy? That sounds cosy. Quite chummy, in fact.'

'She's not a femme fatale, Frankie.'

'If you say so. Seriously, Mother,' Frankie said, accusing.

'What?'

'Why are you cutting the little bitch so much slack?'

'She's not a little bitch and, sorry to tell you,' I said, raising my voice, 'I don't want to rip her hair out.'

'Cool,' Frankie said.

I hated it when he was petulant and curt.

'I'm sorry but right now I'm too tired to think, let alone decide on what happens next. Please,' I said, imploring him. 'Let's not fall out. Are we good?'

He let out an enormous sigh then flashed me a brilliantly mischievous smile. 'Always. Didn't mean to be pissy, Ma. Bit spun out, that's all.'

I smiled with relief. 'As are we all.'

'Right,' Frankie said, bolting the rest of his drink. 'I'm off to my room. Got a date with my XBox. Coco wanted to meet up to give me the lowdown on the fatherly chat,' he said with a facetious grin. 'Thought I'd swerve it.'

'Can you fix your own dinner tonight?' I asked.

'Sure. You going out?'

'Yes.' I fiddled with my wedding ring. 'I'm meeting up with Suki Quant for a drink.'

'God, is that wise?'

'Don't be horrible,' I said, forcing a guilty laugh.

'Have fun,' he said and loped out.

I waited a few beats and then shot upstairs and cleaned my teeth to get rid of the slightly sour aftertaste of white wine. I changed into a flattering peach-coloured sweater over a pair of black straight-legged trousers, and teamed them with a pair of stylish black trainers with an inch of white sole that Coco had persuaded me to buy. Wearing a soft leather jacket and carefully applying a little more make-up than I was used to, I hoped my confidence would return. It didn't. I felt strung out and guilt snapped at my heels for lying to my son, for lying to myself and for the lies I was about to tell Lorenzo. Shouldn't I simply call the whole thing off?

Torn, I decided to walk there anyway, even if the second I arrived, I turned around and came straight back.

Light fading, the streets were grey with the threat of rain. Should have brought an umbrella, I thought, rolling up the collar of my jacket and speeding up.

Past the Jolly Brewmaster pub, I headed towards Park Place and into Suffolk Square, a grand terrace of 19th Century Regency buildings with porticos and columns in dressed stone, with a central bowling green at its centre.

About to cut into Montpellier Walk, I had a strong sensation of someone behind me. Glancing over my shoulder, I saw a girl on a bicycle and an older woman jogging. *Nothing to fear*, I thought — then why was I scared?

Quickening my step, I sped up. It began to rain, the pavement greasy beneath the soles of my trainers. People were heading out for drinks and dinner, family meals and illicit trysts and I was one of them. Was it guilt pursuing me down the road, or something and someone else? What if one of the Mount brothers wanted to make a point? What if beating up Lance wasn't enough?

By the time I reached the hotel my chest heaved, perspiration coated my brow and I was clattering with nerves.

Bowling through the revolving doors, I nodded to a receptionist who greeted me, and headed straight for the Ladies.

Resisting the urge to splash my face with water, I dabbed at my neck with a wet tissue, took out a deodorant from my bag and, rolling up my sweater, sprayed my armpits. My reflection in the mirror told its own story; a tale of desertion, abandonment and foreboding. I hadn't imagined someone following me. I was sure of it.

Ruined financially and emotionally, I was afraid for the future, for my life and for my family. Weak and vulnerable, I needed Lorenzo and hated myself for it.

Is this how Amy feels about Lance?

As if in a trance I headed back out into the lobby and took the lift.

Lorenzo's warm smile, a kiss on each cheek, should have settled my nerves. His hands resting on my shoulders, his eyes finding mine, I swore he'd heard my heart bumping inside my chest.

'It is so very good to see you,' he said.

I stuttered a reply.

When he indicated one of the two chairs I sank into it.

On a table, two flutes and a wine cooler in which a bottle of Bollinger Special Cuvée nestled. I watched as Lorenzo eased out the cork without a pop, fizz from the bottle lifting into the room like smoke. Effortlessly chic, he wore a white collarless shirt that hugged his physique and displayed the depth of his tan over navy jeans. He wore nothing on his feet, which I found alarmingly sexy.

Pouring out two glasses, he handed one to me and chinked.

'To old times,' he said, a dark glint in his eye.

I lifted my glass and took a sip. I felt the weight of his gaze on my every movement. I couldn't quite decide whether I liked it or not. Lance's behaviour had made me tired and worn out. Lorenzo had the opposite effect. He made me feel alive.

'Better?' He looked at me with a wry grin.

'Thank you, yes.'

He sat close. 'So?' he said. 'I don't know the first thing about you. What have you been doing all these years?'

I gave him a highly edited account of my life. He listened and smiled in the right places.

'And your parents, are they still going strong?' he said.

'Oh yes.'

'They must be very proud of you.'

I felt the smile curdle on my face. I was nothing but a constant source of disappointment to my mother.

'Where I come from parents and grandparents are very important,' he continued. 'Do they see much of your children?'

'Not as much as they used to. It's a little different here. Family ties are not so strong.'

'That's a shame.'

'And you?' I said, eager to change the subject. 'You mentioned you were in pharmaceuticals.'

'Medicines,' he said. 'It's big business. The UK imports 1.3 billion in pharmaceuticals a year.'

'Why Cheltenham?'

'There are a number of companies here I trade directly with.'

'You enjoy it?'

'It's what I do,' he said, self-effacingly. 'And it makes a good living.' He leant in with a conspiratorial smile. 'And with two wives and children to support I need to.'

'Yes, of course.' I prickled with anxiety. 'Goodness, it's warm in here, isn't it?'

'Forgive me, let me take your jacket.'

Self-conscious, I slipped it off. Lorenzo hung it in the wardrobe. I sipped my wine, desperate to think of something to say that wouldn't lead to the unsayable.

Lorenzo sat back down. 'I don't want to pry, Susannah, but you sounded upset earlier. As someone whose had his fair share of marital difficulties, I'm a good listener.'

Oh God, I thought, *if you keep looking at me like that, I'm going to either burst into tears, or start talking and never stop.*

And then I did both.

* * *

Chantal was accustomed to pressure at work, never in her personal life. Three missed calls and a visit from Susannah, during which Chantal had cloistered herself in the bathroom, counted as intolerable pressure. She'd thought Susannah had taken on board her advice. She believed Susannah would stop digging around in Lance's past, and by default hers. Evidently, she was wrong. And then there was Coco's rabid reaction to staying with her grandmother. She'd stormed out hours ago, no doubt to get wasted with Frankie.

Now what?

Taking a breath, Chantal approached the safe in her office as if it were unexploded ordnance. She rarely opened the combination because underneath all manner of personal identification, birth certificates and her old marriage certificate, deep below important financial details and the deeds to her home, she held the key to Lance's past, her own, and the two items that could scupper the pair of them. She should have destroyed them long ago. She'd held on because somewhere in the darkest recesses of her mind she thought that they would protect her.

Was she right? Shouldn't she simply destroy them?

Unsure — and Chantal was a woman who had decision-making running through her DNA — she used the combination code to open the safe. Perhaps if she looked at the unspeakable it would help clarify her thinking.

Kneeling on the floor, she reached inside and dismantled the funeral pyre of miscellaneous papers to reveal a selection of newspaper cuttings and a passport and wallet belonging to a man she'd never known. Opening the passport, the serious face of Austen Walsh, a twenty-six-year-old from Australia, born in Belconnen, stared back at her. She knew that he was a backpacker only because she'd read the newspapers afterwards. In her nightmares — and she still had them — she was in court, being choked by accusations from his parents, his sisters, his friends, and finally by Austen himself. How different he had looked when she last saw him. Bile flooded her mouth at the memory. She was not impervious to the damage done, the heartache caused. When she saw Coco and Frankie larking about and full of life, she often thought of the young man she never knew.

Unable to come to a decision, she replaced both items back in the safe, piling everything else of value on top, including the newspaper cuttings, and shut the safe door.

Checking out Veldo was a good deal less emotionally charged and complicated. *This she could do*, she thought, her knees cracking as she stood up.

Opening her laptop and armed with information from her daughter, she carried out a background check on the British end of the Veldo operation. It yielded little of notable interest because it had been in operation for less than a year. There was next to nothing on the Mount brothers, other than both being educated in Cheltenham. So, she asked herself, what is the nature of the sketchy alliance with a business organisation in the States? How on the level was the Florida operation? Was the UK enterprise some kind of franchise deal? Or was one a front for the other? It begged a question: why hadn't Lance carried out a basic check or had he done so and was too terrified to report what he'd uncovered?

Parking that thought for now, and one she would return to later, there was only one way to deal with Susannah. As much as it stuck in her throat, Chantal had decided to play nice. She would empathise and recognise that Susannah was vulnerable. She was seeing everything through a negative lens, she would tell her. She was looking for skeletons that didn't exist. Chantal would reassure Lance's wife and, if necessary offer emotional assistance, even though, along with her hormones, her feelings had dried up long ago. Chantal would do anything to stop the woman poking around in matters that were cold and dead in every sense.

On with her coat, hood up against spitting rain, and off she went only to see Susannah looking exceptionally well groomed (for her) and tripping up the road as if the burdens of her failed marriage were a distant, uncomfortable memory.

Assignation, Chantal thought, sniffing out a potential source of leverage, and deciding to follow. There was one feverish moment when Susannah stopped walking as if she'd spotted her pursuer. Instincts on alert, Chantal had dropped down and crouched behind a Cheltenham wheelie bin before picking up the chase again as Susannah, satisfied that nobody was in pursuit, moved off.

Watching Susannah mount the steps at the entrance of the Queen's hotel, Chantal had a pretty good idea who she was visiting. And it wasn't anyone local.

* * *

Pissed off with Frankie, Coco got pissed.

From work she headed straight for the Brewery Quarter to meet with a couple of her besties. Camilla had greeted her with the news that she was skint and couldn't stay and Savannah had greeted her with the news that, courtesy of WhatsApp, Coco's daddy was the talk of the town. Coco had wanted celebrity, not notoriety.

Fortunately, Savannah, who worked for her father doing some shit job in his office that paid a fortune, had moola for the pair of them and stood her a few commiserative rounds. They were drinking Long Island Iced Teas, an electrifying mixture of alcohol. *Screw five fruits a day*, Coco thought tipsily. *Give me vodka, gin, tequila, rum and triple sec.*

'What are you going to do, hun?' With wide features, a small mouth and a tendency towards a double chin, Savannah could not be described as attractive, but she could wield a make-up palette like a diva. She took a pretty damn fine picture too. *From plain Jane to vixen*, Coco thought, feeling a little foxy herself. Amazing the power of booze to transform a mood.

'I'll think of something,' Coco said, glugging her cocktail.

'Yeah, but I mean it's all so gross. I'd be gutted if it were me.'

'But it isn't you, is it?' It came out sharp and pointy. *Screw this*, Coco thought.

'All I'm saying is . . .'

'Do you know what?' Coco cried. 'I'm so sick of people *sayin*'. I've got my mother threatening to send me off to my

Gran's. My horny father telling me he's cutting off my funds. St Suze is putting it about that the whore who stole my father isn't such a bad person, which is so bloody perverted I could scream, and now I've got you *sayin'*. You're not entitled to say. Your family are fucking loaded.'

She finished breathless and slapped her glass down.

Made-up lips pulled back in a snarl, Savannah leant towards her. 'Poor little Coco.'

'Bitch,' Coco spat.

'*Rich* bitch, if you please.' Savannah slid off the stool and, taking her bag, headed off to the other side of the bar and a group of their mates who'd clearly been enjoying the show. Maddeningly, Coco saw Miles was among them, laughing and joking and looking at her funny.

Furious, Coco grabbed her things, marched towards them, fully fired up. And then she spotted Art with his arm around Savannah. It was like a punch to her gut.

The tittering stopped as if someone had turned down the sound.

'Here comes the freeloader,' Savannah said loudly. 'Hang on to your wallets and purses everyone.'

Coco gaped. Ejected from the herd, she wasn't one of them anymore. All of them were laughing and they were laughing at her.

Stumbling out, hot tears springing to her eyes and down her cheeks, the cold air hit her in the face like a wet flannel. Unsteady on her feet, humiliated and heartbroken, she rummaged in her bag for her headphones. To the sound of "Teardrop" by Massive Attack, she lurched left down the road into Henrietta Street, briefly onto the High Street and into St George's Place — not the nicest bit of town, but she didn't care. On self-destruct mode, she planned to raid her mother's drinks cabinet when she got home. She knew where her mum kept her private stash of weed and she was going to help herself to that too.

In tune with her mood, rain tumbled down from dark skies, soaking through her flimsy jacket and designer jeans.

She didn't see the van approach and slow down. She didn't spot the danger from two men with red hair. She saw nothing at all.

Until it was too late.

* * *

Lance's duplicity, the secrets of his double life had tumbled out in a jumbled heap. Gazing into my eyes, Lorenzo took my hand. It felt warm and solid and dependable, the way Lance's used to not so long ago.

'It's such a dreadful mess.' Red-faced, tear-stained and creasing with embarrassment, I accepted a clean white handkerchief from Lorenzo.

'I cannot believe it,' Lorenzo said. 'And you never knew, you had no idea?'

'You must think me so stupid. I know I do.'

'Nonsense. The man is a fool.'

'Kind of you to say.'

'It's the truth. I'm only sorry I let you go.'

His expression was intense. I found it hard to look away.

'How have his children taken it, your boy, in particular?'

'Not well,' I said hoarsely.

'Very hard for a son to see his father this way.'

My breath caught and got entangled inside my chest. Should I say something? How would Lorenzo take it?

'Remember the day we took the ferry to Capri?' He had a distant smile on his face.

I looked at him fondly, relieved to be spared from making a confession. 'I do,' I said softly.

'That was one of the most beautiful moments in my life. Did you know I waited for you to come back?'

'I didn't know. I . . .'

'If I had not been so poor at the time, I would have come and found you. By the time I could, life had other plans.'

I shivered with regret. If only I'd had the courage to trust my instinct instead of obeying my mother, I would have returned, confessed I was pregnant and somehow we would have made it work.

'Do you still love him?' Again, his dark eyes fixed on me with an intensity that blew me away. Suddenly, I was back where it all began, his skin against mine, his kiss on my mouth.

'I hate him.' The depth of my feeling took me by surprise. Did I mean it, or was I only saying it to impress Lorenzo?

'In my experience the line between love and hate is very fine.' He waited a beat. 'That day at the park,' he said, 'when I saw you after all this time and you were hurt, Lance hadn't . . .'

'Hit me? No, oh God, no.'

'Then what happened?'

'I told you.' I gave a giddy laugh.

'And I didn't believe you then and I do not believe you now.' A smile glanced across his lips. His dark eyes found mine. I felt myself slipping, my resolve melting. How could I keep on lying? 'Susannah,' he said gently.

'I was threatened.'

His eyes flashed fire. 'By whom?'

'We're in real trouble with some very nasty people.' I told him about Lance becoming embroiled with loan sharks to fund his other life, how the cars had been taken in lieu of payment, how Lance had received a beating and there was now the very real threat of stripping us of our home.

'And they hurt you too?'

I nodded dumbly.

'*Bastardi.*' Lorenzo stood up so suddenly it made me jump. 'Who are these people?'

'Lorenzo, you can't get involved.'

'I can help you.'

'No,' I said. 'I didn't come for your help.'

'Then what did you come for?' His expression was so intimate.

I tingled with crazy, mixed-up feelings I shouldn't have. *I'm not a good person*, Lance had said. Well, neither was I. By failing to tell Lorenzo about his son, wasn't I also guilty of leading a double life, one I'd lived for the past quarter of a decade?

'I should go,' I declared, standing up. 'This was a mistake. Please forget everything I said.' I searched around for my jacket before remembering he'd hung it in the wardrobe. About to walk past him, he stretched out, caught hold of me and tipped my chin up so that I was looking directly into his eyes.

'I won't and I can't,' Lorenzo said.

* * *

Coco's brain pounded inside her skull. Pain shot through the back of her head. Immensely cold and, more strangely, wet, she shivered.

She remembered the bar, her *friends*, her drunken rage and the street. Had someone spiked her drink? Was this Miles's idea of a sick joke? Nothing funny about the chair she was tied to by her wrists and ankles, or the dark void surrounding her.

She tried to focus. It was as if her eyes weren't working.

'Hello,' she called out. 'Okay, you crazies, you've had your fun. Let me go. I want to go home.'

Nothing.

She flexed her fingers in a vain attempt to push blood into her hands, get the circulation going so that she could break free. It looked so easy in films: wriggle and wriggle and bingo.

Rope chafed and then cut into her flesh, tearing the skin. In stinging pain, she let out a frightened yelp.

Dry-mouthed and in desperate need of a drink, she called out again. Still no reply.

Terrified, she willed herself to get her bearings.

The strong smell of damp indicated a cellar or basement. She felt cobbles underneath her feet and realised that she had lost her shoes.

'Please,' she cried, her voice cracking. 'I need to pee. I need a loo. I'll wet myself.' With each exhortation, her voice rose in pitch.

Silence bit a chunk out of her.

Concentrating on her bare feet, she flexed her toes. Maybe, if she could shift the entire chair, she could rock it back to a wall and smash it or something. She gave it a try. It didn't budge. With a low moan, she realised that the legs were bolted down.

Psycho, she screamed inside. *Serial killer.*

Terror stamped its ugly great boots all over her and kicked her in the head.

'Whoever you are I won't tell a soul. My name's Coco,' she shouted, 'Coco Stratton.'

Screwing her eyes up tight, through blurred vision she made out a blocky shape, a desk or maybe a table, possibly two pieces of furniture, unless she was seeing double.

'I'm only twenty-four!' she screamed. Life, even the prospect of not a very nice one, had never seemed more precious. She had people who loved her, a darling brother.

Where are you, Frankie? How she wished he hadn't blown her out that evening. He would have protected her from those ghouls at the bar. He would have stood up to them and dragged her home. He would never have let her be pounced on and disappeared from the street.

Ever more desperate, she yelled, 'My parents will give you money.'

'Is that right?' She heard a man's voice in the darkness.

Next, ice-cold water hit her face and chest and suddenly the place was drenched in light so bright it made her eyes hurt. Dripping and spluttering, she gaped at two men with red hair and pale skin. Dressed identically in jeans and navy hoodies and desert boots, they stood with their legs apart, as if they'd been on safari. They had slim builds and faces like dolls, without lines and flat expressions. Menace oozed out of every pore, as if it were an inherent part of their DNA.

'Dad,' she whispered, teeth chattering. 'This is about my father.'

'Who needs to do as he's told.' The one who spoke had a permanent sneer.

'He has and he will,' Coco stammered.

'That's not the impression we're getting.'

'I'll talk to him,' she said, panicking. 'He listens to me.'

'We have fresh demands.'

'Anything.'

'We want the business. All of it.'

Terrified, she nodded wildly, her eyes fastening on a freestanding cooker with a propane gas cylinder. These were the shapes she'd discerned in the dark. The silent man with the thin lips stood gravely beside them. The one who did the talking slipped out a blade and advanced on her.

'Go away,' she screeched, recoiling. She didn't want help. She didn't want the loo or a drink. She wanted to be left alone in the cellar. She wanted the damp and the dark. 'Please, *please.*' She cried and sobbed.

Still with the sneer, he squatted down in front of her with a gaze that was pale and sinister. He reached out and pushed a strand of her hair away from her cheek and tucked it behind her ear. 'What's the problem, little one? We're letting you go.'

She stared at him. A cruel joke, he was screwing with her. She knew she wasn't getting out of there alive. Why go to all this trouble?

Pouncing with the agility of a big cat, he swept the blade once and then twice. Heart teetering on cardiac arrest, she was free.

Relief lasted seconds.

One hand on her neck, the other forcing her arm up behind her back, she was pushed forward. Her toes dragged painfully across a cobbled floor.

First she heard the hiss and then she saw the flame.

'No,' she shrieked, bucking and rearing, like a young filly yet to be broken. Cold sweat erupted and coated her skin. Her mind flew, split apart and shattered into lots of tiny pieces.

'This is a message to your father,' the other man spoke. 'He does exactly as we say or . . .'

* * *

How do you explain to a five-year-old that Daddy is married to another woman? Bereavement would have been more bearable. Easier to explain that Daddy had got run over by a bus than Daddy has a wife and is living with another family.

Amy pondered this while Tana slept fitfully in her bed, next to Wilf. Both of them had played her up something rotten and refused to go to sleep in their own room. It hadn't helped that she'd spirited Igglepiggle away and put it in the washing machine with a ton of biological soap powder. The bloody thing was a health risk, she reckoned. It could give them hepatitis or something. She hadn't told Wilf this, only that Igglepiggle needed a bath and spruce up. Wilf wasn't having any of it. Adele had picked up on the bad vibe and was grizzly and unsettled too. Unforgivably, Amy had shouted at her so loud that Tana had told her off for being horrible.

'Unhappy people make snappy people,' Amy had retorted hotly, before wrapping her arms tightly around Tana, kissing her and saying that she was sorry.

'Why are you sad, Mummy? Is it because Daddy isn't here?' Tana said.

'I miss him,' Wilf said, his little eyes filling with tears. Again.

So it had gone on.

And so did the phone calls and messages from Rollo.

She'd had fourteen missed calls since the morning. Choked as she was for all he had done, she longed to see him again. Every time she heard his voice, a little part of her melted. Taking out her phone, she played his last message again.

'Amy, love, it's me. I know you don't want to speak to me. Who could blame you but, please, pick up the phone. I don't deserve or expect your forgiveness, but I'm begging you: let me know you and the kids are okay. I'm missing you all so very much and I just wa . . .' Tears rolling down her cheeks, Amy deleted the voicemail.

* * *

It was theatre, brinkmanship and pure terror. Coco thought they'd have her eye out. She'd believed they would maim her.

Without a phone, keys or personal possessions, Coco staggered barefoot, bleeding and disorientated, along the pavement. Vomit spattered her clothes. The terror of the last hours had not abated. She didn't think they were coming back to get her. They had no need. There was only one thing worse than torture: the anticipation of it.

When she saw flame she felt heat. When she heard threats she registered promises. Those doll-faced men had not plunged her face into the fire. They had not disfigured her skin. They had mutilated her mind.

Judging from the odd reactions she was getting, people thought she was stoned. Some looked. Most looked away. Her cheeks felt on fire. The smell of singed hair was strong in her nostrils. Like an animal dumped miles away after its owners moved to another county, she had one aim: to reach home as fast as possible. She didn't think beyond getting inside and locking herself in her room. Charged with delivering a message to her father she would do it in her mother's home.

The house was in darkness. Coco rang the bell. Nothing. She rang it again. Still nothing. Frenzied with frustration, she drummed her fist on the door and skinned her knuckles.

'Open up,' she hollered, terrified of the images in her head. Perhaps if she spoke out loud they would go away.

'Mum,' she called. 'MO-THER.'

Coco prayed her mum hadn't taken one of her sleeping pills, although the idea of popping several now and going to sleep forever felt infinitely appealing. Maybe her mother had gone out, although that would be weird. She didn't have a social life, at least not one that was recognisable.

'Come on, come on, open the fucking door,' Coco cried, leaning heavily against it for support.

Still no answer.

Frankie, she thought. *My brother will know what to do.*

Stumbling back into a tangle of darkness punctuated by the odd streetlight, sheer will kept her going against a mess of pain. Not so easy to escape pictures of those ghoulish faces, yellow-skinned against the flame and without expression.

Be there, Frankie, she prayed. *Be in.*

One more step, she told herself, one last push. Finally reaching her father's home, with its lights all on and music playing from Frankie's bedroom, she thought she had never seen such a wonderful sight. With effort, she pressed the doorbell and a great wave of fatigue rolled over her, threatening to wash her away.

Frankie opened the door, the loose grin on his face quickly vanishing.

'Coco, holy crap, what's happened? Who did this to you?'

And suddenly she was falling forward and was swept up into his arms.

* * *

'I don't want you getting hurt too.'

'Neither do I,' Lorenzo said. 'These people, tell me about them.'

Reluctantly, I gave him the lowdown on Veldo. 'The HQ is in Florida,' I said.

'I'll make enquiries.'

'I'm really not happy with that.'

'It will be discreet. Perhaps we can put a stop to this at source.'

'You really think so?' I didn't dare to believe and yet Lorenzo seemed so certain.

'We can but try.' He smiled, willing me to trust him. 'In the short term let me give you some financial assistance.'

'That's so sweet but I wouldn't dream of it. I have a job. Besides, your wives, your dependents.'

'Let me worry about them.'

'I can't take your money, Lorenzo.'

'Then take it for your boy.'

Silence snaked around me. My responding smile was weak. *Tell him now*, a voice in my brain urged. *Do it and walk away.*

And then my phone rang. Seeing it was Frankie, I picked up the call.

'Mum, Mum, you have to come quickly. It's Coco. She's been attacked.'

Fingers of fear closed over my heart. 'Where is she?'

'At home. She won't see a doctor. She won't see anyone. You have to come.'

'I'm on my way.' I glanced apologetically at Lorenzo. He looked as astonished as me. 'Have you called Chantal?' I asked Frankie.

'I've tried to get hold of her. She isn't picking up.'

'What about Lance?'

'Same.'

I cursed under my breath. 'Okay. I'll be with you quick as I can.'

Lorenzo was already reaching for my jacket as I explained the situation. 'I'll come with you.'

'No,' I said. 'I mean that's very kind, but it's not necessary.'

'Then let me order a cab.'

'It will take too long.'

'Susannah,' he said, firmly taking hold of me by my shoulders. 'Your stepdaughter is hurt. She is in good hands with your son. The way you are right now, you could get run over crossing the road. Best you arrive calm and composed.'

Before I could argue he'd let me go, walked away, picked up the phone to reception and ordered a taxi. 'There's one dropping off a guest right now,' he said. 'Will you take it?'

I nodded blindly.

He ushered me out and kissed me softly on the cheek. 'Let me know how it goes.'

I hurried downstairs to the waiting vehicle. I'd barely got my breath when I was outside my home, wondering what the hell I was walking into.

'She's in there.' Frankie indicated the study off the sitting room. 'It's not good,' he said. 'She's completely lost her shit and not making sense. She said she'd been held in a basement.'

'Oh my God, did they . . . ?'

'She wasn't raped,' Frankie cut in. 'She believed they were going to disfigure her.'

I pressed a hand to my mouth. They'd threatened me in a similar way. For Coco, it would be devastating.

'How badly hurt is she?'

'Her wounds are largely superficial as far as I can tell. It's what's going on inside her head that's worrying.'

I touched his arm in gratitude. 'Thank you.'

'Where were you?' he said sharply. 'I phoned Suki and she hadn't a clue what I was talking about.'

'Oh,' I said, guilt washing over me. 'I needed to escape, to walk, to spend time in my own company. You know how it is.'

'You didn't need to lie.'

'No,' I said, chastened. 'I'm sorry.' The suspicion in Frankie's expression nearly undid me.

'I got hold of Chantal finally,' he said, 'and she's on her way.'

'Right,' I said. *Hell*, I thought.

'Oh, and the man responsible for all this shit,' Frankie said with barely concealed contempt, 'is driving back from Worcester as I speak.'

Good, I thought, *Coco my priority right now.*

I found her sitting in the corner of the room, knees drawn up to her chin, arms clasped around them, in a true Coco pose. That's where the similarity with the girl I knew ended. Her hair and eyebrows were singed. Her pale cheeks were livid red and scorched. The soles of her feet were bleeding and raw.

'Oh, Coco,' I said, plunging towards her.

She put the flat of her hand up. 'Don't come any closer,' she said, her voice a rasp. 'Don't you dare come near.'

Bewildered, I knelt down on the floor. 'I'm not the enemy, Coco.'

Her expression told me otherwise. She was like a wild cat cornered by a large, hostile animal.

'Talk to me,' I said.

'What's the fucking point?'

'Coco, I'm trying . . .'

'Stop it, will you?'

'Coco . . .'

204

'You're as much to blame. You didn't stand up to him. You didn't fight our corner. You let him walk all over you.'

And it was true — all of it. 'Are you hurt?' Of course she was.

'Not as badly as expected. Not this time,' she added, glowering.

'They?' I knew who had done this to her. I still needed confirmation.

'The Mount brothers. The doll-faced creeps. The bastards.' She broke into a wet laugh. 'They plucked me off the street, took me to Christ knows where, some dingy godawful basement. They held my face to a flame, not enough to blister and burn, but enough for me to imagine the consequences if they changed their minds. Torture but not torture, clever really.'

'Coco, you don't have to go through this now.' I pulled out my phone. 'Let me call the police. They can get somebody round straightaway.'

'Don't you dare.'

'But, Coco . . .'

'Those guys meant business. They weren't pissing about and I'm not having some copper victim-blaming me about the stupidity of getting wasted.'

'I honestly don't think that's likely.'

'What would you know? You've never done anything even vaguely immoral.'

Heat spread from my chest and wrapped my body in a bear-like hug. Sweat popped out on my brow. I didn't know if it were a hot flush or guilt about where I'd been that evening.

Coco was still talking. 'They had a message for Dad.'

'Yes?'

'If Dad doesn't hand over the business, they will finish what they started.' Suddenly, things fell into place. *Finish what they started.* The competitor that had stolen Lance's Middle East deal — it had to be Veldo. It was all part of a bigger plan to drive him and his family into the dust. In answer to my furious expression, Coco said, 'There's no way out.'

'But...' I began.

'You tell him,' Coco said, 'because I never want to see him again. Not ever.'

As bad as things were I had no doubt that in time she would change her mind. Coco was too close to her father to abandon him for a lifetime.

The door flew open and Chantal entered the room, elbowing me aside. 'I'll take things from here.'

'I should warn you that Lance is on his way.' I got to my feet.

'I'm not seeing him,' Coco said loudly.

'Hush, darling. You don't have to.' Chantal spoke in spooky, soothing tones. Slipping her arms around her daughter she said, 'Mummy is taking you home.'

'She can barely walk,' I pointed out.

'I brought the car.'

'You still have to get her to it.'

Chantal examined Coco's feet, as if she were cleaning out the contents of a urinal. 'Fetch a bowl of warm water and a towel, would you, Susannah.'

Wordlessly, I did as asked. Frankie wandered into the bathroom as I was rummaging through the medicine chest for bandages and antiseptic cream. 'How's things?'

I didn't know how to answer so I didn't. 'When Lance arrives keep him away from Chantal and Coco,' I said.

'I'm not speaking to him.'

'For God's sake, help me out here, Frankie.'

Before he could retaliate I returned to the study, deposited the bowl on the carpet, along with a makeshift first aid kit, and left Chantal to her ministrations.

I was so shaken up, I poured myself a slug of brandy and, after bolting it down, actively prayed that Chantal and Coco would be gone before Lance arrived. A glance at the clock revealed it would rely on split-second timing.

Frankie popped his head around the door. 'I'm staying at Art's tonight.'

'I'm sorry I spoke to you sharply. You don't have to go.'

206

'I do, Mum. You know I do.'

I couldn't blame him. Part of me wanted to follow. I felt terrible for lying to him so brazenly. I'd have to tell him soon, although now was definitely not the right time. 'Call me tomorrow?' I said, hopeful.

'Sure.' His smile was warm. His eyes were cool.

For the second time in days I listened to my son fleeing the place he should have called home.

Chantal didn't say goodbye when she left either. 'You and me will talk soon,' she said, somewhat threateningly, and that was it. Lance arrived, wan and drawn, a few minutes later. How he'd missed Chantal driving out, I'd never know.

'Where is everyone?' he said.

'They've all gone,' I replied. 'You can sleep on the sofa tonight.'

'But, Susannah . . .'

'You don't get it, do you? We're all sick and tired of paying for your mess. I'm going to bed. If we must talk we'll talk in the morning, but, quite honestly, Lance, I don't care if I never see you again.'

CHAPTER THIRTY-TWO

Wired after the night's events, Chantal went for a swim, returned, checked on Coco, who was still asleep, and showered and dressed. She'd got the whole story out of her daughter eventually. It was like prising information out of a seasoned spy taught to withstand interrogation. Most mothers would contact the police immediately. Most would assure a daughter that she was a victim and not to blame in any way. Half-cut and vulnerable when abducted, nobody deserved what had happened. What those men did was grotesque.

But Chantal could not afford to go to the cops. Veldo had a hold on Lance and if her past, so inextricably linked, came tumbling out it would ruin the pair of them.

Calm and composed, with a cup of chai on her desk, she called her ex-husband. He answered after two rings. From the monosyllabic response, he didn't sound as if he'd slept either. She didn't bother with pleasantries or accusations. She came straight to the heart of the matter.

'Our daughter is lucky to escape with her life. She is utterly traumatized and it's all your fault.'

'I never . . .'

'That's the problem, Lance. You never think.'

'Can I see her?'

'You cannot.'

'Five minutes is all I ask.'

'Out of the question. I've made arrangements for her to go away and rest.'

'Where?'

'Somewhere safe where she cannot be abducted off the street and assaulted.'

The abrupt silence confirmed there was no coming back from his sketchy position. 'Your only choice is to disappear.'

'Disappear, what the hell are you talking about?'

'Austen Walsh.' It felt physically painful to assemble those two words in her voice box and eject them through her lips. Judging by the stunned silence, it hurt as much for Lance to hear them.

'Are you still there?' she said, bright and barbed.

'But they don't know, I swear.'

'They're blackmailing you.'

'This is simply about extorting money with menaces.'

'There is nothing simple about this.'

'I know, I know. A poor choice of words and I'm sorry, but the Mount boys have never uttered a word about . . .' He paused, coughed as if he had a fur ball in his throat. '*It.*'

'What about people in the umbrella company in Florida?'

'What about them?'

'Do you know a single thing about who they are and what they do?'

'Financial services a.k.a. lending money at high interest.'

'You are pathetically naïve, Lance. Do you understand what you're involved with?'

'Do you?' he said, bullish.

'I've got a rough idea.'

'And what's that?'

'They're a front for organised crime.'

'*What?*'

'For God's sake, Lance, you're so entangled in your complicated love life you've lost all powers of reason.'

'Leave Amy out of it.'

'Is that what you tell Susannah too? Poor cow.'

After a long offended pause, he said, 'Even if what you say is true, how could men in America know about Austen Walsh? It's all done and dusted and in the past.'

'A cold case is never over. It's always waiting to be inserted into the equivalent of a microwave and reheated.'

'Then why has nobody said as much?'

He had a point, but it didn't serve Chantal's best interests to listen to it. 'Perhaps they're saving it up for when you refuse to give up your business along with the keys to your home. You do realise, don't you, that all your problems are part of a planned, systemic attack on a thriving British company in order to grab it without paying a cent?'

'Why mine?' He sounded indignant, as well he might be.

'Have you not listened to a single word I've said?'

'But I just tol—'

'Because you're gullible and weak, because you're easy to manipulate.' And she should know. 'Your only option is to vanish, get on a plane, go and live in the far reaches of the universe, for heaven's sake *die*. It would benefit everyone's lives immeasurably.' She'd even administer the pills, she thought meanly.

'Chantal, that's low even coming from you.'

'How else are you going to stop those animals from extorting money and using members of your family as a punch bag?'

The line went deadly quiet.

At last, Lance spoke. 'And if I don't?'

'How does twenty-five years behind bars sound?'

'You're bluffing. You wouldn't go to the police.' Lance was right. She'd rather dedicate her life to good works than shop either of them to the cops.

'I still have Walsh's passport and wallet. I could say I found it.'

'What? Decades after the event?'

'You really want to test me? I'm quite sure I could come up with a plausible explanation. I could say it got buried in the wrong removal box after I moved out and has been stowed in the loft all this time.'

'You wouldn't.'

'Try me. Make the necessary arrangements, or else. That's if your wife doesn't beat me to it and go to the police herself, something she's been gagging to do since this all kicked off, I might add.' A vile possibility and one that required her utmost attention; Chantal was not averse to a little blackmail of her own.

She cut the call and set about making arrangements. First, she called her mother to confirm and then she called Frankie. She was amazed to hear that he was awake and sounded it.

'How's Coco?' he asked.

Sweet boy. He cared more for his half-sister than her father evidently did. Chantal gave him a quick précis. 'I know she doesn't want to go to her grandma's, but I was wondering if you could persuade her.'

'She might feel differently after last night,' Frankie said, quite reasonably.

'I'm not so certain. She can be quite stubborn. Would you be a darling and drive her there in her car?'

'Happy to.'

'That's great. Her feet are in such a mess, you see.' It was Coco's mind that worried her more but Frankie didn't need to have that spelt out. 'I'm not even sure she could make the journey on her own. In fact,' Chantal said, inspiration striking, 'why not treat it as a sort of break?'

'You mean stay with her?'

'My mother would be delighted to have you for a few days. It would lighten the load for the oldies.' Mother would appreciate having a good-looking boy like Frankie around the house, Chantal thought, and it would give Chantal time to ensure that life carried on more or less smoothly.

'Well, as long as that's okay with them.'

'I'll give my mother a ring now. Shall we say pick-up about 2.00 p.m.?'

Chantal finished the call as Coco hobbled in. 'Who was that?'

'Your guardian angel,' Chantal replied.

* * *

Amy had been up all night with Adele who had colic. Every time Amy dropped off, her baby would start up again, fretting and bawling. Amy had read that sleep deprivation was an effective tool in torture. She'd tried everything from rubbing Adele's tummy to coaxing her to take warm gripe water. Nothing worked. Going through the gruelling chaos of the morning routine, she'd never felt so ill and alone and was only too glad when her mother turned up, sorted out the lunch boxes and took Wilf and Tana off to the local playground before promising to deliver them to school.

While Adele slept, Amy made a cup of tea and settled down to enjoy the silence. Her phone exploding into life soon put a stop to that. Only one person would be idiot enough to ring at that time: Rollo. Must be an emergency. Amy frowned. The only emergency around here was hers; she was a walking catastrophe.

She peered at the number through bloodshot eyes. Yes, Rollo. Should have blocked him days ago, Amy tutted. Easy enough to switch off the phone, she could do it right here, right now. She pushed it away. He'd probably been on a bender and was in hangover hell. *Good*, she thought. Yet the thought of speaking to a wasted Rollo was better than speaking to nobody at all.

Amy snatched it up. 'What?'

'Thank God, you answered. I had to speak to you. It couldn't wait. How are you?'

Exhausted, sad, broken-hearted. 'What do you want, Rollo?'

'The kids, how are they?'

'Adele's got bellyache.'

'Poor sweet thing. You need to give her some of that colic medicine.'

'I know what I need to do, Rollo,' Amy said stonily.

'Of course, love. And Tana and Wilf?'

Amy's throat felt as if it was clogged with silt.

'They miss you.' *I miss you, too*, she thought, but she'd walk on hot coals before she admitted it.

'Oh my God, Amy, I miss and love you all so much.'

'Then why hurt us?'

'I never meant to. I've made such a terrible mess of everything.'

He had. There was no denying it.

'Believe me when I tell you I'm in hell,' he pleaded.

Amy scowled. 'We're all in hell, Rollo.' Why did he always have to go and ruin it?

'Yes, yes, but . . .' And then he told her about his eldest daughter. *Dear Lord*, she thought. Rollo had got himself mixed up with proper psychos.

'Are me and the kids in danger?'

'No,' he said firmly.

'Are you sure?' She wondered if she'd better have a word with one of the lads who lived opposite her mum's. Amy had gone to school with Laurie Turner and he'd turned out to be a right sort. Heart of an angel, mind, and would do anything for her if she asked nicely. He had serious connections in Birmingham and she'd put him and his crew up against any fancy scumbags from Gloucestershire.

Rollo was still yattering on. 'It's all my fault,' he said.

'Too right.'

'I take full responsibility.'

'Good.'

'Can you ever forgive me?'

Amy wasn't sure whether Rollo was asking for forgiveness for what had happened to his daughter, or for what he'd done to her and the children. 'I don't know,' she replied. 'Maybe.' Which was honest.

'Can I speak to Tana and Wilf?'

'They're with my mum and she's taking them to school.'

'How are they coping?'

She swerved the question. 'They know something is up.' And making their feelings known by taking it out on me at every opportunity, she thought.

'I need to see them.'

'That's not going to happen.'

'Just the once.'

The way he said it you'd think it was for the last time. Shit, she spiked inside. Rollo wasn't planning on doing anything awful, was he?

'I don't know, Rollo.'

'A quick cup of tea and a chat,' he said. 'At ours.'

There was no 'ours'. It was she and the kids and that was it.

'Not today.' She couldn't face it and the house was in a right state.

'Tomorrow, after school?'

'Not convenient. Swimming club.'

'Please, Amy.' His voice screeched with near hysteria.

'All right, all right. Day after. Teatime.' Except there'd be no tea.

'Fantastic, Amy. Thank you, thank you.'

'Keep your hair on,' she said, taken aback by his effusiveness. 'A quick visit, nothing more. You're not stopping.'

'It's fine,' he said. 'Lovely.'

Oh my God, he really *was* planning something final. According to the magazines she read, often men who topped themselves acted super happy with loved ones before they did the deed.

'You take care of yourself, Rollo.' She couldn't help herself. He was really worrying her.

'That's very kind.'

It was, Amy thought. He sounded genuinely touched.

'It will be so good to see you all again,' he said.

Long after Rollo had hung up, Amy stared out of the window, her tea stone cold.

* * *

I had all the "outs": worn out, strung out and clean out of compassion. Lorenzo called before I was barely awake after a patchy night's sleep. Cool and vague, off-hand really, I wasn't at my best. I think I'd used up all my emotions, fond or otherwise. I simply lacked the energy.

'How is your stepdaughter?'

'She will mend. I can't go into detail.'

'It is a terrible thing that has been done to her. I hope she recovers very soon.'

'Thank you.'

'Would you like me to come round? My flight isn't until tonight.'

'That's a nice thought, Lorenzo, but I'm absolutely shattered.'

'I understand.' He stayed on the line. Something was niggling, she thought, possibly her tepid emotional response. 'Those men that attacked her,' he said.

'Yes?'

'They are the same people who threatened you and demanded the deeds to your home?'

'And now they want my husband's business too.'

'He has agreed?'

'I'm not sure he'll feel there's another way.'

'This is *oltraggioso* . . . how do you say . . . outrageous.'

If someone had sat me down and informed me these things happened, I would have been appalled. If I'd been told they would happen to me, I would have laughed. As it was I was reduced to a state of frozen disbelief.

'Let me talk to him.' Lorenzo's voice rippled with urgency and purpose.

'To Lance?' I jolted with surprise. 'How will you explain who you are?'

'I will think of something.'

'I'm not . . .'

'*Please*, Susannah. I want to help.'

No, it was too risky. 'It's his mess, not yours.'

'It's yours too and that makes it mine.'

I couldn't think. What could Lorenzo do that would make it all go away? He couldn't make the Mount brothers take a hike. Bad enough Lance had been beaten up and Coco terrorised.

'Lorenzo, I genuinely appreciate the offer and I thank you for that, but we've all run out of road, do you see? The attack on my stepdaughter was serious and the police must be notified.'

'Of course.'

'I really wouldn't want you to get caught up in it. You do understand, don't you?'

'It is fine.'

It wasn't. I could tell from his short response.

'I'm so sorry, but I envisage a lot of my time will be taken up at the police station.'

'Of course. I hope it works out for you all. I'll leave you to it,' he said. 'Goodbye, Susannah.'

'Safe travels back to Italy.'

But he'd already gone.

Spun out, I went downstairs to the kitchen and found Lance at the breakfast bar, staring into the middle distance. I should have felt sorry for him. I gave him a cold glance and let my gaze settle on his phone.

'Who was that?'

He hesitated. 'Chantal.'

'How is Coco?'

'Traumatized. Chantal is sending her away.'

I didn't comment. After the police were notified, it was probably a good idea — one less to worry about — though to "send away" a twenty-four-year-old grown woman sounded archaic, positively Victorian, and not something I'd attribute to modern, right-on Chantal.

'You don't know where, do you?' Lance asked.

'Why would I?' And why would I tell you if I did?

'Right,' he said aimlessly.

I looked him sharply in the eye. 'You will report the attack, won't you?'

He viewed me with a listless expression that astounded me.

'Don't you care? She's your daughter.'

'Not my place.'

'You mean Chantal is going to report it?'

'You'd have to ask her.'

I intended to. 'So what did Chantal have to say for herself?' My tone was borderline snarky.

A mirthless laugh broke from between his lips. 'She suggested I died.'

'Figure of speech.'

'Oh no, she meant it.'

'Why would she say such a thing?'

His expression didn't change so I answered my own question, the same question that had dogged me from the start.

'Because you're both hiding something unspeakable.'

'Not that again.'

'*Yes*, that again. I swear I'll get it out of one of you, one way or another.'

His upper lip curled. 'She'll never tell you.'

I leant forward, my face in his face. I spoke quietly and with intensity. 'You're stone-cold liars and I swear to God you're going to tell me what you did.'

I don't think he'd ever seen me so furious. His eyes locked onto mine. For a tense moment I thought he would brazen it out. Suddenly, his face fell. Beads of perspiration popped up along his hairline. His hands shot to the top of his head, pressing down as if he were trying to keep every dark and troubling thought he'd ever had locked inside. I watched every move on his face, from anger and frustration to confusion and resignation. I saw something else, something I'd seen before but never been able to put a label to: sorrow. He took a breath and looked at me square. 'I killed a man.'

Hand clasped over my mouth, I sat down with a thud. Cold fear crushed my windpipe. I couldn't speak.

'I didn't mean to,' Lance said beseechingly. He'd stopped clawing at his hair and sat with his hands flat on the breakfast bar. His shoulders slumped as if the weight of the burden had finally bent him double. 'It was twenty-three years ago.'

I fiercely did the maths. Lance and Chantal had divorced twenty-two years ago. She knew all right. Bloody hell, she did.

'It was late at night and I was travelling down one of the back roads near Winchcombe. It was dark, no street lights.'

I briefly closed my eyes. I sensed how this story was going to roll and it was hideous.

'You ran him down?'

'Accidentally.'

'You didn't see him?'

His shoulders bowed a little more. 'It was raining, absolutely hammering. Road was greasy.'

'Oh my God. Were you drunk?'

He shook his head vigorously. 'No, but I . . .'

'Christ, you were driving too fast.'

He sank lower into his seat.

'Did you stop?'

'I did but . . .' He looked away.

'But what?'

'I didn't stay.'

'You left an injured man in the road?' For the second time my hand flew to my mouth. I stuck my fingers between my teeth and bit down.

'He was dying, Susannah. There was nothing I could do for him.'

'You don't know that!' I cried, recoiling. 'You couldn't possibly know that.' I jumped up, grabbed a glass and filled it with water from the tap. My hand trembled as I drank. Suki Quant had talked about Lance's aberrant behaviour stemming from a sense of shame. I didn't know what I expected, but it was never this.

'I panicked, drove away, went home and woke Chantal,' Lance continued, eager for me to buy into his side of the story. 'She didn't believe me so we went back to see. We took Coco with us,' he added before I asked what they'd done with their baby. 'No pulse, no heartbeat, nothing, the man in the road was dead. Honest,' he said, in answer to my stunned expression. 'Chantal went through his things and we took his ID to buy us time.'

I had an appalling image of grave robbers. 'What things?'

'His passport and wallet.'

Christ. No wonder neither of them wanted the police poking around in their lives. 'What happened to your car?'

'Chantal got rid of it. She knew someone who stripped it down and took it to a knacker's yard.'

'You had it crushed to remove all evidence?'

'I'm sorry. I know how this sounds.'

'Christ Almighty, Lance, it *sounds* like a hit and run!' My voice roared. 'What have you done? And what have you done to me — to us?'

'I know. I know.'

'I've lived with your lies for the best part of my adult life,' I said accusingly, 'and now what you did has come back to haunt us.'

He stared at me helplessly. Disgusted, I drained the glass of water and sat back down. 'Who was he?'

'An Australian backpacker.'

'His name?'

Lance stared at the table in shame. I thumped it with my fist. 'Austen Walsh,' he replied.

'How old was he?'

'Twenty-six.'

'The same age as Frankie.' Oh my God, I couldn't imagine how terrible it would be for the boy's parents.

'I know. It's awful.'

'How the hell do you live with yourself? But that's it, isn't it Lance?' I sneered. 'You don't. You haven't actually lived with yourself for a very long time. You've lived with a facsimile, one that's infinitely adaptable. Poor, duped Amy offered you the perfect escape route. With her, you could literally adopt a different persona, pretend you're a man with no darkness in your past.' No, he'd saved that for me, and I wasn't finished.

'And all this time the young man's parents, if they're still alive, his family and friends, have no idea who killed their son.' It was monstrous. *He* was monstrous. And so was Chantal. I'd always glimpsed a bigger, more ugly picture. I just hadn't seen the whole of it until now.

'Is that what the call from Chantal was about?'

'It wasn't her fault,' Lance said, quick to defend her. I guessed old habits died hard. They'd been covering for each other for over two decades.

'Not coming clean, not owning up to what you did, covering for you *is* her fault. Is that what the conversation was about?'

'She issued an ultimatum. Either I vanish or she goes to the police.'

She's lying. Chantal would never cut her own throat. 'I'll save her the bother and do it myself.'

'You don't have to,' Lance said, sombre. 'In forty-eight hours, I'm turning myself in.'

After all the fight and fury, all the times I'd begged him to do what other sensible people did and report what was happening to us, it came as a shock. Had some internal dam burst inside him? Did the physical attack on his daughter finally shame him into seeing sense, or was it because he had no other option? 'Why not do it now?' I pushed his phone towards him.

'I need to say my goodbyes.'

'To Amy and her children?' What about mine? What about Coco?

He nodded sadly. 'And Chantal will need time to make her own preparations.'

'You're giving her a chance to run?'

Lance shook his head.

'You mean get a lawyer so she can cover her bets and wriggle out of any possible charges.' Now I was on a vicious roll, I couldn't stop. 'What happens to my home? Have you handed over the deeds?'

He spoke in a quiet voice. 'Not yet, but . . .'

'Jesus Christ, so I can expect to be evicted at any time, that right?' I should have felt devastation. I think I was beyond it.

'I'll hold them off for as long as I can.' He looked at me with pleading eyes. I hoped he didn't expect gratitude. 'Will you give me that time, Susannah?'

'You don't deserve any favours from me. Not after all you've done.'

'I'm begging you. Not for myself, but for my other children. I've arranged to see them to say goodbye.'

I looked at him long and hard, the man I'd loved, the man I'd have once staked my life on; the man who'd also ripped the ground from beneath my feet. But he'd got me. Three little kids were innocents in all of this.

'Two days and no longer,' I said.

CHAPTER THIRTY-THREE

Forty-eight hours later

'Mind if I stay another couple of nights, Ma?'

'You're having a good time then?' Artificially bright, I found it easier to hide my disappointment on the phone.

'Coco's grandmother is a laugh. Her stepgrandfather — God, that's a mouthful — is old school, closet racist and all that, but he's generous enough. We're being dined and very much wined.'

'Glad you're enjoying it.'

'I'm still getting on with work,' he said, keen to impress me, or reassure me; I wasn't certain which.

'Good, good.' I wished I could bottle Frankie's energy and drink deep from its depths. 'How's Coco?'

'Coco is so-so,' Frankie said. 'Better now that she's away from the scene of crime, if you get my meaning.' My pulse tripped. How would she cope with finding out that her parents were involved in a hit and run? I dreaded to think how Frankie would take the news. I wanted them to stay in a bubble of safety and happiness for as long as possible. 'It's very pretty here,' Frankie enthused, 'lots of trees, ponies and deer.'

I couldn't envisage either my son or his stepsister tramping through the countryside. What works, works, I guessed, genuinely glad that he sounded in better spirits. There was lightness in his voice, less angst and anger. I should have been more appreciative of the toll Lance's dismal behaviour had taken on him.

'I've even had a couple of riding lessons,' Frankie said. 'Coco reckons it's so I can get lit on hoof oil.'

'God, you're not, are you?'

'Joke, mother.'

'It's not funny.'

'Sorry,' Frankie said, contrite. 'Down here I feel a million miles away from up there.' How I envied him. Frankie lowered his voice. 'Any fresh developments?'

Oh God, yes. 'Nothing for you to worry about.'

'So there's actually a home for me to come back to?'

I glanced at the walls in the bedroom, the prints hanging above an old Victorian fireplace, a dressing table I'd bought in a junk shop before I was married, and the feature wall I'd lovingly painted. My life. My things. Talking of home made the thought of imminent eviction harder to bear. I'd barely left the house in the past two days, fearing that if I did, I'd return to find the locks changed with all my possessions trapped inside. I'd promised myself that I'd make a stand if the Mount brothers turned up before the forty-eight hour deadline passed. Could Lance stall them for long enough? If he failed, they'd have to cart me out kicking and screaming. Could the police intervene after the deeds were in the Mount brothers' possession? I didn't know.

'Mum?' he said, jogging me from my thoughts.

'For now,' I told him.

'Things can only get better. Promise.' He spoke with the confidence and naivety of the young. I loved him all the more for it.

'You'll text me before you travel back?'

'Sure thing. Oh, before I forget, Coco sends her love.'

Warmth spread through me. I'd been forgiven. 'Give my love to her too.'

I ended the call with *lots of love* and went downstairs full of apprehension. I'd neither heard nor seen anything of Lance over the past two days. His continued silence put me on edge. Assuming he was with his other family, I pictured a fond reunion in which he was hugged and pardoned. My flesh crept. How long should I wait for my errant husband to call me from a police station and confirm that the Mount brothers were under arrest? How long before he assured me that he'd finally confessed to a crime committed years before? Was time up now, or midnight tonight? I wasn't sure how entrenched I should be about the exact hour. Lance's track record on trust and loyalty had been publicly smashed to bits. Surely, this time, he wouldn't let me down, but if he did and made a run for it, God help him.

But doing the unthinkable would create no sense of payback, or triumph. The prospect of betraying my husband (was that even the right word in the circumstances?) and denying Lance his freedom also impacted on mine, in an indefinable way. Would satisfaction in seeing justice done and providing closure for Austen Walsh's family be enough? And if the Mount brothers were charged with extortion, would I get back all that I owned? Would I get my life back too? Or was I doomed to be forever frightened, distrustful, waiting for the next calamity to strike?

There was still Chantal to consider. Despite her threat of an imminent and important conversation that needed to be had, she hadn't contacted me. She was lying low, I suspected, after Lance had warned of my intentions. I pictured her busy cutting deals with legal people to safeguard her interests when the police turned up. I'd always thought her cold and unreachable and now I knew why. She'd done a hell of a thing that night all those years ago.

What would I have done? Would I have had the courage to report it, or would I have gone along with Lance to protect him? I understood what I wanted to believe: I'd have

224

ordered him to hand himself in. Yet Coco was right when she'd accused me of complacency. Trusting Lance, falling in with what he wanted in our dismal dealings with extortionists and going against my gut instincts, had got me nowhere. It had jeopardised everything. But that was the old me, the new me had to get it together and work out the best way forward to protect me and my family and that meant finding out who was really pulling the levers, who wanted to destroy us so badly. I couldn't discount the fact that someone in the Walsh family had found out and wanted to settle a score, although how that tied in with the Mount brothers I couldn't yet fathom.

Unsettled by the thought, I called Lance. He didn't pick up. He was with Amy, I thought. Heart pounding, I called her.

'Hello,' she answered uncertainly.

'Is Lance with you?'

'Um . . . no.'

'It's important I speak to him.'

'Honest, he's not here. I thought he was with you.'

'He isn't.'

I felt awkward. She felt awkward. Before either one of us rang off, I said, 'Amy, when did you last speak to him?'

'A couple of days ago.'

'And you haven't seen him since?'

'No, although . . .'

'Although what?'

'I'm expecting him later.'

'As soon as he arrives, tell him to call me. It's urgent.'

Before she asked a load of questions I couldn't answer, I hung up and called Lance's office at MultiMax. Someone I didn't know, a man called Faraz, answered. 'I am the new Operations Manager,' he announced with evident pride.

'Could I speak to Lance, please?'

'He is not here.'

'Do you know where I can find him? I'm his wife,' I added, feeling uncomfortable.

'Mrs Stratton,' he said, 'very pleased to speak to you.'

'Likewise,' I said, fizzing with frustration. 'Has my husband been into the office?'

'I saw him last three days ago. I was off sick,' he explained apologetically. 'Mr Stratton sometimes sleeps here, as you know,' Faraz said in a way that suggested he very much hoped I did know.

'Yes, but did he sleep in Worcester last night?'

'This I cannot say.' He paused. He was clearly doing his level best to be helpful. 'Some of his clothes are here and his toothbrush,' he said, as though it worthy of special comment.

'Has he had any visitors?'

'I do not think so.'

'Nobody called Mount?'

'No, I would remember this.'

It didn't sound as if Faraz was conspiring with them. Strange how my mind worked these days; everyone seemed a potential foe. 'Thank you, Faraz. Could you put Sharon on? I'd like a very quick word.'

'I will find her. Is there anything else I can help you with, Mrs Stratton?'

There was but I wasn't going to put Faraz in a tricky position. I needed the entry code for the unit, which was changed regularly as an extra security precaution. If I asked Faraz, a man who'd never set eyes on me, he'd be instantly suspicious and refuse to reveal it. I didn't want to test an assiduous employee who obviously took his job seriously.

'No, you've been most helpful,' I said.

'It is my pleasure.'

I waited. Finally, short and not so sweet Sharon answered. She sounded as harassed as ever.

'Yep?'

'Could you give me the six digit entry code for the week, please?'

'597021.'

'Thank you.'

'Anything else?'

'No.'

She cut the call.

So Lance wasn't at Amy's and he wasn't in Worcester. I smacked the side of my head with the flat of my hand.

'Chantal,' I said out loud.

* * *

'Everything all right at home?' Beady-eyed Miss Ward was at the school gates when Amy collected the children.

'Yes,' Amy lied.

'Only Tana was quite unkind to one of the other little girls today and that's not like her.'

'I'll have a word.' Amy grabbed Tana's sticky hand and scuttled away.

As soon as she'd got the kids inside the bungalow and plonked them in front of the TV with a plate of Jaffa Cakes, she went to the window and waited for Rollo's return. Butterflies were doing acrobatics in her tummy. She was light-headed with apprehension and expectation. She hated him and loved him and she wasn't quite sure which was the stronger emotion. When she saw him she'd know. When he stepped through the door that would be the time to make a decision.

A high-pitched squeal and Amy was catapulted into the dramatic and crazy lives of three children under the age of six. She ran to Tana who stood red in the face, clutching her arm, tears rolling down her cheeks.

'He bit me,' she howled.

Wilf, sullen and belligerent, stared at his sister. 'She wouldn't let me watch *Paw Patrol*.'

'You don't bite people, Wilf.' Tiny tooth marks had left indentations on Tana's skin and some of the blood vessels beneath were broken. It looked sore.

'Go to your room, Wilf.'

'Will not.'

Anger surged through Amy. At that moment she understood how parents could lose the plot. Wasn't right, but she got it. Before she did something she might regret, she swept up her phone and house keys and fled outside, shutting the front door firmly after her.

Stabbing in Rollo's number, she called him. It went straight to the messaging service. 'Where the hell are you? You should have been here half an hour ago.'

She walked out onto the street, cupped a hand over her brow, and stared into the distance for sight of his car. Traffic whizzed up and down. There was no sign of Rollo.

He isn't coming, she realised, prickling with disappointment and anger.

She phoned him again. 'Rollo, are you okay. Just call me, right?' She paused, stomach twisting at the thought of him doing something silly. 'Love you,' she said.

She paced up and down, struggling with whether or not to contact Susannah. *Urgent*, she'd said.

Quickly glancing through the window, she saw Tana's tear-stained face pressed up against the glass. Thank God she hadn't raised her child's hopes that her daddy was coming home.

'Mummy won't be a moment,' she mouthed, holding her phone aloft. She texted Susannah two words: *NO SHOW*. Then, forlornly, she tramped back inside.

'Where were you, Mummy?' Tana asked. 'We were scared.'

Amy was scared too. 'Needed a breath of fresh air, that's all, my love. Where's Wilf?'

'Playing in the bedroom.'

'I'm sorry he hurt you.'

Teatime was a nightmare. Wilf wouldn't eat his sausages and baby Adele grizzled and wouldn't take her bottle. Amy feared she was gearing up for another night of colic. Washing up the dishes, something Rollo did when he was home, had never felt so arduous.

'Mum,' Tana shouted. 'Wilf's done a wee on the carpet.'

'Coming,' Amy called, exhausted. This was her life from now on: long years ahead of struggle and grief.

* * *

Chantal tried not to look startled when she found me on her doorstep, but it didn't quite land. For once in my life I held the dominant hand. It wasn't an unpleasant feeling. Once I'd ascertained that Lance wasn't lurking amongst her eclectic art collection, I told her I was coming in. My tone was *like it or not.* In all the years we'd rubbed along, she'd never heard me so authoritative. Visibly taken aback, she opened the door wide.

I followed her into her study-cum-office. A business-like discussion required a businesslike setting. I half expected a lawyer to pop out of the trendy newly-painted panelled woodwork.

'I know what this is all about,' Chantal began.

'No, you don't. Where is Lance?'

'I have no idea. Last time I had any dealings was the morning after the attack. We spoke on the phone. As you might imagine it was not the most amicable conversation.'

I raked her face for falsehoods, not easy because Chantal was a consummate liar. My phone pinged. A text came through from Amy, confirming my worst suspicions. Was Lance really going to run it to the wire, or was there another reason for his silence?

'He's not at work,' I told Chantal. 'He's not with his other family. He's not answering his phone.'

'Maybe he's actually done us all a favour.'

'God's sake, do you have to be so cruel and callous?'

Chantal's expression didn't alter. For an unsettling moment I wondered if she were capable of murder. She certainly had a motive. If Lance disappeared from her life she could protest plausible deniability about the hit and run.

'You don't seriously think Lance is dead?' A preposterous suggestion, Chantal appeared to suggest.

'It's possible, isn't it? He's desperate.'

'He's a coward.'

'And so are you.'

Chantal's eyes narrowed to slits. I felt the full force of her contempt. 'Who are you to lecture me? The woman who cheats on her husband.'

So it was *you who followed me*, I thought, quickly recovering. 'I am not cheating on my husband.'

'He's Frankie's father, isn't he?'

She had me cold. No point in denial.

'I'd heard he was an Italian,' Chantal said.

No doubt from Lance, I thought.

'I saw you in the park with him,' Chantal continued, 'and made an educated guess.

'It's entirely platonic,' I said, 'and, even if it weren't, it's rich to compare it to aiding and abetting an offender and leaving a young man to choke in his own blood and die on a road.'

Chantal's complexion drained to the colour of curdled milk. Her lips very slightly parted. So she did have a pulse after all.

'How did you find out?' Her voice was hoarse.

'How do you think?'

She sat down. I towered over her.

Sudden fear haunted her eyes. The facade she'd adopted for decades shattered and crumbled. It reminded me of Lance when he'd confessed. Oh, how the mighty have fallen, I thought. Her jaw tightened and when she spoke each word felt as if it were being wrenched out of her.

'I was a young mother and not terribly good at it. Coco was not a longed-for child,' she added with bewildering honesty. 'I'm not like you.'

'That's certainly true.'

'I was doing the best I could.' Her expression was sour, her voice bitter. 'Motherhood is not for everyone.' She briefly held my gaze as if loving my son suggested a terrible character defect in me. 'When Lance told me what he'd done, in all honesty, I didn't believe him,' she continued. 'Then I saw the front of his car and realised he wasn't making it up or imagining it so we drove to the accident in my vehicle.'

She let her gaze drop to the stripped wooden floor. 'I'd never seen a person dead before, let alone someone . . .' Chantal faltered. 'There was a lot of blood,' she said, picking up the thread again. 'Straight up, I panicked.'

'You didn't think to call the emergency services, the police?'

'Kneeling in the dirt on the roadside, I wasn't thinking at all. All those charges Lance would have faced . . .'

Death by dangerous driving, failure to report an accident, these were only the most obvious to me. For all I knew there were other charges that could be levelled at the pair of them.

'. . . I only thought of them later,' she finished, briefly drifting off into some unseen, forsaken place.

'Chantal,' I said, bringing her back.

'Guilt, it's like a pollutant,' Chantal murmured, her scared gaze clinging to mine. 'It poisons every thought, spoils every day and ruins every plan for the future. How can you feel joy when you live and sleep and dream with the shame of it 24/7?'

'You took the young man's passport and wallet,' I said simply.

'My insurance policy, I'd thought at the time.'

'And now?'

She gave a shrug.

'You still have them?'

'I do.' She shook her head sadly. 'I'm not the monster you think I am. I often wonder about that young man's family. There was a time when I nearly caved in and went to the police.'

'But you didn't.'

Her silence was a beat too long. 'It was too late,' Chantal said, with extraordinary self-possession. 'I'd covered up a crime, perverted the course of justice or whatever it is. What would have happened to Coco, with both her parents in prison?'

She could have come to me, I thought sadly. I would have given her a home. But, of course, I hadn't met Lance until later.

Chantal gave me a quizzical look. 'Do you really think Lance is dead?'

'That, I don't know.' I only knew he was missing. Had recent events pushed him over the edge? What if he'd done something really stupid? Men at his age often did. Some resorted to drink and drugs and others . . . I couldn't bear to articulate it. Unable to endure the public acknowledgement of his crime and subsequent prison sentence, seeing a lifetime of work in jeopardy, helpless and unable to protect those he loved, would he do the unthinkable? It brought me up short. Lance never struck me as a man who would succumb to mental illness, let alone what I was considering.

Chantal cut into my thoughts. 'Can I trust you to be discreet?'

Asked by the woman without a moral compass, the question did not take me by surprise. 'Let me tell you something, Chantal. I am the victim of extortion. I have been threatened physically. I have watched my family torn apart. I probably have no home. My job is in jeopardy so no, you can't trust me. You're out of options.' And so was Lance — if he were alive.

She didn't look as scared as I thought she'd be. I swear she had a glint of triumph in her eyes.

'If you think knowing about Frankie's father is going to give you leverage, you're wrong. I fully intend to tell my son about his biological dad when he returns. There are no Get Out of Jail Free passes after what you did.'

I turned and walked away.

'Where are you going?'

'To Worcester.' To check out the unit.

One last chance and then it would be over. For all I knew it was already over for Lance.

Unless he'd fled.

* * *

Friday afternoon traffic meant I didn't arrive until after the unit was closed and everyone had gone home. I was amazed to see Lance's BMW in its designated space, with his name

232

above it, parked next to a Dacia Sandero, the car Lance used in his other life. He must have snuck back when he thought the coast was clear. I had images of him packing up, catching a taxi and heading for Birmingham airport to catch a flight to a country from which he couldn't be extradited.

Drawing up next to the Sandero, I planned to surprise him. More accurately, shock the hell out of him.

I climbed out, walked to the front of the building, entered the code and listened to the familiar thunk-thunk as the lock released. Pushing open the reinforced glass door, I slipped inside into a central lobby and reception area.

Next to an Apple laptop, the nerve centre of operations, two MultiMax mugs of half-drunk beverages sat on a desk from which Sharon would be able to monitor CCTV.

Beyond, and through a glass door, a state-of-the art modern showroom, displaying multiple types of incinerator. Bio-security was big business, particularly in the wake of avian and swine flu, and diseases that afflicted cattle and livestock. Consequently, the efficient destruction of infected waste and diseased carcasses was essential. "In situ" incinerators also took care of the natural mortalities that took place on any large farm, without having to pay to have those carcasses clinically removed.

To the left of reception, another door, again with a glass window through which I could see the new shredder standing idle. Behind it, row after row of shredded paper, like supersized bales of hay that stretched up to the ceiling. It had been Dave's idea to diversify and Lance had been supportive. It ticked the company's recycling credentials and made money in the process.

Offices upstairs housed service support engineers and technicians, as well as admin staff who were also able to give advice on dealings with DEFRA and handle paperwork. Lance's office was right at the end.

Empty factory units at night are creepy. My footsteps sounded too loud, the silence too soft. Lights, timed to pop on through a movement sensor, lit the corridor. I scuttled from one pool of darkness to the next as if I were navigating an underground cave that threatened to fill with water at any moment. It suddenly revealed how vulnerable I was. If Lance was there he might cut up rough. I no longer knew him. What would a desperate man do to maintain his liberty? And if he wasn't there, and was lying in a body bag in a mortuary, the Mount boys might already be here, counting their ill-gotten gains. Maybe they'd stolen his business — like they'd stolen our lives.

My pulse rate spiked. The hairs on the back of my neck tingled. My legs felt thick and heavy. I so badly wanted to turn around and flee and yet I could not. One way or another, I had to see if Lance was alive, lying or not.

With a toxic mixture of fear and dread careering through my veins, I approached Lance's room. Sickness assailed me when I noticed that the door was ajar. I hoped to see him but what if I heard voices, the sounds of drawers being opened and closed, papers pored through, possibly the chink of glasses from the bottle of whisky that Lance kept in his bottom drawer to toast a deal done and if, having beaten me to it, it were the Mounts, celebrating another victim ripped off. I heard nothing except my own breath coming in hot spurts from my nostrils and an insistent drumming inside my own head.

What if . . .

My fingers stretched out as if they belonged to someone else and I pushed the door fully open. A light automatically went on, revealing an empty sleeping bag on a camp bed pushed into the corner, a suitcase, open, with a shirt neatly folded inside. Looped over a two-seater sofa, a favourite dove-grey suit, which Lance wore to meet clients. Beside it, a pair of black shoes that looked new. The only thing missing: the owner.

Off the office, Lance had his own private bathroom. The door to this, too, was open. Faraz was correct: Lance's toothbrush remained together with a tube of toothpaste that he always squeezed from the middle. His shaver was in a small cabinet above the sink. I noted a bottle of heavy-duty antacid mixture, painkillers and antihistamine. Wherever he was he hadn't taken them with him.

I went to his desk, sat down in front of his laptop and attempted various combinations but failed to access it.

Defeated, I leant back to focus my thoughts. Apart from the usual pens and notepads, a single empty tumbler, its base containing a sticky yellow film that I identified as whisky. Sure enough, in a deep drawer beneath a half drunk bottle of bourbon. I wondered whether it was consumed over a period of days, or in one go and whether it reflected a timeline I couldn't yet fathom.

The top drawer revealed an assortment of stationery, the one below paperwork. I pulled a sheaf out and my eyes widened at the sight of Lance's passport, his wallet, the keys to his car, and the keys to our home. A man who obviously planned to go somewhere, yet was nowhere. I picked through his wallet. It contained two twenty-pound notes, no loose change, a credit card and two bankcards. His driving licence, a potential proof of identity, was missing.

Heading back downstairs, I went straight to Sharon's station and checked the CCTV. Nothing notable; nobody driving into the car park; no-one skulking around outside. No cause for alarm, I told myself stoutly while feeling a terrible sense of dread.

I rolled the footage back to two days before and watched Lance's BMW drive into the car park and come to a halt next to the Dacia. The time stamp when he climbed out of his car was at 17.45 p.m. I spiked inside at seeing him in the flesh. The strain on his face was evident. Tense and urgent, he was a man on a mission, a man in a hurry. He moved towards the building purposefully, entered through reception and that was it. I went to the next frame, which showed Sharon and Faraz leaving the premises the following day, on Thursday. What had happened in the intervening hours? I thought I'd done something strange to the machine and rewound, but no. A critical gap stubbornly remained. Lance had entered the building but there was no record of him coming out and no evidence that anyone else had entered and come out either.

Unless the images had been deleted.

Too many people had reason to want Lance dead. The Mount brothers lay in pole position, but bumping off Lance would attract attention and turn off the money tap too soon. Chantal closely followed. Removing Lance removed the threat of exposure. That left Amy, acting hysterically in revenge and, I supposed it could be argued that, in my more disturbed moments, me.

Slick with sweat and sick with anxiety, I picked up my phone and called 999.

CHAPTER THIRTY-FOUR

A man answered, I guessed a civilian. I told him straightaway that my husband was missing and had been for the past
forty-eight hours.

His response was cool and calm and within seconds,
he'd elicited my name, Lance's name, and our address.

'You live in Gloucestershire?'

'I do.'

'Only the call's been routed through to West Mercia
police.'

'I'm calling from his works place in Worcester.' Damn,
I'd briefly forgotten the name of the company. Brain fog had
descended without warning, entombing my thoughts and
robbing me of clarity. 'It isn't a problem, is it?' God, was I
supposed to ring off, go home and phone again?

'Not a problem at all. I can reroute the details to
Gloucestershire.'

'Thank you.'

'You say he's been missing for a couple of days — have
you checked with family and friends?'

'I have, including his girlfriend.' Shit, why oh why did
I blurt *that* out? I imagined the man's cynical reaction. He'd
be thinking *affair; wronged wife seeks revenge; maybe hubby has*

another woman in tow, dirty bastard. 'Although it's completely irrelevant,' I said in a strangled voice. 'He's in trouble with loan sharks, you see.'

'Has he been threatened?'

'Yes.'

'And you believe your husband to be high risk right at this very moment?'

I'd obviously triggered some internal alarm because the voice sharpened. Good.

'I don't know, but he owes them a million pounds and they've taken my car, which they used to ram my other car. They've taken my son's car and want the deeds to my house and . . .'

'Do you consider yourself to be at risk, Mrs Stratton?'

How to answer? I guessed the police had a triage system. Would this be considered low, medium or high risk? 'Not specifically; maybe.' I hoped it would elevate me to "need to take her seriously".

'How far are you from home?'

'I can be there within the hour.'

'I'm going to send an officer to you to make a preliminary investigation.'

'That would be great.' *Thank God.*

'Right, well travel safely and I'll pass your details on.'

I thanked him and, glad to get out of the building, drove at warp speed down the motorway. Inside, I was flying on neat adrenaline.

Crossing into Cheltenham and heading down the road to my house, my heart tripped and I slammed on the brakes.

My Macan was parked outside home. The audacity stole my breath away. It shrieked of power and contempt for the law. And now the law was coming back to bite Veldo hard, where it counted, and I would be vindicated.

I pulled over, bumping up onto the kerb, two wheels on the pavement. Police officers would be here at any moment. All I had to do was wait and hope that the Mount brothers didn't exit my house and drive away.

I watched the minutes tick by. I twisted round and strained to look over my shoulder for signs of the police. I didn't know how things were handled. Surely, the message would be received and responded to by now? Once I'd given more detailed and pressing information, the emergency handler appeared to take me seriously.

In frustration, I got out and crept along the street and onto the drive, cursing that the gravel we'd laid as a security precaution gave me away.

Any damage to my Macan, I noticed, had been repaired and carried out professionally. No scratches on the bumper, no dents to the bonnet. Good as new.

Flustered, I stole up to the living-room window and peered inside. Everything looked the same. I couldn't see anyone moving about. Perhaps he or they were upstairs. Not that I was daft enough to find out. No have a go hero, I returned to the Polo.

Minutes later, a patrol car prowled down the street. I leapt out of my car to flag it down and was perturbed to see a single young uniformed male officer, a rookie perhaps. Would he be able to handle the situation on his own? Should I offer to go into the house with him?

He popped his head out of the window. 'Are you Mrs Stratton?'

I nodded and he introduced himself as PC Mathew Falconer. His strawberry blonde hair was cut short and he had striking blue eyes the same colour as the periwinkles in my garden. His jaw was prominent. I suspected he had a malocclusion.

'Is your husband still missing?'

I confirmed he was and gabbled that the car, which had been taken, was now back on my drive, fully repaired. Said aloud, it knocked a hole in my previous allegation, not something lost on PC Matthew Falconer.

'It's been returned then?'

'Yes and no.'

PC Falconer's eyes contracted to two tiny jewelled dots.

'I don't know whether it's been returned or whether it's parked there by the man who took it,' I explained. 'The point is there's someone in my house and I don't know who.'

'Your husband?' Falconer said hopefully.

'No, well, possibly, yes. I have no idea,' I finished awkwardly.

I couldn't blame him for viewing me as if I'd walked out of a secure unit for the mentally disturbed.

'I'll go and take a look,' Falconer said. 'You've got the house keys?'

I handed them to him.

'Is that your vehicle parked on the pavement?' He tilted his chin in the direction of the Polo.

I said it was.

'Go and wait inside while I give the place the once-over.'

Sheepishly, I obeyed and watched as PC Falconer pulled onto the drive and climbed out. Short, he had a stocky build that signalled he'd be good in a fistfight. He spoke briefly into his radio and approached the front door.

Straining nervously to see what was going on, I realised I was not alone. Mrs Fletcher was also having a good gawp and virtually blocking my view.

Minutes passed. Hungry, thirsty and cold, I switched on the engine and turned the heater up to full blast. I imagined an urgent phone conversation and a request for backup, the arrival of a fleet of police cars, verbal warnings, noise and arrest. I pictured Jack and/or Marcus Mount threatened with a Taser and marched out in handcuffs. That would give Mrs Fletcher something to shout about. Good, she was scuttling back inside. I supposed I should have asked her about Lance. Perhaps the police would do it as part of their investigation.

At last, PC Falconer reappeared, alone. He talked into his radio and walked slowly, as if to buy him time to think how he was going to frame words he wanted to say and yet feared saying. The sick thought that he'd found Lance dead went off like a firecracker inside my head. It vanished like smoke when I buzzed down the window and Falconer gave me the 'All clear'.

Perplexed, I gaped at him. 'That's not possible.' Unless whoever had returned my car had gone into town on foot, intending to come back later. I put this to Falconer. He didn't seem persuaded.

'The keys to your Macan are near the kettle.'

'They are?'

'You didn't accidently leave them there?'

'Absolutely not. Like I said . . .'

'Along with the deeds to your house.'

Hot spots of colour flashed across my cheeks. The sweat breaking out all over my body was, this time, for all the right reasons.

'They were in full view,' Falconer continued. 'Anybody could have stolen them. Best to keep confidential papers and information like that locked away with your solicitor.' Falconer's tone was mildly reproving.

He obviously believed I'd had a memory lapse, which was partly true but *my* car had been forcibly taken. *My* car had been used to scare the shit out of me. With regard to the deeds to the house, Lance had said he'd *hold them off for as long as I can*. If he'd managed to retain them, why not inform me? 'And there's really nobody inside the house?'

'No-one.'

'You've checked absolutely everywhere?'

'I conducted a thorough search, including the garden. Shall we go in and have a little chat?'

Too muddled to speak intelligently, I gave a feeble nod and followed him along the pavement.

Like a stranger stepping over the threshold of a new home for the first time, I sniffed the air. Unless Falconer wore a heady brand of aftershave, which he didn't, somebody had been in my home even if they weren't there now.

The keys to the Macan, together with the deeds to the house were exactly as the police officer described.

'Mrs Stratton,' PC Falconer said, taking out a notebook. 'Shall we?'

I led him into the sitting room where we sat down. Falconer glanced around the room, making deductions, which he failed to share. His body language suggested: nice place, nice life, barking woman. I remained silent and let him lead the conversation.

'Your original report stated that your husband was missing.'

'He still is. I found his phone, passport, wallet and car keys at his unit in Worcester. His cars are there too.'

'What makes?'

I told Falconer and supplied the registration for the BMW. 'He also drives a Dacia Sandero, not sure of the reg.'

'And you say they're both still there?'

'Yes.'

'Did he have cash on him?'

'I don't know.'

'You have joint accounts?'

'For bills only.'

'And nothing has been taken out that you can't account for?'

'No.'

Falconer explained that Lance's card payments would be tracked to pinpoint his last movements. Similarly, his phone records would be examined.

'Now these loan sharks you mentioned.'

I cleared my throat. My accusations regarding my car and the deeds carried a lot less weight. The bigger complaints remained. I rambled on about Veldo and Jack and Marcus Mount, the address from which they worked in Battledown, and their other address in Gloucester Road; that they were part of a bigger corporation in America.

'Could be a franchise operation, or . . .'

Falconer cut across me. 'You say your husband, Lance, borrowed money from them legitimately.'

'Well . . .'

'Willingly?'

'That's right.'

'And how much did Lance borrow?'

'The initial loan was for around £250k.'

Falconer practically whistled through his teeth.

'So Lance went to this company?'

'He met a man in a pub.' I briefly stalled. It sounded ludicrous, like it was the precursor to a very bad joke. 'His name was Martin,' I said.

'Surname, or first name?'

'I presumed surname but I couldn't swear to it.' And that was becoming a serious problem in Falconer's eyes. I soldiered on, feeling silly as he made more notes.

'And when was this?'

'I think around a year ago, but it could be longer. Like I said, Lance had a double life.'

'Okay, we'll come on to that in a moment,' Falconer said, an ominous note in his voice. 'Essentially, he was funding his girlfriend . . .'

'And their family . . .'

'And their family,' he said laboriously, 'with the loan.'

'Yes. And then Veldo started racking up the interest on it.'

'Did Lance pay?'

'Some, yes, but he couldn't keep up with their increasing demands. That's when they wanted the deeds to the house.'

'Except they are here.'

'Well, yes, but I didn't know that, you see.' *Please believe me. Please don't look at me like that.*

'Then they threatened you, is that right?'

'They terrorised us.'

'In what way?'

I explained about the fistfight with Frankie and how I'd been personally assaulted. I waited as Falconer made more notes. 'Oh and I was chased on the motorway and virtually run off the road. My car, the Macan was used as a battering ram. It damaged the car I was driving.'

'I can take a look. But the Macan's been repaired, you said.'

'Um . . . yes.'

'Ri-ight,' he said. 'You reported both incidents?'

'I was too scared.' Before he disputed my account, I told him about Coco.

Falconer stopped writing and looked up from his notepad. 'And this has been logged with the police?'

I shook my head. Falconer nodded slowly. *He was doing his job*, I told myself. He wasn't passing judgement, except I thought he was.

'What's her full name?'

'Coco Stratton.'

'You didn't think to report it?'

'It wasn't my place. She has a mother.' I didn't intend for it to come out defensively, but it did.

'And what's her name?'

'Chantal Kelly.'

'And she didn't think to report it either?'

'No.'

'How old is your stepdaughter?'

I told him.

'An adult and she hasn't gone to the police at all?' Falconer sounded incredulous.

'As far as I understand, no. As I already told you, we were scared. We were threatened. None of us have any experience of this kind of thing.' I felt as if I were not only defending myself but our whole extended family, Chantal included.

'When did the alleged incident occur?'

Alleged? He doesn't believe me. How the hell do I introduce Lance's involvement in a hit and run? 'A few days ago,' I answered.

'And where is Coco?' He glanced around the room as if she might pop out of the drinks cabinet.

'She's gone away with her stepbrother to her maternal grandparents.' I swallowed hard. To my ears, I sounded mad. To Falconer's ears, I was a fantasist.

He paused, fixed his eyes upon me in a way that my mother would have described as brooking no nonsense. 'Lance's girlfriend.'

The flush on my cheeks grew hotter.

'You've double-checked Lance isn't with her?'

'It was the first thing I did.'

'And she wouldn't lie to you?'

'No, I . . . I don't think so.'

He nodded sagely. For the second time that evening I could see how it all looked to an outsider. In the absence of hard evidence it was a classic case of humiliated wife fabricating a tale designed to embarrass husband. I hadn't stooped to cutting all the trouser legs off his best suits, or posting vile personal details about him online. My revenge was of a more complicated and cerebral nature. I'd be lucky to escape the charge of wasting police time. Tears of frustration filmed my eyes. I tried not to cry.

'I think that's all for now.' Falconer closed his notebook with a finality that was not inspiring and stood up. 'We will follow up on the information you've supplied and get back to you. Evidently, if Lance returns, you'll let us know. Do you feel we've covered everything, Mrs Stratton?'

'Yes.' And more.

'Have you any questions?'

I shook my head. No point in telling him another "story".

'Then I'll say goodnight.'

I saw him to the door. Falconer appeared to hesitate as if he'd tumbled to something. 'You'll be all right then?' he asked.

I assured him there was no need to worry and waited for him to drive away. Returning to the kitchen I put water in the kettle for a brew and picked up the deeds. Everything was as expected with one mind-blowing exception: the deeds to the house were in my name.

Oh my God, this was definitely Lance's work, wasn't it? Reparation and redemption, a parting gift, a final farewell before . . .

Bewildered and thick with fear, I stumbled from room to room. The garden received the same treatment. My mind in free fall, I moved mechanically for something to do, letting my body go through the motions, trawling through every possibility. Getting nowhere, I called Frankie.

'Hiya,' he said. 'What's occurring?'

I began with the easy, the functional and unemotional. 'Is it possible to delete CCTV footage?'

'Delete or overwrite?'

I wasn't entirely certain what he meant. 'Either.'

'You haven't got a clue, have you?' he said with a laugh that I didn't find funny. 'Okay, here we go — layman's version: if someone deletes a file from a hard disk, it's empty, which means it's free and can be reused.'

'Can the original footage be recovered?'

'Depends.'

I didn't like *depends*. I wanted certainty.

'If the empty space is filled with new material and overwritten, usually after a period of time,' Frankie continued, 'it's more tricky to retrieve it.'

'But possible?'

'I guess.' He didn't seem convinced.

'How would you go about deleting it in the first place?' I asked.

At which point he lost me. I tuned out as he went into a technical explanation using acronyms I'd never heard of. 'Could be that the HDD is damaged. Why do you want to know?' he asked.

I told him.

'Shit, and you haven't heard from Dad?'

'Have you?'

'Nope.'

'What about Coco?'

'She hasn't heard from him either though she isn't really into taking his calls at the moment.'

'Frankie, I'm genuinely worried.'

'Want me to come back? I can leave now.'

'No. Stay where you are.' It was safer that way.

'You're sure? I can drop everything. Coco will be fine with her folks.'

'Not yet,' I said. 'I'll shout if I need you.'

'Have you spoken to Chantal and that other woman?'

'Yes and I went to the police.'

'Bloody hell, what did they say?'

'They think I'm nuts. Probably have me notched as a fantasist.' I told him how I'd come back home to find my car repaired and the deeds made out in my name.

'But that's wonderful news,' Frankie burst out.

'Yes and no.'

'How so?'

'Who made it happen and where is your father?'

'Yes, I see,' he said slowly, sounding worried. 'Does anybody else know about the house thing?'

'Nobody.' Except, I realised with a thud, somebody did. 'I have to go, Frankie.'

'Stay in touch, yeah?'

I promised I would. As soon as I wrapped up the call, I phoned Lorenzo. He didn't answer.

Shaky and suddenly worried by the Lorenzo connection, I picked through the remnants of past conversations. I knew the shout lines of his life, his work. I had no real inkling of his political and philosophical views, other than, in common with most Italians, he valued family. It's why he'd asked about my parents. *Parents and grandparents are very important*, he'd said.

I felt as if I had a tiger standing behind me.

CHAPTER THIRTY-FIVE

My dad played golf on Saturdays. I didn't want to speak to him. It was my mother I'd come for.

A distant memory of my mother's ire popped out of the mental compartment in which I'd buried it.

You stupid, stupid girl. After all we've done for you and in the middle of your studies too. Dear God, what will people think?'

I hadn't cared what people thought. I cared about how I was going to raise a child alone. Any notion of contacting Lorenzo was quickly squashed.

Marry in haste, repent at leisure,' my mother trotted out. 'And what makes you think some random Italian would want to know about a child conceived in a moment of madness? He'll think you deliberately trapped him.'

'He's not like that,' I protested.

'How do you know?'

Truth was, I hadn't known.

Letting myself in to my childhood home, I found Mum in the conservatory, knitting.

'Oh,' she said, looking mildly annoyed to see me. 'You didn't say you were coming.'

Surprise was part of my plan. Running out of time, too tired to explain, or humour her, I launched straight in.

'When did you meet Lorenzo?'

Shock sped across her face so fast I almost missed it. Confusion followed in its wake. She put down her knitting. 'Lorenzo who? I don't know a Lorenzo.' The little old lady routine didn't suit her and I wasn't fooled.

'Yes, you do: Frankie's father.'

'Oh *him*. Good God, whatever makes you think I've seen that man?'

'I'll explain later.' I had no intention of explaining later.

'Susannah, are you feeling quite well? Your father and I are worried about you. Naturally, we understand that things are tricky at home and you must be under an enormous amount of strain but . . .'

'I asked you a question. When did you last see him?'

The furious expression on her face assured me that I was walking on dangerous terrain. 'Are you accusing me of lying?'

'Yes.'

Her small eyes contracted to slits. 'How dare you.'

'Oh, I dare. How else would Lorenzo know where to find me? Is Dad aware of your deception, or did you keep that from him too?'

Her mouth opened and closed. I had her on a hook and I was going to reel her in. I took out my phone.

'Let's call him.' Whatever I thought of my mum, she had enormous respect for my father, as did I. She wouldn't want him to find out she'd been behaving in an underhand fashion behind his back.

'I did it to protect you.' Her voice along with her gaze dropped like a dead weight to the floor.

'Did what exactly?'

She emitted an enormous sigh. 'It was a long time ago when Lorenzo Bonetti came looking for you.'

'Here? In the UK?' I was astounded. Lorenzo had little or no money and had never ventured out of Italy before we met. 'He travelled all this way?'

'It would seem so,' she said tartly. 'Your father was at work,' she explained keen to keep him out of it. 'I was in the garden and this rather gauche young man knocked at the gate, introduced himself in broken English and said he was looking for you. Well,' she sniffed, folding her hands in her lap, 'I knew exactly what he was after.'

Lorenzo wanted *me*, I wanted to scream, livid that in my mother's eyes *I* was a *what*, not a *who*.

'You should have seen the way he viewed the house,' she said, her mouth forming a short prim line. 'Anybody could see he was a sponger. Couldn't believe his luck, I can tell you. Thought he'd landed on his feet when he impregnated you.'

As vile as her words were, I had a first class honours degree, honed over many years, in not rising to the bait. 'What did you tell him?'

'The truth.'

I nailed her with a look that demanded to know what that *truth* amounted to.

'I said you were getting on with your life quite happily. It was the only way to get rid of him,' she insisted. 'No point soft soaping the man.'

My jaw clenched so hard I thought my teeth would shatter.

'Why are you looking at me like that? I neither regret what I said, nor the advice I gave to you. You would never have thrived in a foreign country. Not the same opportunities.'

'What else did you tell him?'

'Nothing.' Mum picked up the knitting needles again. Knit one, pearl one. I waited.

'But then he came back, didn't he?'

'Damn, I've dropped a stitch,' Mum said, flustered. My eyes bored into hers until she cast the cardigan she was knitting aside.

'All right, yes.'

'When?'

'Eighteen months ago, or so.'

I felt sick and a little faint.

'He was different this time: cocky, assertive, and far too familiar for my liking. Kept talking about *his English girl* and *the one that got away.*'

'Meaning me,' I said weakly.

'Quite. Absurd after all this time.'

'What did you tell him?'

'I don't recall.' The shifty light in my mother's eyes told me she remembered down to the last detail.

'Try.'

'I said you were happily married, that you lived in Cheltenham.'

'You gave my address?'

'Not precisely.'

'How precisely, mother?'

'I might have mentioned the general geography of the Park.'

I had a sudden image of the fleeing figure from my home the evening I'd put out the bin for collection. 'You told him about my job?'

'I *might* have done.' That translated to yes.

'Where I worked?'

'In passing, perhaps. I'm not . . .'

'Did he ask specifically about Lance?'

A pulse flickered below her left eye. 'I daresay he was mentioned in conversation.'

'Did Lorenzo enquire about MultiMax?'

'Only in a general sense.'

'Do you have any idea of the terrible harm you've done?'

'*Me?*'

'*You.*'

My mother sat up a little straighter, drew her chin back and folded her liver-spotted hands in her lap. '*You* were the one who went to Italy and slept around.'

'I did not sleep around.'

'This is your mess, not mine,' she insisted.

I had a strange and highly charged sensation in my head. 'Did you tell him about Frankie?'

'Give me some credit.'

'You didn't discuss Frankie at all?' I persisted.

She glanced through the window and shifted her gaze to a lilac tree. 'I said you had a young son.'

'Christ, mother.'

'I didn't say the child was his.'

But, oh my God, Lorenzo would twig. To every question asked, he'd already known the answer. He'd listened and smiled while I'd lied, evaded and fabricated. It put a different complexion on everything. I recalled the obsessive intensity in Lorenzo's expression as if in his mind we were always destined to be together, except Lance was in the way. I saw now that Lorenzo was Lance's biggest threat and always had been.

I pushed back the chair and stood up. My mother viewed me with a wafer-thin smile. 'I presume Bonetti has been in touch. No good will come of rekindling your romance.'

For once we were in agreement.

Back in my car, I called Chantal who answered like a woman about to receive a death sentence. As far as I was concerned it had been metaphorically deferred.

I cut straight to the chase and convened a Council of War. Chantal's relief at not being turned in to the police immediately gave way to apprehension.

'What's the catch?' she asked.

'There isn't one.'

'There's always a damned catch.'

'Frankie's father,' I said. 'Courtesy of my mother, Lorenzo Bonetti knows all about me, my life with Lance, and has done for over a year.'

'And he never let on?'

'He didn't.'

Chantal didn't exclaim or emote. She asked questions and I supplied answers about Lorenzo's work, where he lived, between homes in Salerno and Matera, about his two ex-wives. Next, I gave a shorthand version of my skirmish with PC Mathew Falconer, including the mysterious return of my car and the even more mysterious appearance of the deeds made out in my name. After I finished, Chantal cut straight to the heart of it. 'Does Lorenzo have a son?'

'No.' I felt as if I'd swallowed stones.

'A straightforward man would simply come straight out and ask. Someone more complicated and devious would act differently,' Chantal said with massive understatement. 'You think Lance is in genuine danger?' Suddenly, she didn't sound so confident and cocky. For all her bluff and bravado Lance was the father of her child. She didn't want him dead.

'I do.'

'You think it's possible we've all been viewing Veldo through the wrong lens?'

I did. 'And why we need to work out a plan of action.' I explained I wanted to include Amy in any discussion.

'What's it got to do with her? She's not exactly at the sharp end.'

'She's the mother of Lance's children and deserves to be warned at the very least.'

'Sometimes you are too noble for you own good.'

'And why I won't be telling Amy about Austen Walsh.'

'I suppose I should thank you.'

'I suppose you should.'

'But it's only a stay of execution, isn't it?'

I couldn't make a promise I wasn't going to keep. Conscience wouldn't allow it. 'First,' I answered evasively, 'we need to nail down the Lorenzo connection.'

'Agreed.'

'How soon can you be at mine?'

'A couple of hours?'

'I'll call Amy,' I said.

* * *

The strain attached to single motherhood with three children under six was gradually breaking Amy into lots of tiny pieces. Everything she tried to do, big or small, to keep things ticking and running smoothly, was doomed to failure. In a stroke of inspiration, she'd bought a brand new Igglepiggle to supplant the old smelly one.

'Don't want it,' Wilf had cried — and boy, could he cry.

'But this one's lovely.' It's not coated in snot and dirt for a start.

Wilf sniffed at it suspiciously and flung it back at her. 'Want my old Piggle.'

Forced to pluck out the original toy from the bin, where it had briefly resided with an empty tin of tuna and last night's leftover meat pie, she had handed it to a delighted Wilf and gone and wept outside with a glass of cheap white wine.

Apart from all her domestic woes, and maybe because of them, she was paranoid. A custard-coloured car, with high sides that resembled a disabled vehicle, had followed her to work the day before, had popped out of nowhere as she'd driven to school pick-up and, she swore, had crawled past her home that evening. With tinted windows, the driver was obscured from view. The bad men after Rollo did not seem the type to drive a Suzuki Wagon R so her fear was unwarranted and purely symptomatic of the pressure she was under.

Still it troubled her.

So Saturday, a day she normally enjoyed with her children, she'd resorted to taking them to a play centre where the noise levels could break the sound barrier and there was always one horrible kid cutting his bullyboy teeth by pushing around the little ones.

Tana and Wilf were evidently enjoying themselves while she nursed an unpleasant tasting coffee, an unpleasant smelling Igglepiggle and, in second place in the stink department, baby Adele who Amy juggled on her lap.

Rollo's silence haunted her. Not given to premonitions, unlike her mum who saw disaster everywhere, she had a really bad feeling that something awful had happened. There were all those horrible people on Rollo's back and out to get him. Susannah claimed she hadn't seen him. Well, she would, wouldn't she? It could be a smokescreen. Bloody hell, what if *she'd* bumped him off? Susannah had every reason to want to get rid of him. Maybe that way she could get her home back. Not much the woman could do about her pride though, Amy thought, chucking Adele under the chin. And who was she to talk? Humiliation burnt through Amy's veins like fresh lemon juice on an open wound.

Her phone rang. She glanced at the number. 'Talk of the devil,' she muttered aloud.

'Have you found him because, if you have, tell him to bugger off.' Amy still had some self-respect.

'There's been a complication,' Susannah said.

Oh my Christ, Amy thought, crumpling inside. 'How, when, is he dead?' Amy blurted out. Thank goodness the kids couldn't hear.

'What makes you say that?'

Amy stood up and walked away from the crucible of noise. 'Say again.'

Susannah repeated the question.

'Stands to reason, doesn't it? Why else would he disappear off the face of the earth.'

Susannah fell quiet. She bloody knows something I don't, Amy thought. 'Hello, you still there?'

'You could be right,' Susannah said. It's why I'm phoning.'

Amy's vision briefly blurred. She clutched Adele so tightly the little mite let out a squeak.

'Amy, can you come to mine?'

'Your house? I thought you didn't have a roof over your head.'

'I'll explain later.'

Fishier by the second, Amy thought. She glanced at her children. Wilf was careering down a slide with an ear-piercing shriek. Tana was pulling another little girl's pigtail and making her cry.

'You want me to come now?'

'Yes.'

'I've got the kids. My mum is away. I can't . . .'

'Bring them with you.'

A rumbling noise from Adele alerted Amy her baby needed an urgent nappy change. 'If you're sure,' she said uncertainly.

'I'm sure,' Susannah said, ending the call.

Amy rounded up her children, wondering where would be the best place to quickly change Adele.

* * *

Rocked by Susannah's revelations, Chantal had made herself a cup of soothing camomile tea and retreated to her office.

She'd been so angry at Lance that, when she'd wished him dead, she'd meant it. His actions had coloured her post-divorce life in dark greys and browns and he had put their daughter at risk. But the thought of him murdered — for that was the language in which they were talking — horrified her.

As soon as Susannah mentioned "pharmaceutical" in relation to Lorenzo's business interests, she immediately thought *drugs*, followed by *organised crime*. Then she thought about extortion, kidnap and torture, and how her daughter had fallen victim. Was Lorenzo Bonetti who he said he was?

Chantal had been doing business in Milan for a number of years and had never knowingly come up against the Italian Mafia, although she was certain that it had touched her. Sometimes, it would be a fast change of subject, a name dropped into a conversation in hushed tones, and the suggestion that it would be better if that name were never openly referred to again. Sitting outside a café watching the world go by, she had seen certain types of men who she'd instinctively recognised were members of a particular syndicate. They were thin, stocky, large, slight, good-looking, ugly, tattooed, clean-skinned, sunglasses on, sunglasses off, all different yet distinguishable by the way in which they carried themselves, how they walked, talked, breathed and inhabited and dominated the air around them. Many were Italian, although Albanians had moved into Milan, as they had in other major cities in Europe, and their methods were equally ruthless and violent.

Susannah had told her that Lorenzo lived in Matera. She checked it out on her laptop and discovered a beautiful ancient city that had begun life as a complex of caves. Densely packed yellow-stoned houses, which would not look out of place in the Cotswolds and an instant draw for tourists, would also provide the perfect environment in which to lay low. But Salerno, where Bonetti also claimed to have a property in which one of his wives lived, was what caught Chantal's eye. Home to a single Italian criminal organisation deemed clannish and particularly brutal, it had connections to a "brother" organisation in the U.S., specifically Florida. Was it coincidence that Veldo's HQ was also in Florida?

She leant back in her seat, stretched her arms above her head and clicked her neck. She'd only grabbed a few hours of nervous and fractured sleep the night before. The likelihood of a better night any time soon seemed elusive. If Chantal was right, Susannah had bigger problems than either of them had ever dreamt of. Information like that couldn't wait. Chantal phoned Susannah straightaway.

CHAPTER THIRTY-SIX

Rain spat on the roof and crackled against the windows. It sounded as if the house were on fire. In a way, it was.

I listened to Chantal in a frozen daze. It's one thing to entertain unpleasant thoughts, another to have them confirmed by a woman who was no fool.

'Extortion runs through these people like a seam of quartz in a mine,' Chantal said.

Was Lorenzo one of *these people*?

'Classic moves straight out of the Mafia manual,' Chantal continued.

Keen to put a reasonable and opposing point of view, I said, 'Not every Italian is involved in organised crime. It's like saying every Irish person is in the IRA.'

'You know fine well what I mean. I'd wager Bonetti is a connected man. Check out the Florida association and tell me what you think.'

I didn't need to. It added up. My head hurt. My heart ached. Chantal was right. If Lance didn't contact one of us soon, it didn't look good for him. I could lay no claim to moral superiority; my mother was right in so far as the fault was mine for first involving myself with a man like Lorenzo Bonetti. My next crime was to deny that my son was his, an act so heinous in Lorenzo's eyes he'd decided to take apart the fabric of my existence. What did Lorenzo really want? Was his only interest in his son, Frankie? Was I superfluous, or destined to be part of the package? *I never found the right woman*, Lorenzo had said, gazing at me with desire. A fake act, or did he really mean it? If in Lorenzo's twisted head, he regarded me as material for wife number three, would he seek to further avenge my reputation by going after Amy and her children too? I wasn't up to speed on vendettas and codes of honour and the way in which people in the Mafia and organised crime behaved.

If ...

'Can we talk about this later? I need to think.'

'Sure, I'll bring booze.'

No matter what he'd done, I couldn't imagine Lance out of my life completely. Returning in one piece, as I prayed he would, was the only hope I had. I'd be happy to be wrong about Lorenzo's baser ambitions.

Eager for distraction, I sliced up fresh fruit; made sandwiches, found a variety pack of crisps for the children to eat while the grown-ups talked. And this was as grown-up as life got.

Amy arrived first with a jolly-looking baby in her arms that instantly melted my heart. At each side, a little girl who was definitely her mother's daughter, and a little boy whose resemblance to Lance was so striking it made me want to weep. Viewing me with curiosity, he clutched a dirty blue-coloured teddy with googly eyes. I crouched down to the little boy's level and said, 'Hello.'

He turned away shyly and buried his face in his mother's skirt.

'Wilf, don't be silly,' Amy said.

'It's okay. He doesn't know me,' I said.

The girl was bolder. 'My name's Tana,' she announced. 'Do you have a TV?'

Amy cast me an apologetic look. 'Don't be rude, Tana. We haven't come to Mrs Stratton's home for you to watch the telly.'

'They can if they like,' I said. 'I've made snacks for them.'
I lowered my voice. 'It might make it easier to talk.'

Amy bit her lip. 'As long as you're sure.' Her anxiety
was plain. She obviously thought her children were going to
wreck my home. Stupid really, my home had been destroyed
a long time ago. My perfect blended family, of which I'd been
so foolishly proud, had been put through a meat grinder.

I led the way to the sitting room where Wilf threw himself onto the sofa, scampered up the back and threw himself
onto the carpet, narrowly missing a coffee table.

'Wilf, behave and stop showing off,' Amy hollered. 'Any
more of that and I'll put you in the car and take you home.'

Red-faced, the little boy's bottom lip quivered. I thought
he was going to burst into tears. I wanted to scoop him up
and tell him it was okay. Except so much was not okay and
it would be a lie.

'Do you like picnics?' I asked Wilf. He nodded, big-eyed.

'Come and help me then.' I held out my hand and,
amazingly, he took it.

'Can I help?' Tana asked.

'Course you can.'

'Can I hold your hand too?'

I looked to Amy. I didn't want her thinking I was taking
over.

'No, you carry on,' she said, bemused. She had Adele on
her hip and pulled a face at her that made the baby chuckle.

The children and me found a tablecloth and Tana
helped spread it out on the carpet in front of the TV. We set
down plates of food and put Wilf in charge of crisps.

'My favourite is smoky bacon.' He selected several
packets.

'That's my son's favourite too,' I told him.

Wilf's gaze searched the room. 'Can I play with him?'

'He's not here today. Maybe some other time.' It
would be a while before Frankie came around to the idea of
acknowledging his stepsiblings' existence.

'My daddy plays with me,' Wilf said solemnly.

I caught my breath. A terrible tug of pain dragged apart my heart. 'I know, darling,' I murmured.

Tana put her arm around her little brother's shoulder. 'He'll be home soon,' she said trustingly. Then, darting away, she inspected every corner, touching surfaces, picking up ornaments and putting them back down.

'Stop that,' Amy said.

The doorbell rang. I turned towards the window to see Chantal slack-jawed at what she obviously perceived was a crèche, and brandishing a bottle of wine in each hand.

'Who's that?' Amy asked.

'Lance's ex-wife, Chantal. Door's on the latch,' I called to her.

'Bloody hell,' Amy exclaimed. 'Doesn't anyone have a normal name around here? Can things get any weirder?'

You don't know about Lorenzo yet, I thought.

Half an hour later, Amy knew all about him and more.

* * *

'Bloody hell, am I in danger?' With each new revelation, Amy had become more agitated. 'So let me get this straight, this man, who you had a child with before you married, is in the Mafia and gunning for Rollo — sorry but that's who he is to me — all because you never told him about his kid?'

'Succinctly put,' Chantal said.

Up until then, they'd danced around each other like a couple of drunks squaring up and wondering who was going to throw the first punch.

'We don't have cast-iron evidence that Lorenzo is involved in organised crime, but we can't exclude the possibility.' I winced at the prim note in my voice. Who was I kidding? Obviously not Chantal, who stared straight though me as if I were sheet glass.

'How much evidence do you need?' Chantal informed Amy of every connection we'd uncovered by counting them off on her fingers.

'Isn't that what they call circum-something,' Amy said, frowning.

'Circumstantial,' I chipped in.

'That's the one.'

'You think?' Chantal said.

Amy bit down on her bottom teeth, opened her mouth to speak and stalled. 'Although . . .'

'Spit it out,' Chantal said.

'I think I'm being followed.' She explained about a strange car.

'A Wagon R?' I said.

'Are you serious?' Chantal burst out, unimpressed.

'No, I made it up for a laugh,' Amy retorted, stony-faced.

I shared Chantal's cynicism, although Amy seemed peculiarly certain.

'One way to find out,' Amy said. 'Go and talk to this Lorenzo character and find out.'

'Would you go and talk to a Mafia hood and ask him whether he drives a motor used by geriatrics?' Chantal was already halfway down her second glass. I was drinking more modestly and Amy, very sensibly, wasn't drinking at all.

'I bloody would if I didn't have three kiddies depending on me. Pay him a visit.'

'I can't. Lorenzo has returned to Italy,' I said.

'You've got a phone, haven't you?'

'I've tried calling him, Amy. He's not answering.'

'See,' Chantal said.

Amy ignored her. 'So this is the only theory you've come up with?'

'There have been others,' I said, 'but nothing that sticks.'

'Like what?'

Chantal eyed me in a way I didn't care for.

'We all have reasons to want Lance to disappear,' I said.

'*I* bloody don't,' Amy said hotly.

'Not my style either,' Chantal said. 'If anyone has a solid reason, it's you.'

'*Me?*' I said.

Two pairs of eyes, not including Adele's, fastened on mine.

'That's ludicrous.'

'Is it?' Chantal said. 'Getting us all together for a girlie chat, it's a pure piece of theatre.'

'And we don't know this Lorenzo character,' Amy chimed in. 'We've only got your word.'

'Chantal,' I said, appealing to her. 'You saw him.'

'I saw a man who you told me is called Lorenzo. It could have been anyone.'

'Well, it wasn't.' Feeling thoroughly got at, I took a large gulp of wine and wished they'd both go home.

An uneasy silence descended like a thick black curtain. I needed to get ahead of the conversation before it trampled me underfoot and stampeded out of the door. 'Let's roll it back,' I said. 'Lance has taken each of us for fools. He's weak and foolish but, whatever I think of him, I wish him no harm. I'm sure you feel the same,' I said looking from Amy to Chantal.

'Lance has the superficiality of a stretch limo,' Chantal said with a shrug, 'but he's still my child's father.'

'Same,' Amy agreed. 'And he's been nothing but golden to me and the kids.'

'One way or another, wherever it leads, we find him. The police can't help and will only make things worse.' I caught Chantal's eye. I could tell she approved of leaving the law out of it. 'If we want to know how this all kicked off and whether Lorenzo is in on it, I say we pick up one of the Mount brothers.'

'As in apprehend?' Chantal asked.

'Yes,' I replied.

'Are you out of your mind?' Amy said.

Quite possibly, I thought. 'We interrogate Jack or Marcus and find out who he works for,' I continued. 'We get him to confirm or deny whether or not Lorenzo Bonetti gave him orders to rip our lives apart.'

'That will be a piece of cake,' Chantal said dryly.

Amy looked from Chantal to me, stupefied.

'It's not so crazy,' I said. 'We know where they hang out.'

'So what?' Amy said hotly. 'Have you forgotten what they did?'

'That's *why* it needs to be done. Think about it, neither of them will see us coming.'

'Susannah has a point,' Chantal said, seemingly warming to the idea.

Encouraged, I said, 'We lay a trap. They don't know you, Amy, so you can act as decoy.'

'Oh can I?' Her tone suggested she wasn't sold on the idea.

'We'd only need you to drive the car, slow down and ask for directions.'

'And what are you two doing while I'm putting my life on the line?'

'We rush one of them.'

'Off the street, in broad daylight?'

'It would spring a greater element of surprise.' I looked at Chantal. 'You've done self-defence, haven't you?'

Amy's expression suggested I'd grown another head. 'What's got into you?'

'Hear me out. I can get hold of powerful anaesthesia from the surgery.'

'Isn't that illegal?'

'My thoughts precisely.' Chantal hit me with a wily expression. I bet she was considering whether one illegal act cancelled out another.

'So is extortion.' I was still bruised after they'd each suggested I might have killed Lance.

'It's gone dead quiet,' Amy said hastily. Think I'll go and check on my children.'

Chantal's gaze followed Amy to the door. She jerked her head in Amy's direction. 'She's not what I imagined.'

'What did you imagine?'

'Someone with more class.'

'Bitch,' I said.

'As for your crackpot and totally illegal suggestion, you can forget it.'

I had to admit I was disappointed. I thought Chantal was up for it. 'Then what do you propose we do?'

'They're all right,' Amy said, bowling back in. 'Wilf's fallen asleep. What have I missed?'

'Nothing,' Chantal said.

I drummed my fingers on the worktop. Maybe a crackpot idea was all we had. 'Lance isn't coming back. You know it,' I said, looking at Chantal, 'and Amy knows it.'

'That's as maybe,' Amy said, flashing angrily, 'but I haven't driven all this way so you can offload your messy personal life and involve me in something criminal. What are you trying to do — get us all banged up?'

'That's not it at all,' I said evenly, 'I invited you because I thought you should be included.'

'Then I'll make it really simple. Consider me un-included.' With which Amy swept out and shook Wilf awake.

'Please don't go,' I said, trailing along behind her. 'Forget my idea. I only want what's best to protect us all. Truly.'

Involved in a tug of war with Tana, Amy hissed and cursed. 'You know what?' she said, turning on me. 'My mum was right about you people. You're all half-cracked.'

I stood aside and watched as Amy bundled the children into her car and strapped them in under protest. She threw herself behind the steering wheel, reversed fast off the drive, almost over my feet, tyres chewing up gravel, and drove away without another word.

Back in the kitchen, Chantal was gathering her things. 'I take it all back about Amy,' she said. 'That was one hell of a classy move.'

CHAPTER THIRTY-SEVEN

Embarrassed and mildly tipsy, I cursed my stupidity for suggesting what was essentially a kidnap mission. Chantal was right to question my sanity. I didn't blame Amy for storming out. In similar shoes I'd have done the same.

Dispirited and alone, I cleared away plates of uneaten and partially chewed-up food and chucked the leftovers in the bin. A grated cheese sandwich took some prising out from between the cushions of a sofa. Something sticky had stained the carpet in the sitting room and grubby fingers had left marks on the windows. It took me back to when Frankie and Coco were little. Happy, carefree, laughter-filled days that I thought would never end. It was sobering to think of Amy's children missing their daddy so very much.

About to wash up glasses in the sink, I heard the front door swing open, followed by footsteps. *Lance*, I thought wildly. Spirits lifting. Relief seeping. Anger, for scaring and giving us the run-around, dissipating. Retribution for what my husband had done, in the past and in the present, could wait.

Relieved and with a smile on my face, I turned as Marcus Mount exploded into the kitchen and grabbed me around the throat.

Wild-eyed, any pretence of a cultured veneer gone, he raged, 'Where is he?'

My hands flew to his, trying to loosen the grip on my throat. 'Who?' I rasped.

'Don't fuck with me. *Lance.*'

'I don't know.' My fingernails dug into his flesh.

'Murderous bitch.' Screaming in my face, he bent me backwards over the sink.

I tried to bring my knee up to his groin, but there was no room to manoeuvre. Pain snapped through me as the edge of the granite worktop cut into my spine.

'I'll ask you one more time.' Saliva tripped down his chin, some of it flecked my cheek. His dilated pupils indicated he was hopped on cocaine, or rage, or both. The grip on my throat increased, the pressure intolerable. Scrabbling madly for something, anything, my fingers brushed against the corkscrew.

'I told you . . . I don't . . .'

With one sweep, I plunged the sharp tip into the side of Mount's head. Bellowing like a wounded bison felled by a poisoned arrow, his release was instantaneous and I sprinted towards the door to the hall. Tantalisingly close to safety, I felt a wiry arm snake around my waist. My head whiplashed as I was dragged backwards.

Mount had hold of my hair, strong fingers entwined in my curls, yanking them out by the roots. My scalp tore and I screamed at the top of my voice and thrashed out. It was no use. Stronger, more powerful and a man who knew what he was doing, I was no competition. Two deft punches to my kidneys left me in agony. Bile and alcohol shot from my gut to my throat.

'Stop,' I yelled. 'I don't know where he is.'

On a vicious roll, he slapped my face with the power and velocity of a runaway truck. My lip split, a tooth loosened and I tasted blood.

'It's true,' I wailed. 'I thought you'd taken him. I thought you'd killed him.'

Wordless, Mount pushed me to the sink. A strong hand gripped the back of my neck and plunged me headfirst into the soapy, dirty water. With no time to breathe in, I quickly ran out of air and choked. The more I pushed up he pushed down, his body a lead weight across my shoulders. Straining to wriggle out of his grasp, I inhaled and tasted washing-up liquid. My eyes stung and so did my skin. I couldn't breathe and then I panicked. When I believed I was done for, he pulled me up long enough for me to gulp and choke and take in a breath, maybe two, long enough for me to waste my energy on denial, long enough for me to experience sheer bright unadulterated terror. *Lie*, I thought, *tell him what he wants to hear.*

'I will tell . . .'

Except he wasn't listening.

Plunged back down, I held my breath until bubbles of air cascaded out of my mouth. I struggled as water entered my nose, my throat, marauding all over my body like an invading army. The more I resisted, the greater the pressure. My reflexes took over and I swallowed and coughed and choked and got nowhere. My head fizzed. My eyeballs popped. Starved of oxygen, my body felt as if it were a tributary of a polluted river, funnelling narrow then wide and joining the sea.

With cruel clarity, I understood that Marcus Mount wasn't interested in answers, no more than he was interested in me. He simply wanted me dead.

* * *

The odds were always going to be stacked against Amy, Chantal recognised. Older men were suckers for young and attractive females. It was no reflection on wives although every dumped wife she'd ever known interpreted it that way. It was connected to the call of the wild and the febrile search for that elusive spark of excitement that afflicts the middle-aged male. Get me a younger, more vibrant model and I, too, will seem younger and more desirable. It wasn't Susannah's fault and it wasn't Amy's either.

Chantal had barely got home when Coco phoned. As soon as she saw her daughter's number, she mentally prepared for at least an hour of emoting and whining. Yes, she would agree that Coco had had a nasty experience no person, let alone a young woman, should have to endure. Yes, Coco had reason to be very upset. But Coco had been expressing herself and complaining for most of her life. Spot the difference.

Gearing up to enquire about her daughter's wellbeing, Coco beat her to it.

'Have you seen the breaking news?'

Not the expected opening gambit, it could only mean one thing: Coco had discovered a new and outrageously expensive cosmetic to contain the years and forestall the aging process.

'What news?'

'The murder in Gloucester Road. I think it's at the address Daddy visited.'

Chantal almost walked into the dining room table. 'Have the police identified the victim?'

'Not yet.'

'And you're certain it's the same address?'

'Looks like it from the picture online.'

"Looks like" aptly summed up the modern world. People were prone to jump to "looks like" before realising that "looking" is not the same as "is". Even so, Chantal was deeply troubled.

'I hope it's one of those bastards who jumped me,' Coco said. 'Serve them fucking well right.'

Yes, but what if it wasn't? Chantal wondered nervously. 'Coco, you don't know it's one of those men.' She couldn't bring herself to suggest that it might be Lance. Whatever would her daughter do? How would she react? It didn't bear thinking about.

'Well, I hope it is and I hope it bloody hurt.'

An appalling sentiment delivered with passion, Chantal was mildly pleased to hear her daughter more like her old self. 'Have you told Susannah?'

'I thought Frankie should be the bearer of glad tidings. He's out on a ride at the moment. Think I should call her?'

'Don't do anything, Coco. I'll let her know.'

'You're sure?'

'Positive.'

Scooping up her keys, Chantal headed for the door. She could be there in minutes if she hurried.

* * *

Amy doubted that Chantal, a right piece of work, had anything but chipped ice in her bloodstream.

Fuming, Amy crawled through town, onto the A40 and was heading in the direction of the motorway when Wilf let out a bloodcurdling squeal.

'Igglepiggle. I want my Igglepiggle.'

Amy twisted around. 'Tana, love, can you see him?'

Tana leant forward as much as she could in her car seat. 'No, Mummy.'

'He must be there somewhere.' Amy viewed her daughter in the rear-view mirror. She was a good little girl. She'd find him. Amy told Wilf this. Not persuaded, Wilf kicked the back of the passenger seat and burst into tears.

Then Adele started to cry.

Quickly followed by an overwrought Tana, who'd never wanted to leave the house in the first place, and whose lungs rivalled the pair of them.

Amy very much feared that in her rush to escape the madhouse — for this was how she viewed it — Igglepiggle had been left behind.

'Stop crying!' She yelled so loudly a middle-aged woman in a Mercedes glared at her. *Piss off*, Amy mouthed, hoping the old bat could lip-read. Like any normal mother, she didn't like the sound of her children bawling their heads off.

It robbed her of logical thought. It upset her balance. But this time their tears felt like an expression of desperation that they all felt. Amy wanted to weep too.

Spotting a petrol station, she pulled onto the forecourt, hoping that this would appease her children. It didn't. They continued to howl lustily. If someone had put her head in a tumble dryer and turned it to maximum load, Amy couldn't feel worse.

Cutting the engine and stepping out, she flung open the rear door. Adele's chubby arms shot up. Wilf, puffy-eyed, snot hanging from his nose, continued to holler. Tana had cried so much dry sobs wracked her little body.

Christ, Amy thought, undoing the straps to her baby's car seat and picking the child up to soothe her. Amy rubbed her back and held her close until Adele quietened, then took a look inside the car. With one hand, Amy picked through baby blankets, empty crisp packets, juice cartons and discarded toys. Tana's tablet had run out of battery, she noticed, which made things a whole lot worse. Among the debris, no Igglepiggle.

Defeated, she raised her voice above the clamour. 'We'll go back to Susannah's. I expect we'll find him there.'

It was as if someone muted the sound. Tana and Wilf instantly stopped crying. They didn't let out *yippee*. They didn't need to. Amy could see it in their eyes.

* * *

I could see nothing, feel nothing but pain as my body, starved of oxygen, went into shutdown. Life drained out of me as surely as blood circling a drain. I was going back to where it all began, to darkness and nothingness and an absence of light.

And then the pressure released. I heard a scream as loud as a battle cry, and it wasn't mine.

Spewing soapy water and vomit onto the tiled kitchen floor, I collapsed into a puddle that soaked through my clothes. My throat felt as if it had been seared with a blow-torch. Blinking furiously, I gaped at the sight of Chantal on Mount's back, like a rodeo rider, her forearm locked around his neck, face contorted with fury. Mount thrashed, tried to unseat her and dashed her against the wall in an attempt to loosen her grip. Still she clung on. With her free hand, she repeatedly punched the wound to his head, from where I'd stabbed him with the corkscrew. I tried to get back up, but my legs defied the impulses from my brain. And then Mount appeared to slip, or was it a feint, I didn't know, but Chantal's grasp slipped too. Scared witless, I watched in horror as, with a tremendous shout, Chantal flew off and landed heavily next to the AGA.

* * *

Leave your ego outside the door, Chantal told herself. *You're down and not out and this bastard is still coming.*

Jumping up, she slapped him hard with straight fingers and then, bunched tight, with her fists. Trading blows, he dodged and jinked.

'Come on, Granny,' he goaded. 'Let's see what you got.'

Nothing more guaranteed to piss her off, Chantal followed up with strikes and punches, some wild and reckless, moving fast, limber on her feet, twisting and turning, a rush of adrenaline coursing through her like never before. It wouldn't last. He had one big advantage: youth. To put him down she had to act quickly and decisively.

She lifted a knee and thrust sideways, pivoting on her other foot for maximum power, and delivered a blow straight into his wall of abdominal muscle. Surprised, the man doubled over.

Seizing the advantage and fired up with righteous maternal rage — a fury she never knew existed — Chantal lashed out, striking at his temple. The man rocked but did not go down. Closing in, she hooked a foot around the back of his knee and tipped her opponent onto his backside. He went down with a satisfyingly painful bump. About to throw herself right across him, he levered himself up and sprang to his feet. Viewing her with heartless eyes, he came at her and she wasn't ready. As she tried to straighten up, he bent over, head down, and charged her. The impact was terrific, knocking the air clean out of her body. Her ribs felt crushed. Bile and booze shot to the back of her throat. Shoes slipping on the wet surface, she toppled onto one knee. Hauled up by the collar of her shirt, she managed to deliver two short smacks to his ears before he drew his head back. She read what was coming but was too incapacitated to prevent it as he whiplashed forward. Obliterating pain shot through from her forehead, reverberated around her skull, and zipped out through her ears. She felt sure her brain was bleeding.

Dizzy, she flailed like a puppet whose strings had been cut.

Mean on his face, the man grabbed her wrist with one hand and clamped his other around her throat, below her chin. His thumb and fingers sank into the skin, gripping her larynx, and squeezed tight. Stopped dead, she couldn't speak, couldn't swallow, couldn't breathe.

It wasn't supposed to be like this, she thought, flashes of silver light and black in front of her eyes. There was no safe word and even if there was she had no way to emit it. Her eyes felt heavy. A dark shadow stole over her. Noise next, like the sound of a bat on a cricket ball. Her trachea cracking and breaking, she believed. Christ, she was so sick of bastards like him.

CHAPTER THIRTY-EIGHT

'Oh, my good God,' Amy burst out.

Soaked through and panting, half of me bent over, I glanced up into her astounded eyes.

Sprawled on the bloodstained floor, Marcus Mount, out cold from where I'd clocked him with that most clichéd of kitchen utensils, a copper-bottomed frying pan. Chantal lay slumped against a dresser, knees to her chest, clutching her throat, and making strange noises. I went straight to her and crouched down. She grabbed my hand and mouthed, 'thank you'.

'What the fuck happened here?' Amy had gone quite pale. 'And who's he?' she asked, jerking her chin in the direction of Mount.

'Marcus Mount,' I answered. 'The man who hurt Coco.'

Chantal's eyes suddenly filled. I'd never seen her cry before, but two fat tears trickled down her cheeks. I slung an arm around her shoulder.

'I should be thanking you,' I told her. 'If you hadn't come back, I'd be dead.'

Amy toed Mount's prone figure with the tip of her shoe, as if she were pushing away a dog turd. 'He's not croaked, has he?'

'More's the pity,' Chantal rasped.

'We ought to put him in the recovery position,' I said.

'Here, I'll do it,' Amy said. 'Did a first aid course when I had the kids.'

I watched as Amy placed Marcus Mount's nearest arm at a right angle and the back of his other hand to his chest. Bending his farthest knee, she grasped that leg and rolled him gently onto his side.

Satisfied that his airways were open, Amy stood up. 'We ought to call 999.'

'No,' Chantal said.

'Not yet,' I said.

'He's got a right belter,' Amy said, viewing the pair of us as if we were serial killers. 'What if he's fractured his skull?'

'We'll find out when he comes round,' I said. 'Probably just concussed.'

'But what the hell are you going to do with him?' Amy's high-pitched voice implied: *don't include me in this mess.*

'Tie him up and question him.' A week ago I'd never have uttered those words. Now it seemed the most logical course of action.

Chantal struggled to get to her feet. Her neck was a mess of welts and bruises. Amy grabbed an elbow and helped her up.

'Thanks,' Chantal said. 'What are you doing here anyway? Thought you'd had enough of us.'

'I came back for Wilf's toy.'

'It's probably in the sitting room.' It felt surreal to be talking about something mundane while a dangerous man lay out for the count in front of me.

'I'll run and find it. I've got the kids in the car,' Amy added, eager to escape. 'Is it all right if . . .' she began. 'You know if . . .'

'Go,' I said. 'This has nothing to do with you. Be with your children.'

'Are you sure?' Her voice was uncertain. Her eyes were bright with relief.

'Absolutely.'

I tore outside to the garden shed, where Lance kept cable ties. Between Chantal and me, we secured Mount's hands and feet.

'We can't keep him here,' Chantal said. 'Basement?'

Sometimes I forgot that this had once been Chantal's home. We now used the lower ground floor to store wine, valuables and stuff normally kept in an attic. Its biggest advantage it had a door with a lock.

'Think we can lift him?'

Amy popped her head round. The colour in her cheeks had not improved. 'You're moving him? Seriously?'

'Seriously we are.' What we did with him afterwards, I hadn't thought through. It was like shifting a sedated and highly dangerous animal. Who knew how Marcus Mount would react when he came round?

'I'll leave you to it then.' Amy didn't move an inch.

'Well, go on then.' Chantal made a shooing gesture with her fingers.

'You'll let me know,' Amy said, still not moving.

'We will,' I said. 'Go before the kids destroy your car.'

As soon as she left I locked eyes with Chantal's. 'Ready?'

'As I'll ever be.'

Somehow, by sheer will, we dragged and half-pushed Mount towards the top of the stairs descending to the basement level. This was the easy bit. Getting him down would be harder.

'Think of him as a roll of heavy carpet,' Chantal said, sweat coating her forehead. 'You get his feet. I'll grab his shoulders.'

Step by step, bump-by-bump, we lugged Mount down, sat him on an old garden chair and, unearthing a length of rope from a pile of random junk, secured him to it.

Head slumped, blood on the collar of his expensively tailored shirt, drool oozing down his chin; he looked a lot less fearsome. *Karma*, I thought. Marcus Mount was having a taste of what he'd put Coco through.

Checking his pulse, which was not as erratic as expected, I went upstairs, followed by Chantal who locked the door behind us.

I went straight to the drinks cabinet and poured out two separate measures of brandy and handed a glass to Chantal. The threat of imminent death had had a sobering effect and I drank mine down in one go in a bid to slow the adrenaline in my system and control an alarming attack of the shakes. Chantal knocked hers back and eyed me.

'There's been a death in Gloucester Road.'

'What? How? When?'

'I don't have the detail. Coco called and told me and I thought you should know. Hence why I'm here.'

'Good God, Marcus was looking for Lance.'

'*Lance?*'

And then I tumbled to it. 'Goodness, do you think the body in the house is Jack Mount?'

'And Marcus believed Lance killed his brother?'

'That's my guess.'

'And what do you think?' Chantal asked.

I felt as if I'd swallowed bleach along with the washing-up water. I didn't know if Lance was capable of murder, but weren't we all if pushed far enough? 'He had the motive and was desperate enough.'

'It would explain how the deeds wound up here, in your name. It would explain him going to ground.'

'You think Lance killed Jack Mount so he didn't have to transfer the property?'

'It makes sense.'

'But seriously, Chantal, is Lance really capable of murder?'

Fear swam in her eyes. I intuited what she was thinking. By accident, Lance had already crossed the great divide by killing a man. Was it such a stretch for him to take out his frustration and anger on Jack Mount and murder him? Had Lance deliberately left his passport and wallet for someone like me to find to make it look as if he'd come to harm? He still had his driving licence, I remembered. Yet I didn't think him that cunning. *You never imagined another life either.*

'I guess it puts Lorenzo in the clear,' Chantal said, reluctant to admit a mistake had been made.

'We'll know for certain when we question Mount.'

'How long before he comes round?'

I glanced at my watch. 'About now.'

'I say we leave him to stew a while longer.'

'I definitely need a change of clothes,' I said.

'I'll clear up the kitchen.' A subtle smile stole across Chantal's lips. 'How do you want to play it with Marcus?'

'No holding back,' I said darkly.

CHAPTER THIRTY-NINE

'Your pathetic fuck of a husband killed my brother.'

Bruised and confused, Mount had spent the opening minutes of his waking existence cursing, berating and accusing.

'You saw Lance do it?' I asked.

'If I had, do you think I'd be here now?' Mount snarled, straining against the rope.

'So how do you know?'

'I *know.*'

'When did it happen?'

'Jack stopped answering his calls last night. I'd been away for a couple of days and he was dead when I got back this morning.'

'How was your brother killed?'

'Stabbed.'

'Where? How many times?'

Chantal shot me a nervous look. Location and number were important, I reckoned. Mount stared at me. 'I wasn't counting,' he said belligerently.

I opened my mouth to push it. Chantal snuck in first. 'Why would Lance murder your brother?'

Contempt tilted Marcus Mount's lips. 'Why do you think, bitch? Didn't like our terms of business.'

'And I don't like your attitude,' I said, 'so you can cut the crap and tell me who's in charge.'

'I am.'

'Doesn't look much like it to me.' Chantal caught my eye. 'I'd say we call the shots right now.'

Mount pushed again against his restraints, muttering furiously under his breath. 'You can't keep me here.'

'Says who?' I said.

'Let's start over,' Chantal said. 'You know who I am, right? The mother of the girl you abducted.'

Mount's expression wavered. 'So what? We let her go.'

'Then you're dumber than you look.'

'And we don't play dumb and we're not of a forgiving nature,' I said. 'You can rot away here for all we care.'

Mount was not a stupid man despite the blow to his head. His expression told me that he sensed he was up against a force that was unique: the collective rage of women against injustice, violence and a casual disregard for decent behaviour. He shifted uncomfortably in his seat. With the cocky attitude dialled down, he was simply another weak man caught in the act and in a precarious situation.

'I can't tell you who I work for because I don't know.'

'So you're not in charge?' I said.

Mount glanced at the wall then let his gaze fall on me. 'If I tell you they'll kill me.'

'Who are they?'

Mount clamped his lips together and shook his head, which must have hurt.

'We know about the Florida connection and its link to organised crime,' Chantal said.

Mount's eyes gave him away first. He thrust his head forward. His lips tightened into a slit. His breathing increased. Ankles, tied together, could not prevent his feet from flexing.

'Was extorting our family their idea, or a job you worked off the books?' I asked.

'Off the books,' Mount stammered. *Lying*, I thought.

'You picked on Lance for no good reason other than you randomly looked up his company on the internet and thought he was good for the money, is that right?'

'Yes, yes . . .'

'Do you know a man called Lorenzo Bonetti?'

On more certain ground and obviously pleased he didn't recognise the name, Mount regained an element of composure. 'Never heard of him, never crossed paths with him.'

I thought I'd collapse with relief. Lorenzo wasn't involved and he didn't kill anyone. Thank God. 'What about Milton?'

'Who's Milton?' Chantal asked.

'The man who approached Lance about the loan,' I informed her.

I turned my gaze on Mount who appeared to be having an internal conversation. *How much to say? How little he could get away with and who to drop in the dirt without any comeback?*

'Milton Bruno,' Mount mumbled.

'Bruno?' Chantal repeated.

'It was all his idea,' Mount said.

'What's your connection to Bruno?'

'We . . . I carry out occasional jobs for him.'

'You mean extortion, shake-downs, that kind of thing?' Chantal said, cold-eyed.

'Sometimes, sometimes not,' Mount replied, evasive.

'And Milton Bruno, what nationality is he?' I asked.

'American.'

'With connections to organised crime in Florida, right?'

Mount hung his head in a way so similar to Lance it made me flinch.

Sound from upstairs alerted me to my phone. Chantal's expression told me that she was happy for me to leave and answer it. Taking the steps to the ground level, I couldn't rule out the possibility that she had an ulterior motive for me to disappear. Snatching up my mobile, my mouth dried when I saw the number. Deep breath and smile, I thought, don't let him recognise the state I'm in.

'Lorenzo,' I said.

'Susannah, I'm so sorry I missed your calls. I visited my daughter and stupidly left my phone there. I've literally just received your messages. Is everything okay?'

'Fine,' I lied. 'Where are you?'

'Back in Cheltenham.'

'Usual place?'

'Same room.' His voice was warm and effusive.

'Are you free, Lorenzo?'

'How about English tea in my room at four?'

'That would work well.'

'I'm so looking forward to it.'

CHAPTER FORTY

'Are you sure about this?' Chantal asked.

We were in my bedroom. I'd showered, washed and dried my hair, and changed into a loose-fitting shirt and jeans.

'I need answers,' I told her simply.

'And so will he.'

'About Frankie?'

'Exactly.' Which wasn't the whole truth.

My sin was one of omission. As for Lorenzo, I wasn't sure how far his sins stretched.

'What do we do about Mount?' We'd left him bellowing the house down and locked him in the basement where his cries could not be heard so easily. Despite his crimes, we couldn't abandon him.

'I'll think of something,' Chantal said.

'That's what bothers me.' My grim grin made her laugh. A rare moment of humour between us lightened the crushing mood.

'Don't do anything drastic until I get back,' I warned her.

'How long will you be, or put another way, how long before I send out a search party?'

'The search party that consists of one?'

Chantal's smile was thin. 'I think we can safely say Amy is officially excluded. God, did you see her face?'

'Poor woman.' I tipped my head and smiled. 'Despite what you said earlier, I do believe you have a soft spot for her.'

'I wouldn't go that far.' Chantal viewed me with rare affection. 'Are we good?'

Did one worthy deed deserve another? Without doubt, Chantal had saved my life. I pushed aside her involvement in the hit and run until I had more mental space to deal with it. 'We're good,' I said. Returning to my visit to Lorenzo, I said, 'Give me no more than a couple of hours.'

'Then what?'

'Call the police and ask for PC Matthew Forester.'

* * *

Like a small animal caught in a trap, my heart flailed as I set off across town. I didn't walk. I drove.

The sky was heavy with cloud, grey and gloomy, with no sign of rain, or sun. How differently I felt to when I'd last gone to meet Lorenzo: excited, a little guilty and rippling with anticipation. This time, I was afraid. Fear was good. Fear kept you sharp. Until now, it had almost destroyed me, robbed me of clear thought. That time had passed.

I slipped into a parking space along the Promenade and put a couple of hours on the meter. Trance music was hammering out of 131, a hotel and restaurant on the Prom. The tribal beat thudded in synch with my pulse rate as I walked the short distance to the hotel.

I entered through the revolving door of the Queens, gave a nod to a receptionist and took the stairs. Reaching the corridor, I slowed. Reaching the room, I stopped. This was it. No going back. No place for me to hide — from Lorenzo, or from the truth. Marcus Mount showed no recognition when Lorenzo's name was mentioned, and yet my old lover's reappearance in my life was too coincidental and not without complication and deceit. Crossing the threshold I would get answers I didn't want to hear, that might put my life in greater jeopardy, but ask them I would. I had to uncover and unpick the poisonous web woven so tightly around Lance and me and, by default, Frankie and Coco.

I tapped lightly at the door. Lorenzo opened it and met my cool expression with a smile I knew so well because it belonged to Frankie too.

He kissed me warmly on both cheeks; the stiffness in his manner on the phone at our last goodbye, missing.

An incredibly English scene awaited me. On a small table a tray of tea, cakes, and scones served with butter, cream and jam. I realised I'd not eaten for many hours. My stomach gave an involuntary groan.

'May I take your jacket?' Lorenzo said.

'I'll keep it on, if you don't mind. I'm a little chilly.'

He pushed a smile and invited me to take a seat. I sat; it felt quite formal, as if we were sounding out each other, which we were. Lorenzo turned his dark assessing eyes on mine. I dived straight in.

'You visited my mother, didn't you?'

Lorenzo sighed. 'I did, Susannah — a very long time ago.'

'Funny, she told me you'd seen her more recently.'

He nodded, calibrating the information, plotting his next move. Before he had a chance to make it, I said, 'You found out Frankie is our son.'

'That is true.'

'You've always known.'

'And so have you and when you had so many opportunities to tell me.'

'I didn't for good reason,' I countered. 'The time wasn't right.'

Lorenzo's slow smile corrupted his good looks. When he spoke it was in scathing tones. 'With you, Susannah, the time would never be right. You took our child, *my son*. Is it so wrong to want to reconnect with my boy?'

'He's not your boy.'

285

Had I slapped Lorenzo's face, he couldn't have expressed more annoyance. And then he slammed me with it. 'Have you any idea of the sacrifices I made to find you all those years ago? I had no money and yet I came back for you. I could barely speak the language and I made the trip anyway. I prostrated myself in front of your mother and was told that you were fine without me.'

'Lorenzo, I . . .'

'There has never been anyone else.'

'I'm so sorry.' I truly was.

His voice accelerated. 'Every year, I wrote a letter, every year for twenty years. You never answered, not even once.'

'What? Because I didn't receive them.'

'I don't believe you. Your mother swore on your life she'd passed them on.'

How could I explain that my life was worth very little to her? 'I promise you she didn't.'

His gaze stripped me naked. Terrible realisation dawned. Whatever Lorenzo felt for me, it wasn't love: it was obsession. And Lance was an impediment in Lorenzo's fantasy. He was the flaw in Lorenzo's narrative. With Lance out of the way I was free for Lorenzo to turn his dream into reality.

'Lance is missing and has been for days,' I blurted out.

'I see.'

I said nothing. My expectant gaze said it all. 'What?' he said. 'You think I have something to do with his disappearance?'

'Do you?'

'Susannah,' Lorenzo said, a tsk-tsk in his voice. 'I would never hurt your husband in that way.'

I viewed him squarely. 'Then in what way would you hurt him?'

He pursed his lips, tilted his head, grudging concern in his eyes. 'I see you are very upset.'

At the patronising note in his voice, so reminiscent of my mum, I bridled.

'Did you think that by getting rid of Lance, you could recreate a bond between us?' I demanded. 'That you could have the son you'd always longed for?' Perspiration coated the back of my neck, underneath my arms, along my hairline. 'Lance was an obstacle in your eyes. What have you done to him?' I didn't shout. Quiet and cold carried more weight.

'I haven't *done* anything.'

I went on a different tack. 'Are you really in pharmaceuticals, or is it a coded way of saying you're in the drugs business?'

Lorenzo's lips tightened. 'My business is none of your concern.'

'But Lance is.'

Gaze slip-sliding away, he poured tea into two fine china cups, added a splash of milk in each. Buying thinking time. There was no comfort in the silence. I took a tissue from my pocket and dabbed at my face, praying to God the heat would subside and pass.

'Lorenzo,' I said softly. 'I need to know.' Whatever it was, I'd come for the truth and I wasn't leaving until I had it.

'All right,' he said. 'I will tell you, though why you are so concerned about a man who cheats on you, who has children with another woman, it's . . .' he struggled to find the right word, 'perverse.'

And Lance's duplicity had played right into Lorenzo's hands. My concern for Lance was as great as my guilt for what I'd instigated. If I'd never met and fallen for Lorenzo, never treated him badly and followed my own instincts instead of taking my mother's advice, none of this would have happened. I held my breath, almost too afraid to listen.

'It is true that I came for my son,' Lorenzo continued, 'but I also came for you.'

Rocked by the darkness in his expression, I opened my mouth to protest. Lorenzo cut me off. 'I love you. I always have and I can make you happy, Susannah, if you will only allow it. As for your husband, I swear on my daughters' and my mother's lives, I have not physically hurt him.'

Not *physically*. Then I knew for certain what I'd only suspected. 'You were behind the attacks on his business.'

'I saw an opportunity and took it.' He held my gaze in his cold eyes.

My pulse pounded. 'You work with Milton Bruno?'

'He is an associate, yes.'

'And he approached Lance and instructed Veldo and the Mount Brothers to terrorise us.'

Lorenzo flicked a fleck of dust from his trousers, as if it were of no consequence, an everyday occurrence, and an intrinsic part of his line of business. Nausea consumed me.

'All the time I poured out my heart to you, you sat there and sympathised and yet *you* set it up.' And set Lance up in the process.

'I was not responsible for the extreme methods employed by the Mounts.' He might as well have said *nothing to do with me*. 'I admit they went too far with your stepdaughter.'

'You knew what they were capable of.'

'As I've already said their behaviour was not acceptable.'

'Not *acceptable*? We're not talking about a slip-up at work. You claim to love me. You say you want to make me happy . . .'

'All of it is true,' he said fervently.

'And yet *you* instigated a terror campaign. *You* stripped me of all that I own. *You* hurt our son. *You* reduced me to a wreck so that I would come running; was *that* acceptable? How the hell else did you think your nasty little plan would turn out?' My voice soared and roared. His weary expression told me that I was simply another woman emoting and full of histrionics and that, with enough flattery and declarations, I would see reason. Ultimately, that I would love him again.

Lorenzo spoke quietly through his teeth. 'You have lost nothing. I made sure of that.'

I gasped. 'It was you who returned my car and changed the deeds?'

'Correct.'

'Oh my God, *you* murdered Jack Mount.' I glanced at the door, measuring the distance. How long would it take me to reach it and hurtle through?

'An unfortunate price must be paid for disobeying orders. The Mounts were only meant to scare you.'

'Only?' My eyes were wide.

'They exceeded their remit. I don't expect you to understand.'

As empty as my stomach was I thought I'd vomit over my shoes. 'You framed Lance, didn't you? That's why Marcus Mount believed he'd killed him.'

'Marcus Mount will also be dealt with.'

I stared at him. 'You murderous, lying bastard.'

Lorenzo elevated an eyebrow, shrugged his shoulders and sipped his tea. 'You wanted my help and you got it.'

I stood up.

'Sit down, Susannah. Let us calmly resolve this.'

How did someone who spoke the language of fear so fluently, who talked of murder as if it were a recreational sport, sound reasonable and persuasive? I glanced at my watch. The two hours was not up, nowhere near. I sat.

'Good,' Lorenzo said with a greasy smile. 'To prove that I am a man of honour, I will help you find Lance.'

'So you can kill him?'

'So that you can finally let him go.'

And be mine, was what he intended. I swallowed. Lorenzo had it all mapped out: he would make me whole again. I would be his and we would be one happy family. How was I to defy a man like him, with his iron will, his associates who were terrible men, and the power at his disposal?

'And will you let me go now?'

'Of course,' Lorenzo said, disturbed, it seemed, that I should think otherwise. 'We will stay in touch, *amore mio*.'

I didn't doubt it. When we stood he placed his hands on my shoulders. 'You worry too much, Susannah. All will be well. You will see.'

Dumbfounded, I left.

CHAPTER FORTY-ONE

Despite her bravado, Chantal was too scared to share oxygen with Marcus Mount on her own.

She went to the kitchen, found a cupboard containing beverages, another housing china, and made a mug of tea. She took it outside into the dull gloomy air, mooched along the boundary of the walled garden, longing for a spliff. Her knuckles barked. Her throat hurt. Her shoulders felt as if her arms had been wrenched from their sockets and reset badly. Not one to dwell or feel sorry for herself, she returned to the kitchen that was not hers. In less than an hour she was supposed to call for reinforcements in the form of a young copper called Falconer who she'd never met and who would be rightly suspicious. It wasn't every home that had a man locked up in the basement. More's the pity.

A knock at the door put her on high alert. She put the mug down, grabbed the nearest implement, a carving fork, and headed for the sitting room window. Two sober-looking men, dressed in suits and ties, stood outside the front door. *Mafia men*, Chantal thought, or mates of the Mounts, possibly cops? None were welcome.

Shrinking back behind the curtains, she dropped to the floor and ducked behind a sofa. If she pretended nobody was in, they, whoever they were, would go away.

Except they didn't.

Peeping up over the back, she spotted the shorter of the two, a man with a square jaw and closely shaved head. He cupped a hand over his brow and stared right through the window. Eyes connecting, he waved and then took out what looked like a warrant card and waved that too.

With as much poise as she could muster, she pushed the carving fork underneath the sofa, sprang up as if she'd been searching for a lost earring, and headed to the hall and front door.

'Mrs Stratton,' the man with the square jaw said.

'She's not in.'

'I'm Detective Constable Andrew Smith.' Glancing at his colleague, he said, 'And this is Detective Inspector Lewis Norton. When are you expecting Mrs Stratton home?'

'I'm not sure.'

'Today?'

Chantal nodded.

'Soonish?'

Mount had gone quiet. With images of him starting up again, Chantal had to get rid of the police officers. 'Maybe. Possibly. Not sure.'

'That's a nasty mark you have on your neck.'

Chantal's hand shot to her throat. 'I'm keen on martial arts.'

'Pity your opponent.'

'Accidents happen,' Chantal said gamely.

'May we come in?' Norton interjected. He was older, in his forties, Chantal guessed. His hair was cut short. He had exceptionally high cheekbones; razor sharp features in general and an expression capable of penetrating armour plating. There was no *may* about his request.

Chantal opened the door wide and both detectives trooped into the hall. To smother potential noise from downstairs, she chattered loudly about the cloudy weather and showed them into the sitting room, which was on the other side of the house to the basement. She indicated seats and both men sat.

'And you are?' Norton asked.

'A friend,' Chantal said, evasively.

'All right if we have your name?'

Chantal cleared her throat and gave it. A gleam of recognition passed behind Norton's grey-blue eyes.

'You must be Coco Stratton's mother,' Norton said.

'That's right.'

'And Lance Stratton's ex-wife.'

Chantal squirmed inside. 'Yes.'

'We understand he's missing.'

Both men's gaze locked onto her neck for a second time.

'When was the last time you saw him?' Norton persisted.

'I haven't seen him for a while. I spoke to him on the phone a few days ago.'

'What did you discuss?'

'Our daughter.'

'She was attacked, we understand.'

'Yes.' Chantal felt as if she had a mouthful of sand.

'She chose not to report it. Any particular reason for that?'

'She's an adult. It was her decision.'

'And how did Lance feel about it?' Smith asked.

'Upset, of course, as any parent would be.'

'How did he seem in general, would you say?'

Chantal cleared her throat, which wasn't easy with so much bruising. 'Stressed.'

Norton elevated an eyebrow in a way that told her there was no escape. 'Because?'

'He has a number of personal and professional issues.'

'I see.'

A dramatic pause, no doubt designed to get her off balance; it made Chantal squirm. She painted on a smile in a lame attempt to make her feel more centred.

'Only we're investigating a murder,' Norton said, 'and we understand your daughter's attacker, and the man alleged to have blackmailed your ex-husband, was the victim.'

'Mind if we ask you a few questions?' Smith said.

So far it had been nothing *but* questions. Chantal sensed danger. Where the hell was Susannah?

* * *

I sat in my car, hunched over the steering wheel, thinking and thinking.

Lorenzo had confessed to killing Jack Mount, which mercifully ruled out Lance as Mount's murderer; Lorenzo was on the hunt for Marcus; Lorenzo had set up Lance but allegedly hadn't murdered him. It contained the ring of truth. Killing, to a man like Lorenzo Bonetti, was no big deal. If Lorenzo had killed my husband, he would have brazenly announced it. Having already taken everything from him, Lance had already lost his potency and value. He no longer posed an obstacle to Lorenzo's grand plan. So where did that leave Lance who was still in the wind, without his car, without access to money, or a roof over his head?

His last known location was the unit in Worcester. With CCTV out of action, anyone could have entered and Lance could have left, alone or with someone else. There was no sign of a scuffle so it seemed that Lance had walked out willingly.

He might have committed suicide, although I still couldn't get my head around that. There was another possibility: Amy had lied to shield him.

I rolled back through the short number of times I'd spent in her company. Was it possible she was acting all along? I shook my head. Children are barometers of truth. They can't help themselves. Tana and Wilf both missed Lance madly. *He'll be home soon*, Tana had said innocently.

I looked through the windscreen, into the distance. Children, I thought, and then a thought so monstrous slammed me between the eyes. Seized with icy terror, I called Chantal. She took longer to answer than usual. When she did I could barely hear her.

'Where the hell are you? I've got two detectives in your house who want to speak to you.'

'About Lance?'

'And the murder in Gloucester Road. They've linked the Mounts to the attack on Coco and, due to outraged father syndrome, Lance's disappearance is deemed suspicious.'

'They think he killed Mount?'

'Yes.'

'He didn't. Lorenzo had Jack Mount killed.'

'Christ! And he let you walk away knowing what you know?'

'It's complicated.'

'How complicated? Did he kill Lance too?'

'No.'

Chantal let out a groan. 'I've just risen to number one suspect.'

'Why?'

'Marks on my neck and bruises on my hands.'

'Can you stall them?'

'No, I bloody can't. You need to get here, spill your dynamite news and come clean about Marcus Mount. It's not a good look to have a murder victim's brother holed up in the basement.'

'I will, but first . . .' The fine hairs along my arms stood up. I felt chilled to my bones. I'd been so caught up in the complexities of Lance's life I'd been looking at it from the wrong angle and missed the obvious. I could barely bring myself to say it aloud. What if . . .

'What is it?' Chantal hissed.

'Coco,' I blurted out.

'What about her?'

'You spoke to her, right?'

'This morning.'

'Where is she?'

Chantal clicked her tongue. 'With your son and my mother and stepfather.'

'Phone your mother and ask her.'

'Susannah, what's got into you?'

'Just do it,' I said.

294

'I will not.'

'Then give me her number and *I'll* phone her. If I'm wrong I promise I'll come straight back.'

'I guess I don't have a choice.'

I memorised the number and, finishing the call to Chantal, punched in her mother's number. Praying she'd pick up quickly, I started the engine. If I were right, Amy and her children were in terrible danger.

* * *

A man in a basement, two posh women fighting like a couple of feral cats, murder, a bloke involved in the Mafia, and Christ knew what else, Amy was never stepping foot in Cheltenham as long as she lived.

Still Rollo's disappearance remained a mystery. It haunted her every waking hour — didn't do much for her sleep either — nagged at her, bit into her, ate her alive.

'Can we watch the telly with you tonight, Mummy?' Tana's little face was earnest.

'We'll see.' A standard answer that could be applied as a positive or a negative.

'With popcorn,' Tana persisted.

'And sweeties,' Wilf chimed in.

And wine, Amy thought, *lots of it*. Her children had slept on the journey back and now they were ready for a second wind while hers had long expired. Her nerves needed settling and she had a nice bottle of Lambrusco in the fridge to look forward to.

'In the garden, you two,' Amy told Tana and Wilf. 'Go and have a bounce on the trampoline.'

'Boring,' Wilf complained.

'We want to stay indoors,' Tana said.

'No, you don't.' Amy hated it when they ganged up on her, something they did far too often these days.

'Can I have your phone?'

'No, you cannot.' No, no, no.

Tana stood tall, hands on her hips. 'I want Dad. Daddy always lets me play on his phone.'

Amy lost the will to argue. A lump of grief erupted and throbbed in the back of her throat. If Wilf started up now she wouldn't be able to hold it together. Swooping down, she picked up Adele, clutching her for comfort. In a shaky voice, she said, 'I want Daddy too, sweetie. It's not fair. It's not right, but we can't have him, see?'

Tana's arms dropped to her sides. 'Because he's with that other lady?'

Wilf looked at Tana. 'I liked her. She was nice. She has a boy I can play with.' A deep frown tugged at his mouth. 'I didn't see Daddy at her house.'

'We're not quite sure where he is,' Amy said gently, looking at her son.

'Do you think Daddy's hungry, Mummy?'

'Or cold?' The tip of Tana's nose glowed red. Her eyes swam with tears.

'I expect he's somewhere warm and lovely, where he can eat doughnuts and sweeties all day long.' Her ribs tightened, putting pressure on her heart. 'Now put your jackets on and mind you change your shoes.' Amy pushed a brave smile and handed her phone to Tana. 'Don't lose it and don't break it.'

Then she turfed them out, popped Adele into her baby walker and closed her eyes tight to stop the tears from spilling down her cheeks. She'd about caught her breath when she heard a sturdy knock at the door.

* * *

'Who did you say you were again?'

Weathered by age, salty and gruff, the person asking the question on the other end of the line sounded male, and not in the best of moods.

I stared ahead through the windscreen, wishing Chantal's mum had answered the phone, and repeated my name.

'Oh, I remember. You're Frankie's mother. Well, he's not here. Barely seen the pair of them. Thick as thieves and up to no good, I shouldn't wonder. They come and go and use the place like a guesthouse. Annette doesn't see it, of course. Blinded by love. Mawkish nonsense, if you ask me.'

Slick with fear, I forced myself to ask the next question. 'When did they arrive?'

'Supposed to have been days ago. Annette prepared both guest bedrooms, made a lovely meal, pulled out all the stops,' he said. 'But they cried off and said they'd be late. We had to chuck most of it away. Terrible waste.'

'I need to speak to your wife,' I said urgently.

'My wife?'

'Annette, Chantal's mother.'

'Yes, I know who she is,' he said, combative. 'I'll fetch her now.'

The line went silent. Bleak with disbelief, I chewed my lip, fixed my eyes on the road, desperate to contain a blizzard of questions for which I already dreaded the answers.

Background noise of rustling paper and footsteps, something heavy being picked up and put down, voices, quiet at first and then louder. At last, Chantal's mother, hurried and harassed, came onto the line.

'I was about to speak to Chantal, but you'll do,' she said.

'Is there a problem?' Catastrophe would be a more apt description. I quaked inside.

'My granddaughter borrowed my brand new motor and I was rather hoping she'd be back by now. You haven't heard from her, have you?'

'I haven't. What sort of car do you drive?'

'A yellow Suzuki Wagon R.'

The dread became a thick dark noxious cloud of fear. One final awful question: Annette's husband had said that Frankie was out. I asked her.

'He's with Coco. They're inseparable, but you already knew that, I suppose.'

297

I let out a low moan. My stomach clenched and went into spasms.

That's when I knew Lance was dead and my son and stepdaughter had Amy in their sights.

I didn't thank Chantal's mother or say goodbye. I cut the call, started the engine and put my foot down. I had to reach Amy and the children as fast as possible. On the way there I called her but got no reply.

CHAPTER FORTY-TWO

Amy made out the figure of a young woman through the frosted glass. Opening the door, her first impression was that the girl on her doorstep was not from around here. Fine-featured, slim, indicating a diet in which pies were not a primary feature, she had what Amy would describe as posh looks. If she were a horse she'd be a thoroughbred. Her skin glowed on her pixie-like features. The only flaw was her chin. Pointed, it looked as if she could stamp holes with it.

'Yes?'

'Amy Meadows?'

'Yes?'

'You don't know me, I'm Coco Stratton.'

'Oh.' Crap, Amy thought.

'I'd like to speak to you.'

For all her good looks she was dead behind the eyes, Amy thought. 'It's not convenient.'

'It won't take long.'

Amy hesitated. 'Does your mum know you're here?'

'Oh, yes,' Coco said with another of her chill smiles. Her eyes were a little too bright, Amy thought. Was she on drugs? She wouldn't put it past her. They were all bloody kinked in that family.

Coco pulled out a phone. 'We could call her, if you like.'

Amy did like, especially as Tana had her phone. While Coco stabbed at her mobile with a square manicured nail, Amy looked out across the street. A yellow car, exactly the same as the one she'd spotted days ago, was parked on the other side of the road. Thundering in her head, she gaped from the empty vehicle to Coco and into the eyes of a dark-haired man who'd materialised out of nowhere. Tall, he had olive skin, black hair, a bit swarthy. Drop-dead gorgeous, she'd have said if she'd met him in a pub. And then with a jolt, she twigged: Susannah's son. Stepping back smartly, Amy yelped as a boot shot out between the door and door-frame, preventing her from shutting it.

'Frankie meet whore-mother,' Coco trilled. 'Whore-mother meet Frankie.'

'Clear off,' Amy said.

Dark eyes pinned on hers, Frankie growled, 'Get the fuck back inside.'

To make the point, Coco gave her a shove. Backing away, Amy's terrified gaze dropped to a red can in Frankie's hand.

'What's that?' Amy asked.

'You burnt our house down,' Coco answered. 'Now we're going to burn down yours.'

And then they pushed their way in.

* * *

Everything fell into place.

I pictured Coco and Frankie faking a desire to patch things up with their father and seal it with an offer to visit him at the unit. Delighted, Lance would have welcomed his children with open arms. He would never have sensed the danger. How could he? He could no more foresee it than I could believe it. I could conjecture a murderous inclination in Coco, but not Frankie, not my son.

Lorenzo's boy, a distant voice reminded me.

Frankie had been given every opportunity to excel. He'd never gone hungry, never wanted for anything. Well-educated and well-travelled, he'd enjoyed a privileged upbringing that far exceeded my own. When he'd struggled Lance and me understood. When Frankie had made mistakes he was not punished. When he'd held a view that was so very different to ours we respected it. I'd never believed that nature was stronger than nurture. Not until now.

I recalled my phone conversation with Frankie about the CCTV in the unit. He'd spoken knowledgeably because he'd disabled it. The raw nervous energy he'd expressed when I told him about the return of my car and the deeds now in my name made perfect sense. He had thrilled that his monstrous actions had paid off and been worth the risk.

Brought to my knees, I choked in anguish. How could he ruin his life? He had so much to live for, so much to prove. I'd given him everything I could and it wasn't enough. It would never be enough. I couldn't bear to contemplate what they'd done to Lance because, as painful as it was, it was *they*. Coco had not acted alone. She and Frankie were in it together.

Frantically, I tried Amy's phone again. It rang out. No reply.

Aching with pain, deeply conflicted, I called Chantal who answered bitter and brittle.

'Yes?'

'Are the police still with you?'

'Yes.'

'Let me speak to them.'

'But . . .'

'It's urgent.'

* * *

Baffled, Chantal handed the phone to Norton, a man whose interview technique rivalled foreign intelligence services without the waterboarding and stress positions.

'It's Susannah Stratton,' Chantal explained. 'She wants a word.'

'Hello, Mrs Stratton. We've rather been looking forward to a . . .' Norton broke off and listened with the same acuity as a laser-guided missile, Chantal observed.

There were a lot of yesses and uh-huh's. Norton's skin colour turned from pink to pale and finally to the colour of dried-out cement.

'Yes,' Norton said, eyebrows drawn together. 'Names . . . yes, I understand . . . yes, got that. The exact address, if you will.' He glanced at Smith and made some coded gesture that Chantal failed to interpret. 'Do you have the registration, Mrs Stratton?'

Registration of what? Chantal wondered.

'Okay, how far are you away . . . don't approach under any circumstances. I'll send a team.'

Norton got off the phone and beckoned for Smith to join him in the hallway. A muffled exchange took place. Afterwards, Norton walked outside, paced up and down and made what seemed an urgent phone call.

Grave and serious, Smith returned and Chantal sensed an immediate sea change. No longer a bad actor she was viewed as a victim. Had Lance been found? She asked Smith direct.

'No,' he replied.

'Then what's going on?'

'We don't have a clear picture.' To Chantal's ears: we do but we're not sharing it.

At Norton's request, Smith made for the hall and closed the door behind him.

While they discussed the "unclear picture" Chantal attempted to fathom what was so earth-shattering in a list of stupendous revelations.

Her mother had spoken to Susannah. No doubt, she would have mentioned Coco and Frankie. Pulse tripping, eyes widening, Chantal's lips moved uncertainly, unable to keep up with the terrible thoughts stringing themselves together inside her head. *Coco and Frankie,* she gasped so loudly she barely registered when the door flew open and Smith burst through.

'Do you know there's a man locked up in the basement?'

* * *

Amy's fear for her children was as great and deep as her love. Silently crying, they cowered behind her. Adele, too, had gone quiet. Her little face snuffled wet and tight into her mother's neck. Amy swore she would die to protect them.

She'd pretended Tana and Wilf were at her mum's. One look outside and the sound of children playing had soon exposed her lie. Frankie, with fake charm, beckoned them in. Amy thought her heart would tear in two. *Don't come. Run,* she'd wanted to shout, but there was nowhere for them to go.

'Go and stand with your mother,' Frankie ordered. Coco grabbed Tana by the elbow, her loathing undisguised.

'Get off her,' Amy roared. 'Threatening little children, your father would be ashamed of the pair of you.'

'He's dead so who cares?' Coco said.

Fear scythed through Amy.

Coco exchanged a triumphant glance with Frankie and expanded. 'We stabbed him through his miserable heart.'

The blood in Amy's body ran unspeakably cold. Her teeth shattered. Her knees shook. Whimpering, her children held on tighter.

Unconcerned, Coco stepped away, her gaze suddenly transfixed by a framed print of Amy and Lance, a treasured reminder of a day at the beach at Borth. Plucking it from the ledge of the fake marble fireplace, Coco hurled it to the hearth where it smashed and shattered into pieces.

Amy gasped. This was what they were going to do to her and her little ones.

'Let my children go,' she begged. 'You can have me, not them. They've done nothing wrong.'

Coco drummed her chin with her fingernails. 'What do you think, Frankie? Should we let the little bastards go?'

'Hmm,' Frankie said, making a pantomime of giving the idea serious consideration. He tilted his head. 'On balance . . .'

Amy held her breath, looked at him beseechingly.

'I think . . .'

'*Please,*' Amy begged.

He looked to Coco. A wide smile spread across her face. Her eyes gleamed. 'I think . . . *not.*'

Speechless, Amy gaped. Heart beating, brain banging, there had to be a way out. There *had* to be. 'Why?' she said.

Coco yawned. 'Why what?'

'This. You're hurt. You're upset. I get it. But I swear I didn't know your father was married. I didn't know about his other life. If your mothers understand and can forgive me,' she said, appealing to each of them, 'why can't you?'

Coco put her face in Amy's so close Amy could see the pores on the woman's skin. 'Because,' Coco said, 'temporary cash-flow problem is one thing, serious and sustained loss of earnings quite another.'

Amy gaped in confusion.

'Christ, she's thick,' Frankie said.

'You've. Taken. What's. *Ours,*' Coco said, 'Skewered our existences. Stolen our futures, our reputations, our plans. *You,*' Coco said, poking Amy in the chest, 'fucked up our lives.' Glancing over her shoulder, she gave her stepbrother a satisfied smile.

'You'll never get away with murdering your dad,' Amy said.

'Says who? No body, no crime.'

'That's not how it works. And what about us?'

'What about you? Christ, I'm bored.' Coco cast another look in Frankie's direction.

'Shall I?' He held the can of petrol aloft.

'No,' Amy yelled, her children screaming. 'For the love of God.'

'Do it,' Coco ordered.

304

Obediently, Frankie removed the cap and splashed petrol on the nearest sofa.

* * *

I screamed into Amy's drive, flung myself out of the car and threw myself at the door, rapping it with my knuckles. I looked through the letterbox and shouted for Amy. I swore I could smell petrol.

'Help,' I heard her yell. 'For God's sake, stop.'

I flew to the window. Amy was right at the back, holding the baby, petrified. Tana and Wilf were either side of her, clutching her dress in their tiny hands. I couldn't see Frankie and Coco straightaway but then they moved into view. Two heads turned and gaped at me. Coco recovered first, flashing with defiance, Frankie's expression strained and threaded with alarm. He had not banked on me showing up, but was it enough to stop him?

'Let me in,' I shouted.

Nobody moved.

'I said . . .'

'Go away, Suze,' Coco shouted back.

Oh God, oh God, desperate, I ran to the car, popped the boot and grabbed the jack and smashed it against the downstairs window. In the distance, I heard sirens. I pushed away glass, cutting my fingers, and climbed inside to where the stink of gasoline was overpowering.

'Stop, I said.' Coco held a lighter in her hand, high and plain for me to see. Amy's terror filled the room. Her body shook from head to toe and the children were hysterical.

'Give it up,' I cried. 'Frankie, look at me.'

'Stay right where you are, Suze,' Coco insisted.

'You can't do this.'

'We can and we will.'

'I'm not talking to you,' I said. 'I'm talking to Frankie.'

They say at the penultimate moment before someone drowns, a person sees a life flash before her. Looking into my son's eyes, I saw Frankie: a child crying when he'd fallen over; a tense ride in an ambulance to a hospital when he'd had suspected meningitis; moments when he'd done well at school, winning his first football match; a precious day when he'd introduced me to his friends quite naturally; when he'd taken me out for a drink on his eighteenth; another to celebrate his graduation; Frankie glowing with a sense of achievement, nailing his first interview; getting his first job. Me, so proud of our relationship that I stupidly believed it was close when in reality we were living in another universe. I thought I'd die if anything happened to my son and now I felt like I was dying because of him.

'You have to stop, Frankie.'

'We're doing this for you, too, Mum.' He wanted to sound brave yet, under my grim gaze, he faltered.

'Murdering small children isn't who you are.'

'You don't know who I am.'

Cruelly, it was true. 'It won't repair the damage done.'

Frankie's face turned ashen. My son was culpable. He was also the weak link.

'Your lives will be over if you do this.' I took a step closer. 'There will be no coming back.'

'Our lives are over anyway.' Frankie spoke in a small voice, as if he'd woken up from a bad dream to discover that life was the real nightmare.

'That's bullshit,' Coco said.

I took another step forward. Where were the police?

'Don't come any closer, Suze.' Coco's warning was etched with threat.

'Why not? Are you going to burn me too?' Another step.

'Mum, mum, please do as she says,' Frankie begged.

'Why?'

'Because she'll hurt you.'

I fixed my eyes on Coco and slipped out my phone. 'Your mother wants to talk to you, Coco.'

Coco's face fell into a frown, her eyes screwed with confusion. *Not so living your best life and being your best self now*, I thought.

'Give it here,' Coco said, extending her hand.

I threw it high up in the air in a big loop. Turning, she fluffed the catch and dropped the lighter. On its impact with the carpet, I swooped, picked it up and barrelled into Coco, knocking her slender figure to the floor.

'Fuck, fuck, fuck.' Scrabbling to get back up, she made a grab for my ankle and missed.

I planted myself in front of Amy, arms low and wide. 'Nobody come near,' I warned. The noise of sirens grew louder. Any minute now, the police would arrive.

Frankie gaped in astonishment. 'You went to the cops? You chose that woman and her kids over me, over us?'

'You had my loyalty and love,' I told him. 'It was never enough.'

The fierce light in Frankie's eyes dimmed.

Tyres screeched. Blue lights flashed. At the sight of police officers outside, Coco attempted to make a run for it. Stricken, Frankie stayed where he was. I met his eye, held his gaze. He was not alone in his trepidation and confusion.

'Bitch, you've ruined everything,' Coco railed, as police arrested her first.

No, you did, I thought.

CHAPTER FORTY-THREE

I was the wife of a murder victim and mother to his murderer.

Sitting in graveyards with the dead had become my new pastime. There I wept for Frankie, for Lance and for the shattered ruins of my life. *In the end we are all stripped down to this*, I thought. I simply hadn't anticipated it happening while alive.

I had a home I could not afford to run. I had the remnants of a business that was on its knees. I had two women in my life that I needed more than they needed me. Was it enough? I couldn't say.

In the dizzying days that followed, with the press camped outside my door, my time was devoured by police officers in police stations. Slowly, I grew to be on first-name terms with Lewis Norton and Andrew Smith. As Lance's widow, I was given a Family Liaison Officer, a compassionate woman called Maria Millman who kept me up to speed with the investigation. The Wagon R, the vehicle in which Lance had made his final fatal journey, was towed away and forensically examined. An on-going search for Lance's remains continued deep in the New Forest, where Frankie and Coco, according to Frankie, had dumped his body. *No comment Coco*, as I'd come to think of her, refused to answer a single question put to her by the police. To my surprise, Chantal did not find a talented lawyer to defend her daughter.

The awkward impromptu stay of Marcus Mount in the basement of my house was tricky to explain. Charged with extortion and blackmail, put into a secure unit to protect him from reprisals from his paymasters in Florida, Marcus Mount had bigger problems than pressing charges against two women who'd taken the law into their own hands. While, technically, the police could press charges anyway, without a testimony from Mount, the Crown Prosecution Service would encounter difficulty making a strong case against us.

This was the nuts and bolts of what occurred. But at night, in the early hours, on my own, it was a very different story.

I felt like an empty building, long abandoned and gathering dust. How could I endure? How could I forgive and love a son who had fallen so very far from the path I'd hoped for him, a murderer, no less. I was not tempted to excuse his actions by blaming his stepsister for leading him astray. Frankie had held that can of petrol. Frankie had terrorised Amy and her children. I'd witnessed it with my own eyes. Lance's murder I didn't dare to imagine. It didn't matter who inflicted the fatal wound. Frankie was guilty and a judge would eventually sentence him.

It's a mother's prerogative to presume a child's crime is a parent's fault, a result of too little love; rarely, too much. I'd never taken the credit for Frankie's successes so why accept liability for his failings? This is what I tried to tell myself again and again. It's what I failed to accept again and again even though I urged Chantal to believe it too. In bad shape, she told me that the blade taken to Lance's heart had also been taken to ours.

She was not wrong.

With regard to Lorenzo's role, I stuck doggedly to the narrative with the police and, despite what we all knew, advised Chantal, who was inconsolable, and Amy, who had

309

the emotional strength of yew, to do the same. Not to protect Lorenzo but to protect us.

When he called not long after the case broke, I was ready for him.

'If you wish to see your son he's in custody, awaiting trial for Lance's murder and the attempted murder of a young mother and her children.'

Shocked, Lorenzo emitted a sound I recognised too well. His cry was for missed opportunities, for regrets, for hopes and dreams dashed. Mine was also for loss. Grief, I discovered, was cold and solitary. In the dead of night I mourned Lance. I grieved for Frankie the boy I thought I knew, now gone from me, as if he'd never existed. I urged Lorenzo to do the same.

'Goodbye, Lorenzo,' I said. 'Don't ever contact me again.'

I cut the call and blocked his number.

CHAPTER FORTY-FOUR

'How are you doing, Amy?'

'Dunno. Drinking more than is good for me.'

'Same. How are the children?'

'Quiet.'

'You still at your mum's?'

'Yes.'

'I'm worried about Chantal. She isn't picking up.'

'I'll give her a ring.'

I waited. Amy called back. 'She doesn't want to talk.'

I tried again. Chantal picked up.

'How are you?' I asked.

No answer.

'Want me to grab a takeaway?'

'No.'

'Fancy a drink. I could bring a bottle, or we could sip tea, or . . . ?'

'No.'

'Shall I come round?'

'No.'

'Talk to me, Chantal. You know you can.'

A silence descended as wide and deep as an ocean. 'I don't know how to do this,' Chantal said at last, her voice so very weary.

'I don't either.'

'It's so raw.'
'I know.'
'I'm in agony.'
'Oh, Chantal.' I recognised that too.
'I can't see a way through, Susannah.'
'But you will. We both will.'
'When?'
'Not now.'
'After the trial?'
'Maybe. Maybe later.' Maybe never, I thought sadly.
'My child, my . . .' Chantal broke down.
'Hold on. I'm coming,' I said.

* * *

'What are you going to do, my love?' The endearment was
a sure sign that Mum was worried, Amy thought, or she'd
been on the gin and blackcurrant. 'You've barely eaten since
it all kicked off.'

Grief had robbed her of appetite. 'As long as the kids
are—'

'I'm not talking about the kids, our Amy. I'm talking
about you.'

'It takes time to get your head straight after something
like that.'

Mum patted her arm kindly.

Whatever her mum thought, Amy was more together
than she let on — mostly and when she didn't cry herself to
sleep — in damned sight better shape than Chantal, for sure.
Crikey, the woman had taken it bad. Not that Amy blamed
her. If her Tana had behaved like Coco Stratton, she'd never
forgive her; daughter or not, she could rot in hell where they
kept paedos and child murderers. Not that she told Chantal
this. Well, she couldn't, could she? Poor woman was in a world
of suffering. She looked that gaunt. All that cockiness had been
knocked clean out of her. She no longer spoke with a sharp
tongue, mostly because she didn't speak. And she'd practically

312

given up washing herself. Last time Amy popped round she'd run a bath for her and helped her in. It was like bathing a bag of bones. Thank God Chantal had a cleaner to keep the house nice. *Only proves that money isn't everything*, Amy told herself.

But, shit, it helped.

Susannah was different. A woman to whom Amy owed her life, Susannah was lost for sure, yet she still had fight in her. At the end of the day that's all you could ask for.

'Any news on the bungalow?' her mum asked.

'The landlady's arranging for the rental to be cleaned up by a company specialising in decontamination.'

Her mum looked dubiously down her nose. 'They can get rid of petrol?'

'Dunno.' Wasn't important. Amy would never return — not in a million years. Bad memories outweighed the good. Neither was she going back to the sweet shop because it was bloody boring and didn't pay enough. She had to find a better way to survive. Couldn't rely on her mum's charity for the rest of her life.

'Want anything from the shops?' her mum asked. 'I thought I'd buy us a nice bit of steak for tea. Kids can have burgers.'

'No, I'm good,' Amy said.

'I'll leave you to it then.' Her mum hovered.

Amy noticed she did this a lot. 'Go — I'll be fine.'

'If you're sure; it's not right to be on your own so much.'

'I'm not.' She had the girls. 'Susannah will be phoning soon.' Regular as clockwork, she was.

'You know I don't hold with it.'

Amy did.

'Why you'd want to be in touch with the parents of that murdering bloody pair makes no sense, no sense at all.'

'It makes sense to me, Mum.'

* * *

Chantal tried to be brave. She wasn't like Susannah, the woman she'd ridiculed in the past and who continued to amaze with

313

her quiet fortitude. She wasn't like Amy whose forgiveness she didn't deserve. Horrified by her daughter's crimes, Chantal struggled to get up in the morning. The shame of it weighed too heavy.

Sitting in her office, staring at the safe, Chantal reckoned that this was her punishment for aiding and abetting Lance all those years ago. She deserved to be brought low. She deserved the odium of others.

To escape media intrusion she'd had her landline disconnected and she no longer went online. Her business had folded overnight. It didn't matter how many times Susannah told her that the universe didn't work on a penalty system, that she was no more responsible for Coco's actions than she was for Frankie's, Chantal refused to believe her.

Sometimes her grief for Lance took her by surprise. As an ex, a hostile ex at times, Chantal thought she would be immunised from loss. Lance's murder had raked up the past, strangely good times were more prevalent than bad and it made her sadder than ever.

But remembering Lance, she also remembered Austen Walsh. Before she lost her nerve, she went to the safe, put in the combination and opened it. Taking out Austen Walsh's passport and wallet, she called Susannah.

CHAPTER FORTY-FIVE

On a day that promised warmth and sunshine, Chantal, Amy and the children came to my house. With so much space, Amy and her brood were staying over. The excitement on the children's faces at having their own rooms warmed me from the outside in.

We sat in the garden on a rug under an old apple tree. Tana and Wilf played hide and seek while their baby sister practiced crawling. We ate and drank and talked tentatively at first then, oiled by wine, we spoke of Lance, the good and the funny and the qualities that made us love him once upon a time. We talked of friendship, of the unshakable bond between us and of better times ahead though we knew we still had the court case and trials of our own to face. Too personal, too intimate, I couldn't bear to talk of my son, no more than Chantal could of her daughter. I'd given up my job at the dental practice to run the unit in Worcester. Dave Spencer was coming back to help me.

'Have you thought about my proposal?' I asked Amy.

'Like I said, I've never sold anything in my life, let alone incinerators.'

'You've sold sweets,' Chantal chipped in. She was looking better, less exhausted.

'Bit of a difference,' Amy said.

'You know how to talk to people and that's the main thing. I can't run it all on my own.' I looked at Chantal, hoping to plant a seed.

No benefit in being scared of the future and frightened of happiness even in dark and difficult times like these.

'Yes, then,' Amy said.

Welded together in a way none of us could ever imagine, I looked around at our tiny gathering: children playing, two unlikely women with whom I'd shared the worst of times and who I was closer to than any friend, and raised a toast.

'To last women standing,' I said.

Rosy-cheeked with wine, Amy said, 'I'll drink to that. Got to get on with it, haven't you?'

Chantal's smile was wistful. I wondered if she were thinking of her daughter and asked her.

She shook her head. Her distant eyes met mine, a moment of conspiracy between us.

About now, a woman called Phoebe, who lived in Rio, Brazil, would be opening an anonymous letter. In it Chantal had explained and expressed deep regret for the circumstances of Austen Walsh's death.

I hoped by holding Austen's passport and wallet in her hands it brought a little comfort to his younger sister.

THE END

ACKNOWLEDGEMENTS

There's a saying in show business attributed to W.C. Fields: never work with animals and children. I confess I've always been wary of introducing children to my novels, despite the fact I have quite a few of my own. I'm so glad I broke my own rule and thanks must go to my grandchildren for providing inspiration. Special thanks to the youngest member of the tribe for allowing Wilf to 'borrow' his Iggle Piggle!

As ever, I'm indebted to my good friend and agent, Broo Doherty, who has walked every step of the way on my writing journey. Many thanks also to the entire team at Joffe, including Becky Wyde for her empathetic approach to my stories and picking up my mistakes. Special thanks to Kate Lyall Grant, my editor, and the man himself, Jasper Joffe, without whom none of this would be possible.

Thank you again to Graham Bartlett, writer and consultant in 'all things police,' for steering me on the right side of the law! As ever, any slip-ups are mine alone. Special thanks to Rebecca Munson for providing insights into the waste and recycling industry, enabling me to make the fictional MultiMax unit in the story contemporary and convincing.

Thank you to my readers and the lovely people who take the time and trouble to write reviews. Writers don't exist without you.

Confession time: I nicked a cracking line from Tim and Rosey Goom and improvised on it, which only goes to show it pays to be careful in casual conversation with a writer, even if she is a close relative! Thanks, guys.

Finally, families come in all shapes, sizes and variations. My own tribe is no exception. I thank Ian for his tolerance in putting up with me spending long hours 'somewhere else,' either literally or metaphorically. I also thank my children and their partners for their support and understanding over many years. You are more important to me than you'll ever know.

THE JOFFE BOOKS STORY

We began in 2014 when Jasper agreed to publish his mum's much-rejected romance novel and it became a bestseller.

Since then we've grown into the largest independent publisher in the UK. We're extremely proud to publish some of the very best writers in the world, including Joy Ellis, Faith Martin, Caro Ramsay, Helen Forrester, Simon Brett and Robert Goddard. Everyone at Joffe Books loves reading and we never forget that it all begins with the magic of an author telling a story.

We are proud to publish talented first-time authors, as well as established writers whose books we love introducing to a new generation of readers.

We have been shortlisted for Independent Publisher of the Year at the British Book Awards three times, in 2020, 2021 and 2022, and for the Diversity and Inclusivity Award at the Independent Publishing Awards in 2022.

We built this company with your help, and we love to hear from you, so please email us about absolutely anything bookish at: feedback@joffebooks.com.

If you want to receive free books every Friday and hear about all our new releases, join our mailing list: www.joffebooks.com/contact

And when you tell your friends about us, just remember: it's pronounced Joffe as in coffee or toffee!

Milton Keynes UK
Ingram Content Group UK Ltd.
UKHW012314030624
443602UK00005B/68

9 781835 262832